The End of Dragons

The End of Dragons

A Collection of Short Stories

A Chipper Press Anthology

The End of Dragons

A Chipper Press Anthology

For permission requests, write to the publisher
"Attention: Permissions Coordinator"
Chipper Press
PO Box 1172
Union Lake, Michigan 48387
mail to: info@chipperpress.com

© 2019 Chipper Press, et al

Published in the United States by Chipper Press
An imprint of Zimbell House Publishing
http://www.chipperpress.com

All Rights Reserved

Trade Paper ISBN: 978-1-64390-111-4
.mobi ISBN: 978-1-64390-112-1
ePub ISBN: 978-1-64390-113-8
Library of Congress Control Number: 2019952312

First Edition: October 2019
10 9 8 7 6 5 4 3 2 1

Chipper Press
Union Lake, Michigan

Acknowledgements

Chipper Press would like to thank all those that contributed to this anthology. We chose to show-case seventeen new voices that best represented our vision for this work.

We would also like to thank our Chipper Press team for all their hard work and dedication to these projects.

Table of Contents

A Dragon in the Human Realm

J. B. Charon

Ryrrŷcrax could hear his soon-to-be teacher telling the class about the new student. He tugged on the tie hanging from the collar of his new white uniform shirt. Both were uncomfortable. Dragons don't usually wear things like this, but his parents said he had "to follow the school rules."

As the seconds continued to drag on, they seemed to get longer and longer as his anxiety grew. *Do I have to introduce myself?* he thought. *What if I'm the only Dragon here?* The small purple Dragon shifted on his feet. He mulled over the worst possible scenarios, so distracted that he didn't hear Ms. Felide the first time.

"Ahem," his teacher said louder from inside the classroom, "you can come in now."

He forced the wood and iron door open to enter the room. The door struck the wall behind it with such a loud *Bang!* that it startled everyone present, including himself. Ryrrŷcrax shuffled into the room. Looking out at the sea of Humans, he realized that he was indeed the only Dragon. Surprised chatter and excited comments met him as he stood at the front of the room.

"Well then, why don't you introduce yourself? Children, this is your new classmate, Ryr-Ryrri—"

"It's 'Riracrase.' I'm new to Inmond, my family just moved here."

"Can you breathe fire?" A blonde boy asked excitedly.

"I-I'm too young. I have to be older."

"Do you have wings? I thought Dragons had wings," a girl near the back said.

Ryrrŷcrax was staring down at the floor, his hands trembling as he gripped the legs of his creased uniform pants. "Not all. I don't. I'm a different kind that doesn't—"

"Alright, well, I'm sure we'll all get to know you very well," Ms. Felide interrupted. "You can go to your seat now. There's an opening at Irius' table."

The little Dragon glanced up, doing his best to avoid any eye contact as he tried to find his seat. A silver-haired boy was waving him over to a table on the right side of the room, and Ryrrŷcrax made his way there quickly. He sat down on the stool, his spiked tail bumping into the table behind him. He wished to be anywhere else rather than this classroom, in this school, in this Human city.

"I like your horns," a cheerful voice complimented. Turning, Ryrrŷcrax saw his classmate smiling politely at him.

"Oh. Thank you."

"My name is Irius and I've never met a Dragon before, but your scales are pretty. I like purple, and your tail is neat. Did your horns hurt when they grew in? Can you do magic? Do you like magic?"

It took the Dragon a moment to grasp what all Irius was saying to him. "No, Dragons can't do magic. My grandfather says not to trust it, but I don't think I've ever seen it."

All the while Ryrrŷcrax was talking, his classmate was scribbling on a piece of paper. Irius nudged him, and he saw a circle of symbols drawn on the paper. The silver-haired child put his hand in the middle of the symbols that shined for a moment. When he pulled his hand away, the page began to fold itself. After a few moments, it had taken on the form and movements of a turtle. The turtle crawled over to inspect Ryrrŷcrax. The Dragon giggled as the paper creature attempted to crawl up onto his hand. He was now sure he hadn't seen Human magic before.

"Excuse me, boys," said Ms. Felide, "but we're starting our history lesson now. If you want to play with magic, you'll have to do it later."

"Yes, teacher." Irius set his hand on the turtle again, and when he removed it, the paper creature became inanimate again.

"You can keep him if you'd like, as a welcoming present," his classmate whispered to him. A small smile formed on the Dragon's face at his new gift.

"Now today we are continuing our look into the erm … the Dragon War," their teacher said, awkwardly. "And how it affected the two realms involved; the Human realm of Inmond and the Dragon realm of Zurŭ … wæn."

She went on with the lecture, with several incorrect facts, Ryrrŷcrax wished to point out. Ms. Felide was trying not to glance directly at him, given the topic and new student. His other classmates were not so discrete. Many of them made overt looks, some even turning around in their seats. The teacher talked about the outbreak of the war, the losses of the battles, and the eventual defeat of the Dragons. He could feel the eyes of the students behind him on his back and heard the whispered comments. He had never felt so self-conscious of his being a Dragon in the Human realm as he did during his first day of school.

"—and she said it was the Dragons who started the war, too!" the young Dragon complained to his parents at home that afternoon. He laid slumped over a round, backless chair in the living room. The air filled with the aroma of spices. The dinner his father was cooking on the hearth sizzled and popped. The familiar smell did lift his spirits a little.

"No one knows which side started the war," Virrêi, his mother, said. "It could have been the Humans or it could have been us."

"That's not what grandfather says."

"Your grandfather fought in the war, but he wasn't there when it started," his father, Brarsīr, added. Flames escaped his father's mouth to the coals beneath the cooking pan.

The young Dragon flattened out further. He thought that his parents would at least take his side. He'd imagined they would agree his teacher was wrong and he couldn't get an honest education in the Human realm. That's what his grandfather had said. Then they'd be willing to move back. Now it was becoming clear that wouldn't be so simple.

"Surely your first day wasn't all bad," his mother said.

"There's a Human who sits at my table that did some magic. That wasn't so bad, I guess." Ryrrŷcrax took out the paper turtle from his bag, which had been flattened and folded up for safekeeping.

"Magic, hm?" She smiled as her son examined the turtle. "You don't see that very often in Zurŭwæn. Did it have to do with your little friend, there?"

"He drew these sorts of symbols on it, and they glowed, then the paper folded up into this turtle. But it moved and acted like a real one until the teacher made him stop. I've never seen anything like it before, but grandfather said not to trust Human magic."

"Ryrrŷcrax, I wish you wouldn't listen to everything your grandfather says," Brarsīr said, shooting a cautious glance at his wife.

"Why not?"

"He's set in the old ways, and although he's never even met a Human off the battlefield, he's still distrustful of them. But they are not so different from us. I'm sure that right now, your new friend is telling his parents all about you as well, and how he's never met a Dragon before."

Ryrrŷcrax smiled, then frowned. "Do you think his grandfather told him not to trust Dragons, too?"

"Well if he did, then your friend's grandfather is just as much of a fool as your—" Virrêi's glare stopped him dead in his tracks. "Oh, would you look at that, dinner is ready. We'll have to finish this talk some other time."

Later that night, the young Dragon was laying on the short bed in his room. It was the first time Ryrrŷcrax lived in a house with more than a living room, though his bedroom was more of a closet. Most Dragon homes consisted of a main space, which served as bedroom, kitchen, and dining room. He did not mind it. There was an extravagance to the Human realm that he was still growing accustomed to.

When they moved through the city to their new house, he could see buildings grander and more immaculate than any he'd seen in the Dragon realm. One was several stories, took up half a street, and had various statues on it. At first, he thought it was a castle, but his father said it was just a post office. In an alley behind it, he saw people sleeping in boxes.

He saw a mansion big enough to easily fit many versions of his new "modest" home inside. Yet, only a family of three lived in it. A seven-member family lived next door to them, in the same kind of small house where Ryrŷcrax and his parents lived. The Human realm was confusing. As he lay staring up at the ceiling, he wondered if Irius would find the Dragon realm as complicated.

He turned over in bed with his eyes closed. Like previous nights since they moved in, he found it very difficult to sleep. He missed talking to his grandfather every single night before going to bed. The young Dragon had few friends in his village but always had his grandfather. He sat up and got out of bed, going over to his trunk in his room.

After a little digging, he found the item his grandfather had given him before they left. It was a chalice of black and gold and decorated with engravings of Dragon bones, and five Dragon skulls with the central and most ornate skull present on the front. "When you feel alone in that Human realm," he told Ryrŷcrax, "ignite coals in this with your fire, speak my name. Then pour them out. I'll always be here to visit with you."

The young Dragon slid the door to his room open, peeking around the corner into the living room. Like in their old home, his parents still slept there, and Ryrŷcrax stared at them intently for a few minutes. With the coast clear, he carefully snuck over to the hearth. A single creaking floorboard could awaken his father—or worse his mother. He'd get into trouble for sneaking around after he's supposed to be in bed. Once he made it to the hearth, he scooped up some of the now-cooled coals used to cook their dinner into the chalice, and just as carefully slunk back to his room.

The next part was going to be trickier. Breathing fire was natural for more matured Dragons, but Ryrrŷcrax was still developing. There would be at least three or four years before he could do it as impressively as his parents.

Opening his mouth and aiming at the chalice, he tried pushing out a fire. All that came out was a sort of raspy, choking sound. He cleared his throat and tried again, drawing up power from deeper within. Still nothing. The third and fourth attempt was as unsuccessful as the first two, and he started growing frustrated. He closed his eyes and tried to steady his breathing. Getting upset wouldn't help it, but ... *I want to talk to my grandfather!* He thought, and with a final push, let out a small flame onto the coals. He looked at them, surprised and gleeful, as little orange lights began to reawaken the lumps on top.

With even the smallest flame present, the empty eyes on the central Dragon skull shined with a red light. Suddenly all the contents within the chalice lit up in a mighty fire. Ryrrŷcrax gasped and almost dropped it but caught himself first. "N-Nŷrucrig," he whispered hoarsely, before dumping the coals out on the floor away from his bed. As they poured out, the great fire died out immediately, as if the air was water. The coals broke apart upon hitting the floor, crushed into embers that formed a ring. The burning orange and red lights then spread inward to the circle's center, where the fire took on his grandfather's appearance.

"It's quite late where you are, isn't it, Tŏrşa?"

Ryrrŷcrax smiled, "Tŏrşa" was his grandfather's nickname for him. He didn't know what it meant but missed hearing it. "A little. But I missed talking to you."

"I've missed you and your mother as well. I have been concerned since your father dragged you to that cursed realm. Are you safe there? Have the Humans sought to harm you?"

"No, we're all okay. This place is strange, and I miss our old home, but I guess things haven't been so bad."

and show your father the foolishness of his decision."

"I tried convincing mother and father to let us move home, but they didn't listen to me either. Grandfather, can I ask you something?"

"Of course, Tŏrşa. You can ask me anything, and I will do my best to pretend I know what the answer is."

The young Dragon smiled. "Well, I was just wondering. Do you think Humans are really so bad?"

"You cannot trust the Humans, ever. They are deceitful, wicked creatures who seek to better themselves at the expense of all else."

"All of them?"

"You know that I fought against their invasion of our realm in the Scjjan Shŏn. On the battlefield, you learn the truth about a person that they would mask in peace. I was young and idealistic then, as you are now, and early in the war, I sought to show mercy to my enemy. Every time it brought only misfortune, death to my comrades, or an assault when I turned my back."

"Well, I met a Human in my class, and he's nice. He used this magic to make a—"

"Stay away from their magic!"

"G-Grandfather, not so loud!" Ryrrŷcrax listened for the sound of his mother or father stirring. The house remained quiet.

"Sorry, Tŏrşa. Humans think their magic gives them strength and entitles them to whatever they desire. It is only vain trickery, and they would just as soon use it as a weapon against you or anyone else."

"The Human I met used his magic to make a little paper turtle, it was nice."

"I love you, Ryrrŷcrax," his grandfather said, as he calmed again, "and I trust your judgment on this. Just remember not to let your guard down too easily around Humans. It is late now, and you should sleep."

"Okay, grandfather ... I love you."

"And I love you. Sleep well."

Nŷrucrig's image disappeared, and the embers grew cold. Ryrrŷcrax sighed a little and brushed the ashes over to the corner before crawling back into bed. He turned onto his side as he contemplated what his grandfather told him. *Irius seems nice. I don't think he'd attack me like those Humans in the war,* he thought as he closed his eyes.

At school the next day, Ms. Felide was continuing her discussion of the "Dragon War," but Ryrrŷcrax had long since stopped paying his attention. He didn't have much interest in the constant lecturing on why the Dragons were responsible and the effects on the Human realm. As if they were the only ones who mattered.

"Alright class," their teacher announced, "to conclude this subject, we're going to see an example of the correct action Humans should take when facing a Dragon. We're lucky to have our very own living Dragon here for this demonstration."

"What?" The young Dragon said as he looked back at his teacher. Ms. Felide was digging through her desk's drawer when she pulled out a sizable blade. Ryrrŷcrax's eyes widen as he jumped up from his seat. "What are you doi—"

"Don't let it get away, children."

At her beckoning, all the Dragon's classmates jumped up and began grabbing at him, pulling him to the floor. He struggled against them and broke free of their grasp. But before he could get up, Irius knelt on his chest to push him back to the floor.

"I-Irius," Ryrrŷcrax coughed out, "please don't ..."

The silver-haired boy said nothing. He glared down at the Dragon with disgust and contempt. The look in his eyes hurt Ryrrŷcrax more than anything, and tears began to well up and flow down his cheeks. Ms. Felide arrived next to him and bent down, grabbing one of the young Dragon's horns.

"Pay attention now, children. This is where to make the first cut."

Ryrrŷcrax screamed as she moved in with her blade, then jolted awake. The early sunlight was starting to shine through his bedroom window. He could hear the sounds of the city waking up. It had all been a dream, and yet his fear and despair remained. While birds chirped outside his home, all he could do was curl up in bed again and cry.

His parents must not have realized he used some coals the night before, for neither said anything about it that morning. Ryrrŷcrax, still shaken from his dream, didn't say much to them that morning either besides bidding his father goodbye as he left for work. When he finished his breakfast, he went to the bathroom and sat in the bathtub. Scalding hot water showered down on him. He thought about his nightmare again. It could have been a warning from Yxræûs, the great five-headed Dragon god. Perhaps it was from his grandfather. A sudden knock at the door drew the young Dragon back to reality.

"Ryrrŷcrax, it's almost time for school. Get ready, or you'll be late."

He sighed a little, turned off the water, and got dressed in his uncomfortable uniform for school. At school, he continued to look at the floor as he had done the day before. Irius greeted him and attempted to be friendly. Ryrrŷcrax's shelled demeanor shut down his attempts. He didn't listen to—didn't care about—whatever Ms. Felide was saying.

All the young Dragon wanted and cared about was being back with his grandfather in person, and away from the Humans. All through class, he could feel eyes on him, but it didn't bother him anymore. He started to grow detached from his surroundings. After school, he would return home in silence, not say much to his parents, go to sleep, and the cycle would continue.

"How was school today?" Brarsīr would ask.

"Okay," Ryrrŷcrax would answer.

"Did your friend make any more paper creatures for you?" Virrêi would ask.

"No," Ryrrŷcrax would answer.

That was the extent of his interactions, his responses growing more and more concise as the days went by. On the first night, his mother and father exchanged confused glances. By the fifth night, they were becoming concerned.

The day before, his first day out of school since starting at Pulmorths Academy, his parents had taken Ryrrŷcrax to a park in the city. Instead of growing more comfortable in his new home, the young Dragon only became more anxious. The human eyes on him, the whispered comments as he and his parents went by, people keeping a distance. It wasn't long until Ryrrŷcrax was practically begging his parents to go home.

That night, he was sitting silently in the rounded, backless chair he enjoyed. Virrêi and Brarsīr looked at each other, and then his father nodded to his mother.

"You know, it's been a while since we've talked to your grandfather," she said. "Why don't we contact him tonight? He must be wondering about how we're all doing."

"I don't want to contact him." The young Dragon could feel himself growing hot as his frustration bubbled up. "I want to go back and live with him!"

Ryrrŷcrax stormed off to his room. He had never yelled at them before. Neither expected such a reaction.

Later that night, the young Dragon shifted and woke up. There was a soft light creeping in from under his door. As he got out of bed, he could hear his parents talking in hushed voices in the living room. Ryrrŷcrax carefully crept over to his door and did his best to listen in.

"But what about you? Can you leave like that?" his father asked.

"It's only tavern work, Brarsīr," his mother said dismissively. "Mrs. Evia can just as easily find someone else to serve drinks. But you know that ever since the war, the employment for silversmiths has dropped off. What will you do if we go back?"

"I'll find work somewhere, anywhere. We may not make much, but Ryrrŷcrax will be happier at home, and with Nŷrucrig. Even though I blame him for this. I don't want our son growing up here miserable."

Ryrrŷcrax had to cover his mouth so he wouldn't shout out in happiness. He hadn't felt this happy in at least two weeks; they were going to go back home! *Yxræûs must have listened to me*, he thought as he crawled back into bed. As he turned over, he thought this might be the first night he'd be too happy to fall asleep.

His parents broke the news to him the next morning. They would all start packing up to move back in the next few days. Ryrrŷcrax did his best to act surprised by this, and before going off to school, he hugged them both.

At school that morning, the young Dragon saw Irius sitting beneath a crooked tree on the school grounds. He was doing his best to draw on a pad of paper. The wind kept blowing, rustling the colorful pages, and sweeping his silver hair into his face.

Then a group of three other students approached Irius. The head boy was saying something to his classmate, but he was too far away to hear what. Whatever it was, it wasn't good, because Irius didn't seem very happy to see them. The head boy pointed at Irius and said something, which made the other two laugh.

The leader was an older student from the next grade above his and Irius' class, with darkish gray hair tied back in a braid. Among the blonde kid's followers was a girl with long red and black hair, and a boy with black hair and glasses who was the shortest of the trio.

After a few more taunts, it was clear that Irius was growing upset. Ryrrŷcrax froze in place. He didn't like seeing Irius being picked on, yet didn't want to become involved with the Humans if this became a fight. Especially if they used magic. *He's not even really my friend*, he reasoned. *I'm leaving soon anyway. It isn't my problem, and he's just a Human.*

As Irius went to leave, the head boy showed that he did have magic. He dragged his foot across the ground, kicking up a cloud of dust. The dust revealed symbols like the ones Irius had drawn the day earlier. Stomping in the center of them, a short pillar of rock shot up in front of the silver-haired boy. Irius tripped and fell to the ground as the pages in his sketchbook broke free and scattered around him. That was enough for Ryrrŷcrax.

"Get away from him!" The three kids turned, alarmed, as the young Dragon ran over to them.

"It's that Dragon!" the short boy said before running off, leaving his cohorts behind.

"Wait for me!" the girl shouted as she followed after him. The trio's leader stayed put, as he looked over Ryrrŷcrax.

"Come back, cowards," he called over his shoulder. "You heard what Erick said, this Dragon doesn't breathe fire or even have wings!"

Ryrrŷcrax stood between the boy and Irius, who was frantically gathering his pages. "Leave Irius alone."

"Why? His magic's a joke, all he does is make little paper toys with it."

"Well I like his paper toys, and it's not even your business what he does with his magic. At least he does it to make people happy, instead to bully people like you."

The boy scoffed at this. "What do you even know about magic? You're a stupid Dragon, the closest thing you can do is breathe fire, but you can't even do that much. Go back and hide in a cave, or whatever it is your kind does."

The young Dragon bristled at this, the spikes on his tail flexing and shifting.

"Ryrrŷcrax, don't," Irius said as he stood up. "He wants you to fight so you'll get in trouble. I'm okay, I swear."

The silver-haired boy was trying to keep his scraped hands out of his friend's sight. But the Dragon could smell his blood. "It's not alright! He hurt you!"

"So, what are you going to do about it?" the older boy taunted. He stomped on the symbols again. Another rock pillar rose between Ryrrŷcrax and Irius and knocked both back to the ground. "This is too easy. I barely have to do anything."

The young Dragon had enough—it was one thing if Irius didn't want to fight back, but now the older boy was harassing him too. Ryrrŷcrax got up and rushed at the bully, causing the boy to stumble back in surprise and step on his symbols again.

Another short column of earth came up in front of Ryrrŷcrax, tripping him as he crashed into the older boy. Irius hurried over to check on them as the Dragon sat up, a little dazed after the collision. When Irius reached them, he audibly gasped and covered his mouth.

"What's wrong?" he asked as he saw his silver-haired friend's shocked expression. Then he felt droplets fall from his horns onto his cheek. From their scent, he instantly knew what they were, and he looked down at the older boy laying on the ground in front of him. The two holes in his shirt were welling up with the crimson liquid where the young Dragon's horns had penetrated him, and he was making gasping noises.

"What's going on over there?" a teacher—nowhere in sight when Irius needed him, of course, but present now—called out, as he made his way over.

"I—I didn't mean to—" Ryrrŷcrax stuttered as he pushed back away from the scene. Irius grabbed his arm to stop him, then ran his fingers over the blood on one of the Dragon's horns.

"It's okay, this wasn't your fault. I can help him, but please don't run away." The purple Dragon could only nod as his friend knelt by the wounded boy. With the blood on his fingers, he drew new symbols around the holes in the boy's shirt and pressed his hands onto the center. Ryrrŷcrax gasped as light shone from under Irius's hands, before fading as the silver-haired boy sat back, exhausted. Ryrrŷcrax saw that the wounds had closed up as if they had never been there.

"Alright, that's enough, you three. You know you're not allowed to use magic—" the teacher's eyes darted from Ryrrŷcrax and his bloodied horns to the older boy and his bloodied shirt, and then to Irius and his bloodied hands. "What is going on over here?"

"That Dragon almost killed me," The older boy said, still laying on the ground.

"That's not true! It was an accident," Irius protested.

"Both of you to the office, now," the teacher commanded, as he helped the older boy up. "I'd better get you to the nurse."

Ryrrŷcrax couldn't even find words to say as Irius helped him to his feet. "Come on, we'd better go," he told the young Dragon.

The pair ended up missing all their morning classes, as they sat outside of the headmistress' outside. Irius had washed the blood and dirt off himself and helped clean Ryrrŷcrax's horns. They could hear the older boy's mother inside the office shouting about how the school should never have allowed "one of those things" into their school.

The encounter had left the young Dragon rattled, but it had worn off by that point. Still, he was silent as the older boy's mother continued her tirade in the room behind them. Glancing over at his friend, Irius saw that he was staring at the floor as he had on their first day of class together.

"His mom acts like he almost died," the silver-haired boy said wearily, yawning. "I bet he won't be such a jerk next time, right?"

"I guess so."

"It's his fault that he got hurt anyway. I know that it wasn't on purpose, and I'll tell the headmistress what really happened."

"You shouldn't have to get in trouble too since you helped him," the young Dragon said, glancing over at his friend. "How did you do that, anyway?"

"My magic is Animancy. It's like—well, my mother's said it's like life-force magic. The easiest thing I can do with it is animate things like the paper turtle on your first day." He yawned again. "I can also use life energy to heal people, but that takes a lot of energy."

"Well, you do look tired." The young dragon remembered what his grandfather had told him the night before. "Irius, could your magic hurt people?"

"Hurt people? I don't know, but I never would. I want to use my magic to make people feel better, like when I made that turtle so you would smile."

Ryrrŷcrax felt pangs of guilt over how he'd pushed his friend away since that first day. The silver-haired boy only wanted to make him feel more welcome. He was the only one who ever seemed to care about him since the move.

"I'm sorry for how I've been acting toward you," Ryrŷcrax stammered. "I thought you and everyone else were going to be like the Humans my grandfather told me about, but I was wrong. I was just stupid."

Irius only shook his head. "I don't think you were. Well, maybe just a little? But I'm not mad at you, and I forgive you."

"You aren't mad?"

"I was nervous when we moved to the city too, but even I've been around other Humans before that. This all must be weird for you. After you wouldn't talk to me, I thought I did something that made you mad at me. So, I've been working on something special for you."

He opened his notebook and pulled out a purple-colored page he was drawing symbols on earlier. On it, he stacked pieces of orange and red paper with symbols as well. Ryrŷcrax watched, intrigued. The silver-haired boy pressed his hand onto the symbols, and the papers folded themselves into a tiny copy of Ryrŷcrax.

"It's—It's me?"

Irius grinned and nodded, "I was working on it last night, as an even better gift than the turtle. And look, it can do this too!" He nudged the paper Dragon, which then breathed out "flames" of the red and orange paper.

"It's even better than the real me," Ryrŷcrax joked, "I wish I could make fire like that. Does this mean you still want to be friends with me?"

"Of course, I do! I've never met anyone like you before, and my mother wants to meet you too."

"I want to be your friend too," the young Dragon smiled. Just as soon as he did, though, his smile faded. "Oh, no. I have to go tell my parents that I don't want to move anymore!"

"And why is that?" a familiar voice said. Turning, Ryrŷcrax saw his mother standing there looking less than pleased.

"Mother!" He jumped up and hugged her. "I'm sorry, I've been acting so weird, I—Wait … Why are you here?"

"I was contacted by your headmistress' office that you had been in a fight. And that you attacked someone."

"O-Oh …" the young Dragon said, sheepishly.

"That was an accident, Irius added. Virrêi's eyes lit up when she saw him.

"Oh my, are you Ryrrŷcrax's friend? The one who made the turtle?" Irius nodded.

"That's wonderful, dear! I'm so glad my son was able to make friends so quickly here, and he still has the turtle saved on his windowsill. I think he likes it quite a bit, don't you, Ryrrŷcrax?"

"Mother, stop," Ryrrŷcrax said, growing embarrassed. She turned her attention back to him.

"Are you ready to talk about how you've been feeling, now?"

"I talked to grandfather on the first night of school, and he told me about the Humans he fought in the war. Then I had a nightmare about my class, and … I made myself afraid of everyone."

"I'll need to have a little talk with your grandfather." She stopped and listened to the continued ravings of the older boy's mother in the Headmistress' office. "Is that the other boy's mother?"

Both children nodded.

"Am I going to be expelled?" Ryrrŷcrax asked.

"Wait here, son."

He let go of his mother, who then went to the headmistress' office and opened the door.

"Can I speak with you for a moment?" His mother went in and closed the door behind her, and the chamber grew deathly quiet. Instead of shouting, there was only quiet muttering, and what the boys could make out seemed very intimidating. They both sat their nervously, looking at each other.

"Your mother is a little scary," Irius whispered.

After a few minutes, the door flew open, and the older boy's mother came out of the office.

"This won't be the end of it," she threatened to the women inside before starting down the corridor. As she got to Irius and Ryrrŷcrax, she glared at the young Dragon but said nothing when she realized Virrêi was now in the office doorway. The woman made her way past him and down the corridor, out of sight. Virrêi thanked the headmistress, who followed her out into the hallway.

"Well, that cleared everything up," Ryrrŷcrax's mother told him.

"I am not going to expel you," the headmistress announced. She was, without a doubt, the tallest Human that Ryrrŷcrax had seen. Yet her calm voice conflicted with the stern expression on her face. "But please try to be more careful with your classmates."

"I will, ma'am. Thank you." He turned to his mother, "What about staying here?"

"Are you sure you want to stay?"

The young Dragon nodded. "I miss grandfather, and I'm still getting used to the Human realm, but I don't want to leave Irius behind." The silver-haired boy smiled. "And I don't want you or father to have to leave your jobs, either."

"Well, I'll talk to your father, but I'm sure we'll find a way to stay here."

Ryrrŷcrax and Irius beamed at each other at the news.

"Now then, you two have missed enough class today," the headmistress said. "I trust you can find your way back to your homeroom without further incidents."

The two children nodded, and Virrêi went over and hugged her son. "I'll see you this afternoon, Ryrrŷcrax. I love you."

"I love you too."

She let go, and the two children went down the corridor together toward their classroom. The young Dragon looked over at the silver-haired boy and found himself smiling. He still found a lot of things about the Human world strange and confusing. Despite that, happiness spread in him as he walked back to the room with children who looked at him like a stranger. As long as he had someone like Irius with him, he knew that he'd be okay.

- 18 -

After the Dragon Was Defeated

Maxwell Czyzyk

Flames scorch the sky. Clarke Cobbler rises to open the shuttered window. Wings crest the tops of the trees that separate the village from the farming fields to the north.

A clap of thunder shakes the tower. Lightning cuts through the air against the red-tinted clouds.

Clarke flinches away from the window at the noise and flash of light. He turns back to see the head of a scaled beast breathe fire onto the tops of the forest trees. Flames arch across the corn and wheat fields.

Bursts of color and smoke strike the beast's wings, its neck, its face. The faint echoes of voices reach Clarke in the academy's tower.

Frozen, he watches as the beast tries to gain more altitude. Then, in the blink of an eye, the wings give out, and the beast crashes to the ground, sending a shudder through the earth.

Dashing from his room, Clarke takes the tower steps two at a time. Rounding the last bend, he almost crashes into a scullery maid, but Clarke doesn't slow his pace. He runs through the narrow paths of the village. The foliage scratches his face and neck, his hands and ankles.

Pulse racing, Clarke stumbles through the overgrown grass on the other side of the forest and reaches the cornfields. Heavy smoke blots out the sun. He can't breathe or see, but now that he's closer to the battle, he can discern the shouting voices. He feels the growling of the giant beast reverberating through his chest.

Clarke slows his pace as he approaches the last row of stalks, stopping at the edge of the field. The scene before him is grim. Losses on all sides, though some aren't willing to stop firing spells. The wind shifts, sending smoke down Clarke's throat. He coughs and retches at the smell. Unable to catch his breath, he falls to his knees, tears stinging his dark brown eyes.

A man with golden eyes and a long blond beard appears and blocks his path.

"Master Lombard," Clarke begins, but a raised hand from Lombard silences him.

"What exactly did you think you would accomplish without your supplies?" Lombard asks coldly. "Running toward a battlefield with no way to defend yourself. You didn't even bring a wand. Here I thought I'd taught you better."

"Y-you did teach me better, sir." Clarke holds up a small sack attached to his belt. "I finished it this morning. It holds ten times as much as my rucksack, but is less than half the size."

Lombard takes the offered sack and opens it to find the space within is indeed much larger than it should be.

"Very good," a small smile touches his lips but quickly turns to a frown. "But you're still an apprentice. A novice. And weak with magic at that. You shouldn't be here."

"I know. That's why I didn't bother with a wand. We both know I'm next to useless with them, but I knew this might be my only chance to see one."

"I'm afraid you were too late," Master Lombard says sadly. "We were all too late."

"Why was it here, of all places? I thought it was being tracked to the east, weeks of travel time."

"The Dragonights," Lombard growls. "Those glorified poachers discovered its location. Our faction tried to chase the dragon into the mountains to better protect it." Sighing, he shakes his head. "Something must have gone awry. More and more people have been backing the Dragonights. They're afraid, though whether their fear is from the dragons or the Dragonights, I can't be certain."

As he returns Clarke's sack, Lombard rests a comforting hand onto Clarke's shoulder. "Go back to the academy where it's safe. We'll do our best to drive the last of the Dragonights away and preserve what's left of the dragon as best we can. Perhaps, even in death, it can help us."

"I-I'm sorry. I can't walk away now. I have to see it!"

Clarke ducks from Lombard and rushes toward the huge dragon, silhouetted in a haze of smoke.

"Stop!" Lombard calls to Clarke's back. Cursing, he follows.

Clarke runs across the smoldering field. He hopes that they're deceiving him, that somehow, it's still alive. If he'd bothered to take in his surroundings, he would have seen the patches of dried grass catching fire. The few errant Dragonights continued to take advantage of the chaos. They struck at those trying to douse the flames. The witch rode up behind his left shoulder and prepared to strike.

"Clarke!" Master Lombard yells.

At the sound of his name, Clarke increases his speed and narrowly outpaces the witch's spell. Another fires at him, grazing the back of his thigh.

Tumbling to the ground, Clarke rolls away from his attacker. Rising to his knees, he withdraws a frozen sphere from his bag and throws it at the witch, hitting her in the shoulder. The sphere shatters on impact. It encases the witch's neck and the side of her face in ice, which continues to creep onto her chest and down her arm, inhibiting the use of her wand. A second sphere connects with her torso and a third the side of her head. Her wide-eyed expression freezes in place. Soon, she's completely encased, immobilized for the time. Still, the heat on the field is already making the ice sweat.

"How many times do I have to tell you! Always analyze your surroundings and prepare yourself accordingly! Especially when you don't have a wand!" Master Lombard scolds as he helps Clarke to his feet. "That was a lucky outcome. Not likely to happen again."

Clarke's shock begins to subside. The adrenaline coursing through his veins recedes. He realizes how dangerous his actions had been.

"I-I know. I'm sorry. I don't know what I was thinking."

With new eyes, Clarke takes in the scene before him. Aa handful of black-clad Dragonights are ransacking the dragon's corpse. The remaining Dragonights littering the battlefield continue to shoot off spells. They have no regard to the laws and regulations governing magical use, of course. The fires blaze unchecked and devour everything within reach.

"Go back to the tower," Master Lombard commands. "I'll follow shortly."

Nodding, Clarke cautiously retreats toward the tree line, conscious of any potential threats. He pauses on occasion to throw a frozen sphere onto smoldering embers to ensure they don't reignite.

Once in the safety of the forest, he combines the remaining frozen spheres with the contents of several vials from his sack. Lining them up at even intervals on the ground, he splashes the closest sphere with a deep blue potion. A shimmering haze rises into the air. The haze encases the trees to keep them from igniting and so the village beyond won't be lost to the fires.

After a sleepless night, Clarke finally manages to doze off moments before the sun rises. Unlike any other day, Master Lombard allows him to sleep well past noon. In fact, it's late into the evening before he interrupts Clarke's rest.

At the knocking on his door, Clarke starts, flinging his blankets from his bed. He nervously runs a hand through his mussed curls before answering.

"You need to comb your hair. It's a mess," is Master Lombard's greeting.

Clawing at the curling black strands doesn't help. Instead, Clarke's hair frizzes into a disaster.

Lombard waves his hand, dismissing Clarke's attempts.

"Forget your hair," Lombard says. He enters Clarke's chamber, taking a seat at the desk. Leaning back in the chair, he thoughtfully strokes his long blond beard.

Clarke begins spewing apologies.

Chuckling softly, Lombard assures him not to worry. "I allowed you to sleep so late for a reason."

"What reason is that, sir?" Nervousness tints Clarke's voice.

"Because I needed you well-rested. You're to pack your things."

"Wait. Pack for what?"

Glancing around the room, Lombard's piercing eyes don't miss a single detail. He takes in every speck of dust settled on the candelabra hanging from the ceiling. Every thread is woven together to create the sheet and coverlet. Every grain in the wood of the desk and chair, every rise and fall of the stones forming the walls and floor.

Clarke follows his master's gaze. He knows his eyes don't see the same things, the same intricacies, though he's doing his best to learn.

Satisfied, Lombard says, "After you left the fields yesterday, we were able to chase off the last of the Dragonights. We salvaged much of the dragon, which was luckily a male. We've had word of an abandoned brood of eggs that was discovered not far from the area this dragon was initially sighted. Plans are in motion to convene with the others in two days. Then we'll make our way to a secure location where we can hopefully reinstate the dragon race."

Unable to form coherent words, Clarke nods, his mouth agape. Once the information sinks in, he manages to ask, "When do we leave?"

"I'll send for you," Master Lombard says, rising from the chair. "Make sure you're prepared at any moment. Once it's time to go, there will be no turning back."

Knowing better than to disobey, Clarke grabs his rucksack before Lombard has closed the door behind him.

Questions circle through Clarke's mind. Many involve what he should pack, though he doesn't have many possessions. Three changes of clothes, a bar of soap, toothbrush, comb, and family portrait. Everything else belongs to the academy. He collects the items and dumps them onto his bed.

Once his things are placed inside his rucksack, Clarke finds he has ample space left. He fills some of it with spare parchment, ink, and several quills. With nothing left to do, he instantly grows restless.

After pacing his narrow room several times, he collapses onto his bed. His foot lazily kicks against the frame. Unbidden images of the previous day surface in his mind's eye. The flames, destruction, and chaos. The expressions on the faces of the black-clad Dragonights are power-hungry and unchecked. They are savage, just as they fought.

A shudder passes through Clarke. Not only because of the unsettling images but because of what is to come. He has spent the last ten years training. Master Lombard accepted him as an apprentice at the age of five. After his father died and his mother could no longer afford to care for him.

Clarke is there to help protect the last of the dragons though he has little magical talent. But Lombard pierced Clarke with his sharp, golden gaze and said that he had great promise.

He didn't want to disappoint his master, his mother, or himself. Clarke pushed his limits every day in exercising his magical abilities. He worked around his weaknesses by pouring himself into Drafting. He also immersed himself in crafting and brewing. Clarke bottled potions, aromatics, tinctures, tonics, and more. He read every book he was allowed to touch.

As he studied from the basic to the advanced, he devised new methods and concoctions, such as the frozen spheres. But in all that time, he never imagined this to be what he would face. Witches and wizards not unlike himself pitted against one another because of a difference in views.

Driving the unsettling thoughts from his mind, Clarke shifts onto his stomach and props open a book. *An Explosive*

Reaction: Combining Drafting with Spell Casting by Hobart Flaminio, and delves into the pages.

Four chapters later, his restlessness returns. Double-checking his rucksack, Clarke believes it to be a shame there's so much empty space. He knows he isn't allowed to take the academy's books out of the building. He's been repeatedly scolded for preferring to read outside in the sunshine.

He stuffs the book next to his family's portrait. Clarke slings his rucksack over his shoulder and ties the supply pouch onto his belt. He makes his way to the library.

Easily the most impressive room in the academy, the library takes up an entire floor. Bookcases fill every wall, every surface, and some follow the curves of arched passageways and cling to the ceiling. The charmed shelves hold the books in place despite being upside down. Others spiral up pillars and tuck themselves into the smallest of crevices.

The scent of old parchment and glue fills Clarke's nose as he enters the room. Due to the amount of time Clarke has spent in here over the years, he finds a dozen useful books. They range from Herbology to Charms to Drafting. Most focus on Magical Fauna, dragons in particular.

Satisfied when there is no longer space to spare in his rucksack, Clarke rushes back toward his chamber.

Moments after returning to his room, a hesitant knock shocks Clarke out of his skin. He draws in a deep breath before opening the door.

Appearing just as nervous, the scullery maid he'd almost plowed over earlier whispers angrily, "Where have you been? Master Lombard sent me to fetch you ten minutes ago, but you didn't answer." However, she doesn't give Clarke time to respond. "Never mind. Master Lombard is waiting for you near the kitchen staff's entrance. You're to hurry—even more so now that you'll be ten minutes late, at best." Her eyes dart around the room, and she glances over her shoulder. "Don't stop to talk to anyone. Don't mention where you're going or who you're meeting."

"Did he say anything else?" Clarke asks.

The maid shakes her head. Before Clarke can press for more information, she disappears into the shadows of the hallway.

With his nerves reignited, Clarke begins to put on his traveling cloak, then decides to shove it into his rucksack. After one final look around his chamber, he extinguishes his candles and makes his way to the academy's kitchen.

"Clarke Cobbler, where have you been?!"

Master Lombard scolds him as soon as he's within view.

"I told you to be prepared to leave when I sent for you."

Not bothering with excuses, mainly because he doesn't have any, Clarke meekly falls into step beside Lombard. Nudging Clarke between the shoulder blades, Lombard prompts Clarke to hurry.

Once in the crisp, cool night air, Clarke is uncertain where they're heading and moves to take a wrong turn.

"This way," Master Lombard hisses, ducking into a narrow alley between two rows of houses.

Minutes later, Clarke realizes they're on the outskirts of the village's market square. In the moonlight, Clarke can make out a small group of people huddled together beneath a stall's canopy. Each is wearing a traveling cloak with the hood drawn.

"What now?" Clarke asks.

"We leave."

Signaling to the others, Master Lombard disappears behind a stall. A few of the cloaked group do the same, reappearing moments later leading a menagerie of magical beasts. There are griffins—their front half that of an eagle, the back a lion. The hhippogrif, kin to the griffin, their front half also that of an eagle, their hindquarters that of a horse, Finally, pennequo appear, creatures with the body of a horse and giant feathered wings and mane.

Eager to see which Master Lombard will have, Clarke rushes over to meet him, only to stop in his tracks as he's greeted by a grimmare. It is a beast that looks like something out of his nightmares. Though similar in build to the pennequo, the grimmare's body is covered in dark, sleek scales. Instead of feathered wings, the grimmare's are comparable to that of a dragon's, complete with a claw at the joint.

"Meet Knightmare," Lombard chuckles as he notices Clarke's hesitation.

"Wait, did you call him 'nightmare?'" Clarke blanches, already knowing the answer.

Laughing harder, Lombard shakes his head. "It's spelled 'k-n-i-g-h-t,' like Knights of the Round Table. This particular steed has quite an impressive lineage. Although the wizard that named him had a questionable sense of humor. Anyway, he'll be our mount for this trip."

Giving the grimmare an affectionate pat on the neck, Lombard swings himself up between its wings.

As Clarke balks at the thought of climbing onto Knightmare's back, the others mount their beasts and begin taking off into the night sky.

"It's now or never, Clarke."

Clenching his jaw, Clarke gives a resigned nod and takes Lombard's outstretched hand. He shifts unsteadily once seated, unable to get comfortable with the idea of the grimmare.

Still unprepared for flight, Clarke stifles a squeal into Lombard's shoulder blades. Knightmare takes off toward the moon.

For the first half-hour of flight, Clarke nervously clings to Lombard's waist. He becomes comfortable with the gentle rising and falling of the grimmare's flight. Soon, he is lulled into a half doze by the subtle noise created by the wings catching at the air.

When the night's temperature dips farther, he wishes he put on his cloak before leaving. But the chilled breeze helps keep him awake until they land at a traveler's inn as the sun crests the horizon.

Despite the group's mounts attracting the occasional stare, their stay passes uneventfully. They make their way to their next rest stop. It's a run-down shack that makes their last inn look like a small palace in comparison.

"Stay close," Lombard whispers as they pay for their room, although there's little need to use hushed tones.

The first floor of the inn is packed to capacity. Voices boom over one another. The warm, humid air smells of poorly cooked food, stale ale, and the earthy stench of sweat. Clarke finds it difficult to stay close to Lombard as they cross the space to the stairs leading to their room. He's jostled by burly men and jabbed in the ribs by the bar maiden's bony elbows.

Rubbing his jawline where a tall farmer clipped him with a flagon, Clarke trips upstairs and gladly collapses onto the lumpy bed. Instead of settling in, Lombard paces the room, his hand anxiously running down the length of his beard.

Propping against the headboard, Clarke asks, "Who are the others traveling with us?"

Pausing in his pacing, Lombard replies, "Some are members of the academy who, like us, don't want to see an end to dragons. The rest are those who saw the havoc the Dragonights have caused and wish to help us put a stop to them."

"But won't they go away now that they've killed the last dragon?"

"No, Clarke, they won't," Lombard sighs. "For starters, many of their ranks don't care about eliminating the dragons. They merely want to fight, so they'll shift their focus to something or someone else. You saw how many lingered after the dragon was defeated. They began attacking anyone left in the fields."

Clarke nods. "I still can't believe how they were acting."

"Believe it. You may have to face them someday." Lombard sighs again and resumes his pacing. "The other reason the Dragonights won't disappear is because of the other dragons out there."

"Wait. I thought the one they killed was the last known dragon?"

"It was the last known dragon," Lombard concedes. "Others looking to protect them have been much more successful at hiding them than we were. They've devised ways to keep them out of sight, to ward them against the Dragonights. Although there aren't any known reports of more, the Dragonights will continue searching until they're certain they've killed every last one. If I had to guess, I'd say they'll never stop combing the globe."

A knock echoes into the room.

"Ah, right on time," Lombard says.

When he opens the door, he allows a girl around the same age as Clarke entry. He pulls a simple, wooden chair from the corner of the room and offers it to her. She's one of the members of the academy he'd spoken of earlier.

"So, Ardelle, what word does Diantha send?"

Taking the seat, Ardelle acknowledges Clarke, then turns back to Master Lombard. "She said she didn't see anything or anyone following us, but all this scrying is taking a lot out of her, especially after flying for so long. She'll never admit to her age having any effect on her skills, though we know it's harder for her the older she gets – and at 86 ..."

"I know. I trust her without question though," Lombard says firmly. "I've never seen someone read a crystal ball with such clarity, nor have I heard of anyone matching her abilities."

"Neither have I," Ardelle says. "But as her apprentice, I've seen the changes in her over the past few years. They're subtle, so much so that most wouldn't notice anything amiss. But there's no question that her sight is getting a bit foggy."

During the conversation, Clarke sits quietly, trying to figure out why the girl looks so familiar.

"The scullery maid?" he finally blurts out.

"Excuse me?"

"Clarke, where are your manners?" Lombard scolds.

Blushing deeply, Clarke apologizes. "I knew I'd seen you somewhere before. I just couldn't figure it out."

Flushing even darker than Clarke, Ardelle nods, "I do work in the kitchens on occasion. Not every Master is allotted enough money from the academy to fully support an apprentice. So, I compensate by doing some meal preparations and light cleaning, mostly in the library."

Before Clarke can embarrass himself further, Lombard cuts in. "Ardelle, thank you for your honesty. I must insist that you keep your suspicious about Diantha's abilities to yourself, for the time at least. We can't afford any hesitations right now. And let everyone know that we'll be proceeding as planned."

Promising she won't tell a soul about Mistress Diantha, Ardelle takes her leave. She knocks on doors in code as she makes her way down the hallway as she informs those within of Lombard's response.

"I can't believe your lack of manners sometimes," Lombard sighs, shutting the door and turning to Clarke. He plops onto the now free chair.

"I'm just so tired," Clarke yawns. "Not that it's an adequate excuse," he adds at the look Lombard gives him.

"It has been a trying day," Lombard concedes. Yawning with a stretch, Lombard pushes the chair back into the corner, then settles into his bed. "For now, we should both get some sleep. It's going to be a long day with an early start."

Even before the sun breaks the horizon, Clarke is shaken awake. He staggers downstairs and swallows the slop passing for oatmeal before taking his place upon Knightmare's back. After his conversation with Master Lombard, he'd been unable to sleep. He was too excited and eager to keep moving forward. But now, he's wishing he could have quieted his mind better. Lombard promises this stretch of the journey will be a long one.

"A few groups will be stopping to replenish their supplies, the rest of us will be scattering and circling back to the meeting point in case anyone has been following us," Lombard explains over his shoulder. "We'll be flying non-stop until we get there. Knightmare is well-rested and going strong."

Groggily nodding, Clarke sighs heavily and rests his eyes. He's far more comfortable with the grimmare than he was before. But he still can't manage to fully fall asleep knowing he's tens of feet in the air.

By noon, the temperature shifts to scorching hot, the sun blazing high in the sky. Clarke and Lombard shield themselves with their cloaks. Knightmare seems to enjoy the heat and sunbeams, swooping in broad arches to avoid the shadows being cast by clouds, whinnying happily.

Within an hour or so, the heat begins to lessen and the scents of dry grass and farmland shifts to the damp smell of forests and streams. Clarke realizes he has no idea where they are, that this is the farthest from home he's ever been. He has vague memories of traveling with his father to nearby towns and villages. Yet those places were two or three days away on foot. By now, he and Lombard have flown for nearly two days – covering much more ground.

A small thrill runs through Clarke's spine at the thought.

Two more hours pass. Clarke's bottom and back are exhausted, his arms ache, and he wants nothing more than to take a nap. However, he knows not to complain. It won't do any good, and Master Lombard is likely just as uncomfortable.

Thankfully, their destination comes into view soon after. The last stretch of the journey is far more bearable.

"There," Lombard says, pointing. "You can see the road cutting through the trees."

Knightmare swoops and spins downwards, landing in a clearing near the road. Clarke and Lombard dismount and walk with Knightmare for nearly an hour and reach another inn.

Stomach growling, Clarke follows Lombard to a table where a handful of their group waits. As he scarfs down cheese and fresh fruit, he listens to the conversation.

"We were nearly knocked from the air," a petite witch says. "Thankfully, we lost the Dragonights after landing on a cliffside and climbing down into the forest below."

A burly wizard with corded muscles, Isband, chimes in, "Got attacked meself. Never saw 'em coming neither."

"Clarke and I didn't have any trouble," Lombard says. "But the sooner we meet the others and leave here, the better."

Murmurs of agreement fill the table. As more arrive, they relate their tales from their stretch of the journey. Most, like Clarke and Lombard, had an uneventful trip. Yet the threat of the Dragonights is ever-present, darkening the mood.

Morale is low until Ardelle arrives with Mistress Diantha. The old seer settles into her seat at the table with much creaking and cracking from her joints.

"Thank magic I'm off that blasted beast – oi!" she groans as she adjusts the many shawls and scarves layered beneath her cloak. "Ardelle, if you wouldn't mind?"

"Yes Mistress," Ardelle says. She quickly sets a crystal-clear orb upon an intricately designed stand and steps aside. While Diantha begins to scry, staring with glossy eyes, Ardelle reports to Lombard.

"No, we didn't encounter any Dragonights, but we had to stop once more than planned so Mistress could rest. Our pennequo has a smooth flight pattern. The saddle you had crafted is most comfortable. Yet, she insisted on trying to look ahead for threats. Doing so while flying put too much of a strain on her."

"I understand," Lombard says. "You made the correct decision, given the situation. Did she see anything of importance?"

"Yes and no." Ardelle replies. "I should let her—"

Clearing her throat loudly, Mistress Diantha's eyes refocus and she answers. "While I wasn't able to see anything in regards to more Dragonights, I did see something of great importance. Our faction in the mountains with the dragon eggs they were attempting to incubate there, have proven unsuccessful." The eager faces surrounding Diantha turn crestfallen. "All eggs, save one. A male has hatched! Healthy and vibrant! There is yet hope!"

Cheers ring throughout the space. Several scowl and wayward glances that Lombard immediately notices.

"This is great news indeed, however, but we should retire to our rooms," he says. "We should all be well-rested and prepared for our next move as soon as the others arrive." Nodding to Isband, he adds, "There are also many preparations."

Several people follow Lombard's lead and retire, others linger to enjoy another round of ale. Clarke is among those following Lombard, being more than happy to once again have a bed to collapse into.

Screams startle Clarke awake. In the windowless room at the inn, Clarke isn't able to tell the hour. Regardless, he stumbles from the bed and kicks off the blankets wrapped around his legs.

Chaos greets him in the hallway. Black-clad Dragonights are kicking open doors as they eject the occupants into the hallway.

Clarke retreats into his room and grabs his supply pouch. With deft hands, he crafts several frozen spheres in seconds. However, before he can return to the hallway to put them to use, Lombard enters, with Ardelle close behind. He locks the door with a charm.

"Listen to me Clarke," Lombard commands. "The Dragonights ambushed the group with the dragon eggs. Only a few of them made it—the people, I mean—to deliver the eggs. Only one out of the five eggs didn't make it. However, our plan from here remains the same. I, along with Isband, another Charms Master, created exact replicas of the eggs. Everyone will have either a real egg or a copy to take with them to our final destination. Here is yours. You're to treat it like it's a real egg, understand?"

"Yes, but what—"

Lombard cuts him off, "No time for questions now. Keep the egg hot, Not warm, hot—at all times. Ardelle has one too. The two of you will be leaving now on Knightmare. He'll fly you where you need to go – toward the mountains. Trust him."

While Lombard gathers his things for him and packs them into a rucksack, Clarke prepares the egg. First, he soaks strips of fabric with a pale orange potion, then wraps the egg in the fabric. Carefully placing everything into a clear jar with a latching lid, he drops a lit match inside. Quickly closing the top, he's soon holding a perpetually burning jar of flames. Though the jar itself never gets hot, the temperature within is scorching.

"Ready?"

"Almost," Clarke replies. He takes a moment to rearrange the things in his supply sack before settling the dragon egg among the other jars, vials, and bottles. "Ok, now."

For the first time since she entered the room, Clarke turns to Ardelle. Dried tear streaks run down her cheeks. Soft sniffles occasionally escape her throat.

Catching Clarke's eye, Lombard shakes his head once.

"When I give the signal, we're going to make a dash for the room across the hall; I'll lower you out the window there. Knightmare is in the last stall of the stable. Blast a hole in the back wall to get to him. There's no doubt in my mind the Dragonights will have a guard stationed at the front."

Waving Clarke toward the door with his wand, Lombard wishes him well. "The rest of us will follow shortly after, once we give the Dragonights some push back. We all agreed that we can't scatter without a fight."

Clarke double checks his things. He dashes through the door the instant Lombard removes his charm. Without hesitation, he swings his legs out the window in the next room, leaning his weight forward as he waits for Lombard's spell. Leaning too far, he slips and loses his grip, dropping half a story in less than a second.

Five feet from the ground, Clarke feels his weight lessen and his pace slow. Craning his neck, he looks back at the inn where Lombard is watching him gently land, his face straining with effort.

Not bothering to wait for Ardelle, Clarke slips through the shadows to the stable. Fumbling through his pouch, he uses the same pale orange potion that he used for the dragon egg. He combines the potion with a frozen sphere. Once certain Ardelle has caught up, he moves several feet away from the wall of the stable, then throws the sphere.

Upon impact, an explosion opens a hole more than large enough for Knightmare to fit through.

The grimmare charges through the gaping hole and leads the way for the griffons, hippogriffs, and pennequo.

One pennequo in particular catches Ardelle's attention as Clarke scrambles onto Knightmare's back. She stares, tears welling in her eyes, as Clarke reaches down to help her mount. He follows her gaze, taking note of the pennequo's saddle, which is more throne than saddle.

"Lombard said to take Knightmare ... Besides, won't Diantha need that saddle?"

At her master's name, Ardelle's shoulders shake with sobs. Knowing time is of the utmost importance, Clarke dismounts an impatient Knightmare. He half lifts, half shoves Ardelle onto the grimmare's back. As he scrambles up behind her, he barely has his leg in place when Knightmare launches into the sky. His powerful wings knock a Dragonight closing in on them to the ground.

Though afraid to ask, Clarke's curiosity gets the better of him.

"So, what happened before, at the inn? You know, before you showed up with Master Lombard?"

Sniffling, Ardelle's response is barely more than a whisper. "Mistress and I were scrying, trying to foresee anything having to do with the Dragonights. That's when they ransacked the inn. They kicked in our door and grabbed Mistress Diantha's shoulder."

Though Clarke can't see her face from his position on Knightmare, he can tell Ardelle is crying again. "S-she was pulled from her seat and hit her head. There was a lot of blood. Lombard came in then with that strong wizard, Isband, and they fought off the Dragonights. He s-said that," Ardelle pauses and wipes her nose with her sleeve, "Lombard said it just looked like a lot of blood, that the forehead bleeds easily. He said that she'd be fine. I still didn't want to leave her like that." After a few more sniffles, she adds, "If Mistress hadn't been so tired, she would've seen them coming."

Unsure of what to say, not very skilled at comforting, Clarke remains silent. Though he understands how Ardelle feels since he too had little choice but to leave his master.

After an hour or so of flying, Clarke wonders how much longer it will take to get to the mountains. For the first time since leaving the inn, he takes a good look at their surroundings. He realizes that they're retracing the same path they took after the second inn.

"Wait. This can't be right."

Swiveling around, he tries to get a better view.

"We're heading back toward that run down, joke of an inn!"

"We can't be. Lombard said that the grimmare was going to take us to the mountains."

Pointing, Clarke indicates the thatched roof of the inn in question in the distance. It's easy enough to see as there's nothing within a mile's radius of the building.

However, no matter what Ardelle tries, Knightmare refuses to change course. He continues to soar toward the inn until he's overhead, then he angles to the west.

Eventually, Ardelle gives up and drops the reigns. Knightmare whinnies happily and begins to swoop in arches across the sky. He dips low to the ground and tilts dangerously, running an outstretched wing through a stream cutting across the open fields. Keeping low, he follows the stream until it converges with a powerful river. There, he lands.

"Guess we're resting here," Clarke grumbles, dismounting onto stiff legs.

Ardelle follows suit, stumbling as she lands. She washes off her face in the stream, throwing a handful of water at Knightmare when he comes over to drink.

"Stupid, stubborn beast," she mutters.

"Hey!" Clarke snaps. "Knightmare's not stupid! Stubborn, maybe, but Lombard said to trust him, and I will – I do. He'll get us where we need to be."

"We'll see about that," Ardelle says as she sets up a small bowl with a wire stand. She collects a few handfuls of dried grass and twigs and places them into the bowl. She sets it on fire with a jab of her wand. Stalking over to Knightmare, she yanks a hair from his tail.

A surprised and indignant Knightmare kicks out with his hind legs and narrowly misses Ardelle's shoulder. With a shriek, she falls to the ground, cowering with her hands over her head.

Rushing forward, Clarke grabs hold of Knightmare's reigns and leads him away from Ardelle. Running a soothing hand down the grimmare's face helps to calm the beast down. Clarke realizes that the once cringe-worthy scales are so fine and smooth they feel almost soft to the touch. He moves his hand to the mane, seemingly thick and coarse. He realizes that it is comprised of exceedingly fine tendrils, also covered by scales.

"No wonder you were so mad," Clarke says loud enough for Ardelle to hear. "Having that pulled out is sure to hurt!"

"Not enough to try and kick my face," Ardelle snaps as she brushes the dry grass from her cloak.

Returning to the small bowl, she drops the "hair" into the flames. She carefully watches the subtle changes in color, the way the "hair" shrivels as it burns, and the curling patterns of the smoke.

Huffing, Ardelle abruptly throws the contents of the bowl into the stream. She repacks her supplies and dusts off her hands.

"I suppose we should get moving again."

"That's up to Knightmare," Clarke says. "He deserves an apology. Especially since whatever you just did showed you that he knows where he's going."

Knightmare seems to agree with Clarke; he refuses to allow Ardelle within ten paces of him until she says "I'm sorry."

Dusk arrives, casting the world in pinks and oranges.

Knightmare has been following the river upstream for hours. He glides over acres of farm fields. Soon, they see a small town below. Clarke and Ardelle both hope he'll land, but after the scene at the juncture of stream and river, they know better than to protest.

In fact, he doesn't move to land until the moon is high in the sky. Shocking Clarke out of a slight doze, Knightmare suddenly drops tens of feet at once. Clinging to the reigns and with his legs, Clarke stifles a shout. Ardelle clings to his back, her face buried between his shoulders.

Knightmare continues to dive so fast, Clarke wonders if he'll manage to stop before crashing into the rushing river.

At the last moment, Knightmare pulls up, his hooves kicking up water. For another fifteen minutes or so, he continues following the river as it disappears into a tunnel, naturally carved into the hillside.

Clarke feels Ardelle's arms wrap tighter around his waist in the dark. He tries his best not to tense and appear nervous as well. Minutes pass by in darkness. A low rumbling begins to build louder as they approach the other side of the tunnel.

When they emerge, they're greeted by an expansive lake, encased on all sides by cliffs. On the opposite side of the lake is a cascading waterfall, the source of the low rumbling.

Circling the lake once, Knightmare takes his time gliding across the mirror-smooth surface. His sharp eyes take in every detail, before putting on a burst of speed. A powerful thrust from his wings sends him and his riders through the waterfall. On the other side is a concave alcove, just enough space to set up camp for the night.

Taking Knightmare's lead, Ardelle and Clarke settle in for the night. The white noise from the falls helps them to sink into a deep sleep.

The sun is rising high overhead by the time Knightmare stirs the next day. Not wanting to interrupt his rest, Ardelle and Clarke take the time to replenish their supplies.

Crafting a rod from a branch and some string, Clarke spends the morning fishing. Ardelle insists on climbing down from their alcove to gather moss and salt from a nearby tunnel.

"Fine, but don't expect me to dive into the lake to save you if you fall."

Ignoring Clarke's comment, she disappears over the ledge.

By the time she returns, Clarke is drying out his catches over a smoking fire and reading several books at once. She finds him sitting cross-legged in an arc of opened volumes.

Flushed from the climb, she tells Clarke, "There are probably hundreds of tunnels all over the lake. It was too dark for me to keep track of where we were going last night. We're somewhere in the mountains now."

Opening yet another book, Clarke flips through its pages. "I've been wondering that myself. I can't find this lake on any of these maps."

"Books can only tell you so much," Ardelle sniffs. "Let me see what I can see."

Settling in with her crystal ball, Ardelle stares into its depths with unfocused eyes.

Shaking his head, Clarke returns to his books.

"Aha! We are almost there!"

Ardelle's voice bounces off the rock behind the waterfall, startling Clarke.

"You don't have to be so loud," he snaps. Knightmare whinnies and paws the ground in agreement.

"And you don't have to be so rude and grumpy all the time, but you are," she snaps back. When Knightmare snorts, Ardelle takes it as a sign of support. "Besides, I have a right to be excited after traveling for so long. Especially since I don't want to have to lug this egg around anymore. It's heavy."

To punctuate her point, she dumps a padded sack onto the ground with a heavy thud.

"Be careful with that! They're big but still delicate."

"Oh please, like Lombard gave us real eggs. We're apprentices."

Ignoring Ardelle, Clarke unpacks her dragon egg, examining the surface for cracks.

"Why is it so cold? You're supposed to be making sure it's kept warm."

Shrugging, she indicates the bag, "It's supposed to be insulated to keep it heated on its own. I don't know anything about how it works."

Grumbling under his breath, Clarke examines the lining of the bag. The padding is indeed warm, obviously the source of heat like Ardelle claims. Yet something seems to have gone wrong and it isn't as hot as it should be.

After some trial and error, Clarke fixes the problem and packs the egg into the now piping hot bag.

When he goes to give it back to Ardelle, he discovers she's wandered off.

"Ardelle? Come on, it's time to go," he groans. He collects his books and the dried fish, stowing them in his rucksack before stamping out the fire. "Ardelle, stop fooling around."

Clarke turns to approach the shadow on the other side of the waterfall. He realizes the figure is far too large to be Ardelle.

Without hesitation, he launches several frozen spheres through the water before turning to scoop up Ardelle's egg. However, he's too late. The figure splashes into the alcove and lands next to the bag—a black-clad Dragonight.

Knightmare springs into action at the enemy's appearance, charging. He succeeds in slamming into the Dragonight's chest and sends him tumbling into the lake. However, the Dragonight had already gotten ahold of Ardelle's bag.

"Clarke!"

Ardelle's voice distorts through the rush of water, but Clarke doesn't hesitate. He wants to dive into the lake after the dragon egg. First, he collects the last of his things and mounts Knightmare.

Once through the waterfall, Clarke sees a Dragonight pulling Ardelle into a nearby tunnel. A tall, lean witch with a familiar face. Clarke recognizes her as the same witch that attacked him on the battlefield so many days ago.

Kicking Knightmare's sides, Clarke drives him toward the witch. Balking at the tunnel's entrance, Knightmare kicks out, catching the witch in the forehead. Her skull smashes into the rock wall. The sound echoes down the passageway and across the lake, making Clarke sick to his stomach.

"Don't … don't look," Ardelle tells him as she mounts Knightmare. "We have to get out of here. Don't look."

With another kick to Knightmare's sides, the trio is in the air.

The better part of the day passes in silence, Ardelle gave up trying to comfort Clarke long ago.

Clarke is the one to finally break that silence.

"Part of me wanted her dead. She was one of the Dragonights that killed the dragon near the academy. She attacked me. But still, I—I didn't mean for that to happen."

"I've told you a hundred times already. It wasn't your fault. It just happened."

Sighing heavily, Clarke mutters, "I know, still …"

Silence settles in again, broken hours later by a shattering noise.

"What in the name of magic?!" Clarke exclaims, yanking his supply pouch from his belt.

More shattering is followed by a long, frustrated screech.

Upon opening the pouch, Clarke leans back in surprise, almost knocking Ardelle off Knightmare's haunches.

"Watch it!" she shouts at the same time Clarke yells, "The egg!"

Pointing, Clarke tugs on Knightmare's reigns.

"The dragon hatched! It can't fly yet! You have to catch it!"

Despite being a tiny gray streak against the pale sky, Knightmare spots the hatchling. The dragon immediately takes action, folding in his wings for a dive.

Realizing that they won't make it in time, Clarke begins fumbling around in his pouch. He curses at the broken mess of glass the dragon left behind.

"What are you doing? Your wand is right there! Use it!" Ardelle shouts. When Clarke doesn't move to grab it, she does, firing off multiple spells. None have any effect on the falling baby dragon.

Clarke yells at Ardelle while pulling on a pair of slick gloves. More cursing follows as he finds the ingredients he needs to form a ball of white fluff in his palm. Pulling back his arm, he launches the fluff at the dragon as hard as he can.

"You missed?!" Ardelle shrieks, shaking Clarke by the shoulders. "I can't believe you missed!"

"I wasn't trying to hit it!" Clarke shouts back. "Look!"

The fluff strikes the ground and expands into a mass twenty times its original size. Seconds later, the dragon lands in its center.

Clarke knew it was a matter of time before Ardelle started bombarding him with questions. He just wishes it would have been later rather than sooner.

Sheepishly, Ardelle approaches him. Clarke works on dissolving the fluff trapping the dragon as quickly as possible. The longer it's active, the harder the substance becomes.

"H-how did you do that?"

Gritting his teeth, Clarke tries to will the red flush tinting his cheeks to recede. At times like this, when people are shocked by his skills, Clarke can't help but feel a rush of pride. Still, he usually feels embarrassed at the same time.

"It's Drafting, but very advanced Drafting," he explains. "I have to infuse the concoctions with magic to speed up the creation process on many occasions." Pausing in his efforts, he digs out a book from his rucksack and hands it to Ardelle. *Wandless Magicks: Risks and Rewards* by Emlyn Hemlock.

"You're using magic without a wand?" she gasps. "But that's dangerous."

"Not really," Clarke shrugs, returning his attention to the purple substance. "Not for me anyway."

Stepping back, Ardelle mutters, "I guess I owe you an apology."

"I don't want it," Clarke says shortly. "I heard what you said when you grabbed my wand—that everyone at the academy was right about me." Turning to face Ardelle, he continues. "I know they say I'm useless, not worth apprenticing to Master Lombard. They say I have no magical skills and I'm not worth wasting a wand on. Isn't it funny how people's attitudes change when they find out I've mastered a skill they couldn't even dream about attempting?"

"That's—I meant—what I'm trying to say ..."

"You're no different. You only felt bad after you realized how much control I have over my magic. Even if my magic isn't particularly powerful. That's why I can do magic without my wand because it's so weak. I've worked hard to overcome that weakness. I've turned it into a strength."

Clapping echoes from the forest edge at the end of Clarke's rant.

Jumping to his feet, Clarke wraps his hand around a frozen sphere. Ardelle faces the tree line with Clarke's wand at the ready.

"I don't think I've even been more proud of you Clarke."

"Master Lombard?"

In his excitement, Clarke drops his frozen sphere. It leaves a patch of creeping ice on the ground and he rushes to hug his master.

"Rather affectionate today, aren't we?" he laughs, patting Clarke's shoulder.

"Sorry," Clarke mumbles, flushing cherry red. "I'm just so happy to see you."

Hanging back, Ardelle looks on.

"Lombard?" a voice calls from the forest. "Lombard? Where'd ya go? Did you find 'em?"

"Isband!" Lombard replies. "Out here!" Facing Ardelle, he says, "Don't worry. Diantha is going to be fine. She returned to the academy with a full escort to recover. Once she's completely healed, she plans on joining us in the mountains. She's already insisted."

Happy tears stream down Ardelle's cheeks. She nods once, unable to form words.

"Um, Master Lombard," Clarke interjects. "I have a question."

"Yes?"

"Why in the name of magic did you give me a real dragon egg?"

At that moment, Isband emerges from the tree line. "A real dragon egg you say? That is fortunate."

Closing the gap between himself and the others, Isband pulls out a wand and directs it at Lombard. A cruel smile crosses his lips.

"Don't even think about moving, boy. Lombard bragged about you for hours and hours, so I know all about your skills. I won't hesitate to blast him."

Afraid of what Isband might do to Lombard, Clarke raises his hands in surrender. He knows he needs to get back to the hatchling. His once fluffy substance is getting harder by the second. So, unless the dragon escapes on its own, it won't be able to breathe before long.

Noticing the worried glances Clarke keeps casting in the dragon's direction, Ardelle knows she has to act. Something isn't right. She fears Isband's threats of injuring Lombard if Clarke makes a move. Still, Ardelle believes she can get a spell or two fired off before Isband pays her much attention.

"Stupefio!" she shouts with a flick of the wand, immediately followed by "debilito!" and "ulcus eruptus!"

Unsurprisingly, Isband deflects the Stun Charm with little effort. He sidesteps the Paralysis Charm. However, the final spell—a mossy green blast—glances his wand hand. A patch of pus-filled boils emerges from the surface of his skin.

Growling under his breath, he says, "You stupid whelp. Like a pathetic Diviner could compete with a Charms Master. Such a pathetic attempt."

He moves to raise his wand. Ardelle is faster, aiming her wand at the sky, then slashing downward in one fluid movement.

"Fulmico!"

A blinding flash cuts a path across the sky, striking the ground next to Isband.

Once Clarke's vision clears from the sudden burst of light, he sees Isband laying prone on the ground. Not taking any chances, he lobs a few frozen spheres at him, freezing his limbs to the ground.

"That was overkill," Lombard says, though Clarke isn't sure whether he's speaking to him or Ardelle. "Clarke, the dragon, if you would?"

Nodding, he finishes dissolving the fluff encasing the hatchling.

Kicking Isband's limp leg, Lombard shakes his head. "I'm still in shock. I never thought Isband would be working for the Dragonights. It does explain how they knew about our plans."

"What now?" Clarke asks.

"Thankfully, Isband didn't know our final destination, so we'll proceed as planned. Wait here a moment."

Briefly disappearing into the woods, Lombard emerges while leading two mounts, a griffin, and a pennequo.

Passing the pennequo to Ardelle, he says, "I believe you're familiar with handling one."

Ardelle nods and accepts the reigns. When she tries to mount, her feet barely leave the ground. She lurches to the side, then leans her weight into the pennequo.

"Took too much out of yourself, didn't you?" Lombard says, hurrying to her side. He helps her up, promising to land as soon as possible to rest. "We just need to put some distance between us and Isband. He's guaranteed to be out for some time, but I have no way of knowing if there are any other Dragonights nearby. What you did was very impressive, but also very foolish."

"I didn't know what else to do. Most people think I'm weak because I'm apprentice to a Master Diviner, but that isn't true," she says.

"Obviously," Lombard agrees with an encouraging smile.

True to his word, Lombard signals to land within an hour. He uses his wand to quickly set up camp, complete with tent and sleeping mats. The site is much more comfortable than the night spent behind the waterfall.

The next morning, Clarke wakes to the scent of frying fish.

Stretching, he grumbles. "More fish."

"It's what we have," Lombard shrugs, tucking his beard away from the flames. "You don't have to eat breakfast if you don't like it."

"Right, like I'm going to skip a meal," Clarke laughs.

While they eat, Master Lombard and Clarke exchange tales, catching each other up on what has happened since parting at the inn. When Lombard comes full circle, he sighs. "Isband has been at the academy for years. I don't think I'll ever be able to accept his involvement with the Dragonights. And I now fear there are others like him hiding amongst our ranks."

"I wish I could tell you there aren't," Clarke says.

"There's no way to tell," Lombard sighs. Glancing at the tent, he adds, "I hope Ardelle wakes soon. We need to keep moving, though I know she needs to rest after using such a powerful spell."

"What was that spell?"

"Fulmico. A lightning strike. Rather advanced. It takes a lot of magic, as well as focus. It's not easy to control. We're all rather lucky she didn't strike any of us."

"She could have struck us?!"

"But I didn't, did I?" Ardelle huffs as she pushes the tent flap out of her way.

"Luckily!"

Rolling her eyes, Ardelle sits next to the fire. Pointing to the fish bones, she asks if there's any left.

Skewering two fish to cook, Lombard makes Ardelle promise not to use another spell like that. "I acknowledge the success you had, but we can't afford to have you drain your magic like that again."

Ardelle looks at her feet. Clarke realizes how exhausted she really is.

Her exhaustion wins out after another few hours of flying, forcing the trio to land again, sooner than planned.

"I'm sorry," Ardelle says for the tenth time in ten minutes. "I feel terrible."

Lombard leads his griffon, as well as Ardelle's pennequo, into the mouth of a cave. He reassures her that he understands the situation and she needn't apologize. Once Clarke convinces Knightmare to join the others, Lombard wards the cave's entrance with several charms.

"We may as well rest too," Lombard says once camp is set up. "It's unlikely we'll find another cave like this, where we're so well protected."

Agreeing, Clarke settles in for a nap when the smell of smoke taunts his nose. Sitting up, he sniffs the air. *Smoke.*

He searches his supply pouch to ensure he didn't miss something after cleaning up the mess the hatching dragon made. Clarke realizes the dragon isn't in the tent.

Clarke shakes Master Lombard awake with one hand and preps several spells with the other. Once Lombard is aware of the situation, Clarke pulls on his gloves and creates a mass of purple goo, then carefully seals it in a jar.

"Should I wake Ardelle too?"

"No," Lombard says. "Let her sleep. We can handle this ourselves."

However, when Clarke emerges from the tent, he wonders if they should've woken Ardelle up since the tent is on fire.

"Master Lombard!" Clarke gasps, pointing.

A burst of water from Lombard's wand douses the flames. Lombard is obviously shaken.

A flash of movement catches his attention before he has a chance to rouse Ardelle. Clarke notices it as well and the pair close in.

The dragon hatchling's pale gray skin, leathery in texture, blends almost perfectly with the cave's rock ceiling. Its tail is twice as long as its body, though its main body is still longer than Clarke's arm. As it stares at Clarke and Lombard, the dragon flutters its undersized wings.

"It makes for a small target." Clarke says, hesitant. "I'm not sure if my aim is that good."

"Mine's not either. Plus, most low-level spells won't have any effect. Its skin seems soft, but it's hard as iron. I can't chance anything stronger that might hurt it."

Tired of waiting for the wizards to make a move, the dragon releases its hold on the ceiling. The tiny beast uses its wings to flip mid-air. Landing on its feet, the dragon dashes deeper into the cavern.

"We have to stop it before it gets too far," Lombard says. He frantically fires off spells in an attempt to startle the dragon into stopping.

However, he only succeeds in startling their mounts. Knightmare brays unhappily and thrashes his head while the griffon rears into the air, kicking its talons at the pennequo, which dashes toward the cave's entrance where it's stunned still by the charms Lombard placed.

The other beasts freeze as well, confused by why the pennequo was unable to exit the cave.

Not wasting a second, Clarke lobs a handful of the purple goo at the dragon but misses. He continues scattering globs in the dragon's path, hoping it will come in contact with some of it.

Eventually, its tail trails across a patch, causing it to stick. When Clarke approaches, thinking he's victorious, the dragon turns and spews a mouthful of fire at Clarke's face. Staggering backward, Clarke steps in a patch of his purple adhesive. Pin wheeling his arms, he falls, landing in more.

The dragon is too young and underdeveloped to manage more than one full flame at a time. Lombard still hesitates when it spits out smoke and embers and douses it with a splash of water, just in case, before restraining it.

Once certain the dragon is properly contained, Lombard turns to Clarke and laughs. He's still stuck to the ground. At first, Clarke scowls but soon joins in, filling the cavern with echoing laughter.

With Ardelle rested, the group covers significant ground. The terrain becomes less green. Rock outcroppings jut from the earth at regular intervals. After half a day's traveling, a proper mountain looms over the horizon, marking the end of their journey.

Though minutes tick by, Clarke feels as though the mountains haven't gotten closer. His back aches, his bottom is numb, and his arms are sore. Master Lombard and Ardelle are likely just as uncomfortable. When Clarke's discomfort crescendos, the mountains seem to leap miles closer. The peaks cast them in shadow.

From the lead position, Lombard traces patterns in the air with his wand. Barely visible in the distance, another wizard on a flying mount is tracing the same patterns. Lights appear, dotting the mountainside at varying levels, tracing responding patterns.

"Are those all people?" Clarke asks, astonished at the number of wizards gathered in the same location.

"They are," Lombard replies with a smile. "And they're all Dragon Defenders."

Once they've landed, Lombard, Clarke, and Ardelle are ushered into town. The wooden and stone houses, gardens, stores, and eateries blend into the mountainside perfectly. They almost appear to be natural formations.

After a hearty meal of fresh vegetables and a steak each, the trio is lead through a series of tunnels. They reunite with many who began the journey with them from the academy.

Everyone takes their turn, sharing the story of how and when they arrived. When Lombard recalls his travels and reveals Isband's betrayal, a somber mood settles in. They all retire soon after.

Smoke and shouting wake Clarke.

"Not again," he groans, unable to discern the time due to the lack of windows underground.

Grabbing his supply pouch from his bedside stand, he stumbles from the bed. Throwing himself into the hallway, he ducks in time to avoid a spray of fire aimed at his head.

"Not again!" he shouts.

Adrenaline erases the last of Clarke's grogginess. He rolls to the side to avoid a second blast of fire.

Wriggling his hand into a glove, he uses the last of his purple adhesive. It isn't enough to fully restrain the dragon staring at him with unblinking eyes.

"Look out!" a girl shouts as she tackles Clarke around the waist, just in time to save him from a third burst of flames.

Rolling onto his back, Clarke struggles to wiggle free from the girl's grip.

"Let go!" he grunts.

Huffing, the girl releases him. "Some thanks that is! You really are rude!"

Recognition registers. "Ardelle? Seriously, let go!"

"I'm trying, but you're pinning my leg."

"You're on my arm!"

Smoke and embers erupt above their heads, cutting their arguing short.

"Move!" Clarke shouts, knocking Ardelle aside.

Pressing into the wall, Clarke watches their attacker – an adolescent dragon approximately sixty-five pounds with a long, thin tail that accounts for most of its size, has undersized wings, and is covered in leathery, pale gray skin. It inhales sharply and tries to expel more fire, but only manages another bout of smoke and a few embers.

"This must be the dragon Diantha said hatched," Clarke realizes. "But why is it running loose?"

"There you are my boy!" A large wizard booms as he spots the dragon stuck to the ceiling by Clarke's purple adhesive. "I wondered where I'd misplaced you."

"Misplaced?" Clarke echoes.

"Manners Clarke, manners," Master Lombard scolds as he joins the large wizard.

"Not to worry old chap," the wizard chuckles. "I was just the same at this young 'un's age. Name's Medwin Dragic. This here's my son, Frederick, but I call him Freddy."

Merely a smaller version of his father, Frederick and Medwin both have ruddy brown hair, bright eyes, and thick-rimmed glasses.

"Pleasure to meet you both, but please, don't call me Freddy," he says. "I much prefer Frederick, thank you."

Uncertain of what else to say, Clarke gestures toward the dragon. The beast gradually tears free of the adhesive.

"Not to worry," Medwin chuckles. "Stonewell here was likely searching for the luminescent leeches I lost. His favorite snack they are. Keep an eye out for them, will you? I've been gorging one of the leeches in particular, to find out how large they can grow. Well, it's gotten to be the size of my head, but Freddy here has a bet with me that it won't get bigger. I'm betting it will though, no doubt."

Turning to Ardelle, Clarke is certain he's as pale as she is at the thought of a head-sized luminescent leech crawling around somewhere.

Whispering so only Clarke can hear, Ardelle says, "If I see anything—and I mean anything—glowing down here, I'm going back to the academy."

Once Stonewell is safely returned to his quarters—a giant cavern within the tunnels closed off by a thick iron gate—Lombard can clarify a few things for Clarke and Ardelle.

"Medwin and Frederick are Magical Fauna experts, researchers of a kind," he explains. "They've traveled the world gathering information on magical beasts that wizards didn't know much about or hadn't cared enough about to study previously. Frederick plans on eventually publishing their findings."

"Indeed, I do," Frederick says enthusiastically. "Everything is laid out, right here in this room."

He indicates the parchment smothering every counter, every table, every last available surface. When Ardelle attempts to read a page, Frederick blocks her outstretched hand.

"No, no, no. No touching. I have an extremely delicate, complex filing system. Not a page can be disturbed by anyone other than me, thank you."

"Freddy, have you seen that dragon Lombard brought with him? I can't seem to find it," Medwin asks as he enters the room, scratching his head. "I could've sworn I had it in my office."

"You moved it, remember? To the room next to Stonewell, so they could acclimate to each other," Frederick assures him.

"Ah, right. I do remember that now," Medwin mutters as he exits.

"What does he mean by acclimating?" Clarke asks Lombard.

A broad smile overtakes Lombard's face. "It means they need to get used to each other. We're hoping that someday when they're fully grown, they'll be mates."

"You mean?" Ardelle starts. Her excitement overwhelms her and she can't manage to finish her thoughts.

"The dragon that Clarke hatched was a female. Another two eggs survived. One male and another female. There's yet hope for our dragons."

A World Without Dragons

Joshua Grasso

My uncle squared away with a dragon. They fought for days, trading blows, swearing oaths. In the end, he had slain it, but it ripped him to shreds, spilling his life-blood on the floor of the Gard. And now he would return to the village to be celebrated in wine and song, his ashes returned to the sea.

Of course, that's not how it happened, not this time. I wanted to believe he had slain a dragon. That's why he went out there, to test his mettle against the hunt. Instead, he found something else, as my father did, and his father, and so many generations before. They called it the Hold.

Maybe that's a polite way of saying he felt the cold fear in his bones and panicked. They found him with his own knife plunged into his heart, one hand still tight around the blade. Instead of marching home like a hero, he had to be dragged back on a sled like the others. My mother took me out to see him after he was ritually prepared for the pyre.

I adored my uncle. I remembered from an early age listening to his stories of the hunt, of the great dragons like Hakki, the silverback. He told me of Habrok, who despoiled the island's sheep, and Galterus, He-Whose-Wings-Block-Out-The-Sun. Where were his stories now? He looked like my father had, his face sunken and lost, eyes were more like the memory of eyes than anything that twinkled with life.

It had been over a hundred years since the last successful hunt. The dragons were gone, the Council insisted. Some even suggested they had never existed at all, but only in whispers. We had no way of knowing.

There were rumors from other islands that the hunts continued as before. People said that dragons were caught, slain, and destroyed many hunters. When pressed on what village reported this, or what kind of dragons were slain, the answers varied or became obscure.

Like the stories themselves, they contained details of this and that warrior's shield and the dying words of a great chieftain. Yet, nothing was said of where a dragon was taken or how long ago.

Yet none of this stopped us from training our entire lives for the fateful encounter. From my earliest years, I was taught about the seven types of ice and the six types of wind. I knew that if we got stranded in the Gard, we should always walk east following Signy the Huntress. If you found a sleeping dragon you had to shout—never whisper. A dragon expected whispers and would bolt at the slightest breath. Whereas shouting sounded like wind to a dragon and he might ignore you.

I learned to climb sheer rocks, camp in a blizzard without freezing to death, walk for days and miles without sleep— better yet, how to snooze on your feet—and how to use the stones. The Seers could enchant certain rocks on our island to make them glow at a dragon's approach. I had never seen them glow, though my uncle said they were as constant as a compass. The rocks had brought him more than once to the encampment of a dragon.

But Seers were a fickle lot, as prone to trick you as lead you to safety. Lucky for me I knew the one Seer who would never trick me. Though she had her own reasons for not wanting to help.

She found me on the cracked boulder overlooking the shore. It's where we used to sit when we were younger before she learned of the Sight, where we talked of running away together once I was in command of a longship.

"Skuri, I just heard. I'm so sorry," she said, pushing the hair from her eyes.

I shrugged. "His seventh hunt."

"You're not thinking of going yourself?" she asked.

I opened my mouth to respond, but she already knew the answer.

"Then I'll have to tell them. Your mother at least. I would be responsible if I didn't tell. When they found your body, everyone would know."

"How would they know? And why do you assume I would end up like him?"

"I'm a Seer, Skuri," she said, with a weary smile. "But my powers are beside the point. You tell me everything; you always have."

I was about to protest when I realized that I had done just that. She was the first person I told. The only person.

"Drifa, I need your help. I can't do it alone. I need the stones."

"The stones," she said, rolling her eyes. "You need stones to find a dragon? A dragon, Skuri. Even if the legends are true, a dragon is still a dragon. You would see and smell it for miles. Or more likely, it would smell you."

"So, I can't have them?"

"Of course, I'll give you the stones," she said, with a little shove. "I'll charm them as much as I can. If you come within a hundred miles of a dragon, or if a dragon relived itself a hundred years ago in this spot, my stones will sense it. But is that really what you want? Some magic rocks?"

I laughed to hear her talk so dismissively of her calling, the very backbone of the hunt itself. But somehow, she knew. Yes, I wanted something else, something only she could give me. What she would never give to anyone else.

"I can't fight a dragon by myself. There's so much I don't know, and can never learn. I need something else."

I watched her eyes. It was the only way I could know. They widened, then dropped to the ground. When she brushed her hair away and looked at me again, I knew or hoped she understood.

"If you're asking me what I think ..."

Her eyes looked up at me with a hidden hurt, a secret which I had just begun to understand. I had been foolish to ignore it so long.

"If you want me to come with you, I'll come," she continued. "I would never let you go alone at any rate. You're right, you don't know what you're doing. But I'm not sure I know any better."

"You think it's wrong?" I asked.

"It's not that. I used to dream of the hunt. Going out in the wild, using my power to track the beast. But whenever I imagined it, I was never alone. You were with me."

"Was this a dream? Or the Sight?" I asked.

"I don't know. Are they different sides of the same coin? It's time we found out."

I told my mother I was going to visit friends across the village. Too careworn to question my motives, she kissed my head and gave me a silent blessing. I kissed her back—I didn't always—but I knew this was more than a casual leave-taking. It might be the very last time.

I took the road for as long as necessary in case my mother watched me go. Then I raced through the fields to Drifa's hut. Normally, she would be housed with the Council, but her father was sick and she was given a few weeks' leave. I waited for some time, watching the moon drift in and out of the clouds. Finally, it was completely swallowed up—a bad sign, if you believed in omens.

"Ready?" she said, grabbing my arm.

We ran for a full hour, leaving the flickering lights of the village far behind and entering the volcanic plain deep in the shadow of Visir, the sacred mountain. In ancient times it was said to smoke like a dragon itself, though monthly gifts of food seemed to appease its fury.

As children, we used to steal from the baskets when no one was looking, and occasionally, strip them whole. I regretted how little I had packed for the journey. I was about to ask Drifa if she had anything worth snacking on when she pulled me behind a boulder. She crouched down, opening the satchel at her side.

"Tired?" I asked, quite winded myself.

"Of course not. But I need to look ahead. I haven't made a vision in hours. Keep watch."

I crouched next to her, scanning the darkness in vain. It was deathly silent. I tried to watch as she removed a small object, more a polished orb than a stone, and rubbed it between her palms. Within seconds it began to shine, outlining her freckled cheeks in its light. This was the Drifa I didn't know, the one who spoke to stones and saw the future. I realized how ordinary I must appear to her, a stripling who had never been on the hunt. I knew nothing of the mystic arts.

"There's nothing ahead, only darkness and cold," she said, as the light went out.

"You can see that far ahead?"

"It's not that I can see, exactly—it's more a feeling," she said, returning the stone to her pouch. "I can feel the future ahead of us, like waves as they crash against you. The stronger the wave, the worse the danger. It's lapping now. We should be safe."

"No dragons, then?"

"That would be quite a wave," she said.

"But you do think they found them? Hundreds of years ago? That the stories, minus exaggerations, were true?"

"I do," she said, staring into my eyes, though it was too dark to see them. "And they still are. I can sometimes feel them passing by. Somewhere beyond the Gard."

"Then why haven't we seen them? Not even once? If the stories were true, wouldn't something remain?"

"It's like a tree," she said, with a shrug. "A tree you spent your entire life with, shading your children and your children's children. And one day—lightning strikes it. Gone. Wouldn't we tell stories about it? And wouldn't someone, centuries later, look at the ground and say, I've never seen a tree here."

"But trees grow back. And there are other trees—an entire forest."

"Not if we chopped them down. It would take centuries for a forest to return to life. Maybe that's who we are—the people stuck in-between. The dragons are here, but growing where we can't see them. Not the giants of old, but something much younger, much smaller."

The people stuck in-between. No one had ever described our relationship like that. My uncle would consider it blasphemy. The dragons haven't changed, he would argue. Perhaps they're harder to find, or we've become weaker, less bold in our hunt. You just had to know where to look. Of course, none of that explained the Hold. Not even a dragon could convince my uncle to fall on his knife. He would rather die on his feet, felled by a dozen men or swallowed whole.

We walked for hours over rocky terrain, crossed a stream, and wound up in a valley bathed in moonlight. Large boulders crisscrossed the landscape. Some were larger than others, but all of symmetrical and worn by time. They seemed to have been shaped by human hands. All were covered in writing, though not in any language I could interpret, at least in the pre-morning gloom. Drifa ran her hands over the stones, puzzled by something; she seemed to be looking ahead, into the future. Then she lurched back in alarm.

"Oh! Skuri, it's here!"

"What? Where he died?"

"Yes, where he died—the Hold!"

I drew my dagger and backed up against the rock, ready to attack anything that moved. Drifa wrestled my blade down, holding me close.

"No, it's not like that—it won't come from out there. It's something else. I can protect you."

"I don't need to be protected! I can take whatever it is! Let me go!" I struggled.

But she proved quite strong and persistent, and only when I heard them approach did I cease struggling. Four ghostly figures, or rather, the merest impression of figures. I saw heads and shoulders, a flicker of chests and arms, but nothing below. They stepped into the ghostly moonlight that spilled over the rocks and vanished.

"Who are you?" I demanded.

"Skuri? Why have you come?"

"How do you know my name? Who are you?"

"The guardians of the hunt," he answered.

"Skuri! It's your uncle," she whispered.

I couldn't be sure, since whatever spoke could hardly be said to be human, much less my uncle or anyone else. Yet his voice bore a close resemblance to my uncle's. Behind him, with even murkier features, I seemed to distinguish my father. I could scarcely remember his face.

"You brought a Seer with you. A cunning approach."

"Is that really you?" I asked.

"The most important part. And this is your father, and others you also knew," he said, with a look behind.

My father didn't meet my stare. I felt a curious lack of interest for the man who vanished so long ago. The best my mother could ever say of him was, he occasionally remembered to smile.

"Why are you here? What is this place?" Drifa asked as I fell silent.

"You're a Seer, you should know."

"Yes, I've seen it. The waves always stopped at this point. There was nothing beyond."

"This is where it all began. The hunt. The story is on these stones," he gestured.

"I don't know the language."

"Language has nothing to do with Sight."

Drifa looked terrified as she met my stare.

"You can read that?" I asked her.

"No, though I can look through it. I never tried. Even when I saw it in visions, I knew, but I never wanted to tell you."

"But they're just words. They can tell us about the Hold."

"Skuri, that is the Hold. Those words. Your uncle read them. Your father, too. If you read them, you'll do the same."

"I will not! I'm not like them—like him," I said, gesturing to my father.

But the quiet assurance of my uncle, father, and the other figures made me question my resolve. They watched and waited as if expecting me to join their ranks. Never—I would never become a coward. To throw your life away, for whatever reason, would disgrace your family and bring disaster upon the village. We needed good men like my uncle. Not corpses.

"Read it, Drifa. Please. Let me show them," I insisted.

She wanted to refuse but I was deaf to all her entreaties, as were the men behind me. Drifa squeezed my hand as she peered into the stones, seeing, looking beyond. The figures shimmered just behind her, their faces stern but unreadable. Drifa didn't say a word, and at times, I wondered if she was reading anything. She finally gasped for breath.

"I understand everything. It's all there. And it's not what you think."

"What? What?" I demanded.

"It's not about hunting dragons … or it hasn't been for a very long time. It's about us—or in this case, you. Your uncle and father were hunting you."

"Hunting me?" I said, incredulous. "Why would they be hunting me? And who were they hunting before? My uncle knew where to find me! At home! Not out here in the Gard!"

"Listen to her, Skuri," my uncle said, a mere outline. "This is no longer about hunting dragons. It's about doing penance. Only the worthy can enter the Hold."

"Worthy?" I repeated. "You killed yourself to do penance?"

"Skuri, our village had an ancient pact with the dragons. That's what the stones explain," Drifa continued. "We allowed them to hunt on our land, unmolested, for three seasons out of the year. On the fourth season—winter—we were allowed to hunt them. This ruled out all but the most fearless, seasoned hunters. The only provision is that we were never allowed to kill a turquoise dragon. They were a special breed, often much younger than the rest, with the powers of a Seer. It was a whole army of Seers."

"We broke the pact," my uncle nodded, his body returning. "It became the ultimate prize—to slay a turquoise dragon. No one had ever done so. And cursed be the memory of the one who did."

"The village executed him and begged the dragons' forgiveness, but it was too late," Drifa said. "They immediately abandoned the island and never returned. But that didn't stop the hunters from seeking them out. They went to other islands, the most distant lands. Most of them perished. However, one man returned with a message: the dragons would return if we paid life for life. The dragon we killed was seventy-five years old, one of the youngest in their clan. If we offered up seventy-five lives as a sacrifice and not just any lives, but the lives of our greatest hunters—the dragons would relinquish the curse."

At first, it didn't make sense. The stories never said anything about a turquoise dragon. You only heard of fierce, scaly monstrosities that were jet black or the fiercest orange. But then I realized why they wouldn't. The hunt had to continue. It would have to produce great hunters like my uncle who could match wits and strength with the best. Knowing our failure might make us lose heart and become weaker, less sure of the call. Only those bred in the hunt, who believed in the traditions like their own blood, would willingly lay down their lives to preserve it.

"How many have given their lives?" I asked, turning to Drifa.

"The stones don't say; they only speak of the past, not the future," she replied.

"Seventy-four," my uncle proclaimed. "And she will be the last."

"Her?"

"You're no hunter, Skuri. But she's both a Seer and a Hunter. We would accept her life."

The words seemed to echo in my mind, repeating at an ever-quickening pace. There was no mistaking his intention. It was my penance for coming too early and cheating the guardians of their prize. I looked into her eyes, fear meeting fear, both losing heart.

"You want her to die?"

"It's what the vision told her. Ask her yourself."

"Drifa?"

"Skuri, he's right. It's why we came," Drifa said, undoing her cloak. "I wasn't sure until I read them, but I always knew I wouldn't come back."

I felt played like a puppet, mistaking the ventriloquist's strings for my own defiance. To lay down my own life was nothing; I had prepared to do that for my uncle, my mother, or the village itself. Yet I would betray them all to save her.

She let the cloak drop at her feet; her intentions were clear.

"It makes sense. Why I could bever see beyond this moment. It's where I end."

"I won't let you. I'm stronger than you. I can stop you."

"Not if I told you no," she said, her eyes shimmering. "Skuri, you've been asked to do the greatest thing of all. Much harder than killing a dragon."

"Why me?"

"Because you came. You risked everything. And some-times, you have to pay."

She unsheathed her knife and held it against her chest. My hands instinctively reached out to grab it, closing on her cold, damp skin. But she stared me down. Told me no in the clearest voice she could summon. Her words flooded into my consciousness, guiding me, and giving me strength. Don't fear my death—accept my love. Death is to be forgotten, and I'll never be far from your thoughts. Always right beside you.

Yet, instead of love I felt overwhelming hatred for my uncle, the hunt, and everything I'd been taught to believe. I had served it faithfully and sacrificed my own life, only to learn it wasn't enough. I had to give up even more so that another generation could do it all over again. Hunt, tell stories, want more, destroy the world.

"Dragons!" my uncle shouted.

My neck snapped up and I could dimly make out something vast and dark circling overhead. The light was erratic, but they spit out snakes of fire. I could see the contours of scaled flanks and jewel-like eyes.

"Why have they come? It's too soon!" he cried.

She dropped the blade and fell into my arms. I knew these were our last minutes. They would soon be upon us. The moon disappeared behind the girth of a tremendous dragon. The air grew heavy and damp. They alighted, each footfall like a thunderclap. I lost my footing and careened into Drifa, who toppled backward. But she leapt up, staring intently at the darkness, mouthing silent words.

"Listen to their words. I can almost hear them," she whispered.

I heard nothing but a deep, pulsating rumble, higher from one dragon, lower from another. The wings beat rhythmically, either as a mark of emphasis or simply to cool themselves off.

"Yes, they've been watching us," she said. "These three, they've remained on the island. Hidden, where no one can find them."

"So why are they here?"

"I don't know. I can't understand what they're saying now. It's too strange. Or maybe I'm not strong enough."

"It doesn't matter. We know the truth. I suppose that's worth dying for."

"Look—the big one's moving! He's coming beside us," she gestured.

I could feel rather than see the giant head settle into place between us, the hot breath matting my hair with sweat. Drifa cautiously reached out to him, and after a pause of deliberation, made contact. She gave a whispering giggle of delight as she ran her fingers over the battle-hardened scales.

"He's talking again. Can you understand him?" I asked.

"Yes, but there's so much, and so quickly. Layers upon layers of thought. I need time."

She focused and listened and almost seemed to respond in turn, murmuring as the dragon cooed.

"These are the last of their clan," she explained. "The younger ones went off to seek adventure ages ago. They never returned. Only these three remained, content to live out their declining years on the island. It could be thousands of years."

"So why can we see them now?"

"Believe it or not, they came to save me."

"To save you?"

"They think I'm your turquoise dragon," she smiled. "They hoped I could understand and explain that it wasn't a question of penance. There's no magic number—not seventy-five or seven-hundred. Or even one. They've simply moved on. After these ones die, they'll never return."

"So, it was all for nothing. All our traditions. It ends with this."

"But it doesn't have to end," she said. "All traditions change. Nothing continues unbroken. Each generation alters the course of the world. We don't need dragons to teach us that."

"Impossible. It means nothing without them," my uncle said, a mere flicker in the moonlight. "A hunter needs something to hunt; he needs the pursuit. We need the dragons."

"But did you ever find one?" she countered. "Has anyone in our village—even the oldest hunter, even their parents—ever slain a dragon? No, the hunt is what mattered, not the shadow of the beast itself. It's better that we can dream and tell stories and share them with our children. The only difference is that now we actually can return home. The hunt doesn't have to end in death, and fatherless sons and daughters."

"Our fathers gave their lives for the village," my uncle insisted.

"My father killed the village—and so did you," I snapped. "I barely even knew my father. He spent his entire life obsessed with the hunt. You were better, you took the time to teach me and tell me stories. In the end, you abandoned me, too. Are these our values, uncle? Is the hunt worth more than a human life?"

"Enough!" a voice shouted.

A shadowy form stepped forward, gradually overtaking my uncle, whose features shimmered into a different likeness. My father.

"For once in your life, listen to the boy, Storolf. Because he's right."

I waited for my uncle to protest, but he said nothing, either indignant or shocked to his core as I was. My father never spoke up at home, largely because he never cared to listen. He was always planning to leave, as if he had entered the wrong house.

"He's right. I did abandon him," he said, moving forward. They meant far too little to me, and only in the small hours of the night, cold and alone, did I miss their embrace. And now that I'm dead and can never return home, never hear my wife's words of welcome, I realize I made the wrong choice."

"You died for a greater life," my uncle replied.

"It's not a choice a father would make. I should have sacrificed my honor before my life. So should all the hunters who had children waiting for them at home. If this is all we amount to, this hunt, then we should burn the village and forget it ever existed. I would give a thousand dragons for one more day with my son, so he could remember who I am."

The words cut deep. I felt shame for not acknowledging him in my thoughts, for replacing him with my uncle at an early age. Whether it was his fault or mine, I should have honored his memory. I should have found a way to love him.

"I want to make this right, Storolf. Let the hunt continue, but not the way we were taught. A world without the dragons. Otherwise, they'll never come back."

My father disappeared. Only the silhouette of my uncle remained, unreadable, but lost in thought. As we waited Drifa took my hand, squeezing it with the emotion I felt but couldn't explain. A heady mixture of love and anger and loss.

"I've always wondered what dragon tasted like," my uncle finally said. "Probably awful. We never hunted dragons to eat them. Still less to hang them up. I never thought of catching dragons. I just wanted to be out in the wild, traversing the border between life and death. That's all that matters."

"Then you'll do it?"

"I yield to the Seer's advice."

"I see it clearly now," Drifa said. "The dragons will leave. Our people will continue the hunt."

My uncle gave a nod of acceptance. Behind him, just for a moment, I saw my father's face with the same wordless approval. Then they vanished forever. Only the dragons remained, though they were suspiciously quiet. I almost feared they had other plans for us both. Within moments, I felt a crash of wings as the dragons announced their departure.

"They're leaving, but they won't go far. They'll always remain on the island," she said. "One day, our people might be able to visit them as friends. Maybe when we tell new stories of the hunt. When the old memories have faded."

"Another hundred years, then," I said.

"Or even longer."

With what I interpreted as a grunt of farewell, the dragons took wing and leapt into the starry night. Their great bodies blacked out the heavens, eclipsing the moon one by one until they, too, fell silent. The darkness settled over us. Drifa nestled close to me, and I took her in my arms, feeling her shiver against the cold.

"I saw this in my very first vision," she said. "I was just a child."

"You saw us here? In the Gard?"

"Yes. When we spoke of running away, I always imagined this moment. I knew it would come to pass."

"You said in the dreams I had a longship."

"That was the dream," she smiled. "Not the vision."

"You can tell the difference?"

"Ask me again in the morning," she said, smiling.

Cason's Secret

John Dewald

Two solid thumps on the door interrupted the melody of the wind blowing. Cason straightened up in surprise, twisting around where he sat to stare at the oak front door. It was rare for someone to venture into the Elderwood after dark. Even if Cason's house was just within the fringes of the forest.

"Who's there?" called Cason.

Two more thumps shook the thick door, and a muffled call that sounded like a name came from the other side. Cason calmly crept to the door, catlike on his feet. He slid open the latch to peep out into the darkening evening. Cason found himself looking into a pair of confident brown eyes that stared back up at him. The eyes were familiar, and he wracked his brain as he tried to place where he had seen them before.

"My name's Jax," said the boy outside, speaking up through the slit in the door. Jax's jacket hid the bottom of his face from the cold, and his words came out muffled. "You're Cason Greenstone, right? They said in town that I could find you here." He held his hands up with his palms open for Cason to see that he was not holding a weapon.

Cason slid the latch shut and began to undo the two massive iron planks and many bolts that locked the door. With a start, he realized the boy's eyes reminded him of his old adventuring companion. The fellow dragon slayer Kase Everheart, who he had not seen in twenty years. Could Jax be Kase's son?

Cason unlocked the final bolt, holding the doorknob with his left hand. He made sure his right hand had easy access to the sword propped against the wall beside the door. The sword was tip down, pommel up. That way, Cason did not need to stoop to grab the hilt. This would not have been the first-time bandits had come knocking at his door. He was not going to lower his guard just because Jax looked like his old friend.

Cason cracked the door open and peered outside. The rich smell of pine trees and dry earth wafted into the cabin. Jax stood unmoving on the front step, smiling. Judging it to be safe, Cason opened the door the rest of the way and took full account of his guest.

Jax was young. Fifteen or sixteen years old at best. He looked to be at most five foot five and around one hundred and thirty pounds. Jax's skin was the color of ground coffee, and his dark eyes were wise for his age. His full lips and straight teeth formed a joyful smile. His youthful face showed no trace of a beard nor mustache. He kept his black hair cut short.

Wearing tan colored pants and black leather boots, he dressed like a traveler. His forest green jacket was a few sizes too large. His hands disappeared inside the depths of his sleeves. Squirrel fur lined the hood and neck of his jacket to help ward off the cold, and a pair of wool gloves covered his hands. Jax carried a backpack with a bedroll strapped to its back and wore a sword without a scabbard on his side. Cason could see Jax's breath in the cold air as the boy poked his face out from under his jacket.

"I can't believe you're Cason Greenstone. It's incredible to finally meet you. Can I come in?"

Cason returned the smile and stepped to the side, allowing Jax to pass inside the house. Despite being in his late fifties, Cason was strong and tall. He stood over six foot two with a straight back and a muscular chest. His grey hair hung around his broad shoulders. His salt and pepper unkempt hair still showed streaks of its original raven black.

Cason's tanned and leathery skin showed his many years spent in the sun, rain, wind, and cold. Grey stubble covered his cheeks. A pair of fixed ice blue eyes perched above his hawkish nose, but his smile was warm and genuine. His pants were the same style as Jax's. He wore a dark blue, loose tunic that exposed a thick scar that ran down the length of his left arm. Despite his minimal clothing, he seemed oblivious to the cold.

"You must be brave to wander into the Elderwood after sundown," said Cason, "or you're misinformed. Even this close to town, the forest can get rather dangerous at night." Cason lived in the outskirts of the Elderwood in a small wooden cabin he had built fifteen years before. The Elderwood was held in ill repute by the nearby town of Thousand Stumps. Cason enjoyed the solitude the forest's notorious reputation provided. The was home to wild animals and magical beasts alike. The wood elves abandoned the area a few decades back, right around when Thousand Stumps was originally founded, Goblins, ogres, and werewolves had been known to roam among the forest's shadowy pines since then.

Jax shrugged and offered a sheepish grin. "I've been traveling for over a month trying to track you down. When I reached Thousand Stumps this afternoon, the tavern's barkeep told me I could find you here. It didn't once cross my mind to wait until tomorrow."

"Which begs the question, why did you go to such great lengths to find me? Cason Greenstone is a name that seems to be further forgotten with each passing year."

"My father often spoke of you when I was a child. He said that you were friends with my Uncle Kase. My father gave me this, it's some kind of stone. It used to belong to my uncle. My father said you would understand when you saw it." Jax reached into his jacket and pulled out a small bundle wrapped in an old rag. He unwrapped the worn cloth. Inside was a flat diamond-shaped rock, around two inches wide by three inches long, with smooth edges. The stone was a dark shade of purple, almost the same color as wine, and it seemed to emit a faint purple glow. As Jax fiddled with it, Cason saw that a complex pattern of dots and spirals covered one of the sides.

At first, taken aback, Cason regained his composure. Making sure no one else had seen what Jax was holding, he shut and locked the door. Cason placed a firm hand on Jax's shoulder. "You can leave your backpack by the door. Leave your sword there too. It's nothing personal, but letting armed strangers into your home is not the recipe for long life." Cason went to walk away but stopped himself. He turned back to face Jax. "You have your uncle's eyes," he said. "Your uncle was a great man and an even better friend. Anyone who is family with Kase is welcome here."

As Jax slid off his backpack and undid his sword, Cason walked to the kitchen. "It's going to be a long night. I'm sure you have many questions, and I'm going to have a few of my own. But first, do you want anything to eat or drink? You must be hungry after coming all this way."

"Yes, please," Jax nodded as he rewrapped the purple stone in its rag and stowed it back in his coat. His eyes had flashed with desire at the mention of food.

"Take a seat by the fire and get warm," said Cason. "Dinner will be ready in a second."

Jax was only half surprised to see emerald green flames flickering in the hearth. The fire crackled and sputtered in the stone hearth. The house filled with the bittersweet smell of burning wood. "At least some of the stories are true," he mused under his breath.

Settling into his chair, Jax was finally able to relax his weary feet. He had been walking since sunrise. He had grown accustomed to long days on the road over the last month. Yet, today had been particularly fatiguing. Climbing the steep hill up into Thousand Stumps under the hot afternoon sun had exhausted him. Since Cason was still busy in the kitchen, Jax allowed his eyes to wander around his surroundings, as he took in the many eccentricities of Cason's home.

He first looked toward the fire. Not only was the fire green, but many of the logs burning in the fireplace floated a foot above the embers. Jax bent down and saw a metal grate dark with soot where the fireplace met the chimney. The grate must keep the wood from floating up to the chimney when it gets too light, Jax thought to himself.

Thousand Stumps was famous for bristle pine firewood, a wood that grows lighter as it burns. Then its diminishing weight and hot air from the fire causes the burning wood to take flight. Jax heard stories of entire burning logs rocketing up into the sky after an unknowing traveler used bristle pine wood in a campfire. This was the first time he had seen the floating wood in person. He smiled in amazement.

Jax only had to shift his gaze a few feet before he once again found himself marveling in wonder. In front of the fire lay a rug made from the orange and black pelt of a giant two-headed bear. The beast must have stood over fifteen feet tall on its hind legs and its teeth were longer than Jax's forearm. Jax heard of such animals before but did not know what they were actually called. He did know that whenever they started to stalk something, only two things that could end their hunt. Either killing the prey or their own death.

Jax's eyes danced among the many daggers and throwing axes mounted on the wooden walls. Then, he saw the sword and bow resting against the wall by the front door. The sword's polished blade reflected the flickering green flames of the fire. A leather quiver filled with arrows with blue fletching sat propped up next to the unstrung bow.

Green and blue tapestries covered the walls, as small as pillowcases to as large as bedsheets. Most portrayed hypnotic combinations of ovals and spirals. A few showed scenes of nature. Thick wooden shutters reinforced with iron bands shut all the windows for the night.

All the furniture and the house itself looked constructed with the bristle pines. On one wall, there were three wooden doors, one of which Jax assumed to lead to Cason's bedroom. A giant stone countertop and a wood burning stove formed the kitchen on the far side of the room. Glass cups, ceramic plates, and bowls covered a few shelves. Three large barrels sat against the wall—Jax assumed water filled them. A multitude of herbs and spices hung from the ceiling in long green strands. Cason ducked them as he moved around. Jax's stomach rumbled as he watched Cason pull food from some of the sacks in the well-stocked pantry.

Jax's gaze returned to the fireplace to see a massive battle-ax hanging from near the top of the stone hearth. Spiraling strips of black leather-wrapped the handle for better grip. The big steel blade had a notch around a third of the way up to its razor-sharp edge. The ax was nearly as long as Jax was tall. Jax looked up to see Cason standing over him, holding a tray heaped high with food.

Cason hooked a footstool with the toe of his boot and slid it across the floor until it stood in front of Jax. He set the tray down on the stool and took a seat in a nearby chair. "I see you were admiring Trovão," he said, pointing to the battle-ax. "She was my favorite weapon. One of my most trusted companions during the Second Dragon War and the Cleanse. She saved my life and that of your uncle more times than you could imagine."

Jax nodded as he attacked his food with enthusiasm, gorging himself on the delicious meal. Cason had prepared chicken sandwiches with onion, tomato, lettuce, rosemary, and a hint of olive oil. He had also made a soup filled with rice, a variety of beans, potatoes, carrots, bell peppers, and peas. There were sweet slices of apple lightly powdered with cinnamon for dessert. Jax was famished, and the food tasted heavenly. Especially the soup which warmed him from the inside out. It had been days since he had eaten so well.

When Jax finished scraping his bowl for every last drop of soup, Cason finally asked the question he had been dying to ask the boy since they had first met. "Let me see the stone again. I want to examine it by the light to make sure it is what I think it is."

Unwrapping the stone from cloth once again, Jax handed it to Cason. Cason ran his hands over the stone, feeling its soft edges, smooth surface, and the many diminutive lines and bumps on the stone's patterned side. Bringing it to his eyes, Cason inspected the stone's pattern, its faint purple glow with a furrowed brow.

To Jax's horror, Cason tried to snap the stone in half. His muscles bulged from exertion as he tried to break the stone with his bare hands. When the stone did not show even the slightest sign of harm, Cason banged it with the heel of his knife as hard he as he could. A dull thunk echoed throughout the cabin. Then, oblivious to Jax's cries of dismay, Cason threw the stone into the fire.

Jax looked as if he might faint. Cason calmly walked over to the fire, reached his hand into the flames, and pulled out the stone. It showed no signs of damage whatsoever. "It's real," said Cason half in disbelief as he sat back down. "This isn't a stone. It's a scale. Did your father tell you what this is?"

Jax shook his head as Cason handed him back the scale. To Jax's surprise, its surface was cool to the touch, even though it had been laying on the red-hot coals of the fire. While the fire's flames burned green, the embers glowed red. "He only told me that it was my uncle's," said Jax, "and that until I showed it to you, I couldn't let anyone else know of its existence."

"Your father sounds like a wise man," said Cason. "Did you keep it hidden? Does anyone else know about what you are holding in your hand?"

Jax shook his head again. "I've kept it a secret until now. My father was very wise. I always did my best to listen to what he said."

Cason's eyes filled with compassion when he heard Jax speak of his father in the past tense. Cason too had lost his father at a young age. Jax looked down and broke eye contact, embarrassed by the understanding in Cason's blue eyes.

"He died when I was ten," Jax explained after a moment's silence that gave him time to swallow the lump in his throat. "Our house caught fire in the night."

"And your mother?" asked Cason, regretting his words as Jax tried to hide the spasm of pain that contorted his features.

"The night of the fire, my father saved me from the flames and carried me to safety in a nearby field. He went back to find my mother. The house collapsed with both of them inside. I spent the night huddled in the field where my father left me praying that my parents were somehow still alive. I didn't accept they weren't coming back until the sun's rays shed lit up the smoking ruins. I'd never felt colder nor more alone than I did that morning." Jax's voice cracked with emotion. He rarely spoke about his parents since the accident. "I never found out what caused the fire, but I guess that doesn't matter. Luckily, one of the neighboring families took me in. They had seven children of their own and said that it didn't make a difference to look after one more.

"They were farmers," Jax continued. "I helped in the fields as much as I could to try to thank them for letting me into their home when I had nowhere else to go. As kind as my adopted parents were, no matter how many times they insisted, I knew that they were very poor. Having another mouth to feed added an extra strain on their family. I ran away over a month ago, on the night before my fifteenth birthday. I left them a letter thanking them for everything. I always promised myself that I would go out into the world and find you," he said, looking at Cason, "once I was strong enough to do so. Now that time has finally come.

"My father always told me stories about you and my uncle from the Second Dragon War and the Cleanse. It was always easier for him to talk about you than it was for him to talk about Kase. My father missed my uncle—they were brothers. I don't think my father ever understood why my uncle never came back. I don't know if he ever forgave him.

"One day when I was picking through the ashes of my old home, I found this," Jax held up the scale for Cason to see. "Besides me, it was the only other thing that survived the fire. I remember what my father had told me about the stone, I mean the scale," he corrected. "I've always kept it with me so that it would remain hidden.

"I ran away to find you. It's what my father would have wanted me to do. You're the only person that can help shed light on my past. I was hoping you could tell me about my uncle as well, and whether you know if he is alive or not. If he is, I'm going to find him."

★★★

Cason had listened to Jax in silence, his eyes never leaving the boy. "How much do you know about dragons?" he asked finally, as Jax's story wound to its end.

"Dragons?" said Jax, surprised. "I guess I know as much about them as everyone else. They were big fire breathing monsters. They slept on huge piles of gold when they weren't busy flying around and destroying towns. Many of them died in the dragon wars. The ones that survived were later killed in the Cleanse by dragon slayers like you and my uncle," he said. "Why?"

"It's far more complicated than that," said Cason. "You're going to need a bit of a history lesson if you're to understand what I have to tell you. It's a long story, so let me know if you have any questions. Don't fall asleep. Your uncle had a bad habit of falling asleep halfway through my stories," Cason said with a smile.

Jax nodded. "Tell me everything I need to know."

"It all began with the dragon wars," said Cason. "The First Dragon War started five hundred years ago. This was when the land was wild, magic was strong, and humankind had yet to outnumber the other civilized races. Dragons were numerous. The lairs scattered from the tops of snowy mountains and half-flooded caverns by the sea to the vast sands of scorching deserts and the most remote misty swamps. One could find dragons in the hearts of old forests, the great expanses of the plains, and even in giant palaces in the most ancient of cities. Occasionally, a young dragon was found serving as the flying steed of an illustrious elven knight, or as the overlord of a particularly powerful tribe of goblins.

"Some of the dragons were champions of good. They were wise and benevolent and put themselves in danger to protect their subjects. Others were cruel and deceitful. They used their power for twisted ends, serving as evil tyrants and forces of destruction. Today, it's claimed the colorful dragons, especially the reds, were evil. The metallic dragons, especially the golds, were good. That isn't true. It's not that simple. Usually by the time you are close enough to a dragon to see the color of its scales you know if it is good or bad. But that is based on its behavior, not on its color. Judging a dragon based on the color of its scales is ignorant and unreliable. It can also get you killed. Some of the kindest dragons who ever lived were red or blue, and some of the cruelest were silver or gold. Like we humans, a dragon's moral code depends on their heart, not on their color.

"Dragons are incredible creatures. While a hatchling is no bigger than a large dog, dragons grow to the size of a bear by the age of two or three. From there, their growth rate slows down. While dragons are capable of reaching well over a hundred feet in length, it takes them many years to do so. They have long lifespans, and so need a long time to reach adulthood. It can take a dragon close to a millennium to reach their full size."

"What do you mean 'dragons are'?" asked Jax. "Don't you mean 'dragons were'? The last of the dragons were killed over twenty years ago during the Cleanse. No one has seen a dragon since. You should know that better than anyone."

"Be careful when you make assumptions," warned Cason. "Things are not always as they seem. When most people say the same thing, this does not mean that it is true."

Jax looked at him. "Are you saying that dragons are still real?"

"Most used to agree that during the start of the Cleanse many of the surviving dragons fled to the North and the West. I've never done it, nor have I ever met anyone who claims to have made the journey themselves. Yet, across the great sea to the West there is said to be another land, far wilder and less developed than our realm. Telica. Unlike Telica, humans are rare there. And to the North, the Great Spine forms a boundary that is almost impossible to cross except by wing. The treacherous snow-covered mountains of the Great Spine deter all but the rashest of adventurers. The frozen wastelands of Sincelo that lay on the far side of the mountain range are desolate and uninhabitable. They are not even considered part of Telica. Most maps stop at the Great Spine. There are rumors that farther north the land is warmed by volcanic activity and becomes more temperate and suitable for life. I have my doubts. If dragons fled to either the North or the West, they would be far removed from the wandering eye.

"You think that the dragons who fled the Cleanse are still alive, hiding out somewhere in the North and the West?" asked Jax.

"I do," stated Cason, "and they might not be the only ones."

"Do you mean there were dragons who survived the Cleanse?"

"There is definitely a chance. I've heard of stranger things."

"Then why does everyone say that all the dragons are dead and gone?" asked Jax. "Most people would laugh if they heard you say there is even the merest chance that dragons still exist. They would call you crazy if they heard what you told me."

"After the Cleanse, we entered the Age of Humans," explained Cason. "The two dragon wars ravaged the world so that Telica was forced to reorganize and redefine itself. This left behind many of the old traditions. Dragons, some of the most powerful influences in the world before the wars, were gone. Many members of the civilized races died during the dragon wars as well. We humans have a far shorter life span than our fellow elves and dwarves. We have also been able to repopulate far faster than the other races. The human population has grown to over ten times what it was at the start of the First Dragon War. Meanwhile, the populations of most of the other races and species have declined, and in some cases, even disappeared.

"As humans have become more plentiful, we have started to settle many parts of Telica that were once wild. Cities and towns have popped up where before there was only wilderness. We have pushed the goblins, ogres, and giants that once roamed the land farther to the outskirts of the realm. We have cut down trees to build cities. We dammed and diverted rivers to grow agriculture and provide drinking water for our growing population. We have constructed towering buildings where once stood impenetrable forests. We leveled entire hillsides to make way for roads. We cut down vast swaths of the jungles in the South to plant crops. No doubt, we are leaving our mark on the land.

"As we humans have continued to spread, the wood elves have retreated deeper into the forests. The high elves have almost completely disappeared. Most have left Telica, sailing across the ocean to the West where the land is still wild and nature still pure. The dwarves too are far harder to find than before. The majority of the hill dwarves have migrated to the less populated reaches of the North. Almost all the mountain dwarves have moved underground, to the great old dwarven cities. Now, they work in the mines to provide for the demand for steel and iron in the modern age.

"The thought that dragons could still exist would cause a threat to the modern way of life. Most people do not want to live with that uncertainty. They prefer to believe that there is nothing that could halt the march of progress. After countless centuries, humans are finally in control. People prefer to believe that humankind's dominance is guaranteed for the next centuries than to believe dragons exist. But they are foolish to rewrite history. Dragons are still out there. They may be far away, but that doesn't mean that they are gone. I would bet my life on it."

Jax felt his veins surge with anticipation as Cason spoke. Dragons could still exist. The possibilities of what that meant were endless. He forced himself to stay focused and keep listening.

"The fact that your father sent you here means that he wanted me to teach you about dragons. He must have thought it would be of use in the future. I agree. What do you know about a dragon's characteristics?" asked Cason.

"A dragon's characteristics?" Jax stared at Cason.

"Dragons can have many different types of appearances," said Cason. "Some have curved horns, while others have sharp spines that run down their backs. There have been dragons with spiked tails that they used as devastating weapons. Others have razor-sharp ridges that run along the edges of their wings. They could slice a grown man in half as a knife cuts through a stick of warm butter. Dragons can be any hue imaginable. Red, blue, green, white, black, gold, silver, copper, bronze, and brass are the most common colors.

"Many of the physical characteristics of dragons differ depending on the individual. But there are a few things that all dragons hatch with. I'm sure you've heard of a few. All dragons have a thick layer of scales that turns away the bite of steel and the sting of iron. The scales also protect against the most searing heat and blistering cold. A suit of armor made from dragon scales is one of a warrior's most sought after possessions. All dragons have a pair of wings, of course. Their aerodynamic bodies allow them to fly gracefully and perform unbelievably complicated aerial maneuvers. They all have long tails that they use both for balance and as weapons. Each of the five claws on each of their four paws is sharp enough to cut diamond. Their mouths are full of giant fangs strong enough to chew through great slabs of rock. A special organ in the back of their throat called an ardente allows them to breathe fire.

"Dragons are also incredibly intelligent. Their long lifecycles give them ample time to further develop their intelligence and study whatever they desire. It is said that you can prove you are a genius if you can last five minutes in a game of chess with a dragon. I think the feat of convincing a dragon to play you in chess is in itself worthy of proving one's genius. But that's just my personal point of view.

"Dragons also can use magic. Wizards need to spend hours studying spells and learning the rules of the arcane arts before they cast basic enchantments. Dragons hatch with innate magical abilities. A dragon's magic grows as the dragon gets older. The more mature the dragon, the more powerful its magic. A dragon's magic varies from dragon to dragon. Both the type of magic a dragon can use as well as the power of the magic fluctuates from dragon to dragon. Some young dragons have magical abilities that only increase over time. Other older dragons have very limited magical powers. Magic, like so many other things, depends on the individual dragon in question.

"Every dragon has a special scale known as a scama which is the source of their magic. They can be found on a dragon's underside, located over their heart. The scama is the same color as the rest of the dragon's scales. But it is marked with a pattern unique to each individual dragon. It also emits a faint glow. If for some reason a dragon loses their scama, they lose their magic as well.

"This is a scama." Cason pulled his necklace out from under his shirt. An emerald green scale, the same color as the fire burning in the hearth, hung from a black piece of twine.

Its green glow matched the firelight. The diamond-shaped scale was roughly two inches wide by three inches long. A mesmerizing swirl of spirals lighter in color than the rest of the scale were etched across the top of the scama. Jax's eyes went wide with understanding, and he instinctively clutched at his jacket.

Cason held the scama out in front of him for Jax to see, but he did not take off the necklace. "This is the reason I am called Cason Greenstone. Most people mistake the scale for a stone. I've worn this necklace since the Second Dragon War. This is the scama of Scythe, an incredibly cruel dragon who could breathe fire, as well as exhale caustic clouds of acidic gas through his nostrils. He was famous for using his acidic breath to strip the flesh from his victims. He would then hang the skeletons from the trees surrounding his lair. He joked that they were his windchimes. Scythe's salvia was also poisonous. So, if you somehow survived his monstrous bite, there was a good chance the poison would get you a few hours later. Taking Scythe's scama nearly cost me my life, and it put a notch in the otherwise unscratchable blade of Trovão." Cason pointed to his ax hanging above the fireplace.

"When I confronted Scythe in the battle of Pike's Plain, he was one of five dragons on the battlefield. The enemy army's dragons outnumbered ours three to two. At sixty feet in length, Scythe was the smallest dragon in the battle. It fell on us dragon slayers to take care of him, while the four other dragons were locked in aerial combat above our heads.

"Our battalion was two hundred strong, consisting of humans, dwarves, and a few elves. We fiercely combated a horde of goblins, ogres, and a handful of evil humans. After five minutes of fighting for my life against a group of four goblins and an ogre so large he used a tree trunk as a club, I was able to break free and get close enough to Scythe to capture his attention.

"Scythe was cutting a devastating path through our ranks, gleefully killing whoever came within his reach. Finally getting rid of the tree trunk wielding ogre, I took off sprinting toward the dragon as fast as I could. Seeing me, Scythe shot a green jet of blistering hot fire straight at my chest. Spinning to the side, I avoided the full onslaught of the flames. My metal armor caught the fire's heat, and my skin seared with pain wherever it touched the superheated armor. I forced myself to stay focused. If the pain clouded my judgment, I would be dead in an instant.

"Seeing that I had dodged his fiery breath, Scythe pumped his wings and took to the air to attack me from above. The wind from his beating wings threw everyone near him to the ground. He flew straight at me with his claws extended, his black eyes shining with malice. He lunged at me, snapping his teeth as he tried to bite me in half. At the last second, I rolled my shoulders and ducked under his chin. I attacked with Trovão in a wild uppercut to the dragon's underside. In a stroke of dumb luck, Trovão must have struck Scythe's scama and wrenched it free from the beast's chest. All I remember was a reptilian screech that made my bones ache and my ears feel like they were going to explode. Then Scythe's flailing tail caught me in the chest and sent me flying. I must have struck a rock and lost consciousness. When I came to hours later, the battle was over. I had a concussion, was covered in burns, and spitting up blood from broken ribs. Yet, I was alive, with Scythe's scama embedded in Trovão's blade at my side.

"I wasn't awake to see it happen, but Scythe fled the battle soon after I lost consciousness. When he lost his scama, he flew into a demonic rage, killing whoever he set his eyes on. He gobbled down man and goblin alike, causing the battle to erupt into even more chaos than before. When your uncle sunk an adamantine tipped javelin deep into Scythe's cheek, the dragon decided to flee. Injured and deprived of his magic, he panicked, flying away as quickly as he could. When Scythe fled, the battle's momentum tipped in our favor, and we quickly routed the enemy.

Cason paused, his mouth dry from so much talking. He excused himself to get a glass of water. As Cason headed back to the kitchen, Jax pulled the bundled rag out from his jacket and unwrapped it. He let the dark purple scale fall into his palm. He traced the intricate spirals and dots that covered the top side of the scale with his finger as if he were holding it for the first time. Clutching the scale in his fist, he held the scama to his heart, sensing the great power that lay within.

Cason returned with a glass of water for each of them. He sat back down and took a long drink. "I see you recognize what your uncle left you. Based on its color, Kale must have taken the scama from Evening, a dark purple dragon killed during the Cleanse. Your uncle and I had parted ways by then. I always wondered if he had taken a scama of his own. He was more wary of them than I was, but you couldn't blame him. When he was younger, he saw one of his friends lose their mind trying to capture the power of a scama. Things like that stay with you forever.

"Wearing a scama as a necklace allows you to harness some of the powers of the dragon from which it came from. The scale must hang at the height of your heart for the magic to work. The older and more powerful the dragon was when they lost the scama, the more powerful it is. All scama provide the wearer with a resistance to fire, as well as an ability to handle intense heat and cold. They make the wearer stronger and more aware of their surroundings. They also slow down the aging process. Besides the standard benefits, my scama has also granted me resistance to poison and acid. Although it took me many years to learn how to control the flames, I can use it to create fire as well." Cason snapped his hand. A jet of emerald flame burst into existence above the tip of his outstretched index finger.

Jax's heart raced with excitement. A few minutes ago, he thought he had been the proud owner of a purple stone for the past five years. *A scama.* His uncle had left him a rare kind of dragon scale that could provide him with magical powers. This was turning into one of the best nights of his life. "How do I harness the power of my scama?" asked Jax, excited.

"You don't," said Cason. "Or at least not until you are older and stronger. Part of a dragon's essence lives in their scama. When someone puts a scama on for the first time, they must fight the dragon's essence for control of the scama in a great contest of wills. If they win, the power of the scama is forever theirs. If they lose, the dragon's essence overwhelms them and drives them mad.

"Some people end up braindead. Their eyes glaze over and they drool and babble for the rest of their lives. Others lose the will to live. They go deaf and mute, wandering off to never be seen again. But the majority face a fate even worse. The dragon's essence fuses with their soul, and they become a bent and twisted mockery of who they once were. They are driven to perform the cruelest of actions by the dragon's wicked will. They have been known to commit the most atrocious of crimes. They have even killed close family and friends.

"Your uncle's friend fell into this third category. His name was Zellers. He was the captain in command of the first squadron Kase fought for during the Second Dragon War. They managed to slay and harvest the scams of Jasper, a giant red dragon known for her incredible size and power. Zellers was blinded by the abilities the scama of such a powerful dragon would provide. He was bent on using the scale. Kase counseled against it. He said Jasper's scama would be too hard to control, but Zellers would not listen.

"Boring a hole through the scale, Zellers hung the scama from his neck. His face grew taught, and he clenched his jaw from the mental exertion, not saying a word. For a minute, it looked like he was winning the battle of wills. But then he dropped to the ground clutching his head and screaming at the top of his lungs. It seemed like it would go on forever, but then his cries stopped as they had started. Kase and two more of his friends pulled Zellers to his feet to see if he was alright. Zellers stood stock-still with his eyes shut and his head hung low. Then he smiled and opened his eyes. His once hazel eyes had turned blood red, and a demonic grin stretched itself across his face. He gave a maniacal laugh, then sprang into action. Drawing his sword, he started to slaughter his men, fueled by an inhuman strength. By the time they were finally able to subdue him, Zellers had killed three of his own men and injured four more. They were forced to rip the scama from his neck and lock him away.

"It makes sense that Kase would not have tried to capture the power of Evening's scama. He never trusted scamas after seeing what had happened to Zellers. I'm surprised he even took one, to be honest. I don't know very much about Evening.

I think she was around forty-five to fifty feet long, which is rather small for a dragon. She was known for her remarkable cunning and magical powers, which surpassed those of dragons twice her size. She was supposed to be an incredibly talented illusionist. I was impressed when I heard that Kase had managed to track Evening down. You should be too. Evening was without a doubt a powerful dragon. That must have been why your uncle saved her scama. That is a powerful scama you have in your hands, and we must act with extreme caution whenever handling it.

Jax tried his best to understand what Cason was telling him, but part of him rebelled. He wanted to capture the power of the scama now. He was no longer a child. He was ready. He was strong. He had set off on his own through the world and managed to track down the elusive Cason Greenstone all on his own. He also knew what it was like to struggle. He had lost his parents, but he had never given up. He could dominate the scama. All he needed was a chance.

Shaking his head to clear his mind, Jax forced himself back to reality. If Cason said it was best to wait, then he should listen. Cason knew far more about scama and dragons than he did. He pleaded with destiny that Cason would help prepare him to harness the power of the scama soon. If he was going to find his uncle, he was going to need all the help he could get.

"Are you ok?" asked Cason. He watched Jax perturbed.

"I'm ok," said Jax. "It's a lot to take in all at once."

A wolf howled in the distance, her call echoing through the night. "It's getting late," said Cason. "I don't have a spare bed, but you can set your bedroll by the fire. It's warm, and you will be safe here. We can finish talking tomorrow."

"No," said Jax, "I'm not tired. I want to know now. Why else did my father send me here? Where is my uncle?"

"Are you sure?" asked Cason, "there's no harm to wait until tomorrow."

"I've waited for this moment all my life. We've already come this far. I'm not going to be able to sleep until I know the truth."

"Your father must have sent you here because he recognized the scama for what it was," said Cason. He realized Jax would not take no for an answer. "Your father likely thought the scama would be safest with me. As a friend of your uncle's and an ex-dragon slayer, I would be the best person to tell you the story behind it. I'm sure he also thought you would be in good hands as long as you were with me. My reputation tends to scare most trouble away, and rightfully so. I have a habit of winning fights. I don't know where your uncle is, however. The last I heard of Kase, he headed north, but that was almost twenty years ago.

"I also have a secret that I've never told anyone, a secret I now suspect your uncle was somehow aware of. It has gnawed at me over the years as I've tried to determine if I did the right thing or not. It is a secret that would horrify most people. A secret that would label me as a lunatic and a threat to society if it came to light. I don't know if your uncle told his suspicions to your father or not, but at this point, it doesn't matter. What matters is that you are here. What matters is that tonight, for the first time in my life, I am going to tell someone the truth. The truth about something I did a long, long time ago."

★★★

A breeze danced through the branches of the bristle pines outside. A pair of owls cooed to each other from across the forest. Jax did not pay any attention to the nocturnal sounds of the Elderwood, though. He sat stock-still in his chair, listening so intently to Cason's tale that he barely remembered to blink.

"The dragons started The First Dragon War," continued Cason. "Before the war, dragons reigned supreme. I would be exaggerating if I said they ruled every square inch of Telica. Yet, they were definitely the most powerful forces of the land. Even the great elven kings of old revered the dragons, treating them with the utmost respect. It was common to have conflicts between dragons back then like it is common to have conflicts between kingdoms or cities now. Most dragons were rather solitary in their adulthood, so conflicts usually stayed contained among a small group of individuals.

"As centuries slipped by, many dragons started to form alliances with one another to strengthen the influence and consolidate power. Most of the alliances were solely among dragons. However, some dragons even made deals with elf, dwarf, and human kings as well. While the purpose of these alliances was to promote stability and solidify order, they led to tragedy and war."

"What happened?" as Jax, intrigued.

"One day, Star Blight, a massive male red dragon, killed Morning Mist, a female silver dragon who accidentally ventured too far into Star Blight's domain. Morning Mist was the mate of Dorado, a giant gold dragon who was one of the most influential dragons in all Telica. Grief-stricken, Dorado called for retribution. Star Blight only laughed in his face, claiming to have eaten Morning Mist's carcass to absorb her power.

"Dorado was a kind and benevolent dragon who had ruled in peace for many years. Hearing Morning Mist's fate was too much for him to bear. Blind with rage, Dorado attacked Star Blight, severely wounding him before the red dragon was able to escape. Star Blight retaliated, sending wave after wave of his minions to attack Dorado's lands. As both Dorado and Star Blight's allies were pulled into the conflict, things quickly began to spiral out of control. Within a few months the First Dragon War had begun to cast its deadly shadow across the face of Telica.

"The First Dragon War dragged on for over three long centuries. Both sides were devastated, and almost all of the alliances formed before the war had crumbled by the end. Great cities were laid to waste, and kingdoms were destroyed. Neither side won. By the end, both Star Blight and Dorado had been killed. While many dragons on both sides lost their lives in the war, the good dragons faced higher casualties. Unlike their evil counterparts, they were more willing to risk their lives in battle to protect their allies. Many of them paid the price for their heroism. The war eventually ground to a halt as both sides became weaker and weaker. The widespread fighting slowed to the occasional regional skirmish until those finally stopped. The First Dragon War had ended, and with it, the Age of Dragons.

"Despite the hundreds of years of war that had ravaged the land, Telica began to rebuild itself. The Age of Equality had been born. Telica was similar during the Age of Equality to how it had been in the Age of Dragons. Kingdoms and cities now held more power than before. The remaining dragons had lost their past position as the supreme rulers of the land. Peace lasted for over two hundred years as Telica was rebuilt. Many people thought it would go on forever, but then war once again reared his ugly head.

"Unlike the First Dragon War, fought between the forces of the good and evil dragons, the Second Dragon War was messier and far more complicated. The war resulted from tensions caused by territorial disputes. These tensions severely heightened when the worst drought ever recorded struck the southern half of Telica. Crops withered in the fields, rivers dried in their beds, and massive wildfires raged unchecked across the land. The political structure could not handle the strain. People went hungry and were displaced from their homes. Once peaceful neighbors turned into bitter enemies overnight. In the course of just a few short weeks, it seemed that the entire world was in flames.

"All Telica was drawn into the war as any semblance of order was forgotten. At the height of the war, there were easily over a hundred different armies vying for dominance. It was a winner-takes-all mentality. Any kingdom or clan with half a name seemed to rally behind a war banner or battle cry. The only way to avoid attack when you weren't looking was if you threw the first punch. As much as the bloodshed was fueled by greed and power-hungry rulers, it was also caused by a lack of resources that crippled cities and brought entire kingdoms to their knees.

"The interim period between the two wars was not long enough for many new dragons to be born. Most of the remaining dragons joined the war. Some saw it as a chance to carve out a larger domain for themselves and regain the power they had held. Others went to the aid of their neighbors and allies. Many dragons worked as mercenaries and sold themselves as machines of war to the highest bidder. While some stayed out of the combat, the war was too big for most dragons to avoid. Despite not instigating the war, the Second Dragon War was named after the dragons because of their destructive capabilities on the battlefield. It also helped shift the blame, so that it once again fell on the dragons.

"The war lasted fifty years. While short in comparison to the First Dragon War, the Second Dragon War was long enough to completely reshuffle Telica politics. Warlords fought their way to power only to be toppled and replaced. Cities burned to the ground and kingdoms changed ownership more times than you could count. Chaos reigned supreme. When the fighting stopped and the dust finally settled, humankind had the largest population and the most power and influence in Telica. The Second Dragon War was over, and the Age of Humans had begun.

"As humans set about reorganizing the world, the rest of the inhabitants of Telica struggled to find their place. No one had it harder than the few remaining dragons. Like in the First Dragon War, there had been far higher casualties among what was left of the good dragons. This only further tipped the scale in favor of the evil dragons. They outnumbered the good ones more than ten to one. Having short life spans, we humans remembered dragons as the savage beasts that killed millions. The only stories from the Age of Dragons that were still told were those of cruel dragon tyrants.

"All nine of Telica's most powerful kingdoms passed a decree that placed one thousand gold pieces on the head of every dragon. There was also a one hundred silver piece reward for any dragon egg brought to the authorities. Once turned over, the eggs were smashed to bits. It was stated that dragons must be hunted down to cleanse Telica of the great threat they posed.

"To this day, we refer to this period of history as the Cleanse. At this time, most of the remaining dragons decided to flee to the North or West. Many remained behind in Telica, unwilling to leave home. Good or evil, a dragon's greatest weaknesses are their pride and greed. Many dragons did not wish to leave their treasure hordes behind. Others thought themselves too powerful to need to worry about the dragon slayers. Unfortunately for them, they were wrong.

"The Cleanse lasted a decade but was mostly carried out during its first three years. During this time that your uncle and I went from being two soldiers from the Second Dragon War to two heroes of the Cleanse. Dwarf forged weapons with adamantine tips and mythril edges—strong enough to pierce a dragon's hide—flooded the markets. Anyone who could swing a sword and wanted gold became a dragon slayer overnight. Only a few survived long enough to see the gold and fame they sought. Being a dragon slayer is quite possibly the job with the lowest life expectancy that there is. Despite as dangerous as it was to try to slay them and as many dragon slayers were lost in the process, the dragons were being systematically eliminated.

"It became harder and harder to find dragons. You needed to go deep into the forest or into the mountains if you wanted a chance of encountering the final few. Your uncle and I only hunted evil dragons. Some dragon slayers hunted what was left of the good dragons. Many were blinded by gold. The head of a good dragon was worth the same as the head of an evil one. Unscrupulous dragon slayers didn't think twice about who was at the other end of their swords.

"Others saw all dragons as evil. They had been raised to think dragons were monsters. They thought they were doing a public service in killing every last one. They did not differentiate between good and evil dragons. They thought that anyone who believed a dragon could be good was weak or deceived.

"Slaying the remaining good dragons became accepted as common practice. Many elves and even some dwarves started to refer to the Cleanse as the Extermination. No one paid them any mind. Looking back, the elves were right. That's was it was. We were not cleaning the land of danger. We were eradicating a species."

"You say that like it's a bad thing," said Jax. He thought of the hundreds of stories of death and destruction caused by dragons that he had heard. "They were a threat that needed to be taken care of, so innocent people did not lose their lives.

Cleansing Telica of dragons was for the well-being of everyone."

"I used to say the same thing," said Cason with a sigh of regret. "And I, as well as many others, were acting on those very beliefs. The dragons were being slaughtered. By the seventh year of the Cleanse, it had become far harder to track dragons down. I was in the Rift Mountains looking for Azure, one of the last of the great blue dragons. I had been hiking through the mountains for nearly a week. I encountered a trio of hill dwarves headed in the opposite direction. They had beaten me to it, having corned Azure in his lair the day before. Originally a group of seven, they had lost four of their fellow dwarves before they had been able to slay Azure. Now they were going home, their pockets soon to be full of gold.

"I camped with the dwarves that night in a shallow canyon. The banks were dotted with the occasional wind gnarled tree. We sat up late into the night, watching the glowing embers of the campfire and occasional shooting star. One of the dwarves told me that they had seen traces of another dragon farther up into the mountains. Having already lost over half of their band, the dwarves were not looking for another fight. They were happy to point me in the right direction, especially when they heard that I too had been hunting Azure. The next day, I decided to go investigate to see if there was, in fact, another dragon nearby. The Rift Mountains are beautiful, and I was in no rush to return home. I said goodbye to the dwarves as they headed down the mountain lugging Azure's severed head behind them.

"Instead of following a ridge line up into the mountains, I decided to stay in the canyon as I climbed. I hoped the steep walls would help me stay out of the scorching sun. There was not a cloud in the sky, and the sun beat down so hard. It felt like it was trying to punish everything within its reach. The Rift Mountains are incredibly arid, as they back onto the Kufkao Desert. There, the desert's dry air saps away what little moisture the mountains would otherwise have. Around noon, I stopped to have lunch and to take a nap under the shade of a rock outcropping. I was not pressed for time and hoped the afternoon would cool off by the time I woke up.

"I was awakened by a big drop of water landing on my forehead. The sweet smell of rain graced my nostrils. I inhaled, savoring the smell. As I stretched, the pitter-patter of fat raindrops slapping against the dusty ground. The gathering clouds had caused the bright day to lapse into twilight. A peal of thunder exploded overhead as a bolt of lightning ripped through the sky. I reveled in the power of the storm, listening to the wind whip through the mountains' crags. Then I panicked. I was deep within a canyon in the barren Rift Mountains, and it was pouring rain. It was going to flood.

"Attempting to clamber up the steep dirt bank to my right, I slid back to the canyon floor. The dry earth gave way underneath me as I tried to climb. The other side of the canyon was formed by a stone wall that reached over twenty feet above my head. The overhanging slab was as smooth as glass, devoid of any handholds or footholds. Having no other option, I started to sprint down the canyon, looking for an exit.

"I heard it before I saw it. The canyon filled with the thunderous noise of crashing water as the flash flood bore down toward me. The ground and the walls of the canyon started to shake. Spurred on by adrenaline, I ran for my life, pumping my arms and driving my knees as hard as I could. It was do or die. The roar of the flood grew louder, and I gave one final burst of speed. Coming around a bend, I saw an overhanging tree dangling its branches down the canyon wall. The tree looked as easy to climb like a ladder. I was going to escape. Then a churning wall of turbid water erupted from around the corner and swallowed me whole.

"I barely managed to avoid being struck by a tree trunk the flood had ripped from its root. I was then submerged underwater and tumbled through the canyon like a ragdoll. Luckily, my armor protected me from the majority of the debris flung around by the flood. I was somehow strong enough to fight my way to the surface to gasp for a big breath of air despite my metal armor. I was pulled back under, completely powerless as the flash flood pulled me down the canyon. I struggled in vain to reach the surface. The weight of my armor and the force of the flood were too much for me to overcome.

"I had been held under for over a minute. I felt my body starting to convulse from the lack of air. Stars danced before my eyes. My lungs burned and my muscles tightened from oxygen deprivation. I was starting to drown. I continued to fight, but my grasp on consciousness was growing weaker. My head began to throb, and the darkness started to close in. I could not reach the surface. I tried to accept my fate as I prepared for the worst. Then I felt the swirling water suck me down through a hole in the side of the rock wall. The rest of the flood rocketed down the canyon.

"I fell over ten feet through the air, landing on my back on a hard-stone slab with a grunt of pain. The only thing that mattered was that I could breathe again. Rolling onto my side, I spat up water and wiped the moisture from my eyes, savoring each breath. I had almost died. I was so busy breathing; it took me a while to realize that I couldn't see. Everything was pitch black. I was enveloped in darkness. I could hear a thick stream of water splashing against the rock to my side, but I had no idea where I was. Snapping my fingers, I summoned a ball of fire to illuminate my surrounding. My breath caught in my chest as the wavering green light filled the chamber. I could not believe my eyes.

"I was in an underground grotto. The cavern was long and narrow, maybe ten by sixty feet. A rock ceiling arced well over twenty feet above my head with a gradual downhill slope that angled toward the far end. The stone walls were bare beside the occasional patch of orange lichen. Water poured through the hole in the rock wall behind me that led to the canyon above. The hole was large enough to funnel enough water through to create the whirlpool that pulled me to safety. It was too small to divert the overall flood stampeding through the canyon above. An underground waterfall shot through the hole in the rock, crashing into a shallow pool at my left. A crack in the rock wall a few feet above the ground allowed the pool to drain. Despite the large quantity of water pouring into the grotto, the water level did not appear to be rising. I was no longer in immediate danger. Besides the waterfall and the pool of water, my side of the grotto was empty. It was what was on the other side of the cavern that made my heart skip a beat."

"What was there?" asked Jax, unable to contain his excitement. Cason was such a skilled storyteller that Jax had been worried Cason was going to drown in the flood. Jax sat on the edge of his seat, anxious to hear what Cason had found in the cavern.

"On the far side of the grotto," said Cason, "with milk-white shells turned a soft green by my fire, over thirty dragon eggs nestled against the rock wall. A dragon egg has the same shape as a chicken egg. Where a chicken egg has a height of only a few inches, a dragon egg stands over three feet tall. Covered in multicolored spots and splotches, dragon eggs are a myriad of different colors. They are fascinating to stare at, one of nature's marvelous works of beauty.

"While it is not unheard of for female dragons to lay up to two or three eggs at once, it is very uncommon. Most dragons only lay one egg at a time, however. Thirty eggs in the chamber meant that someone or something was collecting them. Making sure I was alone, I walked over to the eggs, mentally preparing myself for what lay before me. Pulling Trovão from my back, I lifted the ax above my head, ready to smash the eggs to pieces.

"But something stopped me. I couldn't bring my ax down onto the unprotected shells. I was struck by the barbarity of the culture we had created. I, a grown man, was about to destroy the defenseless eggs of over thirty baby dragons. I did not even know if the dragons inside were evil or not. They had not yet been given a chance to take their first breath, let alone the opportunity to choose their path.

"The Second Dragon War and the Cleanse made me hard and unfeeling. The Cleanse had so successfully lead to the widespread acceptance of killing dragons. Before that moment, I had never once questioned if what we were doing was wrong. I had lost my parents to a dragon as a child. As an adult, I had been celebrated for my uncanny ability to fight against fire breathing beasts. I was a dragon slayer in every sense of the term. Not only was it my job, but it was also my passion. It was in my blood. Every time I tracked down and killed a dragon, I was filled was an incredible sense of accomplishment. It was the most rewarding thing I've ever done. I felt I was saving lives. With each dragon I killed, I was preventing would-be orphans from having their parents killed.

"Yet at that moment, I realized we had gone too far. Dragons were disappearing from the world. So were elves, dwarves, and many of the other magical creatures that once so common in Telica. Without the power to balance humans, we had started to spread at an unsustainable rate. We cut down the forests and caused all forms of life to retreat. As we stripped the land of its resources and continued to expand outwards at breakneck speed, we careened toward disaster. If something did not change, Telica would see another war. This time it would be a war of humans."

"What did you do?" asked Jax, confused.

"I did what I had to," said Cason. "Reaching into my backpack, I pulled forth my glutton's bag. Glutton's bags are bags with interdimensional pockets sewn into them. They can hold far more items than their size would ever permit. I loaded the eggs into my bag. After waiting for the flood to pass, I climbed back up through the hole in the wall and into the mud-filled canyon.

"From there, I started the long and arduous journey north. The Rift Mountains are in the Southeast. I had to trek around the vast expanse of the Kufkao Desert before I could head north. It took me over four months to reach the Great Spine. By the time I reached the mountains, it was winter. Trying to cross them nearly cost me my life. Twice, I was almost buried alive in avalanches. Twice, the savage yetis who live on the mountains' slopes came close to ambushing and killing me. The closest I came to death was when I nearly fell into a crevasse. Sliding out of control down a glacier, I was a few seconds away from a bottomless drop when I managed to bury Trovão into the ice. The great steel blade bit into the mountain and managed to stop my descent before I plunged to my death."

"I thought you said it was impossible to cross the Great Spine except by wing?" asked Jax.

"I said almost impossible," clarified Cason with a smile. "It's possible, just incredibly dangerous. After two weeks of forging my way over glaciers through the pine trees of snow-filled mountains passes, I made it to the other side of the Great Spine. That afternoon, I found an uninhabited cave to pass the night. I watched a beautiful orange and purple sunset over the frigid wastelands of Sincelo from the cave's mouth.

The following morning, I wound my way back through the cave's many passages. I found a small chamber hidden behind a massive pair of ice-covered stalagmites. I hid the eggs there, making sure they were resting on a solid rock layer. Dragon eggs are hot. While they don't give off enough heat to burn you, they will quickly melt through ice and snow. I did not want to leave the eggs in the ice only to have them melt into the heart of a glacier. Having left the eggs behind, I quickly set off on the long journey back south before I could have a chance to rethink what I had done.

"I wandered Telica for over a year before finally settling here. Thousand Stumps had just been founded and was even smaller than it is today. I like the solitude living in the Elderwood provides. I was content to grow old in peace until some long-lost piece of my past decided to come knocking on my door. When you live like me, you end up with many loose ends. I never thought the piece of my past that would arrive on my doorstep would be Kase's nephew. It looks like that's what has happened. Now that I think about it, many of the other options could have been far worse. It's a good thing you're here. Growing old was getting boring anyway."

Jax stared at Cason in disbelief. He could not believe what he had heard. Cason Greenstone, the famous dragon slayer, smuggled over thirty dragon eggs to safety. Over thirty dragon eggs. He couldn't fathom the amount of destruction thirty dragons could cause if they arrived unannounced from the North. His father and uncle had trusted Cason, but Jax was worried they had made a mistake. He held his face in his hands as he tried to make sense of everything, but he was unable to understand. His brain hurt. It was too late for this; he could not think straight.

"I know what you are thinking," said Cason, reading the incredulity written across Jax's face. "You need to understand that I took every possible precaution to be as safe as possible.

The eggs are on the far side of the Great Spine. If the dragons do hatch, they will head farther north. Their ancestors fled there decades before. Nor will they know that Telica lays south of the mountains. Plus, as babies, they will be too weak to cross the Great Spine even if they try. On top of that, dragon eggs can take over fifty years to hatch. There is a good chance that the eggs aren't going to open any time soon. And for all we know, they are the eggs of good dragons.

"I should have smashed the eggs the second I found them. I used to think about it every day. But for some reason, I could not bring myself to do it. I may be a dragon slayer, but I am not a butcher of unborn babies. I also couldn't leave the eggs in the grotto. Someone had been collecting them. They could have been creating an army of dragons for all we know. I needed to get the eggs out of Telica as fast as I could. I know the danger dragons pose. I needed to get them as far away from our world as possible to make sure no one was at risk. Leaving them on the far side of the Great Spine where the mountains merge with the wastes of Sincelo was the best option I had."

It was too late to make sense of everything now. Jax hoped the following day would help shed fresh light on the situation. "You said you think my uncle suspected you of something," said Jax finally, furrowing his brow. "Did you mean that you think my uncle realized you hid dragon eggs in the Great Spine?"

"Something of the sort," answered Cason. "I tried to be as elusive as I could, but word got out of my journey north. It would not surprise me if your uncle put the pieces together. Why would I head north to the Great Spine only to return a few weeks later unless I was trying to hide something in the mountains? The last I heard of Kase, he was heading north himself. For all we know, he was going to the Great Spine to investigate."

"You think my uncle is in the North?" asked Jax, hope glimmering in his eyes.

"There is a chance," said Cason. "Finding your uncle is a long shot, but if I were to look for him, I would start there."

Jax nodded. "Can I stay here for a few days? I'm going to need to gather my strength before I head north."

Cason stared into the fire with unseeing eyes, his mind lost in memories from many years before. "Before we head north," he said finally, having made up his mind. "Kase was my best friend, and I owe it to him to help you."

"I don't need help. I can take care of myself."

"We'll see about that," laughed Cason. He stretched and yawned. "You may be strong, but you would be a fool not to accept my help. I know the land; I've already made the journey once before. Plus, I can use our little trip as an excuse to check in on my eggs. It is long overdue that I head north anyway."

Jax nodded his head. It did him no good to argue with Cason now. He would talk to the old man again tomorrow after they both had a chance to get some rest. As legendary as his past had been, it was obvious that Cason was past his prime. Jax did not want to be slowed down by the elderly dragon slayer, nor did he trust Cason's decision making. Cason had carried over thirty dragon eggs across the length of Telica. What other reckless ideas would he think were good decisions?

"You better get some sleep. Tomorrow is going to be a big day,' said Cason, rising to his feet. "Goodnight Jax." He walked to his bedroom and shut the door behind him without another word.

Finishing his glass of water, Jax spread his bedroll on the orange and black rug in front of the fire and tried to relax. When he closed his eyes, he saw glowing scama, fiery dragons, snowy mountains, and dragon eggs. What had he gotten himself into? He did not know what he had expected from Cason, but it definitely had not been this. Unable to sleep, Jax rolled on his side and watched the dying fire float higher and higher. He sunk into a restless slumber filled with dreams of dragons.

DOWNSTROKE

JEFFREY DAVIS

Soaring North across the dark violet sky, Ironplate felt the wind through the holes in his wing. There hadn't been time enough to get his full strength back and he was already fatigued from the flight. A landing to the West it would have to be. Scouring the land to the West for a place to set down, he spotted a clearing in a small stretch of swamp. At least it hadn't any large trees. It would do, he thought.

Ironplate thrust his wing with extra might and landed in the moonlit mire. His feet sank into the mud until his belly touched lightly down. Fish and frogs, mosquitoes and moths, all swamp life were displaced by his presence. His pointed tail whipped and leveled the brush, slicing every cattail.

Craning his long neck to examine the holes in his wings, the great beast shook his head.

"Never leave the mountain. Hundreds of years and no one found me. What was I thinking?" he grumbled in a deep, booming voice.

He lifted a front claw out of the muck. Poking a single nail dripping with mud through one of the holes, he eyed it. A large turtle lounged on a decaying log inside the hole. Ironplate was impressed that his landing had not frightened the creature away. He circled to face it, slowly lifting each foot from the suction of the swamp. His great spiked tail swung wide, knocking down a youthful nearby tree.

"Not afraid of me, little one?" he spoke to the reptile.

The turtle blinked.

"I don't suppose I have to worry about you telling anyone I'm here, do I?"

Ironplate bent his head down and leaned his face in close to the reptile. The turtle snapped at his nose. It clamped on and Ironplate immediately shook his head to get the turtle off. Releasing its grip on Ironplate's nose, the turtle went flying. It landed on a nearby moss-covered mound sticking out of the swamp.

The dragon narrowed his eyes.

"You're against me too, eh?"

In a giant scooping motion, Ironplate collected the turtle up with his mandible. He raised his head straight to the sky, swallowing the turtle whole and passing it down his long neck.

"There. Now I know I needn't worry."

He examined his wing again. The holes appeared a bit larger than before.

"I wonder how I caused such a stir. Suppose I'll nap while I await the inevitable. All this time and no one will even hear my story."

Ironplate lied down in the mud and curled up into a ball. When he was comfortable, he circled his tail around himself. Pushing mud up against his scaly body, he looked like a large rocky mound. A mound a bit out of place in this swamp, but not something that would cause alarm. When he shut his yellow eyes, the illusion was complete.

★★★

Early the next morning, Ironplate awoke to a cracking sound in the distance. He opened his eye but did not move. There was nothing there to see and he sealed his eye shut once again.

A short while later, there was another crack. It was closer this time. Ironplate lifted his heavy eyelids. Nothing there. A third crack came even closer still. Ironplate raised his head and neck out of the swamp. Large clumps of mud dripped and fell. He stared into the nearby forest at the edge of the swamp and waited. Deep amongst the woods, a shadow began to take shape. A human.

Ironplate lifted his great wings out of the muck and tried to take flight. The holes, in both wings now, prevented any egress. There was no lift. He assessed his wings and laid them back to rest against his body. Sinking as low as he could, he waited and watched the human. It didn't come in a straight line. It meandered back and forth between the trees, taking its time.

Then, finally, the human approached. Ironplate lowered his head. Staying as hidden as he could, but keeping out of the mud as much as possible to leave his movement unhindered.

When the human reached the edge of Ironplate's swamp, it stepped in only a few yards away from him. Ironplate reared up. He spread his massive wings and flared the copper scales all around his face and neck. Then he let out a mighty roar, but a muffled one. No point in drawing more attention than necessary.

The startled man made a vain attempt to turn and run but when he tried to lift his feet, they sunk too deep in the mud. He only fell backward on his rump and became further stuck.

Ironplate was not an indiscriminate killer, nor did he like the taste of human. So, he finished his roar and the two stared at one another, uncertain of what to do next. The man cowered in place awaiting death, but Ironplate only huffed.

"Oh, get up," Ironplate commanded.

Fright faded and left only shock on the man's face. His mouth was agape as he blinked. Lifting his hand out of the mud, he used the back of it to wipe his eyes and check his vision. He appeared to be trying to avoid getting mud on his face. He had failed and coated his gray tinged beard.

The man struggled to rise to his feet in the thick mire. He couldn't find balance inside his unmoving large leather boots. Ironplate wrapped his tail around the man's back and pulled him forward, helping him to his feet. It brought him right up to Ironplate's nose. The man reached a palm out and touched it to balance himself.

"Did you just talk?" the man said, timid.

Ironplate pulled his face back. The man teetered but found his balance.

"Of course, I did. What else should I do? You didn't appear to be leaving."

The man paused for a while before speaking again, "What are you?"

"I am the Red Scourge of Wruenele. The King of Karpinsky. High Chieftain of the Coppershield Clan. The last of my bloodline. I suppose it's more of a de facto honorific at this point. Nonetheless, I am called Ironplate."

"You're a dragon!" the man exclaimed.

"Of course, I'm a dragon."

"But dragons don't exist," the man snorted

"What? I would say that I do," Ironplate asserted with an aside to himself, "At least for now." He glanced at his damaged wings.

"I mean, I see that now, but I have never seen a dragon before in my life. You're myths. Fairy tales, you know?"

"Hmm. I suppose I have slept a while. What you say would explain why I hadn't seen any dragons in my journey here."

Ironplate stopped to reflect, "Every single one finally written out. Can it be?"

"There were more of you?"

"There were many once. We lived in the woods, in the mountains, in the seas. Large dragons, some as much as ten times my size, and puny dragons, no bigger than a wolf. Red, blue, green, white, and black, the absolute best color," Ironplate added with a small bow.

The man looked more astonished the more Ironplate spoke. He continued his inquiries. "Where did you learn English?"

"From an Englishman, you fool."

"Yes, I suppose that makes sense. So, you are friends with humans then?"

"Friends with humans? I never cared for them. They are selfish and greedy. No other ambition matches human ambition. Even a dragon's ambitions are simple by comparison.

"Human progress did intrigue my clan. Despite my objections, the High Chieftain relocated our clan to a human village. Much like many other dragon clans had."

Ironplate glanced at Stan, who looked to be listening intently. Then he lifted his head to the still-dark early morning sky.

"That was before humans had developed. Slowly, your kind gained new ways. Their structures grew complicated and they filled them with shiny possessions. They colored things that they saw onto flat surfaces and carved women from stone. They began to record their deeds. Eventually more and more of my kind would vanish. I became the last of my clan. When I could take no more, I left. Seeking refuge deep in a volcano, I slept.

"If what you say you know of dragons is true, then the clans of old must all be gone. I may be the last to have his story told."

"I can't believe this. This is amazing!" the human shouted and laughed, throwing his arms in the air and twisting. His feet remained firmly stuck in the mire, but he didn't seem to care.

"You are a weird one. What do they call you, human?"

"Me? My name is Stanley. Stanley Scriven. Or Stan. Call me Stan. How do you do?"

"Well, Stan, might I now ask you a question?"

"Sure, anything."

"That metal rod on your back, what is it? Some sort of bludgeon?"

"Bludgeon? This?" Stan said, removing the ornate matchlock rifle from his back, "This is my gun."

"Gun? What's that?"

"Well, it's like a bow I suppose. You know what bows are?"

"I do."

"It's like a bow, only it shoots small bits of metal. At much faster speeds. I use it for hunting."

"Ah! You are a hunter! Now you are speaking a dragon's language. Very admirable."

Ironplate was delighted. The killing was his favorite, it didn't matter if it was hunting or in battle. Spending a few of his fading moments with a fellow hunter might not be so bad.

Ironplate continued, "Never cared much for bows though. I was sad to see humans switch to them. Days were better trapping and getting close. Facing your enemy outright with spears and swords."

"Huh. So, you've been alive a while, haven't you?"

"I will have lived nine thousand years soon."

"Wow. I'll be forty in December," Stan smiled a little and paused before adding, "I suppose you have me beat."

"Yes, my age is greater than yours."

Ironplate had learned about humor and its social usefulness from humans. He occasionally made jokes. Yet, his lessons had not included much identification or comprehension.

"Tell me, young Stan, what do you hunt? Imps? Fairies?"

"Wait. What? Are those things real too?" Stan asked, astounded.

Not able to hold a straight face for very long, Ironplate bellowed out a hearty laugh. He came clean. "No no, of course not. I'm having fun with you."

The two shared a laugh. Ironplate's posture relaxed. He sat back into the mud. The human trudged out of the swamp and took a seat on a nearby decaying log, resting his rifle on the ground.

"No, Ironplate, I mostly hunt geese and boar," Stan said.

"Geese? You mean birds?"

"Yes."

"Ah, I see, Stan. A challenge for humans as they cannot fly. Nicely done," Ironplate said.

"Well, thank you. Of course, a life spent hunting in the wilderness is not exactly what my family hoped I would be doing. My youth was spent learning my father's trade but things aren't the same anymore. His business went under several years ago. After that, my father thought I would join my cousin and be a machinist. Well, my father passed away and I suppose that's when I came out here. When I was a lad, my uncle taught me to hunt in the same woods. It was the most freedom I ever felt. Tell me, what is it that you hunt, Ironplate?"

"Anything I fancy. Tiger. Mammoth. Hunted human once or twice."

Stan's eyes widened, "You're having fun with me again."

"No," responded Ironplate flatly.

Stan gulped.

"You need not worry. I actually can't stand the taste of humans," Ironplate reassured him.

Stan appeared to relax, "I see. Tell me then, Ironplate, is that why you left the humans? You were in trouble for eating them?"

"No, that was long ago, before humans were civilized. I left because my tribe had given up. One by one, they accepted their fates and died. They met their end with the help of their precious humans." Ironplate's tone was distant and increasingly cold, "Afraid at the thought of losing the dragon strength, the humans tried to enslave us. To hold onto our strength as long as they could. When I was the very last, they came to chain me. In my rage, I gobbled one of them up. I was hoping to incite fear, but they were as relentless as ever. I fled the village and headed East. As far as my wings would carry me." Ironplate seethed. He dared not look at the human, he feared he would not be able to stop himself from attacking.

"I can't believe they would try to enslave you like that," Stan said. "That was very wrong of them."

The dragon relaxed. Not every human might have deserved his hatred.

"I appreciate your compassion, Stan. As far as humans go, you are proving to be acceptable."

Ironplate attempted to smile. Unlike his forays into humor, his attempts at friendly smiles always incited fear. For once, the target of his smile did not flee. Stan leaned back on his log. Looking up at Ironplate, he smiled and nodded in response.

"So, you retreated to a volcano? How can you possibly survive inside a volcano?" Stan asked.

Ironplate did not respond. Instead, he compressed his neck, pulling his head in close to his body. Holding it there for a few moments, his whole body began to vibrate. The mud around him rippled and splattered everywhere. There was a low humming sound.

Then Ironplate let loose. His neck stretched straight upwards. It was longer and thinner than it was at rest. He opened his massive mouth and flames poured out with great force.

First was a hit of blinding light. A quick and loud rumbling sound replaced the vibrations. Last came a blast of hot wind that swept over everything around Ironplate, including Stan. The mud, the plants, everything leaned away. Finally, it ended. Ironplate closed his mouth and relaxed his neck. He looked down toward Stan who jumped to his feet and began clapping.

"That was outstanding!" he cheered. "I suppose that answers that! Volcanos should worry about surviving you!"

The dragon nodded. Ironplate handled compliments well. He was decidedly proud and always expected them.

"So, why have you awakened now?" asked Stan, settling down.

"Several days ago, I awoke to an earthquake and was famished. I took a flight to find something to eat. As I began to search, things did not look the same. The human cities are walled and made of stone now. There are many and they are so much larger. Last night, I went in for a closer look but my wings were damaged and I wound up taking refuge here in this swamp."

Stroking his short beard, Stan appeared to be in thought.

"Humans again. Well, I'll tell you what, dragon. My cabin is not far from here. It's in the forest ahead. And not far from that is a river. What do you say you and I head there and clean ourselves up? Get this mud off us. Then you stay as long as you'd like. Let your wings heal."

This plan sounded good to Ironplate. If this human revealed himself to be anything like the rest, he figured it would be easy enough to gobble him up too. The ill taste of human.

"Agreed, young Stan. Let's go."

As the morning sun diffused its orange streaks across the indigo sky, they trekked back to the cabin. Ironplate followed behind Stan on foot as swamp mud dried and crumbled from them both.

***

They returned to the hunter's property that day and did as Stan had laid out. They proceeded first to the river bank and cleansed themselves in the clear blue water. Ironplate stomped in, sending clouds of dirty water downstream. His metallic copper scales gleamed in the midday rays of the sun.

Stan washed his leather boots at the edge of the water as the two continued their discussions. He was now engaged in updating Ironplate on human achievements. The dragon worried his new friend suffered from typical human ambition. He quickly put it aside.

When they finished at the river, Stanley led the lustrous dragon to his cabin. He told Ironplate that he had built it himself a few years prior. He traveled to town around two times each month to trade. He enjoyed his simple life here in the wild.

It was a small, crudely built log cabin, but appeared sturdy. There were even a couple of tiny hinged windows that Stan had recently added to the structure. A rock-lined campfire smoldered to the side of the cabin near some drying leathers.

Later that night, Ironplate set up a makeshift nest in the rear of the cabin with the hunter's help. The two gathered twigs and brush, and the dragon flattened it with his tail. When he laid down, the dragon's body was as large as the cabin. Thankfully, the clearing fit them both.

The two minds were alive with new information and their voices tired.

The pores in Ironplate's wings continued to worsen his first few days there. Then their growth appeared to stop, but they were not getting better.

The two worked together to hunt their meals. Ironplate had proven to be nimble on his feet. He would leap to cut off their prey while Stan closed in with his gun. He continually tried to persuade Stan to use the gun as a bludgeon, but to no avail.

Back at the cabin, Ironplate would start the campfire with a blast of his fire breath. Stan cooked dinner while Ironplate waited patiently, even though he consumed his portion raw.

His new friend was a wonderful host. They chatted late into the evening. Ironplate would recount the tales of dragons. The great sky battles between them, the battles with humans, and the battles alongside them.

For his part, Stan would regale Ironplate with stories of humans and anecdotes from his own life. Ironplate had admitted to Stan that he enjoyed the stories about human wars the most. The greedy and zealous kings, the strong and violent knights and, most of all, the underdogs. Peasants proving themselves in battle and receiving recognition for it. Nothing fascinated Ironplate more as it reminded him of dragons.

Both became lost in their time together.

★★★

The days passed and one afternoon the dragon laid on his back near the cabin, relaxing. Stan had ventured into town to trade for supplies. Carrots, potatoes, spices, bullets, gunpowder, oil, rope. Everything was running low. The two were so engrossed in their new friendship that Stan hadn't wanted to leave and visit the town.

It had become unavoidable and he left the previous afternoon, saying he would return in a few days. It was unexpected that Ironplate should hear his wagon nearing on the path this morning. He could tell from the sound that it was traveling at a greater speed than when it had left.

"Ironplate!" Stan called, "Ironplate, you must come see!"

Ironplate rolled over and made his way around to the front of the cabin as Stan arrived. He jumped down from the wagon. He held a folded, very clean looking parchment paper high above his head.

"Ironplate! They're talking about you!"

The dragon's heart sank. The humans had not seen a dragon in quite some time. If Stan's initial shock upon their meeting was any indicator, the rest of mankind would be very frenzied over the reappearance of a dragon. It did not bode well for Ironplate.

He sighed and asked, "Who speaks of me?"

"In the town! It's in all the papers!"

"Papers?"

Stan held the newspaper up so Ironplate could examine it closer.

"Stan, is this writing? It appears so small and rigid and precise."

"Sure, it's writing. It's in print. It's the town's monthly. Weeks old news at this point, but the most recent off the press. It's all about you! They're all talking about the strange, giant beast that passed over the town. Where did it come from? Where was it headed?"

"Monthly? Off the press?"

"The printing press. It's a machine. Think of it as a way of copying the same story over and over on many pieces of paper, very quickly. They print a new one every month and give it to all the townspeople and travelers. I imagine thousands have heard of you by now. That's where my cousin works. Do you remember? The machinist I mentioned before that." Stanley saw the great dragon's head sink.

"What is it, Ironplate? You needn't worry. They don't know where you are. I promise no one is coming to chain you." Stan's enthusiasm seemed to fade away.

"No, Stan. The more we are resounded, the more we fade away," spoke Ironplate distantly.

"What does that mean?"

"It means my tribe did not die off. They chose to meet their end and sought help from humans to do so. The more a dragon's deeds are heralded, the more they fade away. Each one met with a human who wrote their deeds in a book. The stories within were shared far and wide until I was all that was left."

Ironplate lifted his head. He stood up on his hind legs, puffed his chest out and expanded his majestic ecru wings. Stan gazed upon the proud dragon. Looking him over in awe, he examined the now very large holes in the membrane of his wings. Massive and powerful, and yet vulnerable to a simple word.

"The townspeople don't know anything. There are no details about you in the monthly. How could it have done this?"

"A small piece of a dragon's story shared so vastly is as effective as his grandest story told only once. I don't imagine I will survive long in this world. Unless I were to remain hidden forever."

The two spoke sparingly throughout the rest of the morning.

Later, they collected wood. Stan chopped it with an ax. Ironplate would assist, stacking the pieces with his tail. Occasionally he would pick up an uncut block between his teeth and chop it himself.

They made a bonfire in front of the cabin that night. Ironplate curled up and Stan sat on the ground leaning against his belly as they spoke about life and death. Stan did most of the talking.

★★★

Several more days Ironplate stayed silent. He had awoken early and made his way to the river to wash his scales and feast on the trout there. Collecting several extra fish, he set them aside to bring back to his friend. When he had gotten his fill, he gathered the extras between his teeth and carried them back to the cabin.

Ironplate laid the fish near the fire. Sitting down to enjoy the pleasant morning air and clear sky, he waited for Stan to awaken.

"Good morning, Ironplate," Stan said pleasantly, exiting the cabin.

"You as well, Stan. I have brought you some fish."

"You did? Look at that. What's the occasion?"

"We have something to discuss. I didn't want the daily hunt to impede us."

Stan laid the fish out on a nearby stump. Taking a small knife in hand, he began removing scales. "So, what is it then?"

"Thousands of years it has been since I first met humans. All I ever knew of them was the way they used my kind."

"And that we taste terrible," Stan added smiling.

"Stan, please."

"Sorry. Go ahead."

"I've been thinking about the way my clan met their end in companionship with the humans. In all that time, no human showed the kindness you have shown me.

"But I wonder now if I was being stubborn. My clan did not resist their fates. I now know why they were ready to meet their end. They joined the humans with purpose. Their friendship gave them the ability to strive and overcome challenges. The ability to face all things. Dragons live for battle, but they had found peace with the humans. It's a peace I couldn't even find in isolation."

The human stopped his carving and stared down at the slimy, white fish.

Stan spoke. "These years I've spent in the wilderness I suppose I've been somewhat alone myself. I've enjoyed having you here. We are friends, Ironplate."

"That same peace they shared I have now come to know through our friendship. That is why I would like you to write my story."

Ironplate stood straight, resolute in his decision. Chest out and looking at Stan. Stan took a breath and set the knife down on the large stump was used as a cutting board. He looked concerned.

"I haven't written in quite some time, Ironplate. Are you sure?"

"I am certain you will do well."

"This will mean the end of you, won't it?"

"Yes. I will perish as the story is written and told. I see that it is a noble end for a dragon. But do not worry, it is not an unpleasant one."

"If that's what you want, then so be it," Stan said. "Where do we begin?"

★★★

The next day, when they were both ready, Ironplate positioned his head by the window of the cabin. Stan sat at his desk and prepared his inkwell, some paper and a pen. Listening closely to the dragon's words, he took the pen in hand and began with a downstroke.

They spent their days and nights thereafter going through Ironplate's story. They covered the early days spent with his clan and the alliances and battles with other dragon factions. Then, the eventual cohabitation with humans. They covered daily life. How a dragon could remove mountain goat entrails when they were stuck between his teeth. They even spoke of his time spent in isolation.

Ironplate spoke of war the fondly. Raining walls of fire from his throat that cut through infantry and cavalry alike. Landing in the center of the battlefield, whipping his tail and the area of the troop. Swooping in and putting a quick end to battles by tossing an army general hundreds of feet.

As the days recounting his stories passed, Ironplate noticed scales loosen. They fell from his torso and tail. His energy diminished and his desire to rest grew.

Somewhere along the way his vision failed. This was when Stan took over the duties of hunting for them both. It stymied their writing progress. Feeding a dragon, even a fading one, was not easy.

At night they slept near the window of the cabin. Stan inside, asleep at the desk. Ironplate curled up outside between the cabin and campfire.

They continued until the last tale. The last word was written down one warm evening against the setting sun.

"There. I've got it all written down. It might be the grandest story ever told, my friend."

"Thank you, Stan. I do hope you included the time we have spent together. It was the most important of all."

"Of course, I have," Stan spoke warmly. Though Ironplate could not see a smile, he knew it was there.

"So, how are you faring?"

"Tired. And content."

"What should I do now?"

"Please take my story and share it with all who would listen. I am going to rest," he said, placing his head on the ground beneath the window of the cabin.

Stan readied his pack for town the next morning. He checked on his horse and wagon, then he came back and found a spot on the grass beside the dragon. Resting his head and placing his palm on one of Ironplate's large copper scales, he shut his eyes.

"Ironplate, are you awake?" Stan stood before the dragon the next morning in his traveling leathers.

Ironplate found it too difficult to lift his head. His heartbeat felt faint. His scales appeared almost translucent, yet he felt somehow at peace.

"Good morning, Stan."

"I'm heading into town now. I'm going to speak with my cousin. The whole world is going to hear your magnificent story."

Ironplate wheezed. "I am honored to have had a friend like you, Stanley Scriven."

"And you, Ironplate. I'll be back soon, alright, my friend?"

"I will be here," Ironplate made one more attempt at a smile.

Stanley rushed to his wagon and off he rode.

Arriving in town that evening, Stan met with his cousin at home. They exchanged the briefest of pleasantries, then he offered all the coin he had.

"Get it printed. Get it to every man, woman, and child. Free to all."

Though his cousin offered him lodging, he made it clear he must get back right away. He provided no reason and hurried back to his wagon. His horse was familiar enough with the route and they journeyed through the black of night.

When the daylight revealed the frost on each blade of grass that lined the wagon's path, they arrived.

Stan noted something was amiss.

Ironplate could not be seen on the far side of the cabin. The campfire that usually illuminated the area now shed no light, only a small trail of smoke.

Rounding the corner of the cabin, the final friend of any dragon paused and knelt before the empty patch of matted grass near the window. Ironplate was gone.

The printing press starts early each morning. The town was hungry for more information about the mysterious beast. That day, the entire town could do nothing but read and discuss dragons. After that Ironplate's tale spread far and wide.

So went the last of the dragons. Proud and war-loving. The mightiest of all beasts. In the end, a friend of man. A friendship that would trumpet their greatness forever.

END OF BATTLES

E. W. FARNSWORTH

The battlefield between the two mountain ranges was scorched by Dragon fires. Some still smoldered, while the foul stench of the burning flesh of dragons and humans filled the air. A great flap of leathery wings heralded the dragon kind's final retreat toward the setting sun. Like the brilliant sun, the flying creatures flew over the horizon, never to fight again.

Prince Landron thought his arms would not recover from the exercise of the fight. He had held a giant broadsword in his right hand and a broad ax in his left. From the time the battle started that morning, he had not stopped swinging his weapons. He would not stop until the day had been won. Too terrible was the thought of a dragon victory this day. Slavery under the dragons' cruel sway held few fruits for humans.

The prince knew the dragon ways. For a decade he had been a slave dreaming of this. He had dreamt of the future day when he would take revenge for their treatment of him and all his heroes. The plan was intricate, but it was the only way forward. Princess Fiona, Landron's sister, dared to trick the king of dragons to free him. In the fracas that ensued upon his escape, the dragons vowed to exterminate all humans from Earth.

The escaping prince and princess led the entire dragon army into a valley. A trap had been laid to surprise the hated fire-breathers. Fiona had planned the surprise perfectly. Yet, it still required the utmost strength and efforts of the prince and all other humans, and more. It required the support of wizards and gods too.

The wizard, Ealdring the Wise, taught the warrior humans about the dragons' vulnerabilities, like their soft underbellies. There, a sharp blade could quickly pierce them in the heart. Selander, the god of the humans, foresaw the time and place of the battle as propitious. With his power of prophesy, he knew where every blow would fall. He knew how each combatant would live or die as a result of his prowess and endurance.

The sky this morning was clear and cloudless, and the sun rose unaware of what was coming from the south. Suddenly, the sky was dark with wings. The ground glistened with the iron of spearheads on long pikes on the ground. The dragons were enticed to fall from great heights looking for ground-hugging prey. Their keep vision in the heavens dimmed as they dropped. They could not see the sharp instruments raised to pierce their bellies. Too late, they realized that they had fallen into the humans' cunning devices. Some stopped in mid-flight. Flying nets descended on them. As they became tangled, they could no longer use their wings. They either died by the million spearheads diving or by falling to the slicing motions of swords and axes.

After the first charge of the flying monsters, over half their ranks were slain. Half again were wounded and easy marks. Only the unscathed quarter of the dragons' brood remained without leadership or enthusiasm. Those remnants were still formidable. They breathed fire in every direction out of frustration and rage. Wherever the dragons' fires touched human flesh, moans of pain pleased the demon dragon brains. Now was the time when numbers favored the human. The best stepped forward to engage in single combat.

The prince knew from observation of many years' enslavement how to mount a dragon. You stepped up from the rear just behind the head and above the wings. He knew how to plant two hooks on either side of the beast's head. This way, it had to go forward or from side to side. Other humans knew the secret from watching their leader. A phalanx of dragons with humans riding rushed into the tumult of the flying enemy. The clash of forces resounded through the wide battlefield. Fires of dragons breathed on both sides of the battle. Swords hacked as dragons charged at one another. The field filled with limbs and heads and trembling wings.

The human forces split in two, one led by the prince, the other by his sister. His job was to confront the dragons who still dared to stand and fight. Her job was to kill all those who tried to flee. Soon the dragons realized they faced double jeopardy. If they stayed, the prince and his forces would cut them down. If they fled, the princess would harry them to death.

The smoke from battle rose and filled the sky, but no more dragons joined the fray. No living thing on the ground was not immolated. No dragon was untouched by fire from its kind. Finally, he saw that the battle had turned in the humans' favor. Prince Landron laughed and raised his weapons. He took his makeshift reins in his teeth. He forced his ride to sweep from low to high, then back again. Like a giant threshing machine working tall grass on a summer's harvest, his giant dragon responded to his urgent attack. His sister and her forces held the line of the dragons' escape. She pushed the cowards back toward her brother relentlessly.

The outcome of the battle was now as the wizard and the god had foreseen. The dragon army was dwindling to the point where surrender was the only way for them to survive. As they continued to fight, this eliminated the chance for survival. There would be no sufficient breeding pairs to refresh for later war. Only after the females had all been slain did Prince Landron raise his mighty voice to offer a form of truce.

"Dragons all, I offer a truce with honor now that your females have all perished in this foolish battle. You will never again raise small dragons to grow strong against us humans. The question is whether you want to die with your kind. Or, you can live single until you die alone and miserable. You will never hear the sounds of little ones or witness their first fires."

His words did not comfort the enemy. The remaining dragons for a while rushed at the humans with redoubled ferocity. They wanted blood as revenge even though they were doomed and knew it. One by one the males flew to their certain deaths until only a few remained flying. Then the human god appeared to them to give them one more opportunity to live.

"Dragon Kind," he said, "Desist or perish! There is no scenario by which you will survive. Surely, you'll want to enjoy your remaining years."

The spirits of the dragons flagged. The king of dragons, whom Prince Landron rode, spoke in dragon language: "Enough. We have been vanquished. We surrender, but we have terms."

"Speak your terms, dragon, quickly, or you'll die."

"We wish to continue to harbor our masses of gold until we die of natural causes."

The god looked toward the prince for his agreement to this term.

"I agree with this term. We humans do not need the gold of dragons. They can continue to brood over their hoards and guard them—but only until they perish. At that time, humans will do with the gold what we will."

The wily king of dragons then asked, "May we continue to use our fire, talons, and teeth to keep the peace?"

Prince Landron said, "That you may not do. Sly king, your perfidious purpose is well known to me. You would only use this permission to continue your practice of slavery as you once enslaved me. If you become aggressive against humans for any reason, we shall hunt you all down without mercy."

"At least let us enjoy our lands."

"You may enjoy three hectares each, but no more. This includes the lands of your lairs and the surroundings and no more."

The king of dragons roared and breathed fire through his mouth and nostrils. "I hate this constraint, but what can I do? I agree under protest."

"Then we have a truce among dragons and humans. The god is our witness for the terms of this truce."

Prince Landron called to his sister. "We have a truce with the dragons. Desist from the fighting. Let all surviving dragons return to their homes."

"I hate this truce—and I would like to destroy the dragons every one. Still, I must abide by the god-witnessed truce. My forces will dismount and free the dragons they are riding. I will redirect them to cleaning the battlefield."

Prince Landron dismounted the king of dragon. He watched as the humiliated monarch flew away with his survivors. They did not bother to mourn the fallen. The prince thought they would not feel secure until they had entered their distant caves.

The surviving humans knelt on the blood-manured field. They prayed to their god for delivering them in their hour of need. The prince and princess stood side by side as the prince gave his final order of the day.

"Clean this killing field until no sign of carnage remains. Pile all our weapons so that they may be repaired for future use. Know I honor my sister for her role in our triumph. Know I honor the wisdom of our wizard for his help too."

Some humans grumbled because dragons had been freed to escape.

"I hear your grumblings. I know you are angry on account of my judgments in the matter of the truce with the dragon king and his followers. I shall not let this disgruntlement fester. Therefore, if anyone wants to come with me to resolve the issue by single combat, step forward now. Peace will not be possible until humans have come to terms with the truce. Even after the demise of the dragon kingdom."

Prince Landron's fierce eyes and swelling muscles threatened the other humans. The prince and his sister the princess turned to the tasks of cleaning up. However, they kept their vigilance in case one or more humans attacked them.

As twilight came, the fires of the battle became the campfires of the victors. Music played. Male and female warriors danced for joy.

A few brave scouts peered through the darkness looking for dragons to break the recent truce. All through the night, they watched. In the early morning light, no black web of dragon wings was seen in the south. The humans breathed easy. They continued to pile high the remains of slain dragons and humans. By evening, they were ready to smear the huge pile of carrion with pitch and to light the funeral pyre. Flames rose to signify the communal conflagration and the truce.

"Brother, it is wise to be vigilant. I won't feel safe until the last dragon has died. I am tempted to travel south and confront every dragon until I've killed them all. I would do this to perfect your revenge for ten years' slavery."

"Princess and sister, I value your offer, but we have given our word that the truce will stand. Only if dragons violate the truce will we go on the attack again. As god is our witness, we shall not break the truce. Fear not, because no female dragons remain to produce new threats."

"If the dragons had won yesterday instead of us, tell me what you think they might have done to us."

"There's no question. They would have tortured and killed us as an example to the rest, whom they would have enslaved or killed."

"Yes, I know you are right. Still, you granted these monsters their lives and a sense of peace with honor."

The brother and sister stopped discussing the truce. They focused on restoring normalcy between the two mountain ranges.

vines as far in all directions as the soil will permit. The burnt flavor will enrich the wines we'll ferment from the grapes. We'll call the vintage Dragon's Blood Wine."

"I like the sound of that. Whenever we drink the wine, we'll be reminded of our victory."

The humans planted vines in straight rows through the valley, each vine with its post. Several years of cultivation and watering were required to grow the first clusters of grapes. Viniculture followed viticulture. At last, the first Dragon's Blood Wine was produced in large oaken casks.

By the time the humans were ready to taste the first vintage, most dragons had perished. Only two score ancient beasts remained, and they kept close to their hordes of gold.

A harvest banquet was held, and the wizard and the god were invited to partake of the wine.

The god spoke the valediction. "I'm pleased that you humans could make a truce with the dragons. That you could abide by its terms all these years since the final battle. Congratulations. Now I will sample the wine you made on the battlefield." He sipped the wine and beamed with delight.

"I can taste the ashen flavor from the dragons' fire. I can also taste the richness of the soil mixed with blood. As long as you continue to bless this dragon-free land, I'll extend my favor over you and your children."

The food and drink were plentiful, and the evening was full of dancing and song. At the end of the day, the wizard stepped forward to deliver the salutation.

"Humans, rejoice. Not long ago, we lived in fear of dragons' raids, enslavement, even torture, and death. Because of wise judgments by your prince and princess, peace was established. Under this, the fruits, vegetables, meats, and wines of this banquet are possible. I'm glad to have played a small though significant part in the actions that yielded up this miracle. I advise you to remain fit and ready for battle though no foes have given signs of threatening you. Believe me, as soon as such threats become visible, it will be too late to prepare."

After the day's festivities, Prince Landron spoke with his sister about the future.

"We have prevailed, but we must look forward to our future."

"What do you have in mind, Brother?"

"A husband for you and a wife for me would be the beginning. Recall that our victory over dragons was because we exterminated the females. We must learn from our dictates. Children will assure the futurity of our kingdom of humans."

"If only I could find a suitable mate, Brother. I must rely on you to find someone worthy."

Prince Landron puzzled over the problem of finding a suitable mate for his sister. After two weeks, he came to her with a decision.

"Princess, I believe I have a satisfactory answer to finding a mate for you. We'll advertise a contest, the winner of which shall be your bridegroom."

"I reserve the right to refuse the winner, as I won't have a boor or strong man as my husband."

Prince Landron nodded in assent. He sent heralds with a proclamation throughout the human kingdom. Everyone knew the terms of the contest and the reward of the princess's hand in marriage.

Neither the prince nor Princess Fiona knew the perfidy of eight disgruntled humans. Their hard hearts still resented Prince Landron for making a truce with the dragons. They spread the word of the context in the dragons' lands where the dragon king saw an opportunity.

"Nothing in the prince's proclamation precludes a dragon's becoming the princess's mate. I'll hazard everything in this contest, and if I win, I'll sire a son on this princess and restart the dragon brood."

On the appointed contest day, potential suitors showed up to contend for the princess's hand. Among them was an unusual warrior dressed like a dragon. Prince Landron thought his costume was in poor taste. However, he could not deny him the right to attempt to win his sister's hand.

The combat protocol was for each combatant to draw straws and fight to the death. The final four warriors prepared to fight. The wizard appeared to inform Prince Landron that among the four was the dragon king. This alarmed the prince. He had made no provision against a dragon winning the contest. Prince Landron called a brief respite in the fighting and he consulted with his sister and their god.

"Sister, among your suitors is the dragon king. I fear he is likely to win your hand in marriage."

"Then I'll kill myself now. I refuse to marry a dragon, king or not."

Prince Landron said, "Keep your composure. I will enter the contest as nothing is prohibiting that in the rules. I shall slay the dragon king and become your bride."

The god listened to the discussion between the brother and sister. He said, "Princess, I foresee goodness in your brother's plan. How do you feel about wedding your brother?"

"I embrace the opportunity if there is no other way. With one marriage, we'll satisfy both our requirements to have an heir to the throne."

With his sister's agreement to abide by the decision of trial by combat, Prince Landron pulled on his armor. Grasping his sword and his ax, he stepped out on the plain.

The dragon king had no trouble slaying the three human contenders. That made his fight against Prince Landron the decisive round in the contest.

"Prince Landron, so we meet again on the battlefield. Before you slayed the maidenhood of dragon land. Now, prepare to die so your sister can be the ground on which I shall sow the future bond of dragons and humans. You shall perish so that your humans can continue. However, they shall become enthralled by dragon blood."

The prince felt his nostrils bristle with rage. "Dragon king, you pernicious, foul monster. I once rode you while I slayed your fellow dragons. I forged our truce with you. Now you have snuck into the ranks of my sister's suitors. I won't have you or your dragon brothers as my sister's bridegroom. You'll die by my sword, and no one will mourn your loss."

The combatants rushed each other from opposite sides of the lists. The dragon took off and hovered before he plummeted down at Prince Landron.

The prince feigned fright. At the last moment, he raised his sword and swung his ax. The dragon lost his forelegs as his breast fell on the broad sword. The enormous weight of the dragon fell on the hero. Dragon blood drenched both combatants and the dragon tried to breathe fire. The prince used his ax to open the throat of the dragon king. He wrenched his sword from left to right while it severed the chambers of the dragon's heart. The dragon could not breathe fire before his life ended.

Prince Landron, though blanketed with the beast's blood and gore, took his sister in his arms as his prize.

The finale of the contest was the betrothal of the prince and the princess. The wizard witnessed their exchange of vows. The god presided over the declaration the prince made to their people.

"Humans, we have once again been victorious over the dragons. The last time, we fought together and achieved a truce to end the war. This time, I had to enter my own contest to prevent the dragon king from seizing my sister as his bride. I see in what has happened a marvelous consistency. I have been informed that the dragon king was told about the contest by certain disgruntled humans. They wanted to have revenge for my adjudication of the truce. I call these men and women forward for their reward."

The princess read the names of the traitors who had urged the dragon king to enter the contest. Four men and four women stood forward expecting to be rewarded for their evil deed. Instead, Prince Landron had each one of them held while he lopped off their heads one by one.

The prince and princess invited everyone to partake of the meat and wine set out as the victory banquet. The slain in the contest were piled high with barrels of pitch for a celebratory bonfire.

Prince Landron and his bride stood before the blazing fire, their arms around each other. A slight breeze blew sparks into the air, and the dragon king's wing expanded from the heat of the fire.

"Don't worry, Dear Sister and wife, the dragon king will harm no one anymore. It was a good thing I kept in shape and had my weapons honed for action. Our wizard and god advised us well to remain prepared. I never guessed that humans would sacrifice their freedom for an ancient resentment."

Princess Fiona replied, "Others will be contentious, so we must be on our guard."

"True. We'll be vigilant and ready. Our future children would expect no less."

Flying Free

Inaya Bhimani

"Soha, go get dressed. Now."

I stomped up the winding staircase to my room. I slammed my door behind me, the sound echoing through the empty castle. I hoped my mother heard.

My room was too neat. The massive bed was perfectly made, the floors were scrubbed clean, and the walls were crisp and bare. I yanked my closet doors open to reveal a jungle of clothes. The colors gave me a headache, but my parents insisted on fancy dresses. As the daughter of the Emperor, my father always told me, I had to present myself. I ripped a sky-blue gown off its hangar and pulled it over my head.

I hated wearing dresses.

My mother didn't give me a chance to argue though. Tonight, my father and his army would be returning after almost two months at war. The Dragon War, people in the castle whispered. Some told stories of the dragons trying to take over the Empire. Others claimed the dragons had magic powers—powers that the world had not seen for centuries. Still more claimed that the stories were lies. They said it was just another battle with yet another empire.

I didn't know what to believe. I had been cooped up in the castle during the war. My father refused to tell me anything, claiming that I was too young. He had been saying that since I was six and first started asking questions. Now, at thirteen years old, nothing had changed.

There was a knock on my door. I rolled my eyes. It was probably one of my mother's maids coming to check on me.

"Come in!" I shouted. To my relief, a girl with long, brown hair and matching eyes burst through. I smiled at the sight of my friend. "Hello, Mazie."

"They sent a messenger," she said breathlessly. Her maid's dress was wrinkled. She was bursting with energy, as always. "Your father—I mean, the Emperor—is on his way."

I opened my mouth to respond, but before I could, my mother's maid, Helena, appeared in the doorway.

"Look at you!" she said exasperatedly. "Your hair isn't even done!" She brushed past Mazie and took me by the shoulders, leading me to a chair. She started combing my hair into place. Discreetly, I rolled my eyes. Mazie put a hand over her mouth to mask her smile. She knew I hated getting dressed up.

"There," Helena announced what felt like hours later. She held up a mirror. "Now isn't that much better?"

A green-eyed girl stared back at me in the mirror. My dark hair was tied half-up, half-down, with glittering pins holding it in place. Even after all these years, all the glamour was not me. Still, I forced a smile, as I was taught to.

"It's perfect. Thanks."

"Go now, before you're late," Helena ushered me out the door. Mazie followed me down the stairs, our footsteps loud on the stone floors. She was my escort-the heir to the throne could not be alone at any time. Though she was my age, Mazie was stronger than anyone I knew.

"Aren't you excited the Emperor is returning? You haven't seen him in months." Mazie must have noticed my frown. The torches lining the steps cast her face in a golden light, her expression concerned.

"Yeah, I guess," I said absentmindedly. It's not as though he notices me when he's here, anyway, I thought. But I said nothing more.

The spiral staircase ended on the main floor of the castle. The castle's foyer was large enough to fit a hundred people itself. In front of us towered massive iron doors. To the right of the staircase, a corridor lead to the training grounds, rooftop, and servant's quarters. Behind the stairs was a path that led to the throne room, which was currently empty. We turned left, toward the dining area and kitchens. As we reached the entrance to the dining hall, my mother appeared.

She looked disapprovingly at Mazie. Mazie squeezed my arm and slunk into the kitchens. I frowned at my mother. She had never approved of my friendship with Mazie. She didn't think it was right to be friends with a maid. Though servants were paid well, and it was their choice to work for the castle, they were viewed as lesser by some.

"Have I not told you enough?" my mother said in a low voice, grabbing my arm before I could go into the hall. "There are plenty of girls you could befriend. Why does it have to be the servant?"

I wrenched my arm out of her grasp. "Just because she's a maid doesn't mean she isn't my friend, whether you like it or not." We reached the dining hall. "And besides, the other girls are full of—"

"Soha!" my mother scolded me. She sighed and shook her head. "Just go take your place. They should be here any minute."

The dining hall was a sprawling room made of the finest wood and stone. People of all classes sat at several long tables surrounding a roaring hearth set in the middle of the room. I made my way around it toward the gleaming table at the head of the room.

The royal table. People bowed their heads as I passed, and I gave them a polite smile even as I wished I was back in my room, alone. Servants began to lay food on the royal table. So far there was only a handful of people seated there, all adorned with jewels and the finest clothes.

"So glad you could join us," drawled a girl sitting at the royal table as I approached.

"Nice to see you as always, Celia," I said flatly, taking up my usual seat across from her. If it were up to me, I would be sitting as far away from her as possible. She was my cousin, and though she was a year older than myself, she acted as if she was the heir to the throne instead of me.

"Still hanging around the lower classes, I see," she said. Though her words were poison, her back was straight and her expression pleasant. She was the perfect picture of a princess. Exactly like my parents wished I was. My parents always reprimanded me for not acting as a princess should, and Celia never failed to remind me.

"Still full of yourself, I see."

I smirked as her face reddened. Her blonde hair and blue eyes were the opposite of mine, as was her personality.

A bell rung throughout the castle, ringing seven times before stopping. Seven o'clock. A servant set a steaming platter of vegetables in front of us.

"Hurry up, would you," Celina snapped at the servant. "They'll be here any minute."

The servant hurried away, his head down. I shook my head. Sometimes, I wondered how we were related.

Just as the servant disappeared into the kitchens, a man appeared at the entrance to the hall. His cheeks were covered in stubble and his dark eyes roamed the room. My father's righthand man, Silas.

"Silence," he called. Almost immediately, the hall quieted. "I am honored to present Emperor Zeid Tarik!"

Applause broke out as Silas stepped aside to reveal my father, my mother smiling at his side. My father wore a flowing red cloak decorated by the Astasian Empire's crest. The crown atop his head was a glimmering gold. He raised his hand as his people cheered for him. In this room sat his closest advisors, friends, family, and representatives. Merchants and nobility alike bowed their heads. He was the greatest leader the Empire had ever had, many claimed. He put his people before all else. Even his daughter.

"People of Astasia!" My father's voice boomed through the hall. "Battles have been won and lost. Soldiers have fought and died. But their sacrifice was not in vain—the Empire has emerged victorious, yet again.

"As you feast tonight, let this be a reminder that there are forces out there that are dangerous. Astasia is, and always will be, protected. May the Astasian Empire always prevail!"

"Always prevail!" the words came from every person seated in the hall, their hands over their hearts.

Everyone rose as my parents strode toward the royal table, guards tight around them. My parents sat to my right at the head of the table. The room became loud with chatter as everyone dug into their meals.

"Soha," my father smiled at me, squeezing my hand. "It is good to see you, my daughter."

I knew he was just doing it for show. We were surrounded by his court. He didn't miss me in the slightest. I also knew he expected me to put on the same show. So I smiled back. "You too." I hesitated. "How was the battle?"

"It was difficult but well fought. In the end, the better side won." My father's tone was pleasant enough, but it didn't mask the irritated look he flashed me.

"And which empire were you fighting?"

"Oh, look, asparagus!" My father pulled the vegetable platter toward him, suddenly interested in his meal. If I didn't know better, I would say he was flustered. "I missed the castle food more than anything."

And that was the end of our conversation. I spent the rest of the feast wondering why my father wouldn't tell me who the Empire was fighting. Usually, soldiers would boast about crushing the enemy. There was scarcely any talk of fighting. The feast and did not come to a close until well past nine o'clock. When the bell chimed ten times, Silas addressed the crowd, inviting them to the ballroom. I groaned. People would dance for hours, and surely I wouldn't get the peace and quiet of my room until the sun was rising. I wasn't in the mood, so I did the only thing I could.

"Mother," I made myself appear queasy, clutching my stomach. "I—I don't feel very well."

My mother took one look at me and instructed one of the passing servants to escort me to my room. Whether I was faking or not, she couldn't take the chance of the heir to the throne becoming sick in front of guests.

I kept up the sick act until we reached the staircase leading up to my room. I dismissed the servant with a thank you. I sighed in relief as he disappeared out of sight. I could have a nice, quiet night of—

"Faking sick, huh?"

I whirled at the sound of the sharp voice. Celia stood across the hall, arms crossed, smirk plastered on her face.

"I—" I struggled for an excuse.

"You what?" she grinned. She must have seen me become sick.

"Go back to the ballroom, Celia." I turned to climb the staircase. Before I could make it more than two steps, she spoke again.

"Oh, I'd love to. I think I'll have a little chat with your mother while I'm there."

I froze. I clenched my teeth and turned around. If my mother knew I was faking, she would kill me. And, of course, she would believe Celia over her daughter.

"What do you want." I gritted out.

"Oh, I don't know." She examined her nails. "How about you start by doing my chores tomorrow. And the next day. And maybe the day after that."

"You—"

"Careful, Soha," she warned, taking a step toward me. "Wouldn't want your parents to know what a rebellious heir to the throne they're raising. Why they may even have to replace you with someone much more capable."

Something inside me snapped and I leaped at her, tackling her to the ground. She let out a shriek as we hit the ground. My anger came pouring out in punch after punch.

"Get off of me!" she managed to flip us over and pin me down. She clipped me on the face once and raised her fist to do it again, but she was thrown off of me. I scrambled to my feet, but when I laid eyes on my savior, my heart sunk.

"Soha! Celia! Explain yourselves!" Silas shouted standing between us. We were both breathing hard and staring daggers at each other.

"Soha started it," Celia didn't miss a beat, and immediately started playing the victim. "I was going to check on her to see if she was feeling all right because she left the celebrations you know. And she attacked me!"

I rolled my eyes. "Stretch the truth much?"

She opened her mouth to snap back at me, but Silas cut her off.

"Enough!" he sighed. "I've known you both since you were newborns. And though your parents refuse to acknowledge it, you have been at each other's throats nonstop. A divided court is not a strong court, girls."

"I know, but it's not like I attacked her for no reason!" I protested. "She was—"

"What?" Celia sneered. "What was I doing? Tell him, then."

I looked away.

"Soha, I know you," Silas said to me. "And I know that you wouldn't resort to fighting without provocation. But I also know that you two are bound to this court by blood. Which means, Soha, one day you will be Empress. And one day, Celia, you will be one of the most powerful lords in Astasia. Without an ounce of control, this Empire will collapse. If the people of Astasia see conflict within their Empire—"

"We know," Celia grumbled. On that, I agreed. We had been lectured on this matter countless times.

"Well, I'm sorry, but I have no choice but to tell the Emperor about this. I hate to trouble him, but this is a problem that needs to be resolved."

"Soha is the problem."

"Funny coming from you."

Silas rubbed his temples. "Celia, go to your room."

Celia scowled and turned on her heel. Once she was out of sight, Silas put a hand on my shoulder.

"Look, I know you're strong-minded, but you have to learn to control yourself. One day, you will be the leader of this Empire, and—"

"I know, Silas." My voice must have been tired because he smiled straightened.

"My apologies. You hear it enough. I want you to use your smarts, okay?"

I nodded. I knew there was no point asking him not to tell my father about the fight. I'd always known him to be a good man, but loyal to the core. "Goodnight, Silas."

"Goodnight, Soha."

I trudged up the stairs and shut the door softly. The fight had drained me of my anger and energy. I collapsed to the chair in front of my mirror. A bruise was forming steadily under my eye, and I winced as my fingers grazed it.

I pulled the clips from my hair, the ache in my scalp lessening. I undressed, grabbed a book off my towering shelf, and climbed into bed. I read until I could not keep my eyes open any longer. The faint sounds of music and laughter from the main floor were fading. It was well past midnight when I drifted into a dreamless sleep.

The next morning came much too quickly for my liking. I awoke to watery sunlight filtering in through the window. I squinted. Why were my curtains open?

"Up, up!" Helena's voice broke through my sleepy thoughts. "You're late for training!"

I groaned as she ripped the covers off my bed. "Aw, come on."

"You had better be out of bed by the time I come back!"

Helena was the only servant who had no problem scolding me. If I'm being honest, she was more like a mother to me than my mother.

I forced myself to sit up. I knew I shouldn't have stayed up so late reading. Would I do it again? Probably.

I washed and dressed quickly, pulling on loose-fitting clothes fit for training. Every other morning, I trained along with the rest of the kids my age that resided in the castle.

Servant or nobility, we all learned how to defend ourselves. After that, I had lessons for two hours before I was free.

Mazie appeared at my door as I was tying my hair back.

"Ready to—" her mouth fell open. "Soha! What happened to your face?"

I sighed. "Celia happened. It's nothing to worry about, all right?"

Her expression was stony. She disliked Celia as much as I did.

Helena came through the door. I expected her pleased that I was at least not still in bed, but her expression was troubled.

"What's wrong?" Mazie asked, seeing her frown.

"The Emperor requests your presence," she said to me. I waited for her to continue, but she turned to go.

"Wait!" I called after her. "What is this about?"

She turned back just enough to glance at me. "I'd say it might have something to do with that shiner on your face." She paused, then turned fully toward me. "A piece of advice, Soha; don't make things worse. Go along with whatever your father tells you, all right?"

Then she was gone.

"She never calls me Soha," I said to Mazie. Though I insisted she call me by my name, Helena was one to stick to the formalities. She always called me by my title of princess. I hated that title.

"Yeah," Mazie agreed. "Something must be up."

"Well, I guess we should go," I sighed, heading toward the door. "Come on."

As we descended the staircase, I braced myself. My father would be livid when he heard that his daughter and his niece had gotten into a fight. Though, it wasn't the first time it had happened. I already knew what would happen. My mother would scold me, then somehow find a way to say that the Empire could have fallen because of this. Then proceed to blame it on my attitude before my father calmed her down. We would let us off with a warning, as usual.

I was still deep in thought as we reached the main floor.

"Soha," Mazie murmured in warning, jerking her head. I followed her gaze to see Celia stalking toward us, one of her friends, Shauna, in tow. Celia only spent time with those she deemed "worthy." Her definition of worthy was determined by money and class. Shauna was the daughter of one of the wealthiest nobles in the Empire.

"Why, you're looking nice today," Celia drawled when she noticed us, nodding her chin toward my bruise. "The purple brings out your eyes."

I gripped Mazie's arm. I could feel her tensing in anger beside me. Another fight would not do any good.

"And nice company you've got, too," Celia nudged her friend, who let out a laugh. "Shouldn't you be cleaning or something?"

This time, Mazie had to hold me back.

"Unfortunately, Celia," I said, "you're not worth our time. We have somewhere to be."

We turned and started walking toward the throne room. A moment later, Mazie stopped and turned back around.

"Are you following us, or something?"

"I happen to have a summons from the Emperor, maid."

I gritted my teeth. "You, too?"

She nodded. I sighed as we reached the doors, the guards at either side giving me a salute. "Let's get this over with, then."

"I'll see you later," Mazie said in a low voice. "Good luck in there."

I smiled gratefully at her and took a deep breath. The doors to the throne room opened and Celia and I entered the massive room.

A chandelier hung from the center of the room, though the candles it held were unlit. The room was awash in summer sunlight from the windows on either side. A spotless red carpet led to the front of the room. There, my father and mother sat on their thrones, talking in low voices. The moment they noticed us, they stopped.

"Cassius, Oliver, dismissed," my father said gruffly to his guards. The two young men disappeared out the door with concerned glances in my direction.

Celia's parents, my father's sister and her husband, stood near the throne. They looked equally displeased.

"Well?" my mother demanded the moment the door shut. "What do you have to say for yourselves?"

"I—"

"It was a misunderstanding, Aunt Blair," Celia interrupted me. I had to mask my surprise. She wasn't blaming it on me?

My mother was unable to hide her shock. Of course, she would assume it was my fault. "A misunderstanding?"

Celia nodded. "I thought she had said something, she thought I said something—you know, nothing out of the ordinary. No hard feelings, right, Soha?" She gave me a pointed look.

"None at all," I said, slipping into her lie.

"Well, now that this is all sorted out, may I be excused, Your Highness?"

"I appreciate your honesty, Celia," my father said in a way that made me believe he very well knew she was not being honest. "I must impress upon the two of you the importance of your reputation. If word of the two of you brawling got out—"

"We know," I grumbled.

"Soha!" my mother scolded. "Let your father finish."

"It's all right, Blair," my father placed a hand on my mother's shoulder. "You know the consequences that could come from this. So, I'm sure you will not object to a week's worth of work in the dungeons."

"What?" Celia and I exclaimed in unison.

"Father, you can't expect us to—"

"That's not fair—"

My father held up a hand to silence us. "Now, I understand this may seem harsh. But this is not the first time something like this has happened. My decision is final."

Silas stepped forward from the wall. "Your Majesty, with all due respect, the girls could do with a lesser punishment."

"Silas, you may be dismissed."

Silas gave me a look before he too left the throne room. When Celia and I walked out of the throne room five minutes later, our shoulders slumped. She didn't even bother blaming me. Mazie and Celia's friend, Shauna, waited on opposite sides of the staircase for us. Without a goodbye, Celia disappeared toward the training halls. Her fists were clenched at her side. With a glance at me, Shauna left in her wake.

"What happened in there?" Mazie asked as soon as we were alone.

We started toward the dining hall. "Nothing good," I sighed. "This next week is going to be so much fun."

"Why is that?"

"Every night for a week, I have to work in the dungeons. With Celia, to top it off."

Mazie was taken aback. "For getting in a fight? Isn't that a little—"

"Harsh? Yeah, I know. Not much I can do about it, though."

"I'm sorry," she said with a sympathetic look. "I have to go help Helena, but I'll see you later, all right?"

I nodded and headed into the dining hall. I was starving. I ate quickly, contemplating ways to get out of this mess. I set about my usual tasks. The day passed much too quickly for my liking, and by the time the clock struck seven, I was on my way down to the dungeons. Mazie insisted on escorting me, but bid me goodbye at the entrance to the chilly bottom floor.

"Have fun in there," she grinned, disappearing back up the stairs. I rolled my eyes and yanked the heavy iron door open. I was expecting the dungeons to be right in front of me. Yet another staircase led downwards. This one was narrow and treacherous, the darkness below cold and unforgiving. I made my way down until I reached yet another locked iron door. I knocked on it once, twice, three times before it swung open.

A boy stood in the doorway, dark brown, almost black, hair tousled and clothes dirty. Though his boots were covered in mud, like the rest of him, his face was clean, his chocolate-colored eyes sharp.

"Princess Soha," he said in greeting. He opened the door wider and motioned for me to step through. He looked to be about my age, thirteen. "You're late."

I was surprised by his tone. When people met me for the first time, there was usually a lot of bowing, scraping, and compliments. It was tiring, and I mentally thanked the boy for speaking to me like a normal person.

"You may be the heir to the throne up there, but down here you're one of us," the boy said as if he could read my mind.

"What is your name?" I asked, stepping past him and into a large chamber. Torches kept the cold stone room alight, and at least a dozen hallways branched off into the darkness. The space was much larger than I had imagined it to be.

Faint sounds echoed from each path, but I couldn't make out what they were. A guard stood at the entrance to each hallway, both young and old, male and female. None of them looked too happy to spend their evening here. "And what is this place? I mean, I've never been in the dungeons, but I didn't exactly expect this."

"I'm Theodore," he shut the door behind us with a bang. "But you can call me Theo. As for what this place is—well, you'll find out soon enough. Your father requested you and your cousin to organize the antiques down that hall." He pointed down a dark hallway, then turned to a different one. "We need more help in a—let's call it a different area. Follow me, please."

He plucked a torch off the wall and set off at a brisk pace down one of the hallways, nodding to the guard as we passed. I had to jog to keep up with him. The scrape of metal and some sort of screeching became louder with each step.

"Where exactly are we going?" I panted.

"Your cousin is already here," he said, not answering my question. I could not see his face in the dim light. "We are going to need your help. Since the dragons got here—"

"Wait, what do you mean dragons?"

The hallway abruptly stopped at yet another iron door, and Theo halted in front of it.

"I shouldn't have said that before the oath," he scolded himself. "All right. Before we enter, you must swear upon the Empire. You will not breathe a word about what is in this room to anybody, friend or foe."

"But—why?" When I was told I was to work in the dungeons as punishment, I was expecting cleaning or some other normal task. Not some top-secret society.

"Just do it, please."

I glanced at the door, the sounds coming from behind it reaching for me. My curiosity won out and I swore the oath. Theo knocked on the solid door. As soon as the door opened, the sound of screeching animals and loud voices hit me full-on. On the other side of the door was a long chamber, similar to the one we had come from. Only instead of doors, this one was lined with cells with a vaulted ceiling. Ten or so workers scurried about the room, carrying out various tasks. Before I could ask Theo what this room was for, a head popped out between the bars of the cell nearest to me. It was covered in shimmering red scales, with a long snout and piercing yellow eyes. It took one look at me and roared.

"What in the—" I nearly jumped out of my skin.

"Hey, it's all right Rory," Theo stepped forward, his hands calmly in front of him. "Just relax."

With a snort, the dragon disappeared inside his cell.

"What is all this?" I asked Theo, my eyes wide.

"This," he said, striding toward the back of the room. "Is where you'll be working for the next week."

Celia huddled along the back wall, her eyes wide. Part of me delighted in the terror on her face, but I was too stunned to laugh. She straightened as we reached her.

"Ada!" Theo called out to a young woman tending to a dragon in a cell. The woman poked her head out from between the bars of the cell. Under the dirt on her face, she was pretty, probably close to twenty years old. "Can you show Celia how to clean out the cells?"

Celia started. "I am not—"

"You will do what you're told to do," Theo said sternly. "Emperor's orders."

With a scowl, Celia followed Ada away. I hid my smile.

"As for you," Theo turned to me. My smile disappeared. "You're with me."

"What are we doing? And why are there dragons everywhere, again? Dragons are, or, at least I thought they were, a myth."

Theo grunted as he lifted a bucket of water. "It's what's left of the dragons after the last Dragon War. Hand me that set of keys, would you?"

"The rumors about the war were true, then," I said, giving him the keys that were hanging from the wall. "My father fought the dragons."

"Well, not exactly," Theo said, handing me the bucket of water as we walked back across the room. "Rumor has it they fought the Cartean Empire, which is the empire that conquered the dragons. Was the empire. There isn't much of it left. But your father's army managed to capture the last living dragons and bring them here."

The disgust in his voice was clear, and I didn't blame him. It was wrong to keep dragons down here when they belonged in the sky.

"What—what are they going to do with the dragons?" I asked.

"No one knows. I'm not even sure your father knows what he's going to do with them."

My attention was on Theo's words. I nearly spilled the water as a man darted in front of me, chasing the smallest dragon I'd ever seen. Not that I'd seen any before. I was so focused on the cobalt dragon that I didn't notice when Theo stopped. I bumped into him, splashing his back with water. He glowered at me as he unlocked the red dragon's cell door. "Well? What are you waiting for?"

"There is no way I'm going in there!"

"Well, someone has to give Rory his water."

"You do it, then."

Theo gestured to his clothes, still covered in dirt. "This is what happened the last time I tried to give the stubborn dragon his water. It's your turn."

I scowled at him and forced myself to enter the cell. The space wasn't large enough for a dragon, let alone two more people. Rory the ruby dragon sat curled up against the back wall, his eyes glued to me.

"He must like you," Theo observed. "Last time we brought someone new in here, he tried to bite his head off."

"Thanks for that," I muttered. "I assume I have to give him the water, too?"

"Don't worry," he assured me. "He hasn't hurt anyone in … oh, a week?"

"Oh, fantastic."

I swallowed hard and took a step toward the dragon. Then another. And another. Soon, I was less than a meter away from him and I set the water bucket down. Up close, I could see the detail on his scales and couldn't help but marvel at it. I was so enchanted by the creature that I didn't remember to back away as he rose.

"Soha, get back!" Theo hissed.

I froze. Rory towered over me, bringing his face close to mine. I forgot to breathe as he stared at me. I couldn't tear my eyes away from his. All of a sudden, my fear disappeared. The dragon's eyes were not filled with malice, but rather a sort of sadness I hadn't noticed before.

Rory had settled down on the ground and started lapping up the water and splashing it everywhere. I almost laughed. He was like a puppy. A very large, very scary puppy.

"How did you do that?" Theo breathed from behind me. I turned to see his expression full of awe.

"Do what?"

"Calm him down! Rory is, well, the troublemaker."

I heard Rory snarl and raised a brow at the dragon. "Troublemaker, are you?"

The dragon huffed and went back to drinking his water.

"Well, come on then, Dragon Whisperer," Theo said, making his way out of the cell. "There's a dozen more dragons to soothe before your work is done."

The rest of the night passed in a blur of scales and roars and endless soothing. By the time I'd climbed up to my room, washed, undressed, and sunk into my bed, it was well past eleven o'clock. Though I was bone-tired, I could not sleep.

How many people knew about the dragons in the dungeon? Why were they in cells? Every dragon I saw had the same defeated look on their face. Only Rory and the small cobalt dragon seemed to have fire in their eyes. What had the dragons done to deserve imprisonment? Why was it a secret, anyway?

I knew my father would never tell me. I would get the answers out of Theo tomorrow, I decided.

I dreamt of dragons. Crimson and violet and baby blue, and so many other colors and shapes and sizes. They were not in cells, their wings strapped to their sides. They were soaring through the sky, grazing in grass fields, roaring at each other.

Rory came into view. Before I could take a step toward him, the image dissolved. I found myself staring into the darkness above my bed. The sky was pitch black outside my window. Morning did not come for hours, but I spent the rest of the night tossing and turning.

When I awoke, the rain was pounding against the castle wall. I pulled myself out of bed. After dressing, I pinned a velvety violet rose just above my heart. Today was the ceremony for those soldiers who had died in the battle. It was customary on this day for everyone to wear the flowers in honor of the soldiers.

Mazie came to my room at around ten o'clock.

"So?" she asked as we descended the stairs. "How was it?"

"How was what?"

"Working in the dungeons, of course."

"Oh!" It occurred to me that I was not allowed to speak of the dragons, even to Mazie. "It wasn't as bad as I thought it was to be."

"Well, what did they make you do?"

I was saved from answering by a dark brown-haired boy. Theo was walking up the stairs toward us. He had cleaned up since last night and was dressed in clean-lined clothes. When he met my eyes, they flashed in recognition before he dropped into a deep bow.

"Princess Soha," he said as I passed. "An honor."

"Cut it out, Theo." I rolled my eyes as he straightened, a slashing grin on his face.

"Nothing but the best for Your Highness."

I went to shove him before he stepped out of the way.

"And who are you?" Mazie demanded.

"I worked with him in the dungeons last night," I explained.

"Yeah," Theo agreed. "Couldn't have asked for anyone better to dust the old antiques down there."

I nodded. "Cleaning antiques. Yeah."

If Mazie was suspicious, she didn't let on.

"Well, I should be going," Theo said. "I'll see you tonight."

He scampered off up the stairs, and Mazie accompanied me to the dining hall. I had barely started eating when Silas approached me.

"The ceremony begins in twenty minutes, Soha," he chided me. "You should be in the hall by now."

I suppress the urge to roll my eyes. "Can a girl not eat around here?"

"Not when the girl should be with the Emperor and Empress."

I sighed and, with one last longing look at my meal, followed Silas out of the dining hall.

"So, how was the dungeon last night?" he asked as we walked.

"Could have been worse."

"I tried to convince your father it was not a punishment fit for the royal family, but—"

"Silas, it's all right. I don't deserve special treatment.'

He sighed and stopped outside the doors. "I think it would be best for you not to mention the work you're doing in the dungeon."

I frowned at his tone. He couldn't know I was working with the dragons, could he? "Sure."

Silas smiled and opened the door for me. "Great."

My mother and father were already seated at the front of the room, an empty chair next to them. Other than my father's guards, the many lines of benches in the room were empty.

"Where have you been?" my mother said as I took my place beside her. I mumbled an apology. My mother shook her head but turned away. I hated sitting up here. It felt like the world was staring at me, judging my every move.

The benches began to fill, though the room remained silent. Servants sat in one section, middle class in another, and nobility and lords close to the front. When at last, theroom was full, Silas stepped forward.

"Ladies and gentlemen!" his voice boomed across the room. "We have gathered here today to honor the soldiers who have fought and died on the battlefield. Our enemies were vicious and unforgiving. We would not be standing here without these soldiers who sacrificed their lives. We beat down our enemies because of these soldiers who sacrificed their lives." His eyes burned with anger; his expression more intense than I'd ever seen. "Thank you."

A moment of silence followed Silas' speech. Slowly, the crowd began to disperse until only the families of the soldiers who had died remained. As it was customary, my parents and I paid our respects to the family before they left.

"Our condolences," my father said, his head bowed, as we reached the last family. The mother and father of the soldier both had tears streaming down their cheeks. Their daughter, the soldier's sister, was standing beside them, her young face stony.

As the family made their way out, the girl stopped in front of me. She looked to be about four years old.

"Where is Colin?" she asked, grasping the loose fabric of my tunic in her small fist. "They say he is gone."

I knelt in front of her. "Colin was a very brave man. He is in a better place now."

"So he is not coming back?"

My eyes stung. "No, he isn't."

"Come along, Daniella," her mother ushered the girl away before I could take in the pain on her face.

I felt a hand on my shoulder. I looked up to see Silas standing behind me. I rose, wiping my eyes as nonchalantly as possible.

"Sad, isn't it?" Silas said, his voice far away.

"I know," I said. "I wish there was something we could do. I mean, I can't imagine losing someone so close to me."

"Don't get too sympathetic," the hardness of his tone surprised me. "They fought and they died. That's all there is to it."

"Yeah, but—"

"I have to go. I will see you later, Soha." He walked off toward the guards at the door.

"All right, then," I muttered after him.

By the time night fell, I was making my way downstairs toward the dungeons. The patter of rain on the windows drowned out my thoughts.

"Excited for tonight?"

I turned to see Celia hurrying to catch up with me.

"So excited," I said flatly.

"Well, it could have been worse." She pushed open the door to the dungeon stairs. A blast of hot air hit me and I grimaced.

"In what way?"

"We could've been working the day shift. I've heard the beasts are twice as bad when they can hear everyone going on in the castle."

"They're not bad," I reasoned as we reached the dungeon entrance and knocked. "I quite like—"

The door swung open. Theo stood before us, but I barely took note of his disheveled appearance as roars greeted my ears.

"Quick, we need help!" Theo grabbed my wrist and yanked me after him as he sprinted into the chamber and down the long hallway. Celia followed close behind. We reached the end of the hall and Theo shoved the door open. A wall of sound hammered into me the moment the door swung open. I covered my ears with my hands but it did little to block out the deafening noise.

The room was absolute chaos. Rory sat in the middle of the chamber, blowing fire at anyone who dared approach. He must have broken out of his cell. Several people tugged the chain wrapped around his long neck and wings with all their might. Rory was roaring in pain, and his brethren were echoing his calls from their cells. To my horror, workers were striking any dragons who came close to the bars of their cell with metal chains.

"You calmed him down yesterday!" Theo shouted to me over the noise. "Can you do it again?"

"I—I can try."

I swallowed hard and took a step toward Rory. Then another. And another. The scarlet dragon didn't notice me until I was a mere twenty feet away. His attention turned to me, and I took a deep breath. The room stilled, and it was just me and the dragon, and again my fear disappeared.

"Rory," I held my hands in front of me, keeping my tone as calm as possible. "It's all right. Just calm down, and I can help you."

At the sound of my voice, he snorted, smoke billowing up. I gulped. Was that a good thing? At least he wasn't torching me.

"You're all right. Come here."

Rory lowered his head and took all of one step toward me before he screeched in pain. The workers on the end of his chain had taken the opportunity to attempt to drag him back to his cell. Rory's panicked and desperate pale eyes met mine. I couldn't help but remember the pain in the little girl's eyes earlier that morning. Something snapped within me and I sprinted toward the workers holding his chain.

"Stop!" I shouted. "You're hurting him!"

Before I could make it half the distance, Ada, the worker Celia was with last night, stepped into my path. I made to dart around her, but she grabbed me by the shoulders, forcing me to be still.

"Let me go!" I yelled, straining to see over her shoulder. "They're hurting him!"

"If you interfere, Princess," her voice was irritatingly cool. "We'll never get him back into his cell."

"Why does he have to be in a cell? What did he, or the other dragons, do to deserve this?"

"Soha," Theo approached us and laid a gentle hand on my arm. "Maybe you should calm down."

"Maybe you should have a heart!" I snapped, stepping away from them. I glanced over to Rory. The workers slammed his cell door shut, locking him within the cramped stone room. The dragon threw himself with all his might at the bars, but it did no good. He was trapped again.

"I'll take it from here," Theo said to Ada, who shrugged and walked off to calm the other dragons. I was about to snap at him, but the fire in his eyes surprised me. I allowed myself to be led out of the room. We walked in silence down the dark corridor. We reached an alcove I'd never noticed before, hidden along the stone wall. We slipped in and leaned against opposite walls. I crossed my arms and bit my lip to keep from shouting at the horrible scenes I'd seen.

When Theo finally spoke, his voice was hoarse, his expression grim in the dim light.

"I understand what you're feeling. It's not fair for the dragons to be chained up, and the way they treat them." he shuddered.

"If you understand, then why haven't you done anything about it?"

"I want to, trust me. It's just … this is all I have, all right? My parents died when I was young. All I have is this job."

"You don't have any family?" I asked. He seemed so tough.

"None that care to talk to me, anyway," he said. After a moment, he shook his head, running a hand through his caramel locks. "That's not the point. The point is, no one else seems to get that the dragons do not deserve to be chained up. They should be free."

"I get it," I said softly.

"I wish there was something we could do."

I looked up at him. "So why don't we?"

Theo stared at me for a moment, before a grin began to form on his face. "I'm in."

"Theo?" a male voice called from down the hall. My eyes widened, but Theo calmly stepped back into the hall.

"Just getting some supplies, sir," he replied. "Is something wrong?"

"We need more hands on deck. Hurry up, already."

"Of course, sir." When the door had shut again, Theo turned to us. "The dungeon overseer. A jerk, if you ask me. I've never seen anyone so happy to hurt a dragon."

"We should get back to work," I said. "If we don't, it'll be suspicious. Why don't we meet up tomorrow?"

"Where could a dungeon worker be seen meeting with a member of the royal family?" Theo asked, though his tone was thoughtful.

"The roof," I said. "I know a spot."

I explained how to get there. We agreed to meet the next day and reluctantly returned to the chamber.

Rory was lying in his cell dejectedly. I made toward his cell, but a portly man with a mustache called out to me.

"You, there! Feed the blue dragons, will you?" I recognized his voice—it was the overseer.

His back was half turned, and he didn't seem to have realized who I was, or else he would likely be bowing and scraping. All the better. I wanted to keep a low profile down here. I liked feeling like I didn't always have eyes on me.

Gazing at Rory's cell, I went about feeding the blue dragons. Each one of them had the same dejected look in their eyes, and I was grateful when the clock struck eleven.

I bid Theo goodnight and climbed the stairs with Celia in silence.

We didn't bother with goodbyes as we parted ways. I dragged myself up to the final stairs and into my room. My eyes were heavy, but I managed to wash and undress before sliding into bed.

"Soha, get up already!"

I awoke to a pillow in the face.

"Ow!" I complained, sitting up in bed. My room was awash in light, and Mazie stood at the foot of my bed. "What are you doing here?"

"Do you have any idea what time it is? We were supposed to be at training half an hour ago!"

I groaned. "Sorry. Let me get dressed."

I pulled on the nearest clothes I could find, a long white top and black bottoms. We left my room and headed downstairs. When Mazie turned toward the hall that would lead us to the training room, I grabbed her arm and steered her toward the servant's quarters.

"Soha, where are you?"

"It's a long story," I explained everything as quickly as I could, from the dragons to meeting with Theo. When I was done, my friend only stared at me, open-mouthed.

"You're not joking?"

I shook my head. "So, you'll help us?"

"This is utterly against the rules," she reminded me. I waited, and she sighed. "Of course, I'll help."

Before I could thank her, Silas appeared down the hall.

"Soha!" he exclaimed, strolling to a stop in front of us. "Where are you off to?"

"Dining hall," Mazie said smoothly. I flashed her a look. That was in the other direction. Silas didn't miss it, either.

"Then you should be heading in the other direction, no?"

"Mazie forgot something in the servants' quarters," I said quickly.

"Ah, I see," he said, the corners of his mouth upturned. "Well, I'd best be off. Have a good day, girls."

I didn't relax until he was out of view. I turned on Mazie.

"Dining hall? Really?"

"Oh, shush," she muttered. "Let's go before we run into someone else."

Birds chirping outside and the echo of our footsteps on the stone were the only sounds until we reached the door to the servants' quarters.

We slipped inside and were met by a fork in the corridor. One hall led right to the male servants' quarters and the other turned left to the female'. Mazie turned left and opened the door, which was kept unlocked only during daylight. After sundown, only servants had access to the rooms. We were met by a common room, dozens and dozens of bedrooms branching off of it. The room was empty, most servants either on day shift or sleeping from their night shift.

The tapestry at the back of the room was old and withering, but the burgundy fabric still held together. I pushed aside the tapestry to reveal the secret exit. We entered a wide, rickety set of stairs. No torches burned here. We made our way through the darkness by touch alone. I heard a thud from above.

"Ouch!" Mazie's voice rang out. After a moment, she added, "Well, I found the door."

Sunlight poured into the dusty stairwell. The massive door swung upwards and out, revealing a clear blue sky. We clambered out and onto the roof. I squinted in the sunlight. We stood on a small pad of stone, the sides of the roof rising around us. Theo and another boy I'd never seen before stood on the other side. The boy was taller than Theo, and maybe fourteen years old. His dark skin glowed in the sunlight. He ran his hands through his mop of curly black hair.

"About time," Theo chided.

"Sorry," I muttered. "Theo, this is Mazie. She is the one who told me about this spot, and she has agreed to help us."

Theo eyed her suspiciously but introduced the boy next to him. "This is Atticus."

The boy nodded to Celia and bowed his head in my direction.

"He works as a butler," Theo explained. "His mother works in the dungeons, though, and he can get the keys to the dragon's cells."

"And I swear upon the Empire, I will not betray you," Atticus added. "My mother has told me how they treat the dragons. It's just not right."

"Just remember," I warned. "If you break your promise and betray us ..."

"You have nothing to worry about," he flashed a lopsided grin. Reluctantly, I nodded. We all sat down on the stone roof, and Mazie began talking to Atticus. She had always been the social one.

"You're sure we can trust her?" Theo whispered to me, softly enough the other two couldn't hear him.

"You're sure we can trust him?" I shot back, my voice equally low. Oath or not, how were we supposed to know he wouldn't betray us?

Theo nodded. "I'm sure."

"And I would trust Mazie with my life."

"All right then. Shall we get started?"

I checked to make sure the door was sealed tight behind us before sitting back down on the flat stone of the roof.

"Okay," I said, getting everyone's attention. "We need to make an unbreakable plan. If we get caught, or, worse if we fail."

Theo shook his head. "Let's not even think about that. Does anyone have any ideas?"

We were all silent for a minute, racking our brains. I glanced around at the roof, hoping for inspiration. My gaze caught on a rickety ladder leading to the top of the roof, and a plan began to form in my mind.

"I've got it!" I said excitedly, and everyone's attention turned to me. I explained my idea quickly, a rush of words pouring out of my mouth. By the time I finished, Theo, Mazie, and Atticus were all grinning.

"Five days from now," Theo said, his tone more serious than I'd ever heard it. "We're freeing the dragons."

I was thrumming with elation for the rest of the day. The plan was solid, but there was so much at stake. I admitted my fears to Theo that night, as we completed our daily task of setting out water for the poor caged dragons.

"Look, there's nothing to worry about," he reassured me. "We'll be as careful as we can."

"But what if it isn't enough?"

"We have to free them."

"I know," I sighed as we exited an emerald-colored dragon's cell. "As long as we stick to the plan, we should—"

Water splashed all over me as I nearly slammed into Celia, who stood right outside the cell. How long had she been here?

"A plan?" she asked, a sly smile on her face. "For what? Wouldn't want you to be getting into any more trouble, Soha. That would be just awful."

I gritted my teeth and was about to retort when a roar echoed from the other side of the chamber, cutting me off.

Rory.

"We've got it!" Theo yelled before anyone else could. I shouldered past Celia and followed Theo over to the cell. Theo stopped outside and ushered me in with a meaningful look. "I'll wait here. I should warn you; he hasn't eaten or drank anything since last night."

"What's wrong, Rory?" I asked, crouching before the dragon. He did not scare me anymore. I knew he wouldn't harm me as well as I knew the color of my hair. I took in the sight of him—the beautiful scales around his massive chest and throat marred by cuts and bruises, eyes downcast. The dragon finally raised his dim yellow eyes to me and grunted.

Theo handed me a bucket of water and I set it in front of Rory. He didn't move a muscle.

"Do you want me to tell you a secret?" I asked. The dragon stared at me. I continued, "I'm going to get you out of here, Rory. You only have to behave for a few more days. Then you will be free. I promise."

The dragon raised his head and bared his sharp teeth at me. It took me a moment to realize that he was smiling.

Theo, Mazie, and I spent the next three days preparing. I barely saw Atticus, but Theo assured me he would come through. Throughout three nights in the dungeon, I made my way into each dragon's cell, whispering our plan to them. At least two dozen dragons, blue and yellow and orange and so many more colors.

Rory was the only red dragon, and he'd taken a liking to me. He would only take his food and water from me. I didn't know if all the dragons could understand me the way Rory could, but I could only hope.

On the fourth night, I could not fall asleep. We were freeing the dragons the following night. I most likely slept an hour or two, the rest of the night spent worrying and thinking and worrying some more. Still, when I awoke the next morning, I jumped out of bed. I ran right into Helena, who was opening the curtains next to my bed.

"And what do you think you're doing?" she scolded. I muttered an apology, which she brushed off. "Where have you been the last few days? You've been as scarce as a snowflake in summer! It doesn't matter. Get dressed. Silas wants to see you. He has a message from your father."

My father never sent messages through Silas. He rarely sent messages to me at all, let alone spoke to me in person. I dressed and headed toward the dining hall, where Helena said Silas would be. An older guard I'd never seen before escorted me.

Helena assigned him to be firmly, claiming I was "frolicking around by myself" far too much.

The guard did not leave my side until we reached the dining hall. Silas spotted me before I spotted him, and he waved me over.

"Helena said you wanted to see me?" I asked, approaching him. He sat at the royal table, alone, and motioned for me to sit.

"Indeed," he said, a smile playing at his lips. "I have good news for you. I spoke to your father and managed to get your punishment for tonight revoked!"

A moment of silence.

"W-what do you mean?"

"I mean you don't have to work in the dungeons again! Your punishment is over. Unfortunately, I was not able to shorten Celia's." At the look on my face, he laughed. "Aren't you going to thank me?"

My mind was whirling, but I managed to thank him and excuse myself as politely as possible. Helena's guard waited outside the hall, but he was talking to a servant and I slipped behind his back. I took the steps up two at a time. By the time I'd reached my room, my thoughts were collected. I would find some other way to get down to the dungeons, and the plan wouldn't be affected.

Every minute of that day lasted an hour. The clock ticked in time with my heart, beating faster with every passing second. As nine o'clock neared, my nerves were rocketing sky high. I barely ate dinner and was back in my room by a quarter past eight.

A quarter of an hour later, I slipped out of my room. The guard, Mitchell, was planted outside my door, looking eternally bored. Thankfully, he didn't protest when I said I was going to the dungeons to get my jacket, which I'd "left there last night," despite the warm weather.

I made it all of three steps before I realized he was following me.

"I can make it there by myself, you know."

"Orders, princess," Mitchell replied, shrugging.

I took a breath, hid my frustration behind a complacent smile, and turned on my heel.

By the time we'd wound down all the stairs and reached the dungeon door, I was panicking. I couldn't bring Mitchell with me. But what choice did I have?

I led him down the last set of stairs and knocked on the iron door.

Theo yanked the door open from the other side. "Soha! Are you rea—"

"Theo. I left my jacket here last night."

"Oh, um." His gaze darted from me to Mitchell. "Sure, come on in."

He stepped aside to let me through, Mitchell giving him a suspicious look as he passed.

"Oh, now that you mention it," Theo let the door slam shut behind him. "I do remember seeing a jacket down here. Follow me."

He winked at me as he brushed by, and I decided to keep my lips sealed and hope he knew what he was doing. He led us down one of the many branching hallways until I could barely see my own hands in the darkness. We stopped in front of a wooden door, the cold seeping through the crack in the bottom.

"It was just through here." Theo looked at me expectantly as he pulled the door open with a creak.

The cool air from within washed over me, clearing my mind. I suddenly realized why Theo was doing this.

"Mitchell, would you be so kind as to grab it for me? It's black with a silver lining. You'll see it."

A grunt was all I got in response before the burly guard disappeared through the door. The moment his foot cleared the threshold, Theo slammed the door shut and heaved himself at it. I joined him, pressing my back tightly against the door. Not a moment later, Mitchell's pounding fists and muffled shouts reached us. I felt him throwing himself at the door, and it shook with the force.

"Sorry, man!" Theo shouted to Mitchell, then turned to me. He was panting. "Atticus should be here with the keys soon."

I nodded, my teeth gritted with the effort of holding the door shut. A minute passed, and I could tell Mitchell was close to breaking through.

"Can't hold on much longer," I gasped out. A smile split Theo's face. "How are you smiling?"

"Look!"

I whipped my head around to see a small figure in the distance, in the main chamber.

"Atticus!" Theo and I called out together. Atticus whipped his head toward our hallway, squinting in our direction. He sprinted toward us, and when he reached us, he ripped a chain out from under the teal fabric of his shirt. At least half a dozen keys dangled from it. His mother's keys.

"Lock—the—door," I gritted my and spat out over Mitchell's shouts. Theo and I gave a mighty shove, pushing the door completely closed as Atticus locked the door shut. Mitchell kept pounding, but I collapsed to the ground from relief. The lock held.

"It's quarter to nine," Atticus told us, helping us up. "We need to go."

"Will he be all right in there?" I asked.

Theo nodded as he brushed himself off. "Nothing harmful in there but some old junk. Unless you count rats."

I made a face. Theo laughed, but his expression darkened almost immediately. We all knew what we now had to do, and what the risks were.

"Is Mazie in place?" Atticus asked.

"I sure hope so," I replied. "Mitchell, the guard, was sticking to me like glue, so I wasn't able to check."

A loud bang on the door sounded at that.

We hurried back toward the main chamber, fighting to keep our footsteps silent.

As we ran, Atticus pulled out his chain again and fingered a key with an intricate design carved into it. "This is the skeleton key for all of the dragon's cells." He lifted another key, a golden one. "And this one unlocks the entrance to the dragons' dungeon."

"You're sure about this?" Theo's brow was creased. We stopped in the main chamber.

"Definitely." Atticus frowned. "I mean, I'm nearly certain. Of course, there is a possibility I could be wrong, but—"

"Thanks, Atticus," I said. He handed Theo the chain, clapped him on the back, and then Theo and I were off toward the dragon's cellar.

We strode down the hall before slipping into the alcove we'd discovered what felt like years ago.

Now, all we had to do was wait. I slid down to sit on the cold floor, and Theo sat across from me. The faint sound of dripping water echoed around us. The shrieks of dragons from behind the door nearly drowned it out.

"I can't believe we're actually doing this," Theo broke the silence.

"Neither can I," I said in a low voice. "Listen, if we get caught, I'm taking the blame."

"You can't—"

"No, you can't. And neither can Atticus or Mazie. My parents would banish all of you from the castle for disobeying, treason, whatever. It's just not fair."

"What is not fair?" His voice was quiet and as serious as I had ever heard it.

"Everything," I drew my knees up to my chest. "The way some people think they can do whatever they please. The way people think it's all right to torture dragons into behaving."

"Hey," Theo took one of my hands in his. His palm was calloused, but his grip was gentle. "You are going to be an amazing Empress one day, you know that?"

I must have looked shocked because he chuckled.

"You know how I know? Because you have a good heart, Soha. You care about people, and you always do what is right."

I let out a small laugh. "Considering I'm breaking about a dozen rules at the moment, I don't know about that."

"Maybe it's time for you to make your own rules."

I didn't know how to respond to that. Luckily, I didn't have to. An explosion rocked the tunnels. The floor beneath us shook dangerously. Theo shouted something to me, but I couldn't hear him over the ringing in my ears. Even before the shaking had fully stopped, a flood of people stormed past us. Toward the main chamber and, more importantly, away from the dragon's dungeon.

"Do you think they're all gone?" I whispered.

Theo poked his head into the hall. "Only one way to find out."

We made our way to the door, our footsteps light. I hoped Mazie and Atticus did their job. The distraction had gone well, but if they couldn't trap everyone there for long enough …

Theo was struggling to fit the key in the lock.

"Is that the right one?" I asked.

"Yes, he said the silver one was the key to the entrance," Theo grunted, trying to push the key in.

"I'm pretty sure he said it was the gold one."

"No, he said—"

I snatched the chain from his hand and shoved the gold key into the lock. The door swung open with ease. I glanced back at Theo with a sweet smile.

"Yeah, I, um, I was … joking … I knew it was the gold one—"

I cut off his rambling as we stepped into the room, the door closing behind us with a creak. Our luck was running out—they had left a worker back to stay with the dragons. I glimpsed the long blonde hair, tied back from her face, and my heart sunk.

"Celia!" Theo's voice cracked. "What are you doing here?"

"I work here, remember?" she smiled cruelly at me. "The real question is, what are you doing here? I heard you had been relieved of your duties, cousin."

I tucked the keys behind my back. "We—uh, we were sent to help supervise the dragons."

"Really?" she crossed her arms.

I slipped the skeleton key off the chain. I handed it to Theo behind my back as inconspicuously as possible. I didn't have to tell him what I was thinking. I would distract Celia while he unlocked the cells.

"Actually," I confessed, stepping forward. "I'm here for a different reason."

"And what is that, princess? Perhaps, to free the dragons?"

I swallowed hard. How could she know that? I replied weakly, "No."

"Because I thought it was strange when you seemed to care so very much about your precious pet, the red beast. And when I heard from a source that someone wanted to set the dragons free. Well, it is quite obvious who that someone is."

She advanced at me and I backed away. A glance over her shoulder told me that her attention was completely focused on me. She hadn't noticed Theo sneaking up to the cells. I just needed to keep her talking a little longer.

"Who—who was the source?" I breathed out.

"Wouldn't you like to know," she sneered. "I must say, though, I never truly thought the heir to the throne would be the one to betray Astasia. Although, can you be both heir and traitor?"

Before I could work out what she meant, she shoved me and my spine collided with the wall. She spun me around and pinned my arms behind my back.

"After I turn you in," she hissed, pressing me hard into the wall. "You will be declared a disgrace to the Astasian Empire. And I, of course, will be given the glory of capturing the traitor. Your parents will no longer see you fit for the throne, and guess who will be the perfect replacement?"

My heart sunk further. If Celia was on the throne, she would destroy everything good about the Astasian Empire. Out of the corner of my eye, I could see Theo creeping toward the last cell block. I only had to keep my cousin's attention for a little longer.

"I'm not betraying Astasia," I managed to say. "What's happening to these dragons isn't right! And no one knows about it."

"Oh, trust me, no one will know about it." She twisted my arms and I gasped in pain. Wasn't Theo done already?

"Listen, Celia, if you let me go—"

"Not going to happen, princess."

"Then I guess we'll just have to wait for my backup. They're all waiting outside that door, you know." My lie was smooth, and I felt her tense.

"You lie."

"Really? Why don't you see for yourself?"

There it was. She wasn't sure whether to believe me, and I took the opportunity. I wrestled an arm out of her grip and drove my elbow into her throat. I whirled and threw her off me.

"Soha, catch!" Theo's voice. He tossed something through the space between us. I caught the rough plank of wood in a swift motion, splinters digging into my palms as I swung—

Crack.

"Ouch," I said, leaning over Theo's crumpled form on the ground. My hit to Celia's head had knocked her out cold.

"Oh, no, you don't think you hit her too hard, do you?" The corners of Theo's mouth were pulled down in concern as he knelt.

"We did what we had to do," I assured him. "And she'll be all right. Right now, we need to focus on the—"

A shadow fell over me, and I stopped mid-sentence. I heard the scrape of claws against the stone and immediately relaxed. I whirled around, a smile on my face.

"Rory!" I'd been so distracted I hadn't noticed the cell after cell that was thrown wide open. Rory snorted, lowering his head to nuzzle my cheek. I laughed, stroking his snout. "Ready to break out of this place, buddy?"

He tilted his head up and blew a small burst of fire into the air. The other dragons, some of them still bound in chains, echoed him, each of them spouting flames. The room instantly heated, and even after the flares died, it was like the light was still there.

Theo grinned. "We'll take that as a yes."

The two of us made short work of releasing the dragons from their chains. When we finally had them organized, we led them out of their prison. The hallway beyond was a tight squeeze for most of them, but we made it through to the main chamber. Mazie and Atticus waited for us there. All of the hallways were quiet except for one. Shouts and angry yells echoed from the darkness.

"They aren't very happy about being locked in there," Atticus winced, tugging off the black mask. Mazie did the same, tossing hers to me.

"Better that than having them see who we are," Theo reasoned, taking the mask from his friend.

"Good job with the diversion," I nodded to them.

"We'll see you at the top, then," Mazie grinned as if she was having the time of her life. I shook my head as she and Atticus disappeared up the narrow stairwell. I don't think she understood the concept of danger. She had always gotten a thrill from it.

"Soha," Theo's voice was full of concern. I snapped out of my thoughts.

"What is it?"

"We didn't exactly think this part through," he gestured to the narrow set of stairs. "There's no way the dragons will fit through here."

The dragons began to shift restlessly behind us as if they could sense the tension.

I took a deep breath. "It's all right, we just have to think this through. Are there any other exits?"

"Well, one, but—"

"Then let's go."

"But—"

"Theo, we don't have any other choices."

With a sigh, Theo led the group down a different hall, this one tall and wide. Rory brushed my side, trotting alongside me. I stroked his scales.

"Almost free," I whispered.

It was ten minutes before we reached the large, heavy-looking door. Mazie and Atticus must be worried, I thought. We were supposed to be at the servant's quarters by now.

Theo pulled the door open with a grunt, and we were greeted by a set of stone stairs. Much wider than the other set. I blew out a breath, relieved. We climbed the stairs in silence. Finally, we reached a wooden door, arched and worn.

"Can you tell the dragons to stay here and wait while I scout?" Theo asked me.

"Why? Where does this door open to?"

He was quiet for a moment. "The dining hall."

"Theo!"

"Hey, I did try to warn you. Besides, it's late. It should be empty."

"Fine, but I'm scouting with you."

He took one look at my determined expression and gave in. I told Rory to wait until we came back for them, and slipped out of the door with Theo.

We were greeted by a dozen spears, all aimed at our hearts.

A line of guards stood there as if they were expecting us. And in the middle of them was Silas.

"Well, isn't this a nice surprise," he said in a way that made me think it wasn't a surprise to him at all. He stepped forward, a cold smile on his lips. I'd never seen Silas with that expression.

"Silas, what is this?" I asked.

"I'll be asking the questions, Soha. Can you tell me what you and your friend here were doing in the dungeons?"

"Soha forgot her jacket there last night," Theo supplied. "I was showing her some passageways. It seems this was the wrong one, so we'll just be going n—"

"Lies! Guards, arrest them!" Silas' voice was shrill, but the guards looked unsure.

"Sir, with all due respect," one of them spoke up, removing his helmet. "She is the princess. I don't think—"

"Arrest them. That's an order."

There was no point fighting as we were forced to our knees.

Silas smiled. "Now, we can talk. Tell me, were you not attempting to free the dragons?"

My mouth was dry. How did he know? Celia must have overheard us the other night and reported straight to him.

"I'll take your silence as a yes," he chuckled, pacing in front of me.

"Silas, you don't understand!" I protested. "They were torturing them down there."

"I don't understand?" he laughed again, but without humor. "I don't understand? I'm the one who ordered them to be trained!"

A moment of silence.

"What?" I was in shock.

"That's right, your precious father had no idea what was going on in his dungeons. He barely knows anything! It's always Silas, do this and Silas, do that. He has no idea I am planning to train them to serve me, to be my personal army. Wait until the people of Astasia see I have an army of dragons at my service." The look in his eyes was wild. "Well, Emperor Silas Andreas has a nice ring to it, don't you think?"

"That's so wrong!" Theo shouted. "You'll never get away with it. The dragons deserve to be free."

Silas cast an irritated look in his direction, then turned back to me. "I'm surprised Celia was unable to stop you."

"You were the source," I realized.

The sick smile on his face grew. "I hope you two have enjoyed your freedom for this long. You failed in saving your precious dragons. When I turn you in to your father and say you were trying to steal gold from the dungeons, it won't be pretty."

I knew my father would believe Silas. Up until then, I would have trusted Silas, too. I scowled up at the man who had once been a mentor to me.

"Theo is right. You will never get away with this."

"Oh, but you see," he leaned down. "I already have."

His words were swallowed by an echo of roars. There was the splintering of wood, and a blur of crimson smashed into him.

The guards around me and Theo were attacked by a rainbow of dragons. The remaining guards were smarter. Their eyes widened in fear and they dropped their weapons, fleeing for the door.

"You all right?" Theo shouted to me over the chaos, hurrying to my side. He offered me his hand and pulled me to my feet. It didn't take long for the sounds to fade until only a soft whimpering remained, coming from the corner of the room.

"Rory, it's all right," I told the dragon, who was towering over Silas. The man was cowering on the ground, arms over his head, blood leaking from a cut on his forehead. Reluctantly, Rory settled on his hind legs.

I knelt next to Silas.

"All these years," I said. "I thought you were a good man. You've destroyed yourself for power, Silas. But you can still fix this. Turn yourself in to my father, tell him the whole truth, and we can move on."

"Oh, you'd like that, wouldn't you, princess," he snarled. At his tone, Rory gave a warning growl. Silas spat, "Filthy beast!"

I sighed. "You had your chance." I turned to Theo. "Let's lock him in the closet until after we've freed the dragons. Then we can take him to my father."

Silas was about to protest, but a vicious roar from Rory was enough to make him shrink back. I almost laughed at the sight.

Two minutes later, Silas was tied up and locked in a nearby closet. We crept through the halls toward the servants' quarters. Luckily, the halls were empty. There was no one around to see the colorful circus of dragons parading through the castle.

"It's about time," Mazie said as we entered the common room with the secret exit, but I could see the relief on her face. She was sitting next to Atticus, their backs against the wall.

"We were scared you'd been caught," Atticus scrambled to his feet.

"We were, too," Theo said.

True to her word, Mazie had ensured the common room would be empty and left the door open a crack. At least that much had gone right.

"We still could get caught," I reminded them. "Let's free these dragons before we have to lock someone else in a closet."

Mazie and Atticus exchanged a confused glance. They opened the secret exit and led the dragons up the stairs.

Finally, only Theo and I remained below.

"Well, this is it," he said.

"This is it," I agreed, taking a deep breath.

"Would you care to set some dragons free with me, princess?" He bowed, his hand extended to me.

I brushed his hand aside with a grin. "Race you to the top."

He only looked stunned for a moment, before he tipped his head back and laughed. We set off up the stairs.

"I think we can call it a tie," Theo panted as he clambered onto the roof behind me.

I raised a brow at him.

"Fine, you won."

I laughed, the sound echoing in the small space. The night sky was dark and open above us, decorated by twinkling stars. A soft breeze ruffled Theo's hair. His eyes were bright as the small royal blue dragon—Horus—rubbed against his legs.

"Hey there," Theo laughed, crouching down. I got distracted when something brushed against my shoulder and I turned. Rory's pale eyes stared back at me in the moonlight. For the first time, there was light in them.

"You're finally free," I smiled, reaching out to stroke his snout. He purred, then nestled his head against my cheek. I realized that I wouldn't be seeing the dragon every night, maybe never again. I felt a lump in my throat. "Yeah. I'll miss you too, buddy."

I patted Horus on the head, gave Rory one last hug, and then they took off. Like splashes of color on a dark canvas, the band of colorful creatures beat their wings as they blew fire.

Mazie, Atticus, Theo and I remained on the roof, shoulder to shoulder until the dragons disappeared into the darkness.

"They're finally free," Atticus said in disbelief, but he was smiling. "I still can't believe we did it."

"We have one last thing to do," I reminded them. "It's time to see my father."

We filed down the stairs with smiles plastered on our faces. No matter what my father said, I knew we had done the right thing.

"Follow my lead," I whispered to my companions as we reached the throne room and stopped. Cassius and Oliver were standing at the doors, backs straight.

"Princess Soha!" Oliver exclaimed. "What are you up to at this hour?"

"You should be in your room," Cassius added.

I suppressed the urge to roll my eyes. They meant well, but they were like overprotective older siblings.

"I have to talk to my father," I said. "I know he is in the middle of some business or the other, but this is important. Please?"

They exchanged glances.

"All right," Cassias finally agreed. "But only you. Your friends must wait here."

"No, they have to come with me!" I gave them my best pleading look. "Come on."

Oliver sighed. "Fine. But you had better make it quick, you hear me?"

I beamed. "Thank you!"

They opened the grand doors for us. Before we went in, I leaned in close to Cassius and whispered something into his ear. His eyes widened, but he nodded and strode off. When we strode in, I could feel Theo, Mazie, and Atticus slowing down and tensing. But my attention was on my father and my mother, seated on their respective thrones. The moment we entered, my father rose.

"Soha, this is not the time—"

"I need to speak with you, father." I stopped in front of him, the others nervously standing behind me. "And no, it cannot wait."

"Well, then perhaps we can speak alone," his tone may have been pleasant, but the look he gave me was anything but.

"No," I said simply. I ignored my mother's shocked look. I continued, "Your trusted right-hand man, Silas, is currently tied up in a closet."

"What?"

"Perhaps not the best way to start," Theo murmured, and I shot him a look before continuing.

"The reason is that he was training the dragons in the dungeon to serve him. He wanted to overtake you as Emperor."

"This is a very serious accusation, Soha," my mother said, her voice full of stress. "An absurd one, at that."

"I'm inclined to agree with your mother," my father chuckled. "Are you feeling all right?"

As if on cue, the door opened behind us. We all turned to see Cassius yanking Silas into the room. Silas' red face was covered in dried blood. He met my eyes, his expression beyond angry.

"Silas!" My father, for once, looked shocked. "What happened?"

"Emperor, sir, with respect," Theo stepped forward, to my side. "Soha already told you what happened."

My father looked down at Theo as if seeing him for the first time. "And who are you?"

"A friend of mine," I said quickly. "Why don't you ask Silas about the army he was attempting to raise with the last of the dragon race?"

I was surprised to see that it was my mother who put her arm on my father's shoulder.

"Silas, is this true?" she asked. "You truly wanted to overthrow the Empire?"

"Of course not, Empress, I simply—"

"He confessed to me less than a minute ago," Cassius tightened his grip on Silas. "Soha is telling the truth."

Silas went an even darker shade of red. "This Empire is a joke! We are superior to all other empires! As the most powerful empire, we should be conquering territories and reaping the benefits. The dragons should be serving me!"

"Silas, how could you say such a thing?" My father's expression was full of hurt. "All this time, you've served me faithfully."

"That is exactly the problem, Emperor," Silas seethed. "Serving. I deserve to be on the throne for all the work I've done for this wretched Empire."

My father took a deep breath, steadying himself. "Cassius, please take Silas down to the prisoner's block. I will deal with him afterward. Can you do that for me?"

That was the first time I had heard my father ask rather than order.

"Um, of course, Emperor," Cassius said. "You don't have to ask."

My father sighed, his words ragged. "I'm realizing now that I do."

After Cassius had disappeared, taking a thrashing Silas with him, my father turned to me.

"I'm sorry I did not believe you, Soha. Can you forgive me?"

"Only if you can forgive us for setting the dragons free," I replied tentatively.

"You what?" he gripped the armrests of his throne. "I had told Silas to keep them in the best conditions possible until we could decide what to do with them."

"Yes, well, they were in cells, father. All chained up and hurt."

"It's not fair to control them," Mazie spoke up from behind me, then added a sheepish, "Sir."

"They are the last of their race left," Atticus said. "They deserve to be free, Emperor."

"I presume the three of you were the ones who freed them alongside my rebellious daughter?" my father said. I didn't like the flatness of his tone.

Theo, Atticus, and Mazie nodded. Pride sparked in me at their bravery. There was a tense moment of silence as my father considered. I braced myself for the worst.

Before he could speak, my mother rose from her seat. "Then I suppose we will have to reward these brave children for their good work."

"Wait, what?" I blurted out. "I mean, reward us?" That was the last thing I'd expected her to say.

"Without them," my mother turned to my father, "the dragons would have been at Silas' mercy without our knowing it. What gives us the right to keep them?"

My father looked at my mother and some unspoken conversation passed between them. Finally, he nodded.

"You're right," my father turned to me. "I didn't know how the dragons were being treated, but I did know we were keeping them here. Perhaps I was wrong in this."

Another thing I had never heard from my father—admitting he was wrong.

"So we are not being punished?" Atticus cut in, and my parents smiled.

"You are not my mother said. "What are your names?"

"Atticus."

"Theo."

"Mazie, but I believe you know me."

"Indeed, I do," my mother's eyes twinkled. She paused for a moment. "Thank you for being a good friend to my daughter all these years."

I exchanged a glance with Mazie. Had my mother truly said something kind to her? This was turning out even better than I could have expected.

"In any event, we will be rewarding each of you," my father said. "For now, I think we should all get some sleep."

I was about to follow my friends out of the throne room when I heard my father call out my name. I turned, one hand on the door.

"Yes?"

"Thank you," he said simply, but the words were heavy with sincerity.

"For what?"

"For opening my eyes."

I smiled. "Goodnight, father."

That night, I slept more peacefully than I had in days.

Two Months Later

"So, how did you convince your father?" The deep voice startled me.

I stood on a balcony, overlooking the castle grounds when Theo slipped through the door behind me. I turned to face him.

"What are you talking about?"

"The new regulations," he said, walking over to stand at the railing with me. "How servants and workers must be treated well by all, and if they are not, there will be consequences."

I smiled. "How did you know it was me?"

He shrugged, returning my smile.

"It didn't take much convincing," I admitted. "Ever since we freed the dragons, my father's been listening to me."

"I miss the dragons," Theo said after a moment with a sad smile. "But I'm glad they're free."

"Me, too."

The sky was painted hues of orange and pink, and everything glowed in the dying light. Fall evenings were always cold, but tonight was unusually warm. I leaned against the railing, and Theo did the same. Together, we stood there, silent, and peaceful as the night.

As the sun set behind the mountains, I could have sworn I saw a flash of crimson in the distance, and I smiled.

The sky was becoming darker, but the world was bright.

LEFTOVER BITS

KELLY BEDBROOK

Sunshine on cotton sheets and vanilla granola mix. Laundry soap and cut grass, bubbling up with the breeze. The fragrance of Lucie's earliest memories was warm, bright, and clean. If she closed her eyes, she could fall back, the scent of the outdoors tangled in her mother's thick locks. She could feel the soft faded blue cotton of a familiar housecoat pressed against her cheek. There she laid her head, flushed with wonder and heavy with sleep, down on her shoulder.

Lightning ripped open the sky, whipping Lucie's curls about. She turned her face upward, breathed in and grinned. Nine years old, she sat on the small concrete balcony of her mother's downtown apartment. Paper and pencil crayons littered the fragile folding table in front of her. Buttercup was worn down to a stub. She was fiercely attached to yellow. Rain boots, umbrellas, and wheat fields when the clouds rolled in.

Other strange smells had entered Lucie's life over the last few years. They were almost sweet at first. They crept in like a whisper.

Run.

Everything would turn sharp and sour.

Hide.

There was a shift in the air that followed. It would approach her with an ominous embrace that wrapped its arms around her. This constricted her chest until she could only muster little breaths. As her world began to shift, she learned she couldn't trust what was underneath the surface layer. One misstep could take her from a haven made up of blankets and old books to somewhere dark and unsettling. This place was full of broken plates and upheaval.

This was why Lucie adored thunderstorms as much as she did. The air was thick and full of pressure. It wasn't a tiring, burdensome weight. It was charged. Humid and heavy, it was saturated with new beginnings. She could smell the freshness in every drop.

It was the 13th of July and this year it happened to fall on a Friday. People were busying themselves on the ground beneath her. Some tried to sneak in a few last-minute errands and beat the storm. Lucie sat on her perch, watching the horizon grow dark, as it billowed up with drama and nobility. Once again, the sky ignited, lighting up her pages, her face, her heart.

★★★

It was a hot, muggy July afternoon and all Murray wanted was an ice cream cone. The problem was, Murray could not be seen in daylight. He, and those like him, had not been able to do so for centuries.

They had been called many things over the past millennia, though rarely accurate. Most warned of their unsightly appearance and strange calls. Names are spoken in varying languages that roughly translated to Howling Storm Chimera, or Cloudy Mocking Babbler, and Disfigured Feral Nether Elephant. There was Murray's personal favorite, Deadly Shadehags. They resembled a hodgepodge of creature-parts that didn't quite blend. In one dialect they had simply been referred to as "confused mixture" or "leftover bits."

His kind was small stock, with cloven hooves and leathery, pale purple skin. A shock of red hair sat between large ears. They were surprisingly nimble despite their cumbersome appearance. At one point in history, they roamed free in forested landscapes, swam in clear streams, and drank open air. They had survived earthquakes, hurricanes, volcanic eruptions, even the occasional meteor. All forms of natural disaster. Disease. There was resilience in being small, quiet, and loyal to your herd. Yet, there was something else entirely unexpected that would lead them into seclusion. Humans.

Time fell away and people continued to push and stretch their boundaries. The discovery of Murray's kind had led them down a much different, darker path. There was a mystery that enveloped the creatures like an early morning fog. Due to their shy nature, sightings of them were rare. This was combined with the fact that they were distinctly bizarre-looking, appearing otherworldly. Humans get spooked when they can't identify what's before them. Inevitably, they had the terrible misfortune of being labeled bad omens.

As it were, Murray and his kind were a gentle breed, sweet, and, in fact vegetarian. People were initially so startled by their unusual looks. This meant that shock, fear, and distraction would lead them to tragedy. There had been the high-frequency, low-mortality instances. Tripping, the occasional clip of a head on a tree branch. Then came the less common, but slightly more injury-inducing. This often meant falls into bodies of water. It had taken humans a while to learn how to swim. And of course, there had been the time when the bearded man had tried to ride his poor horse cleanly off the cliff. The horse had stopped abruptly, sending him catapulting over top. Beard-man, may he rest in peace.

Rumors swirled, blaming the tiny herbivores for these series of wretched events. Some stories were dismissed as coincidence, however, humanity remained unwilling to tempt fate. Doing so offered zero rewards and left everything to chance. What had resulted was the creatures' frequent capture and subsequent murder. Promptly, they were burned. Their flesh was not consumed, for fear of repercussions. Those that remained of Murray's kind went deeper underground. They shielded themselves from mankind until they dissolved into myth.

Murray and his family currently lived in storm drains beneath the city. That earth-shattering day Murray had first tasted ice cream had been like today. Hot and humid.

He was about to leave his spot under a sewer grate, having taken in a few rays of sunshine before the steam became too hot. He rose, stretched his front legs, and wriggled his bottom to let loose any dirt. *Plop.* The heavenly substance landed on his forehead.

A cry echoed from above from the small child who had lost this delight.

It rolled down the sides of Murray's oblong head. He opened his mouth and his eyelids began to close in ecstasy. He allowed the welcome cooling sensation to take over. That's when he tasted it. Chocolate peanut butter swirl. He was instantly hooked. From that day forward, he vowed he and his newfound love would be reunited once more.

★★★

A bolt of forked lightning staggered its way across the sky and Lucie's face lifted to greet it.

She had been drawing dragons flying off into the thunderous sky, wild and unafraid. They were layered with color. Spiny beards grew out of their skin from temple to jawline, a mane woven of fire, rust, and wind. Their bodies were rounder than one might expect, a dull shade of mauve in contrast to their radiant locks. Their wings appeared dangerously small for such a chunky frame. Nevertheless, they raised long pointed noses as if in song. They trumpeted their way forward into the heavens.

And then there was the familiar scent in the breeze, dripping scarlet berries about to go rancid. She turned to find her mother staring at her from the sliding door. Her eyes were incredulous. Dark purple posies bloomed under her lower lids. Lucie searched her pupils, trying to determine if the Terrorthing was present.

She couldn't remember how old she'd been when she first met the Terrorthing. It was a few years back to be sure. Perhaps it had always been there. To Lucie, it felt all-of-a-sudden, something she didn't recognize stepping into her mother's body. When the glasses smashed, and her face contorted, and she spat her words at Lucie.

"What are you doing?" Her mother asked, voice low, struggling to talk through fatigue.

Lucie drew her papers and her pencils in closer in an attempt to make the scene look neater. "Stuff," she shrugged and sank deeper into her chair, trying to appear small.

Her mother surveyed the drawings. Lucie's stomach dropped, and her cheeks felt hot. She willed herself to shrink away and not be noticed. Her mother's face was furrowed in confusion. "Why are they so bulbous?" she said, at last, casting Lucie a disdainful eye. At least she didn't appear angry. "Don't you think you should draw something people would like?"

Lucie only whispered to her lap.

"What?" Her mother looked stern. "I'm going out, draw something different." With that, she left the house, taking Terrorthing with her.

★★★

It had been 723 days since Murray had last tasted ice cream. He had been plotting ever since. Tonight was going to be his night.

With the storm rolling in, people would be busying themselves getting indoors. Certainly, there would be an ambitious few intent on zigzagging from vehicle to store. He could never understand it. Why humans would shelter themselves from rain, especially in the summertime.

Sometimes during an early morning storm, he would sneak outside to allow the water to roll down his back. He would splash in puddles, the fresh spray giving him energy. The rain was healing and enriching. With each clap of thunder, he would slam his hooves on the ground. He'd shimmy his backside and flick droplets off his tail. He didn't make a sound, but would lift his trunk silently in the air, and sway his body from side to side. No one on the streets or in the alleyways.

The air in the sewer drain was warm and fetid. His round, chocolatey eyes narrowed with purpose. He was ready.

Over the last few months he had done some surveillance. Intent on discovering where his love lived, he had braved daytime. Rolling in plenty of mud first, and keeping close to shrubbery, treetops, mailboxes. Thank goodness people were so busy on their phones nowadays.

He had witnessed the ceremonious handoff hiding in a dwarf lilac bush at Bellwoods Park. An elusive jovial tune had caught his attention. Once he tracked its source, the magic revealed itself.

A box made of painted swirling stardust pulled the miraculous substance in shiny packaging. He hadn't seen a more stunningly attractive human invention in all his years. He watched the child unveil its contents with bated breath. Oh, the pure splendor of it all.

Then it came time to find where the chests were kept. This could best be done between the hours of 4 and 5 am. The shops were closed. He could walk the streets and peer inside to see which ones had the musical boxes. He so desperately longed to open them. There had been some nights where he'd gone out too early. He once had the misfortune of encountering a college student purchasing a taquito.

Poor Murray had been squinting through the convenience store window. The door swung open with a friendly "da-ding!" Out stumbled a young gentleman, up too late studying for the exam he had tried to ignore.

The security light overhead lit up with sudden movement and hit Murray on the bridge of his trunk. He raised it in momentary blindness, trying to block out the intense rays.

"Duuuuuuude." There was a soft plop as the bag of taquitos slid out of the kid's hand and landed on the pavement. Hot fried cheese and spices oozed out. Murray's mouth began to water before the situation took hold of him. Alarmed, he lifted his gaze to the young man in front of him. "Woaaahh," the kid said.

Murray's body felt like it had turned to water, and he couldn't find his limbs. Moments later, the door made its cheery chime once again. By some miracle, the sound ignited Murray and he dashed into the alleyway.

A second man around the same age stepped out. He looked at his friend, confused to find him staring open-mouthed at the empty sidewalk. "Y'alright bud? What is it?"

"It was a baby hippo, man," said the bewildered kid. His friend laughed and smacked his shoulder, "What are you talkin' about?" The first kid shook his head, blinked his eyes a few times. "I dunno, some freaky hairless dog I guess."

Murray had stayed in that alleyway for a good forty-five minutes after the incident. It took thirty minutes just for him to stop shaking and unfurl his ears from his eyes. Since then he had been more careful. With a sharp eye, extensive memory, and meticulous documentation, he had gathered all necessary intel.

★★★

Lucie was making her favorite easy dinner: fried eggs on buttered toast. She loved gooey yolks. Combined with a giant glass of orange juice, she felt as though sunshine was sliding down her throat.

She moved back to her sacred outdoor space. The sky was growing dark, which made it appear much later in the evening than it was. She carried her little plate like a lantern, plopping it down on the corner of her pages. She'd been using a water bottle as a paperweight in her absence and pulled it off to take a sip.

She examined her dragons with great care. Lucie's world could be a lonely one at times. She traced tiny fingertips over their noses and backs. She would make them all their favorite snacks. What would those be? She chewed at her toast absentmindedly. Something sharp bit Lucie's tongue. She must have dropped a shell into the frying pan.

As she moved to pick the shard from her teeth, her elbow knocked her plate over. Yolk splattered all over the concrete. The wind seized its opportunity, rustling at her papers before lifting them high into the air.

Lucie lurched, desperately reaching to pull her friends back in. The storm flipped and twirled them in the air, taunting her. As they dipped close to the balcony railing, Lucie shot forward. Her knee smashed on the metal spindles.

She was too late. Tears stung Lucie's eyes as such sunk to the ground, wrapping her arms around her legs. An angry red splotch was already blooming across her kneecap.

★★★

It was 6:47 PM. Stormwater was coursing through Murray's home chamber. Each clap of thunder revved up his confidence. He could do this. The cloud cover was dark and thick, and the pelting rain would drown out any sound. He would be able to slip past anyone who was still out. He had this, he told himself, nodding his nose.

His destination was the corner store on Queen West. It had a large chest of the goods located in the far-left corner of the shop. He would be able to enter through the back exit. The door was usually propped open with a milk crate for approximately 15 minutes while one of the workers went out for a bite.

By 6:56 PM, Murray was standing shivering beneath the cover of a sodden cereal box. The kid would be returning shortly before seven. The problem was, he hadn't quite left yet. He was standing outside the doorway, typing on his phone. With each passing moment, Murray's heart began to sink. Perhaps tonight wasn't his night after all. Wait - the kid was starting to move. He shifted his weight from leg to leg and then began to turn the corner to the side of the shop. A little further to go.

Now, straining to not make a sound, Murray crept his way up to the back door. He knelt low, winding his body up. With a surprising amount of grace, he glided over the milk crate.

It was a strange back room he was in; everything was painted the same shade of eggshell. He heard footsteps behind him. He slid under a discarded jacket. The young man returned through the back, kicking the milkcrate inside on his way. Murray's gaze followed him through the swinging door into the shop. As soon as the kid was back at his register, Murray tiptoed his way over and pushed through.

Hot spots began pinging all over Murray's tiny body. He had to steady his hooves to keep them from clattering across the linoleum floor. It was a short distance to the freezer, but by the time he had reached it, he almost collapsed with anxiety. He could feel the warm hum of it pressed against his torso. This, he thought leaning into the purr of the machine, this had been worth all the strife. It had been written in the stars. He felt at one with his colorful treasure chest, breathing in and indulging in its warm buzzing. For a couple of moments, he remained still as it massaged him back to tranquility. Finally, he stretched his trunk to slide open the glass doors to his heart's most coveted desire.

Then there was a scream. A twenty-something girl in full-body spandex and fluffy boots stared, wide-eyed. The paper cup in her manicured hand quivered. Murray knew better than to freeze this time. He turned away. This only caused the young woman to flinch, spilling hot, frothy coffee down her front. She stumbled. She began falling sideways in the direction of an elderly gentleman. Even though she was a slight human herself, the frail man did not stand a chance. In a flurry of glitter and syrupy caffeine, they collided.

Her scream had drawn the attention of everyone else in the convenience store. Thankfully, their focus had shifted to assisting the pair. They ran to catch the gentleman before his slender frame made contact with the hard ground.

Murray was out the door like a shot. As fast as the warm rush of muggy air hit him, his problems followed. There was a screech followed by the loud crunch of crumpled metal. Someone had seen him and doing an instinctive second look, had driven off the road into a light post. The luxury vehicle had crinkled like a pop can. And it didn't stop there. The light post was now balanced on phone lines that were beginning to sag and spark.

Murray's body was turning to jelly by the minute. He needed to get away and hide somewhere. Then, he could regain bodily functions and return home to his stinking but safe oasis. He vowed never to leave again. He darted into the nearest carpark. He searched for boxes, garbage, recycling, anything to hide behind.

★★★

Lucie was finishing her latest atmospheric landscape when she heard the commotion below. She didn't want to turn away from her newest creature creation, but her inquisitive nature wouldn't let her be. She pulled her water bottle to the center of her page. Pressed the corners down to reassure herself, before climbing off her chair.

Across the street, sparks were flying as a silver utility pole leaned on telephone wires. It made her think of a friendly robot taking a nap where he shouldn't. Her gaze fell to the pretty cream car that had smushed itself at the base of the pole. She hoped everyone was okay.

A crowd was forming, and she could feel the electric chatter as people emerged from vehicles. Curiosity was building in her body and she wanted to get closer. She checked the clock, 7:03. Lucie was always instructed to be home by 7:30, so she had a bit of time. She threw on her favorite yellow raincoat and made her way to the elevator.

She was making her way out of the underground parking exit when she saw something strange. A pile of cardboard boxes stacked next to the overflowing paper receptacle trembled. Something was making small, muffled squeaks. Her heart leapt. *What if it was a kitten?* She took a step closer, then another one.

Suddenly there was a loud sneeze followed by a rush of air.

One of her dragons fell out of a pizza box.

Race of the Dragon Ships

E. W. Farnsworth

Autumn was the time of harvest for grapes and pressing of grapes for the Dragons Blood wine. Spring was the time for racing boats in the ocean surrounding Earth Island. Young men and women would vie in racing gear to pull the oars. The swift vessels circumnavigated the circle of firm land, both human and dragon land. In ancient times the most hazardous part of the race was the stretch to the south. There, the farthest point was the huge mountain. The largest dragon dwelled there in the largest cavern, surrounded by his piles of gold.

The prize for winning the race varied each year. This year a solid gold cup was the prize. The proclamation for the race was posted far and wide. It came to the attention of dragons, whose lust for gold was stronger than any human impulse. Nothing in the rules for this year's race prohibited dragons from competing. The dragons held their own competitions in the winter months. The five winners would surely win the prize as dragons could swim at least as fast as the fastest boats of humans.

Prince Landron's son and namesake chanced to witness the dragons playing in the waves one winter's day. An intelligent lad, he ran to tell his father that the dragons were preparing to win the spring race. The news surprised the prince and princess. They conferred with their wizard to form a strategy to foil the dragons' plan.

"We never should have allowed the council of humans to decide the prize this year would be solid gold. That brought the dragons out. What should we do?" With these words, Prince Landron opened deliberations.

The wizard spoke when everyone else seemed flummoxed by their predicament. "I see only one way out of our situation. It will take a lot of preparation. Five warriors must train hard to be ready. Upon their efforts, everything will depend."

It required one hourglass of explanations. Prince Landron saw the brilliance of the wise man's strategy. He appointed people for each of the required tasks. His shipbuilders fashioned dragon prows for five boats. They carved wood so cunningly, the humans could not distinguish the wooden from real dragons in the ocean. The five heroes, three women and three men, he and his sister then trained to swim deep underwater. They sported sharp knives that would be used to rip open the soft bellies of the dragon competitors. Humans had only ever fought with dragons on land and in the air. This trial by water would be a new adventure. No one could guess the outcome.

Princess Fiona offered sacrifices to the humans' god for his blessing. The jealous deity demanded the solid gold cup as his in the event the humans won the prize. Crestfallen, she agreed to the terms. She told Prince Landron the bargain she had made, and he was hard-pressed to offer a better solution than hers.

The most dangerous part of the plan was the combat between the heroes and the dragons at sea. Both the prince and the princess spent long hours rehearsing every scenario possible. They fashioned model dragons and exercised every twist and turn of those long bodies. They showed where to insert the deadly knives and how to twist their blades to tear the dragons' innards. The beaches of the humans' side of Earth Island became red with wine. The royalty used it to simulate dragon blood. Prince Landron lectured all sailors about what to do if the dragons should dive beneath the waves.

Princess Fiona said, "What are you thinking, husband?"

"Our early focus was on the five contesting dragons as if they were the only dragon participants. What if they decided to witness the event on the land and in the air. They would not sit idly by when they saw their brothers become a seething mass of gore and blood in the ocean."

The wizard heard the prince and said, "That is why we've fashioned our dragon prows. We'll erect them as we slaughter the real dragons. That way, spectators will think their kind are winning the contest. Meanwhile, they'll be dead beneath the waves."

Princess Fiona urged the three female warriors to steel their hearts. One of the three was injured in practice, so the princess's daughter replaced her. The princess was proud of her daughter for volunteering. But she was also terrified that she might be slain in combat.

Naturally, her brother felt he must also join the heroic team. He practiced in private and stood by to be called into action.

A dress rehearsal for everyone belonging to the racing team and the heroes went flawlessly. Witnesses could not distinguish the dragon prows from the mockups of swimming dragons.

Within a week of the race, the plans finalized. Prince Landron's son decided to witness the dragons' practice one more time. He was impressed with the new formation the dragons had devised—a wedge with one dragon forward and two on each side. As before, he ran to tell his father this news.

Prince Landron announced, "We must make one more practice round. This time, we'll use the new formation that the dragons have devised as our target."

The wizard oversaw the final practice and smiled with approval at the results. He told Prince Landron, "As the ten contestants start the race, five human boats and five dragons must mingle. Each human will be paired with one dragon in the wedge formation. That way, it will appear as if the humans, not the dragons, will have perished. It will seem that only the dragons will have survived to win the race."

The dragon competitors arrived in a flying wedge formation. Like sea birds, they plunged into the ocean where the race was to begin the next day. The humans kept their dragon prows hidden deep in the holds of their vessels covered with tarps. Guards were posted to assure no dragon eyes espied the cunning prows.

The night before the race, the dragons built a fire and danced in their hideous antic motions. Shadows of pointed wings stretched out over the land they once terrified. Prince Landron's son watched the hated monsters. He saw their size and strength. A thrill ran up his spine as he watched them leap into the air like the flames of their fire. They seemed so fast and sure in their movements. He had lived among those creatures for two years, and they never ceased to amaze him.

The five dragons and five human teams in boats formed a line in the water. The first light broke over the horizon. They needed no one to voice the start of the race. All shot forward heading south along the shore of Earth Island. Humans watched from the mountain tops and cheered their favorites on. High in the sky a phalanx of dragons flew nattering in their dragon's language. Soon the ten were out of sight. As the dragons formed their secret wedge, the humans' boats did likewise. This surprised the dragons, but they had trained well. They kept to their plan and maintained the distances from each other.

The dragons did not notice as the five heroes plunged below the water to do their fatal work. Meanwhile, the oarsmen pulled the boats, even with the swimming dragons. The blades of the warriors found the dragons' bellies and opened their innards. A wake of blood and gore streamed aft of the combined formation. One dragon's head went down to the trail and fell behind the racers. The hero who had killed that dragon climbed back aboard the racing vessel.

So it happened with the other four dragons. The heroes prevailed. The teams aboard the human vessels turned their craft into boats with dragon's prows. Five dragon bodies and innards bobbed in the ocean. The five dragon-prowed vessels kept a tight wedge formation. The phalanx of dragons flying high above the racers was fooled, just as the wizard had intended them to be.

As the boats rounded the bend at the farthest point south of the island, dragons on the mountain's peak clamored. They thought they were surely winning. None bothered to fly near the boats to make sure they were not seeing a deception. Some did wonder what had become of the humans in the race. The oldest dragon decided to check out the wake to be sure no signs of dragons' perfidy lay on the surface of the ocean. He saw no human remains, but he did see what appeared from a height to be the thrashing of many fish feeding on offal.

The five dragon boats crossed the finish line. The vessel that rode at the apex of the wedge held the daughter of Prince Landron and Princess Fiona. By the rules, she was declared the winner of the contest and recipient of the gold cup prize.

The dragons, who expected the award to be theirs, swooped down to see why events had turned against them. They saw the dragon-prowed boars and realized the trick. They stood on the shore in a line of hissing monsters. They protested and waved their wings in anger. They objected that their contestants had been betrayed and slain.

Prince Landron stepped forward to say that, in effect, the dragon prows had won the race. He maintained that adjustments must be made to the allocation of the prize.

"We should all have the prize for the brutal murder of our five dragon contestants." So spoke the oldest dragon, who was the most gold-greedy.

Prince Landron was caught in a dilemma of his own making until his god appeared to voice his objection.

"Princess Fiona promised she would sacrifice the gold cup to me as the god of humans if humans won the race. Since that happened, I claim the prize. His hands closed around the gold cup as the dragons flew up into the air. They dove upon the god, who burst into flames to satisfy the sacrifice. The dragons were slain in the holy fire of the god. Princess Fiona observed as the prophecy was fulfilled. A stench of dragon flesh filled the air. Black smoke rose from the place where the god had stood with the gold cup. A funeral pyre had been lit by the blaze, and no human could approach for fear of the heat of the combustion.

The humans were too horrified to applaud. The dragons could not help themselves from entering the sacred holocaust. The princess's daughter was the only mourner among humans. She was proud of her award. Now she witnessed the transitory nature of prizes of all kinds. Especially those sanctioned by a god.

The feasting lasted late into the night. The heroes told their tales of daring during the contest. The craftspeople bragged about the fidelity of the prows to their models. The humans rejoiced that they had achieved victory over the dragons once again.

Invisible among the revelers walked the god smiling. The wizard accepted accolades from Prince Landron and Princess Fiona. Prince Landron's son was happy that his father was proud of him for the intelligence he brought to the contest. Without the lad, the humans would have had no insight into the dragons' plans.

Princess Fiona told Prince Landron, "We should find a special award for our daughter. She not only earned the right to be called a hero but also steered the winning vessel to the goal."

He swelled with pride. "A thing well done is its reward. Still, I agree that our daughter deserves something special. Likewise, our son is due a reward for his timely intelligence. I have an idea that might prove worthy of both."

The next morning, the two young royals were summoned by their parents.

"Congratulations. You have been selected to take one of the dragon-prowed boats and retrace the path of the racers. You should be able to find the corpses of the dragons who perished in the contest. Your reward will be the hides and teeth of those creatures. From the hides, you will fashion armor stronger than any we humans can create. As for the teeth, you will fashion knives. The sharpness will be unlike anything our metalsmiths can devise."

The two young heroes did retrace the racers' journey. They located dragon bodies floating in the ocean and washing up on the shore. As Princess Fiona had instructed, they harvested the dragon skins and teeth. They also towed the carcasses of the victims ashore where they buried them with honor.

When the brother and sister returned to the shore of the broad grapevine valley, they were doubly acclaimed. First, for their heroism as regarded the race. Second, for having paid respect to the dragons from whom they took the hides and teeth. The spoils were taken by the armorers and weapons makers of the kingdom. The hides were fashioned into suits of armor. The dragon teeth were set within handles as knives. Three dragons' teeth were kept separate at the wizard's request. This was his reward for having advised at the early stages of the race preparations.

Prince Landron was both amused and intrigued by this. "Wizard, you don't usually care for rewards. I agree that you should have whatever reward you choose, but why did you choose three dragons' teeth?"

The wizard smiled shyly. "An ancient tradition suggests that sowing dragon teeth can produce a harvest of young dragons."

"That's bad news, I fear."

"It's especially bad if the dragons that spring up from the planting are female."

A special garden was prepared for planting the three teeth. The wizard cultivated the ground and manured it with Dragons Blood wine. He set the teeth in the ground with the pointy end upward. He covered the teeth with soil and watered the garden every day. After nine months, the ground broke where the dragon shoots emerged. Another month and fully formed baby dragons appeared. One appeared to be male, and the other two were female.

Princess Fiona heard about the three baby dragons and asked, "What will we do with these creatures?"

The wizard said, "I am not the maker of policy. That's the job of you royals. My advice would be to think this through before you take any irreversible action."

While the prince and princess thought about the conundrum, their children played with the babies. The baby dragons became obedient and dependent on humans. The human population became protective of the dragon brood. They would not hear of motions to kill them or take them back to dragon land to be freed. The more the news spread, the less likely it was that the presence of the babies would remain a secret.

The oldest living dragon flew down for a conference to discuss the three young dragons.

"I have information that you produced three dragons without a dragon's permission. I claim those children by ancient rights and precedents. My fellow dragons are excited to have the three babies reunited. Otherwise, there will be war. So, what do you say?"

Prince Landron said, "Your words have weight. Your dragon children belong with you in dragon land. We have tended them and raised them. We only ask that you honor their love of humans and not turn their minds against the race that fostered them."

"I can't speak for how a dragon will react when it becomes an adult. I do promise to teach these offspring about the terms of our truce. If you please, I'll take possession of these young dragons and return to their rightful home now."

The ancient dragon seemed gratified when it leapt into the air with the three small dragons. They flew south, and Prince Landron that night had a hard time answering his wife's questions.

"I do wonder whether I have done a good thing for our people by turning over the young dragons to their kind this way."

"You did the only thing you could under the circumstances. If you had tried to withhold them, the war would have been inevitable. Did you tell the dragon the secret of the baby dragons' birth?"

"No, I did not. And he didn't ask me about that. I presume that the dragons already knew the secret. I'm going to start tomorrow with a new program of training. Our children must be ready to combat a new dragon force."

"All this with no evidence of the dragons' perfidy?"

"We can count on the dragons for two things. They hate us humans and love all gold."

"I hoped we would never have to fight dragons again."

"We may not have to fight them, but we must be strong enough to deter them from attacking us."

"The children will be disappointed that their pets are now in dragon land."

"They'll understand why I had to make the decision. I only hope their affection for the dragon babies does not cloud their vision when—and if—we go to war again."

The couple summoned the wizard to discuss the new problem with dragons. He listened to what the prince and princess had to say. Then he gave his judgment.

"I agree that the dragons are likely to have bred new dragons from the teeth of their dead. I also agree that they will attack us when they feel they are strong and we have weakened. I suggest that you renew the people's faith in our god so they may pray while they exercise for war."

Prince Landron took the wise man aside before he left the palace. He said, "we have numerous dragons' teeth in our armory set with handles. If ever we need to breed dragons of our own, we can cultivate another dragon. We would raise the baby dragons just as you did with the three that flew home. Isn't that so?"

"That's true. Any time you want, you can grow an army of dragons, but beware. No matter how you nurture them, they will be true to their nature as dragons."

Prince Landron began the next day by assembling all the young men and women of the land. He taught them in the manner and means of protecting the realm against dragons.

"The threat of dragons belongs to all. There's no telling when the air will become dark with malevolent wings. There is no preparation then against the threat. We must be ready from this time forward to combat the dragon hordes. They will come in large numbers and blacken the sky. You have heard the stories that your parents and grandparents have told. If we had not avoided defeat, you would not live surrounded by green pastures and vineyards. Instead, you would be chained to rocks and forced to do the work of slaves in deep caverns in the mountains to the south.

"You may laugh at the idea in private, but I am addressing the most grievous issue of your time. Practice hard. Learn your skills carefully. Be ready. When the dragons come, you will be in the fight of your lives. Now form your lines for exercises. It doesn't matter whether you are surrounded by boys or girls, or a mix of both. Dragons will not care about your gender when they kill, maim and enslave you. To them, we're all the same."

RESOLUTION

CAMERON CORDICH

The scales were still warm.

That should have alerted him that something was amiss, but he was cold. The dim heat from the dragon's corpse was a refreshing turn of events from the biting chill that clung to him. Henry could recognize that it was more from his blood loss than the state of the environment.

"A little rest," he said as he leaned against the dragon's armored hide.

A glance revealed that he hadn't managed that great of a distance. He felt as though he had run a few miles without pause. Part of him wanted to lie down on the ground and shut his eyes, but he didn't dare risk it. He knew that if he closed his eyes for even a moment, he wasn't going to get them back open again.

Henry glanced down at the makeshift bandage.

The cloth had long since soaked beyond repair. It was hard to say if it was assisting him much, but it was all that he had. He knew enough medicine to take care of himself, that was a requirement growing up on a farm. But a wound such as this was well beyond the scope of his abilities.

He needed a dedicated healer. He needed to get back to camp.

They had marched for miles before they came to this desolate place to throw their lives away. They should have men and women searching for survivors or patrolling the route.

If he could get back to camp.

If he could find someone to help him.

The beat of wings drew the farmer from his depressive spiral.

His eyes met the beady black orbs of the observing raven.

He had seen plenty of them before on the farm, always looking to steal his hard work. Always being driven off in the end, but always coming back. Staring at one now should have been a joke compared to the nightmare that he faced mere hours ago.

His already pale flesh lost what little color it still possessed. The grip around his blade trembled, the terrible answer to the question flooding the back of his head despite his internal protests.

"I'm not food," he said. "Go away, find something else to eat!"

His free hand lashed out at the bird, though it was far short of hitting its mark. The raven did nothing and continued to stare at him with glassy eyes. Henry reached down, ignoring the flaring pain that pierced his leg.

The rock he managed to grab was flung through the air, missing its target by inches.

The raven screeched and flapped its wings in protest. Worse, others of its brethren joined in. The black birds landed in the trees and charred remains of the former battlefield.

"Get back! Get back!" Henry screamed again and again until his throat was raw, his strength spent.

"Such a compelling argument."

Henry knew that there was some clever way to describe the deepness of the voice that shook his very bones. All he could do was stumble back in fear as the body he had been leaning against shifted.

His leg screamed in agony again, but that was a distant thing now.

The dragon's body twitched and twisted until a serpentine neck pulled out from behind it. A single blazing eye glared at him. The gaze narrowed in recognition. The nostrils flared in fury as smoke curled around his jaws.

Despite himself, Henry could hear the whimper escape his throat at the sight of the beast. Most notably, he saw the space where a single tooth had been torn from its gums.

"You."

"PEST!"

Any rational thought of engaging the dragon was shredded in raw panic. His hands clasped at the ground as he struggled to pull himself away from the looming beast. The creature's hellish gaze bore down on him. Its maw cracked open, revealing row upon rows of flesh piercing teeth. The air around the creature's mouth started to warp with heat. The young farmer could feel his skin break out into a hot sweat.

He was going to die.

At least, that was the single coherent thought that ran through his mind. He had seen what that fire could do to people, how whole buildings could be brought to ash with but a single blast.

CRACK.

Something smashed against the dragon's armored head, shattering into pieces. It was less than an annoyance, but the white powder that coated the dragon's snout was a different matter. The creature reacted almost instantly, pulling back in a blind panic. The gigantic dragon snorted and choked on the powder and stumbled as the effects took hold.

Dragonsbane.

He didn't know what was in it or how it was made, but truthfully, he didn't care much. It was very good at hurting dragons.

From what he understood, the powder extinguished their flames and sapped their strength. They would become lethargic and helpless before even the most inexperienced of fighters. It was an old tactic that had worked for hundreds of years by villages that lived in the shadows of the monsters.

Granted, most dragons were intelligent enough to recognize the signs of Dragonsbane. The stuff wrecked the environment as much as it did them. But the threat of death was enough to keep most dragons away.

Now the army had chosen to weaponize it.

More and more glass jars cracked against the beast's hide and released their contents. The dragon staggered for a brief moment. At that moment, the fighters charged forward with swords and spears. A few reached their mark. They quickly learned that even a weakened dragon could still be dangerous.

The farmer did his best not to flinch as flecks splattered against his face. He focused on crawling away from the danger. He had done his part; nobody would fault him for wanting to get away and be safe.

Right?

"Going somewhere?"

Agony, unlike anything he had ever experienced before rolled up his leg. The pain burned his waking mind. His heart threatened to rip itself out of his chest. At some point, his mouth started making a noise he didn't think humans could produce. Only through sheer luck did he manage to wrap his hand around his blade before he was torn from the ground.

Up became down. Left became right.

The entire world spun in his vision as he twisted in the air like a doll in a child's hands.

For a single instant, his vision lined up with the beast that had taken him captive. At that moment, Henry was granted a clear view of his leg trapped in the monster's maw. The creature's malicious gaze met his, filled with hate and amusement as he toyed with him like a cat would a mouse.

It made him angry.

In that perfect moment of clarity, there was no thought, no consideration.

Only action.

With a single thrust, the blade wrapped in his hand found its new home in the one spot it could reach from where he was.

The dragon's eye.

What escaped the dragon's throat wasn't so much noise as it was an experience. The bones rattled beneath his armor as the monster released its grip. The beast screamed fury and hate while he flew through the air.

The air left his lungs as he crashed against something hard and unyielding, and then, darkness.

"I must admit, this is something of a surprise. Who would have thought that you would have survived the battle?" The dragon mused, with the kind of calm tone that did little to hide how blindingly enraged he was. Even down one eye, the creature's glare was a terrifying sight to behold. It had been frightening enough facing down the monster on his own. Now Henry was acutely aware of how alone he was.

"J-just have t-the gods on my side, I guess," he managed to get out.

"Yet here you are, delivered to me." The dragon's smile was anything but kind. Henry flinched as the beast's head drew itself in, engulfing his field of vision. Henry wanted to stand back up, but he doubted the creature would let him. Nostrils flared, and hot breath washed over him like a furnace. "I should return what you have done to me. What is it that you humans say? An eye for an eye."

What was there to say?

The farmer's voice caught in the back of his throat at the realization of how helpless he was. It had taken dozens upon dozens of men to leave the dragon like this, and it had still taken a heavy toll on them. He had a single sword and not even the ability to use it properly.

He was only a hapless conscript, not a hero of old.

It would take a miracle to get out of this.

He was pretty sure he had already spent his.

"What's this?" The dragon asked with a mocking smile. "No words? No threats? Not but a few hours ago, you were willing to strike my wing and tear my flesh. Or are you only brave when hiding behind others of your kind?

"I'm almost disappointed. I would have hoped that when I finally met a human capable of wounding me, I would have had a greater story to tell. A mighty battle befitting of the ages that would be woven into songs. Now all I have to show for it is a witless worm."

He wasn't sure what set him off.

Maybe it was the mocking tone.

Perhaps it was the seeming inevitability of his passing.

He supposed that it didn't matter in the end what it was. A terrible and mighty fury washed over him. For the briefest of moments, he might have been able to stand and fight the dragon from that fuel alone. But instead of rising to his feet and swinging his sword, his tongue loosened, words pouring out his mouth.

"Is this a joke to you?" he asked. The towering creature blinked, head reeling back as though it had been struck. "Do you think I wanted to come out here and fight you! You think any of us wanted to fight you? We would have been perfectly fine, sitting in our homes and living our lives. But your kind can't let us have that, can you? You take what you want and murder when it pleases you! You burned down an entire town! For what? Because you could?"

The rational part of his brain was screaming at him to stop. That reaction was buried underneath a tsunami of anger and spite as he cursed the dragon. "You talk as though you're some civilized thing, but in the end, all you are is an overgrown beast—"

"Do not speak to me as though your kind is blameless in this battle," the dragon snarled. The growl was deep enough to rattle the bones in his chest. The creature's neck twisted as though it wanted to lash out at him and strike him down. Aside from its neck and head, the rest of the dragon's body was motionless. Not a single beat of a wing or twitch of the tail.

"You claim we are nothing more than beasts. Then you must claim that title for yourselves as well. The seeds for this conflict were planted by your kind, worm."

"What are you talking about?" Henry asked, confusion piercing through the shroud of anger. "You burned Crossroads to the ground. It was one of you who set this up."

A laugh bubbled up from the dragon's throat.

"For a species that claims to be civilized and learned, you miss so much."

"Then enlighten me."

Henry did his best not to fidget as a single eye glared down at him. Something was going on in that monster's head, as though he was considering his request. He had heard stories and legends of people talking their way out of being a dragon's dinner. Those usually revolved around appealing to their ego and pride, not insulting them.

Something was wrong, something he couldn't quite see.

"Crossroads was not an unprovoked attack, it was retribution," the dragon said. He spoke as if he was discussing the weather, as though the destruction of an entire town was nothing to him. The farmer could feel his anger rise but he kept his mouth clammed shut. "The town, at the behest of the mayor, had taken something from one of our nests. They had scaled the mountain, snuck into our very homes, and stole what was rightfully ours. How they managed to accomplish this exactly, I do not know, but they did."

"And that justifies burning it to the ground?" He asked, a sick and twisted feeling rolling in his stomach.

"You have not asked what they stole."

"Let me guess, some sheep? A few trinkets of treasure?"

"Our hatchlings."

"What?"

"Newborns, or close enough to it." The anger was still there. Now the dragon just seemed tired. His head hung a little heavier on his neck, the hellish glow of his eye dulled a bit. It wasn't hard to imagine him as his father, sitting on his rocking chair, exhausted from working the farm. The kind of tired that sapped your will and stole your strength. "A single score, most of the next generation."

Arguments about how the creatures would grow up to hurt and kill others flooded his mind. But those all seemed so empty. Yes, they were dangerous, but one didn't kill a littler of pups because their mother had attacked you. "Why?"

"There is any number of rituals that pieces of my kind can be used for." The dragon appeared to shrug. "I do not know the specifics or care to learn them. When we sought to save our young, we found that we were already too late. So, we burned their homes, destroyed their fields, and smashed their goods. Their leaders burned in the fires of our judgment. We graciously allowed the townsfolk to flee, and what do we get for our mercy? Death, battle, and the slaughter of our kind."

"How do I know that you're telling the truth?"

"You don't, I suppose. Are you denying reality because you don't believe it to be true, or because you don't want it to be true?"

Henry didn't have an answer.

"You're dying, aren't you?"

The question escaped his lips as the dragon snapped at another raven that had perched on his back. The black-feathered fiend darted away, narrowly avoiding ivory fangs. Henry doubted it would be too dissuaded by the action, none of the others did. They stood there, watching them with their cold empty gazes.

"No."

"I mean, you don't have to lie to me, I'm pretty sure I'm dying too." The admission hurt in more ways than one. It meant that he was giving up on getting back home, but he didn't see any way out of this. He lacked the strength to pull himself back up. This meant that he would simply bleed out if the dull throb in his chest didn't kill him first.

"I don't need your pity."

"Well, I'm not giving you any." Supposed retaliation or not, he was still a dragon. He had taken great joy in ripping apart countless people who had little to nothing to do with the killing of those hatchlings. The fact that a murderer had a tragic backstory didn't change the fact that they were a murderer. "I'm just asking."

"And why should you care?"

"I suppose I don't, but we've got nothing else to do but talk." Had he been in his right mind, the farmer might have realized how calm he sounded about own impending death. Maybe it was the blood loss or shock. He knew he should be panicking at the thought of his soul leaving this mortal coil, but couldn't work up the energy.

"You think I would want to speak to vermin such as you?" The dragon snarled, but it lacked heat and power, the things that had made it so very terrifying before. The growl that had rattled the very bones in his chest now only tickled his ears.

"I mean, you're talking to me already," Henry noted as he stared up at the sky. The thick overcast wasn't much to look at. At least he could track patterns and maybe get some amusement out of it all.

"I spoke to you because it was within my interest at the time."

"And what interest would that be?"

"Perhaps I wanted you to suffer from the knowledge that you died for a band of murderers. That the king you hold so dear has left you for dead. Your passing will be marked by nothing. Those who commanded you to charge into certain death are rewarded with titles and wealth. You and your sacrifices were worth nothing in their eyes."

He could feel something cold inside of him squeeze at every word of the dragon. What he knew to be the truth rang in his head like a gong. It wasn't as if he had some grand idea of being rewarded. Not being left to die would have been nice. Still, there was something odd about the dragon's tone. It sounded empty. "And what were you worth?"

The dragon's head snapped around with a sharp crack, his slitted pupil glaring at him.

"What?"

"Seems to me we're in the same boat, so to speak. I haven't seen any of your friends coming back to pick you up," Henry pressed, unable to help himself. "At least I have the excuse of just being a grunt they picked up to add more meat to the grinder. But you, they've left you behind, haven't they?"

"You assume that there's anyone left."

"Oh." Henry wasn't quite sure how to react. Excitement that the kingdom would never be threatened by dragons ever again? Mournful that a species, no matter how dangerous or cruel, was extinguished from the face of the world? "There are no dragons left?"

"Perhaps a few elders and younglings too weak and powerless to do anything. But functionally, yes, there's no one left to come and search for survivors. I doubt there's even enough to bring our population back up once this is all said and done. It isn't as if we were ever particularly fast breeders. Not like your kind, you breed just as quickly as any vermin."

The insult might have roused some indignation from him if the tone hadn't been so morose.

Gone was the bluster and pride that could have filled an ocean on its own. Instead, loss clung to every word in a way that he wasn't sure he could understand. He had lost friends and extended family before, his own parents' survival to old age was a minor miracle.

But to lose your entire race?

The dragon fell silent, and Henry took a few moments to chew on the knowledge. As he considered the information, anger bloomed back in his chest. Wrath and hate boiled over in a way he hadn't felt since that time a neighbor tried stealing one of the prized pigs.

"Then, why did you do this!"

"What?" The dragon asked, bewilderment flashing across his crocodilian snout.

"You're telling me that your entire race fought a battle knowing that they were the only ones left of your kind? That you risked the entire future of your species for—for what?"

"Those thieves needed to pay," The dragon started to say. His voice grew in strength and anger with each word. However, before he could build up his steam, Henry cut in.

"FINE!"

The dragon's head snapped back a little at his uncharacteristic roar. Henry could feel his chest squeeze in protest as the outburst. His breathing grew heavy and erratic, but that didn't dissipate the anger under his flesh. If he had been standing, he would have certainly been punching the dragon, futile as it might have been.

"Fine," he said again. "Your hatchlings got kidnapped and killed, that's bad. You had every right to want to kill the people who took part in that. But you just didn't do that, did you? You burned an entire town to the ground and ruined the lives of countless others. Even if you didn't kill them then, they'd die eventually. Most of them will likely starve or freeze to death when winter hits."

"You speak as though I care," the dragon rumbled.

"I doubt you do," he admitted. "But you don't get to claim that we're the only ones in the wrong when you've done just as much damage to us. How many herds of livestock have you stolen, how many fields have you left in ruin? I don't even want to ask how much gold and wealth you've taken over the years."

"Those were ours to take by our right."

"What right is that?"

"The right of strength!" The dragon howled, his voice regaining some of its vigor. That illusion of power was quickly overtaken by a coughing fit. The creature's black scaled neck rolled in protest as the convulsions rose up to its spine.

"And where has that strength gotten you?"

The dragon didn't answer.

"The stars are pretty tonight."

Specks of light danced across the empty night, patterns emerging through the clouds. Henry could remember a time when his father had sat him down in his youth and walked him through every constellation, every star, every story.

The young farmer found himself reciting those stories in the back of his head as he stared up at the sky. At the very least, as he passed, he would have something to do.m.

"Yes. Yes, they are."

"Do dragons tell stories about the stars?"

"Some. The story of the Great Wyrm and his attempt to breach into the heavens is often shared with hatchlings," the dragon mused.

"Could you tell it to me?"

"Why?"

"Do you have anything better to do?"

"I suppose I don't."

The dragon's deep voice started to weave the tale of a titan of a dragon. In that instant, Henry was back on the farm, listening to another one of his father's stories. So even as another raven joined the growing unkindness, Henry relaxed.

It could be worse.

"I'm surprised I haven't bled out yet."

He was no expert on wounds. Certainly, something as big as the hole in his leg would have caused enough blood loss to pass out. The dizziness gripped at his skull. The mere act of twitching his arms felt as though we were trying to lift a boulder. He had long since given up on his legs. The young farmer had managed to shoo off a few ravens, but it was delaying the inevitable.

It was only a matter of time.

"Venom," the dragon's voice came. While it was still deep and booming, a quality of his size most likely, it lacked the strength from before. Weakness clung to every word; the slow sapping of power so great that he couldn't even raise his head. "We have a mild venom laced in our fangs so that our prey doesn't bleed all over the place when we bite them."

"Ah. How long does it take to wear off?"

"Hours. I suspect that you're nearing the end, but it seems to be keeping you alive well enough. If your comrades had not left you, you could have survived."

That didn't make him feel better, but he supposed there wasn't much point in complaining.

"How long will it take for the Dragonsbane to wear off?" He asked.

Henry wasn't aware of the specifics of the poison. He certainly hadn't asked about how long it took from a dragon to shake the stuff off. All he had cared about at the time was how it could save his life when he came face to face with a hungry dragon.

"Never. The poison only grows in strength with each passing hour. Some antidotes can be taken, but I have long since passed the threshold for such measures. My passing is just as assured as yours at this point," the dragon said softly.

The defiance of death was gone, replaced by a quiet acceptance. He hadn't even referred to him as vermin.

"Are you leaving anyone behind?"

"No. My mate perished long ago, and she gave no hatchlings. Even if I lived, I would have little to return to."

"I'm leaving my parents behind. We talked about what might happen if I didn't come back. I guess I didn't expect that to happen." He supposed that was how they made it seem so appealing. Yes, there was a chance that you might die in battle. The odds of it being you that gets gutted is insignificant. A comforting little lie to keep them all in line as they marched off to their doom.

"I said goodbye."

"But it didn't feel real?"

"Yeah. I thought after the winter was over, I'd be able to return to the farm, and everything would be alright. Mom's going to be devastated, she was crying so much when I left, begging me not to go. Dad kept telling me I was an idiot, and I—I told him off." His stomach rolled in his gut at the thought. "The last time I'm ever got to speak with my Dad, and it was a shouting match."

Would he blame himself?

Would he regret the words, or would he regret that he hadn't convinced him?

He might be dying, but they were going to have to live with the fact that their son was dead. Worse yet, they wouldn't know for sure until winter passed, which meant months of waiting. Tears probably would have gathered in the corner of his eyes if he wasn't so dehydrated.

He had broken his family. For what?

"If it is any consolation, I do not think that your father would hold it against you. Your reasons for wanting to defend your fellows was not without merit. You fought well, Eyestabber."

"But we're still going to die."

"The Reaper does not come at a time of our choosing. We simply must accept that our time in this world is at an end."

"It doesn't make it easier."

"No. No, it doesn't."

"Henry."

"I'm sorry?"

"My name, since, you know."

"Kirsad."

"I'm cold," Henry murmured, the words barely passing his lips. Even that action felt as though he were trying to move a mountain. Flesh grew stiff and lifeless as more of his crimson lifeforce poured out onto the ground. The ravens circled overhead, a few brave ones taking positions on his legs.

He could feel the pecking, if only slightly, but he didn't dare look down.

Not knowing for sure made it easier to ignore.

"My fire is fading as well," Kirsad said, his voice a whisper in the winds. The strength that had made him such a formidable creature on the battlefield was all but gone. Embers of a dying fire whose power had been extinguished. He supposed it should have been funny, feeling empathy for a being he had been taught to hate and fear. But in the end, what did any of those differences matter in the face of death?

They were going to die.

That didn't mean they had to die alone.

"Are you scared?"

"Yes."

"That's okay, I am too."

"Goodbye, Kirsad."

"Goodbye, Henry."

The Dragon Maiden

Taylor Rigsby

The rain pounded against the windowpanes as thunder rumbled in the distance. Dazzling white lightning flashed across the sky. It had torn her from her sleep. She thought she had heard the roar of a dragon. Cassandra peered through her bedroom window. She searched the wild sky for any trace of wings and fire. The door cracked open and a little voice whispered.

"Sister? Are you awake?"

"I am," Cassandra answered without turning. She put one hand behind her back and motioned for her little brother to join her.

Her brother obliged, slipping through the door, and shutting it before racing for her bed. In a single bound, he leapt onto the mattress, agile as a house cat. He crawled over the sheets to join his sister as she watched the storm from behind the curtains.

"Have you seen any yet?" Aaron asked, excited. Cassandra, still watching the storm, shook her head.

"No, not yet," she paused and thought for a moment. "I'm not sure if we will see one."

"But it's like grandfather said!" Aaron protested. "When the skies burn white and the thunder roars, there is bound to be a dragon flying by! So, this means the stories are true, right?"

Cassandra bit her lower lip and recalled the old tale their grandfather told them. He was old and sweet and loved his grandchildren dearly. He also liked to tell stories and was, in fact, very, very old now. Cassandra knew it was more than likely that their sweet old grandfather was confused. Dragons, after all, hadn't been sighted for almost a hundred year now. Sometimes Cassandra even doubted that they ever existed at all.

"Cassandra?" Aaron murmured. At last, his sister met his eyes. They were the eyes of any other six-year-old, innocent, and curious. Cassandra made no reply. She only smiled, unwilling to share her true feelings with her baby brother.

At that moment thunder crashed again and the door to Cassandra's bedroom creaked open. The warm glow of candlelight filled the room. In the threshold stood their sweet old grandfather, watching them.

"Looking for Dragons again, I see," he said in a low, knowing voice.

"Yes, grandfather," Cassandra said.

"Granddad, we will see a Dragon tonight, do you think?" Aaron asked.

"Someday, but not tonight, I'm afraid," their grandfather answered. "Not when there is work to be done tomorrow. Not when little heads should be asleep in their beds." He then motioned for Aaron to join him at the door. The little boy, pouting and disappointed, did so. Grandfather then turned back to Cassandra.

"To bed now, young miss. I'll be back to tuck you in shortly."

"Yes, Granddad," Cassandra said with a nod as she climbed under the sheets. As he left, her grandfather left the door cracked. Cassandra turned on her side and watched as the candlelight bounced away down the hall.

"When will I get to see one, Granddad?" she heard her brother whisper in the dark.

"Someday, my boy," the old man replied with a chuckle, "Someday when you're all grown-up. This I promise you." Cassandra grimaced in the dark and then rolled over to face her window. She reached up and tugged back one corner of the curtains and watched as the storm outside raged on.

She was four years older than her brother, Aaron. She knew better than to expect much from the promise of a dragon sighting. Her older brother, Toby, who was fifteen and a blacksmith's apprentice had warned her as much only a few years ago.

"Granddad is a very good old man, Little Sandy," he had said to her before leaving for the village. "But he is still a very old man and gets very confused sometimes. I think, more than anything, he tells you those stories to help you sleep better at night."

Cassandra sighed and shut her eyes for a long time. Maybe Toby was right all along. Their grandfather was just trying to entertain them. That wasn't so bad, though, right? It only showed how much he cared about them. There were no dragons.

The door creaked open again, rousing Cassandra from the stupor she'd slipped into. She turned over and rubbed her eyes as Grandfather shuffled over to her bed and sat down on the edge.

"Ooh! Old bones aren't as kind as they used to be," he muttered under his breath as he struggled to get comfortable.

"I was almost asleep, Granddad," Cassandra yawned wearily. "You didn't have to come to tuck me in."

"Then it's a good thing I came with an ulterior motive," Grandfather replied with a wink.

"What do you mean?"

"Cassandra, my love. How old are you now?"

"I'm ten years old, sir. But I'll be eleven two months from now."

"In that case, I believe you are old enough to learn the real stories of the Dragons," her grandfather said. He set the candle on the nightstand.

"The real stories?" Cassandra repeated, "But Granddad, I don't understand."

"There are many stories about the Dragons, my love," her grandfather explained. "Stories from all over the world. Stories about the different Dragons and their many kingdoms."

"Dragons had their kingdoms?" Cassandra interrupted; her eyes wide with fascination.

"Oh yes indeed," her grandfather answered with a smile. "There were once all kinds of different Dragon kingdoms scattered all over the world. In every single one of these kingdoms was a Dragon King or Queen. Like any other king or queen, they watched over the safety of all Dragons in their kingdom."

"What happened to these kingdoms, Granddad? The books don't say anything at all about them."

"Well, like any other kingdom, the Dragon kingdoms often fought with each other. They fought with other Dragons and other kingdoms that didn't belong to Dragons. Everyone from the giants to the fairies, and of course, even humans like us. That is how the Dragons were exterminated, through war and centuries of fighting."

"But that's so silly," Cassandra protested. "Why should they all fight like that, Grandfather? Couldn't they have talked over their problems?"

"I'm afraid that I don't know, my love," he said, sounding sad. "I never understood it myself, and I don't think I'll ever understand it. But that is why you are ready to hear the real stories about the Dragons and how they managed to escape."

"They did?!"

"Oh yes," Grandfather said with a smile, "At least a few of them anyway. So did their Queen."

"Their Queen!?"

"That's right. And that is the story I will tell you tonight: the tale of the Dragon Maiden. Now let me see," he added, wrinkling his brow, "How should I begin it. Ah, yes! I think I know exactly where to start!" he then cleared his throat and looked to his granddaughter.

"Many, many years ago, long before even your mother was born, I ran this farm with my three older brothers. We never thought once about the Dragons or their wars. Out here we were safe and content, having everything we needed to live quiet, peaceful lives. We believed that the last of the Dragons had been vanquished. We had not seen hide nor hair of one for quite some time.

"But all that changed one day when our flock of sheep got loose from their pasture. My oldest brother sent me out to fetch them from the foothills where they had wandered away. And in my search for the flock, I stumbled across the most shocking thing I would ever come to find."

★★★

"What's this?!" Leon murmured as he knelt beside the bones. They were white as if bleached by the sun but very fresh. But that was not what frightened him. What worried him most was that they were the bones of a sheep.

"Oh no!" he muttered as he jumped to his feet and looked around. He searched through the surrounding landscape for any sign of the missing flock. Only when he stood very still and listened closer, did he hear the distant bleating of a little sheep in trouble. Leon whirled around and followed the sound. He raced through the thickening woods of the mountains' foothills. The sound grew louder and louder until Leon burst through a small group of trees.

"HEY!" Leon cried as he glimpsed the sheep in the arms of a beautiful young girl. She gasped when she saw him and then turned and raced in the opposite direction.

"Hey, get back here you!" Leon called as he chased after her. He ran as fast as he could, gaining on her once as she zigzagged through the trees. When she was within his sight, he reached out one hand and sprung forward. He sailed through the air for a single moment as his fingertips grazed her long, ebony hair. He missed and was sent crashing into the ground with a loud and painful shout.

The girl raced on and disappeared around a wall of limestone without looking back. The little lamb cried out all the way. Leon groaned as he pushed himself onto his hands and knees. He blinked away the flashing white spots appearing before his eyes. He rose, groaning with pain and humiliation. He began searching through the woods where the girl had disappeared.

"Alright, I know you're here!" he called out into the forest, "And that you're the one who's stolen my sheep! Come out right now and return my lamb, thief!" No answer came as Leon tiptoed through the trees. He stilled himself and listened again, hoping the same trick would work a second time. Echoing from inside the opening of a cave came the urgent bleating of his sheep followed by a whisper.

"Shush, insolent creature!"

Leon followed the noise and stopped before the cave. He squinted inside as he strained to see. It was pitch black within the depths of the cave. He couldn't see how deep it retreated into the mountain. There was no way the thief could escape him now.

"Alright, enough hide-and-seek," Leon commanded in his most authoritative voice. "I know you're hiding in there, so come out right now with my sheep!" When no reply came, Leon grunted and stamped one foot.

"If you don't come out now, then I shall have to come in there and take it from you, thief!"

"I am not a thief!" the girl called out from within. "I found this sheep wandering about and assumed he was abandoned!"

"Then that makes you a fool and a thief!" Leon snapped. "Who would think that a single sheep was just abandoned in the woods? A wise person would've sought to return to the sheep to his home. Now, bring it out right now, or I shall be forced to take it from you!"

"Alright already, I'm coming!" the girl shouted. She stepped out from the shadows and revealed herself in the bright afternoon light. At first, Leon was bewildered by this girl, mainly in the way she was dressed. She was covered from head to toe with thick brown leather. She wore a vest of black chain-link over her thin, bellowing tunic. Her long, raven hair had been pulled back into a fashionable, elaborate braid. That was the only thing about her that was feminine. In truth, she looked more like a knight's apprentice than a dainty, fair maiden.

But Leon could not deny that she was fair. This was the second thing that struck him—infatuation. Her black hair and black eyes glittered in the afternoon sun, catching the light. Her skin was smooth, pale and flawless, and appeared soft to the touch. This was a profound contrast to the thick, rough exterior of her clothes. She was lean and athletic, unlike so many other girls his age. She stood with a sense of regal importance and wisdom uncharacteristic for one so young. Even when she grimaced at him, as she set down the sheep before him, her beauty was never failing.

Of course, as she made this face, it brought about the third and final emotion that struck him to his core—anger.

"Now then," he said, as the sheep trotted over to his side. "I would like to know why you felt justified in stealing my sheep?"

"I already told you, I didn't steal it," the girl defended. "I found the poor thing wandering about in the forest over there."

"But you still ran when I called you," Leon snapped. "That means you must have realized he wasn't a wanderer." At this, the girl blushed, her lie unmasked, and she cast her eyes away as she muttered,

"I didn't mean any harm in it, alright? I was trying to find food for my father."

"Your father?" Leon replied, incredulous. "You can't be serious. You can't expect me to believe that nonsense."

"Whether you believe it is up to you," the girl retaliated. "That is the truth and that's all that matters. Anyway, you have your sheep back, so why don't you take it and go?"

"Wait a minute," Leon said, his brow wrinkling as a thought came to him. "You said you were looking for food for your father? Does that mean you're the ones responsible for that dead sheep I found in the woods?" The girl started but made no reply. Of course, with that reaction, Leon already had his answer.

"So, it was you! You stole and ate my family's sheep!"

"Look, it's not what you think!"

"You are correct young master," said a deep voice from deep within the cave. "It is true. We stole your flock and regret it."

"Father, no!" the girl cried as she faced the cave. "Don't give yourself away!"

"Sir," Leon commanded like a nobleman, "I demand to speak to you to discuss compensation for the loss of the sheep." The being inside seemed to pause inside the cave, as if he were mauling over the idea.

"Very well," the deep voice sighed.

"No father, no!" protested the girl, "Please stay inside—"

"Dahlia," the voice interrupted, "Stand aside, child." At this, the girl lowered her head and did as she was told. As she slunk away from the mouth of the cave, a giant yellow eye opened in the darkness. It glowed from the shadows as the cat-like iris came to rest on the now trembling Leon.

The dragon pushed his massive head through the shadows, settling in the cave entrance. Leon nearly tumbled backward as he gaped at the size of the creature. He soon realized there was nothing to fear about the mysterious Dragon.

The Dragon, you see, had grown very old. This was made evident by his scales. Once, they were a proud and deadly shade of black. This had now faded to a weary, flaky light gray. The Dragon didn't even have the strength to lift his head as he eyed the young farm-boy outside the cave. His yellow eye was clouded and weary from the passage of time. The girl, meanwhile, stood at the side of her so-called father. She stared daggers at the young Leon as if daring him to take a single step closer.

"I imagine you have many questions, young man," the Dragon chuckled. "I fear there is no time to answer them all. There is only enough time to say what needs to be said."

"Father, please don't speak that way," the raven-haired girl said softly. She reached one hand up and stroked the Dragon's muzzle. The Dragon seemed to smile at this and went on.

"I am Morodo of the Night," he explained in his slow, tired voice, "Last reigning King of the Sky Dragons. This is my youngest daughter, Princess Dahlia of the Stars. The Queen-in-waiting of the Sky Dragons. Or at least, what remains of them," the Dragon added sadly.

"If I may ask, sir … your majesty," Leon inquired, "What in the world are you two doing way out here? Where is the rest of your kind?"

"Gone," Morodo answered. "All gone forever more, and never to return." Dahlia glanced to the ground and again stroked her father's snout. After a pause, the Dragon explained further.

"Our kingdom was the last to fall, in this centuries-long war. We were the strongest and the bravest of the noble Dragon race. Alas, we too fell before the combined might of the humans and the Giants. Surely you, my young friend, know all that has transpired?"

"Only some," Leon admitted. "My family's farm is in the middle of this region, and out here we are sheltered from the affairs of the kingdom." Leon shrugged and added, "we don't ask questions and the kingdom never thinks to report to us."

"I see," Morodo muttered softly. He fell silent again and in his glowing yellow eye, Leon could see a plan forming in the Dragon's mind. At last, the Dragon King spoke again and asked,

"My young friend, may I ask you your name?"

"I am called Leon, sire," he answered politely. "Only Leon, as my family is small and has no other name."

"I see," the Dragon replied, "And now Leon, I must ask you a small favor. I ask that you escort my daughter to the witch of the woods."

"What?!" Both Leon and Dahlia cried at the same time.

"Sir, I can't!"

"Father, no!" Dahlia protested, "I will not leave you alone out here! Not until you are well again!"

"My beloved," the old Dragon said to her, as he turned his sad gaze upon her black, sparkling eyes. "That is something, I fear, we cannot hope for any longer." At first, Dahlia said nothing but only glared at her father, her lower lip trembling.

"You are our kingdom's last hope," the old Dragon went on. "You and only you can lead what remains of our people back to prosperity on the Isle of Halos. You must go on without me now, child, for I only slow you down."

"No," Dahlia insisted, blinking away the tears in her eyes, "No, father, for you will be well again. You will! I'll see to it myself!"

"My beloved. I am dying. Even you so fierce and so strong, as a future Queen should be, must know this much. There is nothing more I can do for you. This is where we must part."

"Father," Dahlia protested, but the old Dragon paid her no attention and instead spoke to Leon.

"I ask you, young Leon, to escort my daughter to the Witch of the Woods. Only she can guide the princess to her people, now in Halos," the old Dragon paused and closed his single eye. He needed a few minutes to recover before he was able to speak again.

"I know it is much to ask of you. Especially from an old dying Dragon. I humbly ask your assistance for there is no other way for my daughter to reach Halos Isle. Please fulfill an old father's final wish."

Now young Leon realized he was facing quite the conundrum. He had never before heard of the Witch of the Woods or knew where she lived. He was at a complete loss. It seemed very strange. Why him, why Leon? Why would such a powerful creature ask a lowly human for such help? On the other hand, these Dragons were the last of their kind. Even Leon, as ignorant as he was, knew better than to listen to the stories that said Dragons were greedy and evil. He turned to the princess Dahlia, who eyed him with thinly-veiled distrust. Leon thought long and hard, weighing his options carefully until he came to a decision.

"I can assist her, your majesty."

"Many thanks," the Dragon sighed. He then turned his eye back to his princess and said, "Go now, my love, for soon I will be sleeping." Dahlia leaned forward and rested her forehead on Morodo's nuzzle.

Meanwhile, made himself scarce and waited for her at the edge of the woods. When Princess Dahlia's sobs had finally subsided, she joined him there with his sheep.

"I am very sorry for your father," Leon whispered.

"Many thanks," Dahlia replied without looking at him. "Now, let us be off, for I must return to my subjects. I am Queen now after all."

"But my sheep," Leon protested, motioning to the little creature. "I have to see to it that he returns home safe. And my brothers … I must tell them what has become of our flock if we are to survive this winter."

"We must be off now, for I have already been away from my subjects much too long. And I will see to it that you are compensated for your flock," Dahlia replied. "After all, father did promise you that much already."

"But—"

"Listen," Dahlia insisted, "Trust me on this, okay? I swear you and your family will not suffer from our mistake. You must fulfill your promise first and help me find the witch. Alright?"

"Well, alright then," Leon conceded. "But Shepply stays with us the whole time." Leon motioned to the little lamb, who bleated at them. "He's a baby, you know, and needs some protection now that he has no mother."

"Of course," Dahlia agreed, "Then we shall bring the lamb." With that, they set off toward the east, deciding to search first in the deepest part of the woods.

"Exactly who is this Witch of the Woods?" Leon asked after a while, as Shepply the lamb trailed after him.

"I don't know," Dahlia shrugged, "I remember father only spoke of her rarely. She is supposed to be very old but very powerful, omniscient even."

"Omni—what?"

"It means she knows everything."

"Oh. Well, do you at least know how to find her?"

"I'm not sure," Dahlia admitted. "Father told me that she lives somewhere in this area. That's why we landed in the caves back there, so that I may find her and bring her back to father."

"Are you sure it wasn't so that you would be able to find her alone?" Leon asked. Dahlia paused, and replied in a small voice,

"Father was very sick from fighting in the wars. His magic was almost completely spent, you know. And with his magic extinguished, so was his strength."

"Dragons can do magic?"

"Of course. Well, only the oldest among us, anyway. Can't humans do magic, too?"

"Only a few of us," Leon replied as he stopped to help Shepply over a log. "Even then," he added, the sheep still in his arms, "It's not very good magic. Does that mean—does that mean you can do magic, too?"

"Only poorly," Dahlia laughed, "I'm afraid I'm only a hundred and two years old."

"One hundred and two years old!" Leon exclaimed, fumbling the lamb.

"Why yes," Dahlia replied matter-of-factly. She paused and waited for him, "Father did tell you I was the youngest of my siblings."

"There are more of you?"

Dahlia nodded.

"Exactly how many more of you are there?"

"Well, let me see. I have about thirty-five brothers, and twenty-seven—no, twenty-eight sisters."

"And, uh, how old does a Dragon live to be?"

"Well, my oldest brother was over a thousand years old," Dahlia explained. She turned and led them on through the woods. "My mother claimed to be a little over three thousand years. Everyone thinks it was closer to four," she added with a wink.

"I don't know how old my father was, so in truth, even I'm not sure how old a Dragon can grow. I don't think even father was sure of his age. What's wrong?" Dahlia asked as she turned back to Leon. He had sat down on a log, still holding the sheep, his face a sickly shade of gray.

"Oh nothing," Leon replied quickly, leaping to his feet. "It's just a–a lot to take in for someone as ignorant as me."

"I am sorry. I didn't mean to make you feel uncomfortable."

"There is something I wanted to ask you though," Leon said as he put the sheep down. "If you're a Dragon princess, then how come you don't look like a Sky Dragon?"

"Because she is the youngest of her lineage!" a voice from above cried out. Leon and Dahlia whirled around. Glaring down at them were the twisted, gnarled faces of three Screeching Crowthals.

Now, everyone has heard of a banshee, and probably a few tales of the winged Harpies. The Screeching Crowthals are a breed of lesser-known monsters but are far more deadly. With the torso and arms of a human and the legs, wings, and head of a vulture, Crowthal inspire the worst of nightmares in the bravest of men. Their screeches are so sharp, they can be heard from over a hundred miles away. The smallest cut with their claws can prove lethal. What truly makes a Screeching Crowthal dangerous is their skillful form of magic.

Before Leon and Dahlia could think, thick, powerful roots burst from the earth and wound around their chests. Dahlia screamed and Leon cried out in pain, as the roots carried them up and closer to the female Crowthals. The sisters cackled and leered disgustingly at them, relishing in their obvious victory. Shepply bleated out and scampered away as fast as he could.

"Hey, that tasty dish is getting away!" cried one of the sisters.

"Oh, never mind that one," replied another, "We've got a much better prize right here!" At this, the three sisters cackled and howled again. Leon struggled in the grasp of the roots, twisting this way and that in the hopes of forcing himself free. Nothing worked. The grip of the roots only seemed to tighten, threatening to crush him in a single instant.

"Vile creatures!" Princess Dahlia spat, her cheeks burning red. "I demand that you release us this instant—"

"Or you'll what, highness?" sneered the eldest of the three, "Whack me with your massive wings? Spit fire straight into my face? Ha! Don't make me laugh, child. You haven't even had your first molting yet!"

"Do you know the penalty for murdering a Dragon Queen?" Dahlia growled. "My fellow Dragons will not stand for such an insult. They will have their retribution if anything were to happen to me."

"Oh-ho, you mean the proud, unstoppable Dragons who fell to the humans of all creatures? That, majesty, I would think would be the greatest insult to your race."

"Yes, yes!" declared the Crowthal's sister, "Besides, what does remain of the Dragons? How many of them were able to escape their doom and flee to that accursed island of theirs?"

"Few, I would think," the youngest sister gloated. She smiled and revealed sickly, yellow teeth, all filed down to a sharp point. "Not even the mighty Morodo of the Night could escape such a grim fate."

"Shut up!" Dahlia snapped, "Don't you dare speak my father's name, you hear?!"

"I see." smiled the eldest sister, "That wound is still very, very fresh. Well, fear not my dear," she licked her lips in hunger as she leaned in for Dahlia's face.

"You'll soon be out of your misery."

"No, wait!" Leon cried. His lungs protested, screaming for him to be silent, but he ignored them. "Leave her alone! You can have me instead!"

"We intend to, dumpling," said the Crowthal to a chorus of screeching cackles from the others. "But I would rather taste a young Dragon first. They are so hard to come by, you should know."

Dahlia grimaced and turned away, bracing herself for the worst. Leon shut his eyes tight unable to stand the sight but hollering for them to stop all the same. Then, another cry reached their ears,

"Baaa!"

The Crowthals looked around, startled by the interruption. Leon and Dahlia looked behind the Crowthals, equally startled. On the forest floor, standing on top of a rock overlooking a crevice, little Shepply had appeared. The oldest of the vulture-women blinked and then said to the lamb,

"I say, how in the world did you get over there, morsel?"

A round of snarls and barks erupted from the crevice. A pack of giant, black wolves burst forth in a charge. The Crowthals shrieked in alarm and panic, lifting their curse on the trees. The roots loosened and fell away. Leon and Dahlia tumbled down to the ground and landed with a painful thud. When he looked up Leon realized that the wolves were still coming. He rolled over and threw himself on top of Dahlia, shielding her from their fury. The wolves leapt over them, charging, it seemed, straight for the Crowthals.

A young wolf snarled and jumped, grabbing one of the sisters by the leg. She screamed and tried to shake the beast away, but he held on tight and clamped his jaws. One of her sisters swung at him with her powerful wings, knocking him clear across the forest floor. The ugly Crowthals took to the skies and screeched down at the wolves. The pack's disdain was mutual as they barked and growled at the hideous creatures.

"Filthy beasts!" snarled the oldest sister, "What do you think you are doing?!"

"I could ask you the same thing, hag!" replied the leader of the pack, "How dare you assault the Dragon Queen in Lady Grezelle's forest?!"

"Foolish mutt!" hissed the Crowthal, "That insolent Witch has no power over us!"

"Lady Grezelle is the keeper of all the forest! How dare you challenge her authority, you disgusting, miserable old crone!!" The Crowthal hissed again and prepared to charge. She was stopped by her sister who whispered into her ear,

"No, there are too many of them! We must retreat while we still have the chance!" the Crowthal shot her a nasty look, but still heeded her warning. Turning away, she shouted over her shoulder,

"We won't forget this, wolf! Mark my words, we will be back!" With that, the three Crowthals flew off in a hurry, screeches echoing around the forest. When it was over, Leon let out a heavy sigh of relief. He stood up slowly, never taking his eyes off the pack that surrounded them. He reached out and took Dahlia's hand, helping her to her feet as the wolves started encircling them.

"We don't want any trouble, mister wolf," Leon began, nervously.

"And you shall have none, my boy," answered the leader of the pack. Then, with a graceful bow—one that was imitated by every single wolf—he said to the princess,

"We are honored to make your acquaintance, your highness."

"Please, the pleasure is mine," replied Princess Dahlia as she bowed. "I cannot thank you enough for your rescue. I am forever indebted to you, Sir Wolf."

"There is no need for such formalities. You may call me Morgan if you desire."

"Thank you, Morgan."

"Come," Morgan the Wolf said, "Lady Grezelle is expecting you. It is most urgent that we deliver you to her."

"Indeed," answered Dahlia as she turned to follow him. However, Leon grabbed her by the wrist and stopped her, then whispered to her,

"Are you sure that's a good idea? I mean, can we trust a pack of wolves?"

"Oh? Would you rather stay here in the forest, with the Screeching Crowthals? They don't take too kindly to failure, after all."

"Well, uh—"

"Besides, it will be night soon," Morgan added, turning away. "Worse things are lurking in the night out there."

Leon realized that she was right, and with that, hurried along to join Dahlia. The wolves led the way to the Witch of the Woods. Leon picked up the lamb and carry him for the rest of the way. He thought he saw that distinctive, hungry look in the wolves' eyes. It was better to be safe than sorry.

They walked and walked for many hours. At last, as dusk was settling in, they came to a large oak tree that seemed to appear from thin air. The bark shined like gold in the early starlight. The leaves, as pure as silver, glinted brightly, swaying in the evening breeze. They stopped just before the tree, and Morgan the wolf turned to Dahlia and said,

"You must knock three times and say these words to gain an audience with Lady Grezelle." The wolf spoke slowly. When he had finished, Dahlia faced the tree and knocked on it three times.

"I seek the wisdom of the Witch of the Wood, sovereign to all of the Grezling Forest."

The breeze died almost immediately and the sliver leaves shivered. A bright, white beam of light burst from the tree. Suddenly a door appeared before them, carved into the bark. The door slowly opened. From it peered out a tall, beautiful woman wearing a long black dress with wide, billowing sleeves. Her hair was sleek and silver, flowing down her feet in a thick braid. Her eyes were a deep shade of purple that resembled the evening sky. Leon swallowed and forced himself not to stare at the witch's third eye, set in the center of her forehead.

"I am Grezelle, the three-eyed witch," the woman murmured. "I have been expecting you, Dahlia of the Stars."

"Lady Grezelle," Dahlia began, "we have come to seek your treasured aid."

"I know why you are here," the witch replied. She opened the door for them and beckoned them inside. "This way please." Dahlia, Leon, and Shepply disappeared into the tree. Grezelle turned back to the wolves and said,

"I thank you for your assistance, Morgan Wolf."

"You are most welcome, my lady," replied the wolf politely. "Do keep in mind, it is not like wolves to be so lenient with humans who wander into our territory."

"I will remember that in the future," Grezelle assured him. "In the meantime, please do no harm to the boy until he has returned home. I suspect he will remain much longer than anticipated." Morgan Wolf grunted, but nodded, seeming to accept these new terms. Then, he led his pack away back into the forest. Grezelle then disappeared inside the tree and shut the door with a light thump.

At first, Leon couldn't see anything as the door shut and plunged them into total darkness. A few moments later, a candle chandelier burst to life and bathed the tree-house in a warm, welcoming glow. Leon blinked and gasped at the sight of the house. Small as it was, it contained a never-ending library of books neatly arranged on a spiraling bookcase, which climbed the length of the tree. Leon looked up and had to brace himself against a small table to keep from falling over. Below the spiraling selves of books sat a little bedroom with a bed pushed up against the wall. Opposite the bedroom, a little kitchen led into a little nook. In the center of the room stood a large black cauldron, proof of the witch's ancient powers. Its contents bubbled and steamed without fire.

"So, the mighty Dragons have fallen," the witch Grezelle commented. She tossed a handful of herbs into the cauldron. It bubbled rapidly and turned a bright red, fizzing out.

"All but a few, yes," Dahlia replied.

"You must return to Halos Isle, the fabled homeland of the Dragons."

"Yes. My father sent us to you in the hopes that you could lead us there, and fast. Otherwise, anarchy will break out as the remaining Dragons fight for the throne."

"Yes, I am well aware of the urgency of your quest. And I do know of one way to return you to your people. Still, I am the guardian and protector of these woods and all the creatures within. I cannot in good conscious leave my charges, all for the sake of restoring a dying breed."

"Please, Lady Grezelle, I beg you for your assistance," Dahlia pleaded. "I have no idea of knowing how many of my kinsmen have survived, nor do I know of how long they have been without a leader. You must take me to Halos as quickly as possible, or I fear the worst will befall our entire race!"

"I am sorry, young Majesty," murmured Grezelle with compassion, "But I simply cannot. I cannot leave these woods unguarded. They have an abundance of magical power and would be vulnerable to any being who desired to steal it."

"Excuse me, my lady," Leon stated. The princess and the witch turned to him. "I've thought of something."

"Yes?"

"You cannot leave the forest unless there is someone else here guarding it, is that correct?"

"It is."

"Well then. I know this might sound a little forward, but what if I watched over the woods for you?" Grezelle tilted her head, making Leon flush with embarrassment. So, he went on,

"I mean, until your return of course. I could stay here in your place so that you can lead the princess to her people. And then I leave willingly as soon as you get back."

The three-eyed witch was a scrupulous and clever maiden. She was all-knowing and all-seeing and therefore had foreseen this event some time ago. She was also one who did not trust humans. After centuries of life and experience, she considered them greedy and selfish. Still, there was something about this boy that must have left a favorable impression. When Grezelle at last spoke again, she replied,

"Very well, I accept your offer, young Leon. You shall remain here, in my stead, while I escort the princess to her new kingdom. But I warn you, my young friend, it will not be an easy task to undertake."

"I understand, your ladyship," Leon replied, "and I am not afraid."

"Very good then," Grezelle motioned toward the little bedroom. "The Isle of Halos is very far away. I must make preparations tonight if we are to reach it quickly. Please, rest yourselves here for a while. Dahlia and I will soon leave for the island."

Grezelle the witch left the tree and Leon and Dahlia retreated into the bedroom. Since he was not tired, Leon offered the bed to Dahlia who had a long trip ahead of her. She accepted it gratefully, ready for a little bit of sleep.

"I cannot thank you enough, Leon," she muttered after some time had passed.

"There's no need to thank me," Leon replied, as he stroked the sleeping head of Shepply. The little lamb had fallen fast asleep in his lap some time ago, sighing and bleating sweetly in his sleep.

"Yes, there is, especially after all the trouble we have caused you," Dahlia said. "And," she added, her cheeks blushing, "after how I treated you when we first spoke."

"I understand," Leon smiled. "You were only trying to save your father. The same way you are trying to save your people now." Dahlia nodded and then said something that Leon would never forget.

"I fear we are beyond saving. I fear that no matter what we do, this will be the end of us, us proud Dragons. You see," she added as she propped herself up on one elbow, "we Dragons didn't always fight with each other. Or with anyone for that matter. We only wanted to live in peace with the rest of the world's creatures. But we were the most powerful creatures in the world, and that made us arrogant. Even a little nasty. I think that made others fear us in the end, and that was how all the fighting started."

"You mean you don't know?" Dahlia shook her head.

"No, the warring began long before I was born. I've seen many of my brothers and sisters killed in battle, each one fighting for reasons we can't even remember. That is why the youngest born is heir-apparent for the throne," Dahlia yawned as she lay back down on the pillows.

"The youngest of us are never sent into battle. When we are so long-lived we can be taught to be good leaders for when the fighting is finally over. It was one of father's ideas, though, for a long time, it wasn't very popular."

"I think it is a good idea," Leon replied softly. Dahlia smiled at him.

"I like to think so, too."

"You will make a great queen. Just look at how far you were willing to go for your people."

"What do you mean?" Dahlia asked, furrowing her brow.

"Well, I was a silly, country human who mistook you for a thief. Yet, you were willing to accept me as a friend, and trust me to help you. Talk about a leap of faith!" he laughed with a wink. At this Dahlia smiled and closed her eyes, her mind finally growing drowsy.

"You don't give yourself enough credit," she said sleepily, "You're an amazing person, I think. Why else would father have sent you with me?"

"What do you mean?" Leon asked, then he saw the peaceful look on her face and decided to ask her in the morning. He looked down at Shepply as the lamb turned over in his sleep, and stroked his wool gently as he turned over in his sleep.

"Leon?" Dahlia whispered sleepily. "If we never see each other again ... promise me you won't forget me?"

"Only if you promise, that we'll always be friends," Leon replied gently. Dahlia smiled in her stupor, and muttered,

"It's a promise." With that, she fell fast asleep. Leon smiled down at her and reached out and stroked her hand. *Who would've ever guessed I would've had a Dragon for a friend*, he thought. He waited there by her side until Lady Grezelle finally returned.

★★★

"Don't stop now, Granddad. What happened next?" Cassandra asked, her eyes wide and round with curiosity. Her grandfather shifted uncomfortably at the edge of Cassandra's bed. His back was beginning to ache, and in his mind once again he cursed the ravages of time.

"Dahlia the Dragon Maiden left not long after, with her guide, Grezelle the three-eyed witch. They set off in a boat along an enchanted river that the witch had conjured in the middle of the forest. I, meanwhile, remained behind and watched the witch's forest as promised. Oof!" he muttered suddenly as he rubbed his back.

"Oh, these old bones! It's one of the curses of age, Sandy my girl. Look," he added pointing to the candle on the nightstand. It had burned down to almost a nub and threatened to go out at any minute.

"It is well past your bedtime now, my love," he grunted as he rose to his feet.

"But Granddad, what about the story?" Cassandra protested, bolting upright in bed. "What about the wolves and the Crowthals, and the witch and the Dragon Maiden? Did the Dragon king know you were coming and would remain to protect the forest? Did you ever see Dahlia again? Did she ever make it back to her people? Did she ever become Queen?"

"She did indeed," her grandfather chuckled with a smile. He laid Cassandra back down and tucked her gently into bed. "She went on to become a marvelous queen. She safeguarded the remaining Dragons for years to come."

"But, how do you know this Granddad, if you didn't go with them to the island? How can you know that the Dragons have survived if you haven't seen one since?"

"Who said I haven't seen one since that day?" the old man muttered with a sly look in his eye. Cassandra's eyes lit up and he chuckled once again.

"But that, my dear Sandy, is another story for another time."

"Will you tell it to me tomorrow night, grandfather?"

"Oh yes, my dear," he replied as he kissed her cheek, "It and a thousand other stories just like it. Now, lie still and go to sleep."

"Alright. Goodnight, grandfather," Cassandra yawned as she rolled onto her side.

"Goodnight, my love. Sweet dreams," he answered. He then picked up the fading little candle and shuffled out the door. When it closed with a click, Cassandra turned over again. She watched as the withering storm rolled along into the night. Little stars from worlds away blinked beyond the fading clouds. The rain lightened more and more until it was only a soft pattering against the window. The thunder and lightning had long since faded. As Cassandra's eyes grew weary, she sleepily thought,

They must've all gone back to Halos. Pretty soon she was there herself, gliding through the skies with Queen Dahlia of the Stars.

THE FINAL QUEST

ADRIANA ZADRAVEC

Almanzar, the last commander of the desert dragons, clawed at the ground. With the last of his strength, he dug a small hole in the dry sand below. Tugging the precious amulet off his neck, he stared at the yellow stone for a moment, then placed it in. He covered the priceless artifact with as much dust and dirt as he could.

He smiled, even though his vision began to fade. At least someone might find it and save their history. He could only hope that this historic battle wouldn't be forgotten. Even with the power of elemental magic, the dragons were no match for the strength of the wizards.

In the beginning, the dragons had the upper hand. The water and ice dragons froze and swept away hundreds of the puny sorcerers. The desert and fire dragons covered the enemy with molten glass to burn and trap them.

Halfway through the battle, many days later, the wizards unleashed a secret weapon. The jade dragons of disease and death. They were thought to be long gone. Their attack caught the dragons by surprise, and a plague laid waste to the entire water dragon army. The battle went downhill from there, leaving only one troop of desert dragons on the battlefield. Three of them managed to escape with their lives, but barely. They hid deep underground, far away from the end of the war.

The wizards, or the Karafan as they called themselves, whisked away the aftermath of the battle with their magic. The dragon's bodies disappeared into thin air, and any damage to the land was repaired with a simple wave of a hand. All traces of the war and dragon race itself vanished. Or so they thought.

Ezmir, Kamkha, and Wrenn, the last desert dragons on Earth, hibernated deep underground. They had all been injured during the battle and needed to heal. So, they waited. They hid in their dark underground cave until their safety was ensured and their wounds soothed. Months passed, then years.

Then, one day, Kamkha finally decided to dig her way out of the cave. Her sharp claws sliced through hard rocks and soft sand as she made her way to the surface. Soon, the sand became warm against her rough orange scales. She hadn't felt warmth in a long time. The surface was so close. Kamkha roared as she shoved her head through the final layer of sand, exposing her to the sun and fresh air. She climbed out of the hole and stood proudly in the sand. She looked around, expecting to see the beautiful desert that she had lived in for years.

Instead of soft, golden sand, dry bushes and spiny cacti, the land was covered with wooden buildings and flat grey rocks. Kamkha was puzzled. How long had they been underground? She roared down the tunnel again, signaling her friends to climb up to the surface. The ground rumbled as the two large dragons ascended through the sand. Ezmir clambered out first, his golden scales shining in the hot sun. Wrenn followed him, talons digging into the crumbly ground. The two of them huffed in amazement at what had happened to their home. Their beautiful desert was gone; it had transformed into some sort of civilization! Not the best news to wake up to.

In Crathidian—the language of the dragons—Kamkha asked, "How long do you think we were gone? How could an entire town of new creatures appear in our home so quickly?"

"If a settlement like this was built while we were underground, years may have passed," Ezmir answered.

Wrenn sighed.

"Fantastic. Now, what do we do? The war is over, our kind has all but died out, and we have no home," he said. His jagged brown tail thumped on the ground in defeat. Ezmir nudged him with the edge of his wing.

"Don't be so gloomy, Wrenn. As long as we live, the history of the dragons lives on. In the meantime, we should find out what creatures live here now, and what happened to the Karafan," Ezmir suggested. Kamkha nodded and sniffed the air. It smelled strange. The air never used to have such a sour scent. Desert air was supposed to be dry and fresh. The worst part was that Kamkha caught the faint scent of one of the evil wizards. This must have been their work.

"I don't know about you guys, but this stinks of the Karafan to me. They must have built it after we disappeared," she growled.

"Something tells me that they're not the ones living here," Ezmir replied. Wrenn shrugged and began walking into the town. He cringed when his claws touched the strange flat rock that covered the ground. He shook his head and continued walking through the city. Ezmir and Kamkha followed him. They stared at the wooden houses along the road. There were holes in the walls of these buildings that had been filled in with thin sheets of glass. The dragons knew what glass was, but they didn't understand how these creatures had made it so flat and clean. When other species of dragons blew fire at the sand, it became all clear and hard, making glass. However, glass made by dragons was lumpy and dirty. How interesting that they've created a purpose for it.

When Kamkha peeked into one of these windows, she noticed animals that looked like the Karafan, but less magical. Were they wizards without magic? Or some other simple creature? The three of them continued wandering around the town. Then, the creatures started screaming. Some of them would take one look at the dragons and fall to the ground. It was very strange. In the time of the dragons, they were all respected, not feared. Now, these puny wizard-shaped animals with strange clothing ran in terror at the sight of them.

"Hey, we're not here to hurt anyone! We want to know what's going on in this village," Ezmir tried to explain. The creatures didn't understand his language and kept running away.

Then, in the middle of the crowd of people, a small child stood and stared at them. It wasn't afraid. Wrenn glared back at it. The child stood his ground. Kamkha stepped toward it. Her eyes honed in on a bright yellow stone hanging on a chain around its neck. She turned around and yelled, "This child has Almanzar's amulet! Our history is not lost!"

She bared her teeth in a sort of smile, then crept closer to the creature. As she approached, it spoke in Crathidian.

"Hello, I'm Mint. What's your name?"

Kamkha blinked in surprise.

"My name is Kamkha. What type of creature are you, little one? How do you know my language?" she asked.

"I'm human! That's such a weird question to ask. As for the language thing, I can't explain it. I guess it's good that I understand you. The rest of the town doesn't seem very happy to see you guys," the child answered.

"I have never heard of humans before, dear Mint, but that is not important right now. I must ask where you got that pendant. It is an artifact of my kind," Kamkha said.

Ezmir and Wrenn walked up behind Kamkha. They glanced at each other, then at the human child. It resembled a small wizard, but with tan-colored skin instead of the deep green of the Karafan. What an odd little creature.

"This necklace? My dad gave it to me. He said he found it in the sand when he was my age," Mint explained. "Would you like to hold it?" he offered.

Kamkha nodded, so Mint pulled the pendant off his neck and held it out to her. She took it in her large claws and stared at it for a moment. The beautiful yellow gem shined in the sunlight. Kamkha took a deep breath, thinking of all her kind had lost in the war. Then she smiled.

"Thank you for keeping this safe, small one. It is the last artifact of dragon kind, and it may still be able to tell our stories. Now, I must ask you one more question. What happened to the Karafan? The wizards that defeated us and built this village, where are they?" she asked the boy. Mint blinked in confusion.

"Wizards? I've never seen any. My mom told me they don't exist. I mean, she also said the same thing about dragons, and here you guys are!" he answered.

Wrenn growled.

"You must be lying. They were an enormous force of powerful wizards. There is no way they could have disappeared with no trace!" he said, angered. Mint stared at him with concern.

"I'm sorry mister, but I have never seen or heard of any wizards. If you want, I could help you find them?"

"Relax, Wrenn. It is just a child. It has no bad intentions. Perhaps we should take his offer. After all, he knows much more about this world now than we do," Ezmir told him. Wrenn sighed.

"I suppose," he said. Removing himself from the discussion, he lay down in the sand next to one of the houses. He curled his spiked tail around himself and closed his dark green eyes for a while.

Kamkha handed the necklace back to Mint.

"Do you think we could communicate with the elders of your town? They may have heard something about our enemy that you have not. If they haven't all run away like the rest of the village, would you be able to lead us to one?" she asked.

The boy tilted his head in thought. "I know that there's a house a couple of minutes away that a lot of the old people live in. We can go there!" He waved with his hand for the dragons to follow him down the road.

Wrenn grumbled as he stood up but followed him anyway. Their large claws scraped the rock below as they walked down the now-empty street. They passed by many small wooden houses, but also some that had signs out front. The dragons had no written language and never learned to read in any language. Especially not that of the Karafan.

The three dragons and Mint approached a long building with a tall roof. It seemed to be the only place that people hadn't run away from. That was a good sign, at least. Mint opened the white door and frowned.

"I don't think you guys are gonna fit. Wait here while I go ask some of them if they know anything," he said. Ezmir nodded, so Mint stepped inside and began asking questions.

Kamkha and Wrenn lay on the ground in front of the building, while Ezmir paced around the block. Down the road, Ezmir noticed a small group of humans. They were small, like Mint. He tilted his head to the side, then began walking toward them. Like Mint, these children didn't run away. Instead, they stared curiously at the tall dragon in front of them. Ezmir stopped to think. Would these humans be able to understand his language? Or was Mint special in a way they weren't? There was only one way to find out.

"Hello, small humans. What are you doing still in the city? All the grown-up humans ran away in fear," he asked. The children frowned. They only heard a bunch of grunts and growling. Ezmir tried to communicate with them differently. He turned around and walked back toward Kamkha and Wrenn. He motioned with one of his claws for them to follow him. A few of them stepped forward and followed him, staring in wonder. Kamkha and Wrenn hummed in confusion as Ezmir returned.

"Why have you brought these children here? One small human was enough for me," Wrenn said, glaring at Ezmir. Kamkha shoved him.

"They're small children, you must stop worrying! We can judge them once Mint talks with the elders," she scolded. Ezmir nodded in agreement. Wrenn shook his head and sat on the road. The group of children stood in a nervous circle. None of them understood what was going on, but the dragons looked very interesting. Curiosity always wins. One especially brave kid walked up to Ezmir and petted one of his shiny gold scales. The dragon snorted in amusement. The sound startled the poor little girl and she jumped backward.

Before anyone could say anything, the door to the elders' home creaked open. Mint stepped out, followed by a frail, grey-haired man. They spoke in a language that the dragons didn't understand. When the man saw the three mighty creatures, his eyes widened, and his arms began to shake. Mint reassured him with more words from that strange language. Then, he turned to Kamkha and spoke in Crathidian.

"This man says that he remembers when the Karafan brought his family here! He was very young, but he says he was there when the village was built, and when the wizards left. He might even know where they're hiding," he explained. Kamkha, Ezmir, and Wrenn all stared at the man in amazement.

"Ask him if he can show us their hideout. This is our chance for revenge!" Wrenn shouted.

"I get that you want revenge, but don't you at least want to find out what happened at the end of the war? Why they did this and what the future holds?" Ezmir asked.

"I suppose we can do it your way, but I will avenge our species," Wrenn declared. Kamkha rolled her eyes, then turned back to Mint.

"Could you ask this kind elder if he would be able to lead us to the Karafan?" she asked. Mint spoke to him. The man frowned, then nodded slowly. Excitement bubbled up in Kamkha. They would finally be able to learn about what happened after the war. Some closure, finally. Maybe some bloodshed too. Only time would tell.

"He says to follow him. We're lucky that he's still able to walk. Who knows what would have happened if he wasn't as healthy! Let's get going, it's a pretty long walk." Mint told them.

"Wait, we need to do something about these other children that Ezmir brought over. Can you talk to them and tell them to stay here?" Kamkha asked. Mint nodded and wandered over to the group of kids behind Ezmir. He explained the situation to them. Their faces all fell as they realized they couldn't follow the dragons.

Kamkha wished she could understand the human language. She and Ezmir wanted to tell them that they would return, but Mint had already begun following the elder. Ezmir waved goodbye to the children before he trailed behind the other two dragons. The five kids wandered back into their homes and waited for the rest of the townspeople to return.

As soon as the two humans and three dragons left the village, a strong gust of wind stirred up all the sand around them. At first, the party brushed it off and continued walking. Then, the wind blew harder and didn't stop. The gusts of wind turned into a sandstorm. Wrenn shielded their guide with his tough wings and Kamkha protected Mint with hers. Ezmir tried to use his magic to direct the storm away from them, but it failed. Something was blocking his spell. He growled and covered himself with his wings, mirroring the other two dragons.

"We need to get out of this! There's a mountain not too far away. If we stay in a group, we might be able to make it behind the side of it," Ezmir yelled over the whistling wind.

"On three, we start walking straight forward and don't stop until we're under shelter! Ready? One, two, three!" Wrenn called out. When he said three, the group of them took quick but careful steps forward. This carried on for several minutes. The sandstorm never even slowed down. Finally, Wrenn cheered in victory as the sand stopped bombarding his back and sides. Kamkha shook the dust off out of her scales and wings. Mint and the elder sighed in relief.

"Well, that was unfortunate. We must wait for the storm to end before we can continue. In the meantime, would you be willing to ask our guide some more questions, Mint?" Ezmir said, looking at the boy.

"Well, I did learn his name before we got ambushed by the storm. He calls himself Jann. Is there anything specific that you want to know?"

"Yes, did he know about the war between the Karafan and the dragons? Also, why did he decide to help us?"

Mint smiled and shuffled over to the man. In the weird human language, the two of them spoke quietly for a few minutes. Ezmir watched them, then turned to Kamkha and Wrenn. The two of them were lying on the ground, grumbling. Ezmir laughed softly. Then, Mint came up to him and tapped one of his legs.

"Hi, Mister Ezmir. So, Jann says that he only heard stories about the war from his parents. Our old kingdom was very far away from the dragon kingdom, so neither of you knew the other species existed. The wizards came and destroyed your kingdom, then brought the humans to expand theirs. They've been here ever since. Also, he said that he wasn't sure why he decided to help you. Maybe he felt guilty that you guys lost your home and your friends. I'm not sure. Anyway, I hope that helps!" he said.

Ezmir smiled sadly. "Thank you, young one. I'm happy that we finally have some answers. For now, though, we still have to wait for this sandstorm to pass." Mint nodded and sat down on a large rock nearby.

For many minutes, the group of them waited as the wind howled and the sand pelted the side of the mountain. Wrenn had dozed off and was snoring loudly. Kamkha rolled her eyes. Luckily, the storm slowed to a stop soon enough, and Ezmir smacked the side of Wrenn's face to wake him up. He snorted and jumped up onto his feet. Ezmir chuckled while Wrenn glared at him.

"It's time to head back out, snoring beauty! Let's get a move on," Kamkha announced. Wrenn growled at her, then sighed and waited for Jann to lead the way again.

"Mint, while we walk, I'd like to test a theory of mine. Would that be ok?" Kamkha asked the boy. He nodded.

"Ok, good. Could you give the amulet to Jann for a moment?" Mint tilted his head in confusion.

"I can get it back after, right?" he asked. Kamkha nodded, so Mint tapped Jann's shoulder and handed him the amulet. He took it carefully with a confused expression.

"Jann, are you able to understand what I'm saying?"

The man's eyes widened.

"Yes. How is this possible? What sort of power does this amulet hold?"

"It belonged to our commander, Almanzar. I didn't think it held such power, but we've never talked to humans before. It adapted to help us."

"Incredible! If it has this sort of magic, do you believe it could help us get to the top of this mountain?"

Mint frowned.

"But you guys are dragons, can't you fly up?" he asked.

Kamkha laughed and shook her head.

"Most dragons can fly, yes, but we are desert dragons. We live underground. We have wings, but they aren't strong enough to carry us if we try to fly because we don't use them."

Ezmir coughed. Well, as much as a dragon could cough. It was more like a choked growl with a snort mixed in somewhere.

"Isn't anyone wondering why Mint can understand what we're saying even though he doesn't have the amulet?" he asked, looking at the others.

Wrenn, who was walking at the front of the group, whipped his head around.

"Wizard magic! It must be! I told you we shouldn't have trusted him," he growled, blocking the path up to the top of the mountain. His eyes glowed a deep purple.

"What's the matter with you? I know you're angry, but all this boy has done is help us! You should be careful, yes, but this is a child! They are good and kind, they don't want to hurt us" Kamkha answered, angry.

"You're wrong! Everyone lies, even the small ones. I can't trust any of you, I have to finish this quest on my own!" Wrenn slashed the air with his claws, trying to cast a spell on the others. Purple sparks sizzled in the air, then faded. The yellow amulet around Jann's neck glowed. Ezmir's eyes lit up in understanding.

"Wrenn, enough of this! The amulet is the key to it all. It's stronger than we thought, it showed me a vision. Our quest is pointless."

"No! Revenge is the only answer and I won't let you take that from me!"

"You can't have your revenge. The wizards have all disappeared for good. Their species is gone, just like ours. All these traps were left here a long time ago. They caused the sandstorm and your anger, but these curses have been here for years."

Wrenn shook his head as if he was trying to get something out of his mind. The amulet glowed again. When he looked back up at Ezmir, his eyes had returned to their natural brown.

"I see that now. But it also showed me that the boy is related to them. I wasn't wrong about that, he is magical."

"Can't you see that he has a good heart, though? That we can trust him?"

"I-I think so. But if this journey is pointless, what do we do now? We're the only ones left," Wrenn said sadly.

"I mean, if we get down off this mountain, we could build a place for you all to live near the village! I'm sure those other kids would love that!" Mint suggested.

Kamkha smiled.

"That's right. It was our final quest, finding all the answers. Our friends passed so that we could live in a new world, and that is what we will do. All we can do now is live."

THE FORBIDDEN FEAST

KARIN OSTERBERG

Paola ran her fingers across the rough flesh of the dragon's wings. It felt like the paper Mama Misha had taught her to make by drying reed grass with cotton fiber. The wind hummed beneath the dragon's wings, lifting them higher. The girl squeezed her legs tight around the dragon's back as they flew. The wind blew through her hair like water flowing through a river.

"Wooo-ooo!" Paola howled, throwing her head back.

The dragon roared too, a deep rumbling bellow. The beast dove straight through a cloud full of rain. They burst through the other side and water dripped off the ends of Paola's curly hair.

"Sassa!" Paola cried. "I'm soaking wet!"

The girl shook droplets off like a wet dog. Then Paola saw the sun nearing the horizon and got a worried look on her face.

"We had better head back to the village. Father will not be happy if we are late for the ceremony."

The word Father was closer to Owner in her village. Paola was chosen at birth to be the Daughter of the Dragon Master. That day, Father had swaddled Paola in dragon leather and taken her to the dragon's cave. Lucky for Paola, she had been a curious and quiet babe. If she had made so much as a squawk, the dragon would have likely eaten her. However, the dragon didn't eat her. That moment on Sassa, the village dragon, became her mother. Paola was the Dragon Girl, destined to tame the beast and serve Corath village.

Though Paola knew it was a great honor to serve the village, she felt unrest growing inside her. The world around Corath felt small and she longed to see more. As the years passed, Paola began to realize she and Sassa would never be free.

Sassa and Paola flew over the lush forests, past Corath village, to the Circle of Warriors. It was a great henge with seventy stone pillars rising forty feet into the air. It was by the strength of the dragons that such enormous stones were placed. Each stone pillar represented a fallen warrior killed in the Last Dragon Battle. The story of their sacrifice in defeating the old, wild dragons was retold at every Solstice. The Circle of Warriors was a reminder of humanity's rightful victory over the dragons.

Paola saw things differently. She yearned for a time when dragons flew free. Truth be told, she hated these stories. Paola thought their dark jagged cracks looked like monstrous faces. As she and her dragon neared, Paola saw Father waiting in the center of the Henge.

"He looks mad," Paola whispered to Sassa.

The dragon snorted.

They landed in front of the Dragon Master. He grabbed the dragon by the chain around her neck and tied her to a pillar. The rope was so short that Sassa could barely lift her head off the ground. However, the dragon did not struggle. The old dragon had served the villagers of Corath for over two hundred years and knew no other life.

Paola slid from the dragon's back and bowed low. The sarsen stones loomed over her like evil ogres.

"Paola, you are late," Father reprimanded. Paola feared him, not that he had ever been cruel, but because he had never shown weakness. The Dragon Master was tall and strong. He wore a burnt red cloak with a hood of black feathers. To Paola, Father looked like a smoldering fire raven.

"I'm sorry, Father," she replied.

"Never mind, Paola, the ceremony is about to begin. Go and kneel on the altar. The sun is almost in position," he ordered.

Paola did as she was told. The other villagers gathered around. The sun began to set. An otherworldly light shone through the sarsen stones. First orange, then pink, settling into a final deep purple-red. There was a pinhole in the sarsen stone nearest the dragon. As the Solstice sun set, its light condensed into a single ray. A beam shot out from the stone and onto the golden lock on the chain around the dragon's neck.

In the lock's center was a large ruby-colored stone. It glowed as it soaked up the magic of the Solstice light. This ancient magic of the Solstice bound to servitude for over two centuries. At least, for the dragons who survived the Fall of the Dragons had been.

Paola snuck a glance at her dragon mother. The light shimmered off the dragon's scales like the ripples of a lake. She looked at the villagers gaping at the spectacle.

"I am more dragon than human," Paola thought.

The ritual songs were sung well into the night and another Solstice was ushered in. A full moon rose high in the sky. Finally, Paola and Sassa were allowed to return to their stone cave just outside Corath. Sassa and Paola were not allowed to live inside the village, but Paola didn't mind. She preferred the wilderness to the company of people.

From the outside, the cave looked much like the burial mounds that surrounded it. The stones were now covered with grass and peppered with blue and white flowers.

When they landed, Paola saw Mama Misha waiting outside. Paola suspected the old woman had magic. She was always showing up.

"How did you beat us here, Mama Misha?" Paola asked, sliding off the dragon's back.

"I took a shortcut," Mama Misha replied with a mischievous grin. "Well now, would you like to hear a story or not?"

"Of course!" Paola exclaimed. The girl built a small fire to keep them warm, as the old woman spoke.

"Long ago the land was ruled by the beast with the leather skin. Dragons, as you know, were the sworn enemy of man.

Many brave battles were fought. Those warriors are the ones told of in our songs of old. Our ancestors had a single great weapon that alone could have defeated the dragons."

"A sword?" Paola asked.

"No, it was sharper than the sword and stronger than the stone," Mama Misha replied.

"What was it?"

"It was the Book of Dragons," Mama Misha said with an ominous tone.

"How can a book be stronger than both the sword and stone?" Paola asked.

"Oh, child, words have always held a secret power. This book was filled with all the secret magic of the Dragons. The spells within it had the power to heal, to control the weather. It also had the darkest magic of all, a spell to grant immortality."

Paola's eyes went wide.

Mama Misha continued, "Immortality is very dark magic indeed. One must prepare a Forbidden Feast of dragon heart. Only in consuming the heart can the magic of the beast be transferred to another. Yes, it was dark magic, for a dark time. Any person who partook in the Forbidden Feast paid a terrible price. Paola, dark magic is like black tar. It sticks to the soul of the one who uses it and poisons them. All that is left to live for all eternity is a demon with red glowing eyes."

Paola shivered. She had never been afraid of the dark before, but now she thought she saw demon shadows lurking in the woods.

Mama Misha saw that the girl was frightened. "Yes, it is right to be afraid of dark magic and evil deeds, but that is not what I have come here to tell you. In this book, there is also a spell to End the Dragons."

"How terrible!" Paola cried out.

Mama Misha shushed her and explained, "It was never used. Our ancestors and the dragons of old made a truce after the Last Dragon Battle was won. It was decided that the remaining dragons would serve each clan, until the end of their days. The book would be hidden away until the time came when it was needed."

Paola breathed a sigh of relief. All this talk of magic, demons, and the end of dragons made her feel uneasy. Sassa must have noticed because the dragon curled up behind Paola.

"I have said too much," the old woman said, shaking her head, "Let us see what the Spirits tell us, hm?" Mama Misha took out a small leather pouch and shook out the contents onto the ground. Sun-bleached bones tumbled out into a pattern. Mama Misha frowned when she read them.

"I fear for you, Paola," the old woman said after a long silence. "The Spirits tell of a great change coming. They speak of a child, marked by the dragon, bringing about this great change on her eleventh year."

"Do you think they are talking about me?" Paola asked.

The old woman didn't answer. She gathered up the bones in her leather pouch and wrapped her shawl around her shoulders. With great effort, she climbed to her feet.

"What will be, will be. Now hold out your hand," Mama Misha said. Into Paola's palm the old woman placed a tiny jade stone with a hole drilled in the top. "Happy Birthday, Paola," Mama Misha said with a sad smile before walking away.

Paola watched Mama Misha disappear into the darkness toward the village. Then she took the jade stone and strung it on the necklace she wore around her neck. Her eleventh birthday bead.

★★★

A woman named Veldis, clad in dark armor, walked slowly up to a dragon that lay bound with rope on its side. With each step, the woman's metal armor clanked. On her waist hung the talons of nine dragons that she wore like trophies.

Veldis leaned over the dragon and smiled.

"Just one more after this and I'll be immortal," she said, running her iron gloved hand over the beast's throat. The dragon cried out in fear.

Nearby stood an old man shackled in chains.

"Prepare the heart for my feast, Bacchus," Veldis ordered.

The man looked weary, but the scars on his arms and face were a testament to his broken spirit. The old Dragon Master did not argue or resist. He set down the torn yellow pages, drew his knife and made a large circle in the dirt, chanting in a low mournful voice. The air stirred and dust billowed around them. The other men took a step back, frightened by the dark magic. Veldis stood in the center of the circle and stretched out her hands. The Dragon Master stabbed the dragon and removed the still-beating heart for the Forbidden Feast.

The villain Veldis held the heart in her hands and took a bite. Suddenly, a dark cloak of smoke engulfed her. Her eyes flashed red in the moonlight and from her erupted a terrible and sinister laugh.

***

Paola awoke in a cold sweat. She ran to the door, half expecting someone or something to be waiting for her, but there was no one. The girl leaned against the cold stone of the cave with her hand over her heart. Paola had dreamt of dragons being slain by horrific stone ogres. The nightmare had been so real, that when Paola awoke, she swore she could still hear the cry of the dragons. As Paola stood in the doorway, she felt her dragon mother nudge her back.

"I don't know, Sassa. It must have been a nightmare," Paola said, her brow furrowed. "Well, there's no use trying to sleep now. The sun will be up soon. What do you say we have some breakfast?"

Paola went to the offering chest near the dragon cave. The girl pulled out three dead ferrets and tossed them to Sassa. The hungry dragon ate them each in two bites. Paola cut a piece of bread crust and grabbed an apple for herself. Despite the restless night, Paola couldn't help but hum to herself. She had been looking forward to today all year. The day after her birthday was the only day Paola was free to do as she liked. A day free from village obligations. It was the only day all year where she got to taste what freedom must be like.

"Let's go to the waterfall," Paola said, munching her apple.

The dragon huffed and rolled sleepily onto her side. Though Paola rarely thought about it, Sassa was an ancient dragon. There were scars along the dragon's belly from the Last Dragon Battle over two hundred years ago.

"Okay, okay, we'll have a lazy morning first," Paola laughed. She grabbed the stick she had been carving and climbed to the top of the cave. Paola found a soft spot of dewy grass and plopped down. Then she pulled out the small but sharp knife that she kept hidden inside her boot and began to whittle. This particular white cedar stick would be a wand. She was carving a long curling dragon into the handle.

Paola had heard of wands from the old stories Mama Misha told her. It was a magic forgotten long ago. Still, the idea of holding magic in your hand fascinated Paola. It had taken her three months to carve this wand and she was almost finished. All she had left to carve was the dragon's tail.

As Paola sat whittling, the sunrise painted the sky blood-red. Paola thought again of Mama Misha's words and the demon with red eyes. She glanced back at Sassa. The dragon yawned at her and slowly rose to her feet.

"Ready then?" Paola asked, stowing her knife in her boot.

Paola stood tall and stretched her arms to the sky. With the loudest howl she could muster, Paola leapt from the top of the stone mound onto the dragon's back. Then the dragon took to the sky. They flew over forests of dew-covered leaves that sparkled in the sunlight. Paola took a deep breath, filling her lungs with cool morning air.

After they had flown thirty miles, the dragon dove below the canopy of trees and into a hidden tunnel. The cave was no more than a mile long, but the cool damp air within felt like another world. Water dripped from the ceiling onto Paola's head. Sassa weaved through the stalagmites and stalactites. Once they came out on the other side, they were greeted by a lush green waterfall oasis.

"Hold steady, Sassa," Paola said, climbing to her feet. She stood balancing on the dragon's back. Then, with her arms stretched above her head, she dove into the clear and cold water below. Underwater, Paola imagined she was a merperson who could cut through the water with fins. She resurfaced, laughing. Sassa circled her twice. The dragon used the tip of her wing to splash Paola.

"That's not fair!" Paola cried, trying to splash water up at the dragon, "Flying is definitely against the rules!"

Sassa grunted and landed on a large rock under the ribboning waterfall. Paola swam to meet her. The dragon spread her majestic wings wide, letting the water flow over them. Paola swam under the dragon's wings to the secret cave beyond. The cave was hidden and unspoiled. Quartz crystals shimmered on the walls and cast tiny stars onto Paola's brown skin. The girl looked around the cave and smiled. It was here that Paola felt safe to dream about things she knew would never come true. She dreamt about all the adventures she would have. There were incredible places she would find exploring the great wide world.

The first time Paola saw this cave, she wondered what other magical places remained hidden in the world. How she longed to search for them! Paola knew she would never have the chance. Her life was bound to serve Corath village. Paola knew she would never be allowed to leave, but tried not to think about it.

"Someday, Sassa. Someday, we'll find the other hidden places of the world," Paola said dreamily.

The dragon snorted and laid upon the cool cave floor.

Paola's stomach rumbled.

"Time for lunch," she said eagerly, jumping up.

The dragon, once again, used her wings like an umbrella and Paola dove back to the oasis pool. The girl swam to the shore, broke off a nearby branch, and used her knife to sharpen it into a point.

Crouching low and quiet by the water, Paola waited. Suddenly, as if shot from a bow, Paola plunged the spear into the water. When she pulled it back, there was a wriggling fish skewered on the end. Paola took the fish and killed it with a rock. She then speared two more fish until, at last, she had three little fish sitting next to her, ready to eat.

Since Paola was raised by a dragon, she felt no need to gut nor cook the fish before eating it. Paola simply brushed off the grass and dirt before sinking her teeth into the fish's raw flesh. Paola ate the sweet meat all the way to the bone, saving her favorite part for last—the fish eyes. Paola sucked them from the fish heads, savoring each salty morsel. What little remained of the fish, Paola tossed to Sassa. The dragon gobbled up the fish guts eagerly. The dragon had already used her long talons to catch and eat six more fish whole.

The girl and dragon spent the entire day by the clear waters. As the evening rolled in, so did dark and ominous storm clouds. The dragon chuffed at the sky.

"You're right, Sassa. We better head back," Paola said.

The storm only grew taller and darker as they flew. Soon, they faced a towering nimbus wall, angry with lightning and windy rains. Paola held on tightly as they flew into the storm. The thunder was so loud it made Paola's teeth chatter and she feared she'd vibrate off the dragon's back.

"Fly higher!" Paola shouted to Sassa over the storm, "Maybe we can get over the worst of it!"

Sassa obeyed, climbing higher and higher into the swirling black clouds. Rain pelted Paola's face. The drops turned to hail that felt like pebbles falling from the sky. Paola's skin was freckled with tiny red welts as she held on for dear life. Paola couldn't remember ever flying into such a dangerous storm.

Lightning flashed all around them. Suddenly, a bright streak reached across the sky, like electric fingers reaching out. CRACK! There was a sharp thunderclap and Paola felt her hair stand on end. She lost her grip and tumbled from the dragon's back and began plummeting to the earth at an incredible speed.

"SASSA!" Paola screamed.

***

"Well?" Veldis said impatiently, "Where is the next dragon?" Veldis had her ironclad arms crossed over her chest. Ten dragon talons now hung from her belt and a cape of black smoke curled and waved around her. She looked less and less human as the days passed. The whites of her eyes had turned black and her pupils elongated like a snake's. Her fingers were now jagged claws. Even her skin had a strange grey roughness to it.

Bacchus, the old Dragon Master, trembled with fear when Veldis looked at him. He held out the Finder's Stones. They glowed faintly in the moonlight as he walked in a circle chanting. Suddenly, the stones glowed like stars in the old man's palm. He pointed his long, crooked finger North, toward Corath village.

"We ride through the night! There will be no rest until we find the dragon!" Veldis cried, raising her sword. Her eyes flashed red.

★★★

Paola somersaulted through the air, falling faster and faster to the ground. She squeezed her eyes shut just before impact. But to her surprise, she was lifted back into the sky. Sassa had saved her.

"I knew you would catch me!" Paola laughed, kissing the dragon's back. But the dragon's flight was erratic. The two of them barely made it back to the dragon cave before Sassa collapsed onto her side.

"What is it, Sassa?" Paola asked. Then she saw the scorch marks on the dragon's wing.

"Stay here, I'll be right back," the girl said, running into the forest. Paola gathered fern spores and lemon balm, crushing them in her palm. She applied the mixture to the dragon's wing.

"That will have to do. Perhaps Mama Misha can do more for it tomorrow," Paola said stroking Sassa's head. "Now let's go to bed. I've had enough excitement for today."

In the middle of the night, Paola awoke. Her heart raced. The nightmare had been worse than the night before. In it, she had seen the red eyes of a demon approaching from the woods. They were followed by wolves of fire and smoke, who devoured every home and person in the village. Now that she was awake, Paola could not shake the feeling that something was coming. Something dark and sinister. Sassa felt it, too. The dragon was pacing back and forth outside the cave. Her golden eyes mirrored the moonlight.

"Do you think you can fly?" Paola asked. The dragon nodded and bowed low for Paola to climb onto her back. "Come on, Sassa, let's have a look around," Paola said.

The moon was still quite full and, as they flew above the treeline, Paola saw smoke curling up from the South.

"There!" Paola yelled, pointing toward the smoke.

The dragon dove low, her wings brushing the forest canopy. Paola saw men with torches that slashed and burned their way through the underbrush. There was a woman yelling orders at them. Paola saw the woman's red glowing eyes and gave out a cry.

Veldis looked up. She saw Paola and Sassa's silhouette against the moon and pointed savagely.

"Bring me that dragon!" Veldis screamed.

Out of nowhere, a rope attached to two large stones catapulted into the sky. It wrapped around Sassa's tail, sending the girl and dragon falling to earth, like rocks in a pond. Paola screamed. The dragon wrapped her wings around the girl and used her body to cradle her from the impact. They landed with a thud on the wet muddy ground, one hundred feet from Veldis.

Paola heard the woman's clamoring steps approaching. The heavy clank of Veldis's armor seemed to make even the forest cower.

"I expected my final dragon to be more of a challenge. It seems you aren't much of a dragon protector, little girl," Veldis sneered.

Sassa snarled and Paola trembled with fear.

"Secure the beast down! And bring me Bacchus!" Veldis ordered the nearby men. Long ropes flew over Sassa and were staked into the ground on either side of the dragon with large iron rods.

"Bacchus, prepare the final Forbidden Feast! On this night I shall be immortal! With the power of the dragons in my blood, all the world will bow at my feet!"

"No! You can't!" Paola cried, throwing herself between the Dragon Master and her dragon. Veldis stepped toward the girl and slapped her hard across the face, sending her flying to the ground. Paola tasted blood on her lips.

"Nothing will stop me! Certainly, not a child," Veldis said, "Tie up the girl."

Paola's arms and legs were bound together with rope. The large men tossed her aside, like a bag of rubbish. Paola felt utterly helpless as she heard the old Dragon Master begin to chant the dark spell. She fell in a heap to the ground, wishing she would melt right into it. Suddenly, Paola remembered the knife hidden in her boot. Mama Misha had given it to her on her sixth birthday.

"A girl needs a knife," Mama Misha had said, "Now this will be our little secret. Never leave without it, and Paola, keep it hidden."

The men charged with keeping watch on the girl were too preoccupied with the dragon. Paola twisted her hand left, right, then around and around until it slipped free from the knot. She retrieved the knife from her boot. Then, as quiet as a mouse, Paola crawled toward the dragon's bound tail. Carefully, she cut through the thick rope. The first loop broke free, then she cut another and another until the rope and stones lay useless on the ground. Paola crawled around the backside of the dragon and sliced through the ropes.

Paola peeked over the dragon's neck. In the firelight, she saw that the old Dragon Master, Bacchus, had his knife raised above Sassa's chest.

"Wooo-ooo!" Paola howled with all her might, jumping onto the dragon's back.

The dragon reared up onto her back legs, raising her wings high. She roared so loudly that the old man Bacchus fell backward, dropping his knife. Sassa flew into the air carrying Paola away.

"Faster Sassa! We have to warn the others!" Paola cried, urging Sassa to fly higher, but the dragon was clearly in pain. The fall had left the dragon battered and the wound on her wing was much worse.

When they came to Corath village, Sassa skidded onto her belly as they landed, kicking up dirt in her wake. Paola leapt from the dragon and cried out, "Father! Mama Misha! Come quickly!"

Soon they were both outside trying to understand what Paola was saying.

"The demon! The demon is coming to Corath! We have to do something!"

"Slow down, child, what demon?" Mama Misha asked.

"The demon with red eyes is coming! It is just as you warned, Mama Misha! This woman, Veldis, has tasted the Forbidden Feast!" Paola exclaimed.

Mama Misha put her hand over her open mouth. "So it is as the Spirits have foretold," the old woman said to the Dragon Master. Paola looked to Father for guidance.

"We will evacuate the village," Father said. "We can hide in the forests for as long as we have to. Paola, blow the horn."

The girl nodded and ran to the huge bell-shaped trumpet by the watchtower. Ever since Paola was little, she had wanted to blow on that great instrument. Now, when there was a need to sound the alarm, she felt overwhelmed. Her breath was shallow and fast. She felt as though a constrictor had wrapped around her chest. She couldn't breathe. She looked to Mama Misha for help, but the girl saw the old woman was busy tending Sassa's wounds.

They are all counting on me, Paola thought. *I may be afraid, but I will not fail them.*

Paola took a deep breath and blew into the great copper horn with all her might. The long clear note rang out over the land. Soon, all Corath was awake and the villagers were fleeing to the North Woods.

The Dragon Master stood beside Paola. In silence, they watched as the smoke drew ever nearer from the South. An eerie quiet descended. The village was empty now. The Dragon Master turned to Paola.

"You are the protector of this village, Paola. Do you understand?" he said with a softness in his tone that Paola hadn't heard before.

"Yes, Father, I understand," Paola replied, her voice trembling. She knew she must be brave for the sake of the village, but she was afraid. After seeing the wickedness in Veldis, Paola wondered how she would find the courage to face it again.

"Misha, it is time. Give Paola the book," the Dragon Master said to the old woman.

Mama Misha stepped forward, carrying a large and very ancient book in her arms. The old woman pulled Paola close and whispered in the girl's ear, "Paola, ignore your Father. You should go to safety with the others." Mama Misha's voice sounded like wind blowing through dry leaves.

Paola shook her head, "No, Mama Misha. If Sassa stays, then so do I."

Mama Misha looked like she wanted to say more. Instead, she nodded solemnly and handed Paola the ancient book.

Paola took the book. It was bound with dragon leather that felt like the bark of a tree. The pages within were yellow with time. She flipped through the book and saw some pages had been torn out. *The immortality spell*, Poala thought. She remembered the yellow pages Bacchus had clutched in his hands.

"Take the Book of Dragons, my child. It will show you what you must do," Mama Misha said.

Paola gazed at the yellow pages of the book. "But there are so many. How do I know which spell to use?" the girl asked.

"You are the Dragon Girl. You have a power in your veins, Paola. Let the Spirits guide you and you will do what is needed to protect the world," Mama Misha replied. She ran her hand on Paola's cheek. For the first time, Paola felt the soft touch of another person. The old woman's hand reminded her of the dragon's wings, delicate but strong. It made her heart feel full and gave her courage.

Mama Misha wiped a tear from her own wet eyes and turned toward the forest to join Father and the others. Paola wanted to run after her, to thank her for all her kindness, but that was not the way of her people. So, instead, Paola sat on the dirt and examined the book in her hands. The spells were ancient and full of symbols that Paola didn't understand.

"How will this help us?" Paola asked Sassa.

The dragon didn't answer. She was weak and lying on her side taking labored breaths. Soon Paola felt the ground beneath her vibrate. The dark one was coming. Paola put her hand on Sassa's side. How she wished she could climb onto Sassa and fly far from this place. Paola looked at the scorch marks on the dragon's wing and sighed. Sassa's injuries were bad and the flight home had left the dragon weak.

"At least the villagers are safe," Paola said. "I have fulfilled my duty to Corath."

The dragon nudged at Paola, urging her toward the forest with the other villagers.

"No, Sassa. I'm am staying here with you," Paola answered.

The dragon nudged again, but it was too late. From the woods shot a net woven from the spiny black locus. It wrapped Sassa in a blanket of sharp thorns.

"Sassa!" Paola cried.

Then a familiar clank, clank, clank came to Paola's ears.

The dragon snarled at Veldis who now walked toward them through a cloud of black smoke.

"So, we meet again, Dragon Girl," Veldis hissed. Her face looked like a cracked stone, jagged and hard. "And here you are, all alone, with only a broken dragon to protect you. How quaint."

Paola tried to run, but Veldis grabbed her by the arm. Paola scratched at the woman's iron grip. She threw Paola to her bloodthirsty men and the Book of Dragons tumbled to the ground.

"What's this?" Veldis said picking up the book. "The fabled Book of Dragons? And here I was made to believe that three little pages were all that remained of it." She shot Bacchus a look so full of venom it could have killed a bull. "Don't worry, little girl," Veldis said with a hideous sweetness. "I will take good care of your book. Just after I'm done taking care of your dragon." She laughed. "Men! I want you to keep a knife at the girl's throat. If she so much as moves, kill her." Her henchmen were all too eager to follow her orders. The knife was held so close to Paola's throat, that the girl scarcely dared to breathe.

Sassa the dragon began to tear at her bonds. Paola had never seen the dragon so agitated.

"Tell your dragon to be still or I will make her suffer before I kill you!" Veldis ordered.

"Sassa! Please!" Paola cried. "I'm sorry. I'm so very sorry, Dragon Mother."

After the words 'Dragon Mother' left Paola's mouth, Sassa lay very still. The dragon moaned in a way that only a mother scared for her child can. Then the dragon roared with such heartbreak, it sounded like a prayer. The Book of Dragons began to glow. The pages of the book blew open, as if by a phantom hand, to the last spell, Finis Dracon. The dragon, Sassa, raised her head high to the moon and sang in a voice that Paola didn't recognize. Sassa's eyes glowed golden and powerful in the moonlight. There was a flash and the thorny net that held the dragon burned up like leaves in the fire. The thorns fell to the ground, like ash, at the dragon's feet. Sassa spread her wings wide.

"No, Sassa! Please, save yourself!" Paola cried out. Somehow the girl knew the spell Sassa was preparing for was the End of Dragons, but there was nothing she could do. The dragon's roar rose and fell like an ancient song of magic and so did the tears down Paola's cheeks.

"What is happening?!" Veldis screamed at Paola.

Ash swirled around the dragon, like a dust storm. The dust transformed into beautiful leaves of every color of the rainbow. The leaves danced around the dragon until the colors mingled into a brilliant white. Paola felt an overwhelming feeling of love wash over her as the dragon Sassa, her dragon mother, sang. Then there was an explosion of light. The circle of light emanated from the dragon and rippled out like a wave over the hills and valleys, all the way to the ends of the Earth. The spell Finis Dracon was complete. And, at that moment, all those who had tasted dragon blood were bound to the spell.

Sassa spread her magnificent blue and green wings wide and gave one last roar. All the dragons of the world joined in. Paola closed her eyes and felt the rhythm of the song travel on the swift wind through all the hidden places of the world. It was the Dragons' Final Song, a parting gift to a world in which they had long-lived. The notes sang of days long past when magical creatures roamed freely across a thousand seas of time.

Paola looked on in wonder as Sassa's talons dug deep into the earth, stretching ever longer. As her talons grew, they changed into the deep roots of a tree. The dragon's scales became smooth white bark. A tree was growing, taller and more beautiful than anything Paola had ever seen.

A cry came from Veldis as she scratched at the spiny black scales now covering her skin.

"What have you done to me?!" Veldis screamed at Paola who now stood alone, the men holding her having already fled.

Paula's eyes were fierce and her voice clear and brave. "You have brought this end upon yourself," she said. "You have bound your fate to the dragons. Now you will have what you have always desired, a life that extends beyond the ages."

Veldis screamed and stumbled into the woods, tearing at the long thorny brambles that shot from her fingers and toes. The vines dug deep into the ground, and Veldis's body became a twisted black tree. Her arms would forever stretch toward the sky. Her wicked men ran for the hills from whence they came. They saw that the Dragon Girl was more powerful than Veldis ever was.

Then all was still. A peaceful, quiet, blanketed world. It was a sad and sacred calm. The world was now without dragons. Paola ran to the tree that now stood in place of her beloved Sassa and threw her arms around it. She ran her fingers over the smooth bark of the white pine towering above her and cried.

Even in her mourning, Paola could feel the dragon's love. Sassa had saved her life and given her the freedom she had always yearned for. Paola knew that it was just as Mama Misha had always told her.

"What will be, will be," Paola whispered, drying her eyes. Dragons were now the watchers and protectors of the forests and the wild places of the world. Wherever Paola went, they would be, also.

The villagers returned and Paola was heralded as the Great Hero of Corath. Mama Misha broke through the crowd that surrounded Paola and wrapped her in a tight embrace.

"You are the child with the dragon mark. Our beautiful Paola. May you be forever free from this moment on," Mama Misha said.

Father, the Dragon Master, nodded and bowed low before Paola. Soon the other villagers bowed too. Paola alone stood tall above them and was filled with such a feeling of pride, she felt she might burst. She was the Dragon Girl.

★★★

The next day Paola left Corath village to begin a new chapter in her life. She would search out the Dragon Trees in the wild places of the world. She wanted to tell the tale of the End of Dragons to all she met along the way.

But first, Paola climbed the branches of her dragon mother, one last time. She climbed higher and higher until she was one hundred feet above Corath. When Paola reached the highest branch a gust of wind blew up the trunk and danced through her wild hair. Paola closed her eyes and felt as though she were flying on Sassa again.

"Goodbye Mother," Paola whispered to the wood.

Then something caught her eye. A ruby red stone sparkled in the sunlight. On a nearby branch hung a necklace made of braided branches. The necklace curled around the very ruby-colored stone that had once held the dragon's chains. Paola smiled when she ran her fingers over the stone and put the necklace around her neck. Sassa would never be chained again. The dragon was free at last. Paola climbed down and the stone shone brightly on her chest. With Sassa's spirit within her, Paola left the village and did not look back.

The Noblest Dragon

Rebecca Coyte

In my ninth winter, I met my first, and I fear my last, dragon. My father and the other men were off pursuing a herd of elk, and they had been gone for several days. When they returned, the village had plenty of meat to feed our swollen bellies for days. The women began to salt and dry what they could. The aroma of cured meat of the smokehouses filled my nostrils. The stew bubbled in several large pots placed over open cooking fires. Peppercorns, berries, and taters were added to the mix. We all had our fill that evening.

Once we had all feasted to our heart's content, the hunters gathered around the big fire. They began to tell tales of their escapades. Father, the leader of our village, described the chase in great detail. He jumped about and acted out every moment of the hunt. They had been following the herd for days. When they finally reached the creatures, it took three men to take down a large bull. I was entranced with the story and dizzy with food and smoke. I envisioned myself one day joining in on the hunt with the men.

Next, Callan, one of the wisest and bravest of men, stood and began to tell of the abandoned fishing village they found. There, they encountered the still-smoldering ruins of several thatched huts. The cooking fires had long been extinguished, yet the food still sat idle and uneaten within the pots. It looked as if the village had been deserted quickly. The people had left without a chance to take their prized belongings. Many men believed it to be a cursed place and would go no further, choosing to head back from whence they came.

Our people are very superstitious and believe in evil spirits. We believe that the dead should be left alone and not disturbed. Still, there was no dead to be found in that village. Instead, they discovered the prized egg, the possession which would become the secret of our simple village.

In the glow of the flames, Callan then slowly to unveil his prize, freeing it from several layers of cloth. It was the largest egg I had ever seen, oblong and shiny black, with green scale-like bumps covering it. He walked around and beckoned us to touch it. It was warm and felt full of life, full of danger. The egg seemed to come alive in the firelight. At that moment I became immediately enraptured with this stroke of amazing fortune.

Unlike the others, Callan had no fear of the dead and only thought of the living and starving family back in the village. He discovered some good metal tools and jewelry, and several pieces of tanned seal skin. He thought of the wonderful, supple shoes that the women could make from them. It was then he saw the wooden crate sitting atop a cot in the middle of the hut. The box was filled with straw, and on the straw rested a single, enormous egg. Callan knew exactly what he was looking at. He had heard stories of dragon's eggs from his father, and his father's father before that. He grabbed his prize and left the hut in exhilaration.

In our village, we share everything and all are considered equal, both children and men. We are a peaceful people. Our lives are simple because we choose to live that way, away from the troubles of the mainland. We would often have too little to eat, but the ocean and the land provided for us and kept us sustained. This was a choice that my ancestors made many winters ago. We had escaped the fighting on the mainland and felt grateful for the sanctity of our lives. The egg was seen as belonging to all of us, and I became its guardian and caretaker. That egg was the most fascinating thing I'd ever beheld, and I became obsessed with its safety. Callan was more than happy to allow me the indulgence of nursing the egg. He had other work to do.

Long after the stars appeared in the sky and the children had wandered off to sleep, hushed whispers filled the huts.

Would it hatch? What would become of the dragon inside? Should we fear this creature—a creature that no member of our village had seen for hundreds of years?

"We should seek the dragon hunters' advice," mused Dónal, an elder of our village. Excited chatter followed this suggestion.

"Nay!" exclaimed his wife, Caitríona, standing up to face the others. "We shall do no such thing. The egg is ours now, and it is to be protected. If we rear it, it shall not harm us, for it will know its family."

More debate followed. This continued night after night, until it was finally decided by my father that the egg would not be harmed. We would not speak of our find to others. We were very distrustful of outsiders and this distrust had kept us safe for many years. The entirety of the village respected my father and followed his advice, for he was the wisest of our people. It was known that he could read and write in the markings of the mainland folk, and for this, he was revered.

What relief I felt to learn that the egg would not be harmed, nor the dragon within it. I knew in my deepest heart of hearts that this dragon was honorable and would never harm us. It was a strong sense that I felt inside my being. I felt this every time I held the egg. This dragon was a good dragon.

Every day, I cared for the egg. I wrapped it in blankets of furs, talked to it, rubbed its bumpy surface. I wondered about the life that was transforming within. Oftentimes, I fell asleep next to the egg, cradling it as one would cradle a small child or a beloved dog. The egg became more than an egg to me—it became a member of my family.

One day when the sun stayed in the sky long after dinner, I went to check on the egg. As I held it, I noticed a small crack in its surface. It was time! Nobody had seen a dragon for hundreds of years. Perhaps I would be the first to witness one being born, the first of many generations of man to meet a live dragon. I lay there for several hours, but there was no more movement. I fell asleep in Callan's hut, cradling the egg between my arms.

When I awoke, I realized that I was covered with several sharp fragments of thick black shell. Scanning my surroundings, I looked to the glowing hearth and saw him there. A small, beautiful, perfect creature. The dragon was black as onyx, with iridescent purple and green scales. He had a long, spine-covered tail which he had curled around him, and his wings had still not opened up. His eyes were deep and expressive, his face long and pointed. The poor creature sat staring into the fire and uttering a low chirruping sound. I ran to him and grabbed him in my arms. He stared at me with his huge marble-like eyes and croaked. The creature seemed to recognize me. He nuzzled up to me and chirruped as he rubbed his head against my chest. He began to purr a deep rumbling sound from his throat. At that moment I knew that this dragon would love me as I loved him.

The next several weeks I spent all my waking hours tending to the baby dragon. I fed him a slurry of seal fat, water, and insects, which he seemed to relish. The dragon's growth was surprising. He had tripled his birth size in only a manner of two weeks. I gave him the name of Rígán, for to me he was a little king. Gentle in manner and loving, he was unlike any dragon of lore. The village was proud of our very own dragon, and we loved him fiercely and kept him safe and secret.

He took his first steps with me by his side. I taught him to fish and hunt for small animals. When he grew strong enough, I brought him to a small ledge and encouraged him to jump, flapping his wings. As he grew stronger, we went higher and higher, until he could soar from the highest cliffs of our island. Rígán instinctively knew how to harness the gusts of wind to his advantage. He saved his energy for quick dives and climbs which he also began to master. He was the king of the sky. The village children would sit at the shore for hours on end and watch him dance through the clouds like a winged god.

Rígán continued to grow quickly, now reaching a fathom in length. His wingspan was twice that length, and he outgrew his surroundings. We set him up in a small cave near the coast. There, he could come and go as he pleased, hunt seals, and soar through the chilly salt air. To watch him fly was a miracle. He possessed such grace and nobility as he soared over our humble village. We feared that soon he would leave us. Dragons are notorious for wanderlust and curiosity. I knew I could no longer protect him. Thankfully, it was at this time that he began to produce fire, with which I hoped he would be able to protect himself.

One day, we spotted several whaling ships approaching the coast near Rígán's cave. A sense of despair filled my belly, and I immediately ran to find Rígán and warn him to stay hidden. When I arrived at his cave, he was not there. I scanned the skies. To my horror, I saw Rígán in the distance, soaring over the water. No doubt, he was curious about the ships beneath him. I wrung my hands, unsure of what to do to help my friend who had never known danger or the threat of his mortality. A hunting party from the mainland would surely want to capture such a creature as Rígán. He would fetch a fine price at the market, or even become a part of the Queen's palace menagerie. Those were the best possibilities I could envision. At worst, he would be pursued and hunted like a monster. His blood and bone and hide would be sold at auction to the highest bidder. Everyone knows that dragons' blood has magical healing properties. Bone could be powdered and used in black magic rituals. The hide could be worn by the very wealthy as a sign of dominance and power. I pondered just how I could stop Rígán from being pursued. I was just a boy and this was a problem that even my father did not have an answer for.

The sailors anchored their ships and lowered their canoes to the water. They easily rowed in the high tide toward the shore. Rígán had again disappeared. I hoped he would stay away for good. Yet, I knew he always returned home after his excursions. It was only a matter of time. Perhaps the men did not see him. The sight of a juvenile dragon soaring in the distance is certainly not one that most would miss.

Running at full speed, I went to search for my father and the other village men. I found them and told them of the approaching group of strangers. I began to cry for fear that my dear Rígán would be discovered. My father calmed me and gathered his bow and quiver before heading down to meet the party.

The strange men were now pulling their canoes onto the sand. My father and the village men were there to greet them. They exchanged pleasantries. I stood at my father's heel; my mistrust of these newcomers scrunched in my small, sun-baked face.

"Is it true that you have a dragon? We would gladly hunt him and protect your village from harm. One dragon could do terrible destruction to your homes, as they have done to many others before you." The man seemed sincere. His blue eyes twinkled with the possibility of hunting the greatest creature known to man. Surely after killing so many whales, a dragon would be a welcome prey for these men to vanquish.

My father shook his head. "Nay, no dragons here, sir. You must be mistaken." Father stood and studied the intruders, waiting for their response.

Their leader squinted and peered at my father in condescension. To him, we were heathens, simple hunters and foragers. He knew that my father was not being truthful. Still, he said no more and asked politely if my father was interested in trading goods. They had brought spices from the mainland which we did not harvest in our village. There was also the offer of good whale fat, which we could use to light our lanterns and make soap and candles. Father accepted the offer and led the men back to our village.

My heart was beating so hard, I was sure that the men could hear it and see that I held a great secret. Still, I remained silent and followed the group back to the village. There, the trading of seal skins and whale fat and spices took place. My eyes never left the sky, and I dreaded the thought of seeing my dear friend Rígán sailing overhead. Yet he did not appear. Soon, the men had filled their leather water bladders at our spring, and they headed back to their canoes. As I watched them push off back toward their ships, I breathed a huge sigh of relief. Yet it was a sigh most premature, for as they neared their ships, Rígán reappeared overhead.

There was much clamoring and chaos as the men began to paddle harder. They scampered back up to their ships. Rígán dove down closer to examine these strange humans. I saw at once that the whalers were now manning their harpoons. I mustered up all of my energy and shouted at Rígán, "Rígán! Go! Go far away! Quickly, Rígán! They mean to hunt you!" Tears streamed down my face as I feebly watched Rígán take another dive. One of the men fired a harpoon, and it missed the dragon by a hair. Rígán became agitated, and pumped his wings, quickly ascending out of firing range. He continued to circle the men. Harpoons began to fly more quickly now, and I knew that Rígán didn't understand what was happening. He did seem to sense that he was now in danger, for he flew higher yet, circling the ships in a maddened fury.

Another series of harpoons flew toward my friend. This time, one pierced him directly underneath his wing in his shoulder joint. Dragon hunters know this spot vulnerable and not covered by tough skin. Rígán gave a great cry and began to fly erratically. I sensed what would occur next, and I wanted it to happen. I cared not for those men, those intruders, those monsters that were trying to hurt my friend. At once, Rígán gave a thundering cry and plummeted down again. This time, he opened his mouth and breathed his deadly dragon fire in a rage. The ships became immediately ablaze. Soon, they were incinerated to ashes. Men jumped overboard and screamed in confusion. Rígán flew up again, and I could see how labored his movements were. He was badly injured by the harpoon that still stuck under his majestic wing.

He came down again upon the men, this time with the ferocity of ten dragons. He released his fire upon the rest of the ships and survivors. The sea combusted with dragon fire. I could now smell the acrid smoke that was billowing across the water. Rígán had killed those men, and I was glad of it. He had never harmed a person in all the time he lived with us. He was simply defending himself and possibly defending our village. My heart swelled with pride and sadness, for I knew that this certainly would be Rígán's end. Someone would come looking for those men. Or one or two would escape, spreading the tale of our deadly and fearsome beast.

"Rígán!" I called my friend, and he at once cocked his head toward the shore. He gave one more great heave of dragon fire at the already burning ships. Then, he soared toward me, sinking lower and lower until his wings scraped the top of the water. With a tremendous effort, Rígán made it to shore and landed at my feet. He looked pathetic and broken as he lay upon the cool white sand.

I ran to him and cradled his beautiful head in my lap. I spoke to him quietly, telling him everything would be okay. I knew that it would not be, for my friend was dying.

My mother ran to us with a basket full of fresh plantain leaves and a healing poultice of powdered herbs and flowers. She looked to me with that dear, mothering look in her eyes and I could see that she was crying. Soon, she was applying the poultice to Rígán's wound, trying to stop the bleeding. She waited for the menfolk to arrive and remove the harpoon from Rígán's body. They knew that doing so could be Rígán's end. The bleeding did subside. But Rígán had lost all his energy attacking the ships. He had never before used so much dragon fire in one instance.

I prepared a bed for him on that beach. I collected branches and thatch to comfort him. He crawled into the bed and soon fell into a fitful sleep, his body jerking and stiffening in pain. He chirruped and croaked quietly, and my heart broke into a million pieces every time he uttered a cry. There was nothing more I could do for him. I sat and kept him company, singing to him and talking to him as I stroked his head and held him near my body to keep him warm.

Soon, most of the villagers arrived to take in the tragic scene. Rígán and I lay there, and I rocked him back and forth as my tears covered his majestic face. Other children of the village now approached and joined me. Many tears were shed and little was spoken from that point forward. We kept vigil at Rígán's side until the sun began to set in the horizon. It was at this time that Rígán took three deep, rattling breaths, and then breathed no more.

We constructed a simple pallet of leather and sturdy branches. It took four strong men to lift Rígán's lifeless body and bring him up to the cave. We placed his body in the cave and left gifts for him to cherish in the afterlife. Rígán deserved the freshest, sweetest berries, fragrant blossoms, and bowls of fresh water for his spirit to drink. The children came up one by one and placed an item of importance inside the tomb near

Rígán's body—jewelry, straw dolls, wooden flutes, and leather drums.

"We shall guard this cave for all our days, and our children's days, and their children's days. Never shall we let the body of our dragon be disturbed. This is our sacred duty now," said my father. He began to seal the opening of the cave with large boulders. I helped as much as I was able to. I placed smaller stones into the gaps and chinks in the wall until it was completely sealed. We left no marker. We should never want his grave discovered, only to be pillaged and desecrated by greedier men.

If this is what it feels like to lose one you love, then I decided at that moment that I would take no wife and sire no children. I could not ever stand to feel this pain again. This was a decision that I stayed true to for all of my life. The devastating loss of Rígán never quite left me, and I was never the same after that day. My loving mother seemed to understand the pain that I felt, for she had lost two babes to the sickness. "It is quite a thing to have known a dragon," she told me one night as we stared at the stars together. She was right, of course, for I had truly known a dragon, and I loved him as he loved me.

Now I am an old man, and since that day I dreamed of Rígán every night, he never returned to me. I wonder where dragons go when they die. Was Rígán soaring in the heavens again, free to wander? The village children often gather around me and ask me questions about Rígán. I love to tell of him and how he was the truest and dearest of friends.

The hurt of losing Rígán faded, but has never completely disappeared. Although I am old and withered, I still dream of dragons. It is said in our village, and amongst those that discuss such things, that dragons are no more. That their kind is extinct and never to return. There is still a hope in my heart— the faintest steady flame—that dragons still exist in this world.

The Red Dragon's Treasure

Lillie E. Franks

It was two days after the battle between the Telion sisters and the Red Dragon of the Tallis islands. You'll have heard all about that, of course. The oldest and fiercest of dragons against the cleverest of dragon hunters. We played it like a game when I was your age. One friend would be the dragon, one would be Yarris Telion, who could cast magic, and one would be Seave Telion, who could split a twig with a bow from forty feet away. At least that's how it worked in theory. Usually, it came down to two of us arguing over who got to be Yarris and who had to be the dragon. By then, my brother, who had his own bow and was always Seave, would shoot both of us with whatever he could load. Good fun.

The Telion sisters fought the Red Dragon near the Ketangut caverns. It was one of the places the dragon would appear, and one of the caves was chock full of gold. Really, anyone would have assumed that was the Red Dragon's horde. It wasn't.

The Red Dragon had been the last dragon. We all knew that. So, there was no real hurry for anyone to go poking around its cave. For the first day, people celebrated. For the second day, they cleaned a little bit and went to bed early to get over all the celebrating.

On the third day, representatives of the three families who had lost gold to the Red Dragon went to the Ketangut caverns to split its riches. They were not expecting interruptions. They were not expecting to be mid-negotiation by the tide rising and water filling the cave. The next interruption was very annoyed sea serpent with a mouth full of jewels. Their escape from that cave is a good story in its own right, but it's not this one.

The three of them all came back to the town together, very wet and talking fast. If you've ever been attacked by a sea serpent in a cave you thought belonged to a dead dragon, you'll know how scary it can be. If not, you'll have to imagine.

Soon enough, people figured out what had happened. Soon after that, people realized what it meant.

"The Red Dragon's cave is still out there."

The news passed from ear to ear and got bigger and bigger as it went. "The Red Dragon's cave is still out there and it's full of the gold of three families. Also, watch out for seas serpents near the Ketangut caverns."

Once that got out every idiot with a suitcase and some hiking shoes was off to find the Red Dragon's treasure and make a fortune. Everyone had a clever method and a reason they were destined to find it, while everyone else would fail.

One of them was your grandmother.

She was only twelve at the time, but like everyone, she had something no one else did. She liked dragons.

You might not think that sounds odd. Dragons are cool, right? They can fly and breathe fire. Who doesn't like dragons? Well, back then, the answer was a lot of people. For many reasons, not least of which the fire breathing, dragons are easiest to enjoy from a certain distance. It's easy to think that a huge lizard that eats anything is awesome. It's harder to appreciate them if anything, its eating is the animals you had planned to live off of for the winter.

Your grandmother, Remenor, had seen her family's fields burnt by a dragon. She still loved them. She loved them so much, she held interviews with all the people who spied one. She asked them where the dragon had come from, what it had done, and anything else they noticed about it. She took notes of the clues the dragon left behind. She looked at its footprints and measured exactly how far it could shoot its breath.

She loved dragons so much, she persuaded her mother to let her keep a pet iguana she named Ivonna. It wasn't the same, but it helped.

A lot of kids at school thought she was weird, but that didn't change how cool dragons were. What it did mean was that when it came time to go looking for a dragon's treasure, she had studied for it and they hadn't.

The same day the mix-up was discovered, Remenor was at home, forcing herself to do her homework and not doodle dragons. Her mother, my grandmother, and your great grandmother returned from the town, breathing heavily.

"Oh, thank goodness," she said when she saw Remenor. "I was so afraid you would have left already."

Remenor looked up from the homework. "Left to do what?"

She began and stopped. "Nothing. Forget I asked."

Remenor smiled and nodded.

She returned to her homework, and her mother, pleased that she hadn't given anything away, headed out.

As soon as she was convinced her mother was out of hearing, Remenor set her pen down and tiptoed after her. As she had thought, her mother had gone to the fields to have a word with her father before going back to town to try to sell more. Luckily, Remenor knew all the places in the field where you could hide to listen to someone else talking.

She picked up Ivonna, who was lying in the sun of the doorway and crept her way as close as she dared to her parents.

"No, see that's why I had to come home. What they found wasn't the dragon's cave. Wherever the red dragon put all that gold it stole, it's still out there somewhere! You see why I came racing home. There's no telling what Remenor would do if she knew."

"Good thing she doesn't," her father said, missing the sound of a stifled giggle somewhere among the wheat. "Who knows what one of those money seekers might do if they found her."

Remenor didn't hear the rest. She was already on her way back to the house to pack her bags and get going. Her parents had understood her quite well.

"Let's see, Ivonna, she said, emptying the bag she kept her school things in. "What do we need for a trip?"

As she packed, she thought about how she would figure out where the dragon's cave was. She had her interviews with people, and she was sure there would be a clue in that. Once she had her bag full, she started reading them over again. She noticed something she hadn't noticed when she first wrote them down. Almost all of them included the direction the dragon had come from and the direction it had flown off in.

She grabbed her history book. On the third page was a map of the Tallis islands. She lived on the biggest one, but she had gone to all the islands at some point. She started to draw her findings. First, she drew a dot where the dragon sighting had happened. Then, she drew on arrow leading toward the dot and one arrow leading away from the dot.

She had drawn about twelve dots when she noticed a pattern. The dragon was flying in figure eights, looping in one direction one day and in another the next. Some of the sightings that had happened on the same day showed what must have been the same loop. Other sightings showed the dragon taking similar paths even on different days.

She charted a few more to be absolutely sure and was finally satisfied. Every figure eight had a center, the same center. That center had to be the dragon's lair.

She drew an X on the map in the spot where the dragon was starting from and returning to. It was on another island, among the mountains, but that wasn't a problem. There were ferries between the islands every day and she knew how to take them. Now it was a matter of speed.

She set Ivanna on her shoulder.

"Mom didn't tell us that we weren't supposed to go find the dragon's cave. If your parents don't explicitly tell you not to do something, they must be okay with it."

Ivanna said nothing.

"You're right. That's not true. But that's only because she thinks it'll be dangerous, and I won't do anything dangerous."

Ivanna again said nothing.

"You're right. Leaving on a quest to find a dragon's treasure is dangerous. And my parents don't want me to do it."

She considered.

"But I wanna do it anyway!"

Ivanna seemed satisfied with this reasoning, and with that, Remenor set out.

★★★

Her first obstacle came when she reached the dock. It was crowded, full of various adventurers and treasure seekers. When she got to the boat to the island she needed, it was full and with a line in front of it.

One of the adventurers, a tall man in extremely heavy chain mail was arguing with the boat captain.

"You don't understand. The dog star, the morning star, and the wandering star were all in a line at the moment of my birth. In case you've forgotten what stars are, that means I have a destiny no one else does! That means I deserve to be on that boat!"

Before the captain could reply, another adventurer, carrying a large shield, chimed in. "Stars, schmars! If the stars wanted you to succeed so bad, they'd row you across themselves. See this shield? It costs money, unlike your chain mail. And people who have money are important and deserve to be taken across the water in boats so they can get more money!"

"You think I should wait for the next boat?" Remenor whispered to Ivanna. "Normally, I'd agree, but in this case, my parents might come and get me by that time. Or the treasure might get found! No, this is a moment we should do something clever."

"Oh, any old idiot can buy an expensive shield!" the first adventurer snapped. "But what about the stars? What are you going to tell them when they come out tonight?"

Remenor slipped in between the adventurers and their heavy packs, weapons, and bits of plate armor. She made her way right up to the captain as the situation was starting to heat up.

"You know what? With my Dad's money, I could buy the stars! The dog star chose you? Well, I own it! Or I will, once I find someone to buy it from!"

She stepped in between the shouting man and the captain and slipped off the bracelet she was wearing. It was a very pretty golden thing she had gotten for her birthday.

"I don't have much," she started, raising her voice. "I'll give you this pretty bracelet I found outside a cave if you let me board."

The adventurer in chain mail stopped in the middle of answering the one with the shield. "Even if you could buy stars, they'd be so expensive that … sorry, gecko girl, what was that you said?"

Remenor forced herself to say nothing about being called gecko girl. It was obviously an iguana and even more obviously meant to be a dragon. She kept her eye on the captain. "I need to get to the other island to buy some things from the market. I can't give you money, but I found this bracelet near a cave in the mountains and you can have it if you'll take me!"

"Which mountains were these?" asked the adventurer with the shield.

"Over there." She pointed. "It was by the tree with the big scratch on it."

"On second thought," the adventurer in chain mail said, "you can have the boat. I'll wait for the next one."

"No, no, I insist," the adventurer with the shield said, and they walked off, still arguing.

They weren't the only ones. Within a few seconds, the boat was empty and everyone was running in the direction Remenor had pointed.

"Do you want the bracelet?" she offered.

The captain shook her head. "For dealing with them, you can ride for free."

Remenor stepped into the boat. Ivanna looked at her, accusingly.

"Oh, it wasn't really a lie!" she said, finding a place to sit. "Well, it was a lie, in that it wasn't true. But it wasn't a mean lie! Well, okay it was a mean lie. But I don't want to feel bad about it!"

Ivanna nodded slowly and watched the waves go by.

While the boat sailed, she studied her map and its X so that when she landed, she would be ready to go. It wasn't a very long distance and she could manage most of the way on big roads. She also talked with the captain. He told her all about the sea serpent, the missing cave, and all the people who had come to find it.

"I don't care who finds it," the captain said, "so long as it's quick and people stop asking for boat rides."

Remenor smiled, glad she could help.

When the boat arrived, she set out so fast she didn't even hear the captain telling her the market was the other direction. She sped off straight down the track, passing townspeople, sailors and of course, others convinced they knew where the treasure was. She wanted to go home and let her parents be angry at her but also a little proud.

This whole quest was silly and she had been silly to go on it. Her parents hadn't wanted her to go, she had tricked away all the more experienced adventurers with a lie that would get them mad at her. At the end of it, she wouldn't even get to see any dragons. Just some stupid cave full of gold.

"Should I turn back?" she asked Ivanna. "It's not like my parents will be any less mad at me if I find the cave than if I don't. They'll be less mad because I'll have done less. Anyway, just because I've come this far doesn't mean I have to go any further. Mom says you're always allowed to change direction."

For some reason, she kept walking.

"Then again, it would be pretty cool to see a dragon's cave for the first time. What do you think they do in those caves, besides collect gold? Sleep, maybe? Play, eat? Where do they go to the bathroom? And what do they need all the gold for anyway? It's not like they spend it at the market the way Mom does."

She kept on walking. She was starting to get toward the border of town.

"Maybe I could visit the cave later. That would sort of be like discovering it, right? There'd still be all the stuff to learn there. Just not the gold."

She continued silently for a while.

"Sometimes you're not a very helpful conversation partner, Ivanna."

She came to the place where it was time to leave the road. A thick forest of pines and hedges with large rocks and red, dusty ground waited for her as soon as the stamped earth road ended. It was all uphill.

"I guess this is what being a dragon investigator is like," she said. She started pushing through the branches. Sometimes one would scratch her or she'd step on a rock wrong and it would fall all the way back down to the road.

"Dragon investigators get tired and take a break for a little, right?" she said, resting against a tree. The forest around her was quiet except for all the usual nature sounds. This wasn't an area any other adventurers were searching.

She pulled out the map. The sound caused some birds in the trees to fly away. If she had judged her directions right, the cliffs in front of her ought to be just about where the X was.

It hadn't struck her that finding a dragon-sized cave would be any challenge. As she approached, she realized it might be. The trees were thick and there were a lot of twists and turns in the earth walls rising around her. She had no idea how high a dragon's cave would be and it wouldn't be hard to miss it among all this.

Nearly an hour later, during which time she had gone back and forth several times, she was more convinced than ever. She stopped to eat some of the food she had packed.

"I guess they were just lines on a map," she said, offering a bit of bread to Ivanna. "Dragons don't have to follow patterns. That's even assuming I read the map right anyway. Maybe this whole thing was dumb."

That was the moment she noticed the cave mouth.

It had been purposefully hidden. There were bits of leaf and hedge piled in front of it, well enough to make it very tricky to spot. Remenor noted that dragons took the time to hide their horde when they left it and climbed in its direction. It was higher than the halfway point, which would give the dragon space to take off in.

After about five minutes of climbing, she reached it and pushed aside some of the branches and leaves to make a hole big enough for her.

The cave and its treasures were just behind.

The cave was low at first, then opened up into a much larger rounded chamber. Pillars of rock hung from the ceiling, dripping water onto other rocks that rose from the ground. They looked like teeth in a huge drooling mouth. A dragon could make itself quite comfortable here and one obviously had.

Rising in the center of the room was a huge pile of silver, gold, and precious gems of all sorts. Remenor had never seen or imagined anything like it. When she thought of wealth, she thought of the piles of crops at harvest time. This was larger than those and sparkled like water in the dim light of the cave.

She approached the pile, realizing there was no one to stop her. She could touch it all she wanted, even take a piece. She laid her hand on it and had a surprise. It was warm, not like the cool cave. And as she plunged her hand in, she realized there was something else there.

She dug among the gold and gems like dirt, throwing them behind her to see what it was. It was a whitish-yellow, smooth, round and large. There were more than one, she realized, continuing to dig. She refused to let herself believe it was what she thought until she was absolutely sure.

Finally, she was.

They were eggs.

"Real dragons!" she yelled, waving her arms in excitement. This was cooler than anything she had expected.

There was a sound and a movement from inside one of the eggs, like something tapping on it. These eggs were closed to hatching. When they hatched, there would be at least five of them, maybe more.

"Real live dragons!" she cried again, waving more.

"Did someone say something?" came a voice from behind her.

She froze.

She hadn't actually considered the possibility of someone else coming to the cave. She'd gotten as far as finding it and then assumed her parents would pick her up and take care of the details. There must be a process for dealing with huge piles of gold, but she didn't know it. What if the person lied and said he had found it and not her? Would anyone believe her?

What if they wanted to destroy the eggs?

She remembered all the kids who made fun of her for liking dragons. They said dragons were monsters to destroy. A lot of people thought that way, even grownups.

It was her job to protect them.

"Uh, no," she said, the smartest lie she could think of off the top of her head. "And don't come in!"

"I am Tokano, the truth bringer, sword bearer, despair of my enemies, bane of the unrighteous, scourge of the Eluniad, the Iletian fox, champion of the Tokano line, who comes to lay claim to the dragon's treasure in their name!"

"I'm Remenor. Nice to meet you."

Remenor wasn't sure what all Tokano's words meant, but it didn't sound like the way nice people who wanted to take care of cool dragons talked.

"Who's Remenor?"

Remenor stepped closer to the branches and leaves that obscured the entrance of the cave. She lowered her voice to sound more grown-up.

"I'm a sea serpent."

"A sea serpent?"

"That's right. And this is my cave."

"In the mountains? Nowhere near the sea?"

"I got lost."

"I didn't know sea serpents can talk."

"I didn't know people could, but I didn't bring it up, now did I?"

There was a long pause. "Are you a big sea serpent?"

Remenor smiled. "Yeah, I'm totally huge. Can barely fit in here at all."

"Do you have sharp teeth?"

"Oh, yeah, all over."

The voice outside paused to think again. "I'm gonna head back to town."

"Thanks for stopping by!"

She could hear footprints heading back down the side of the mountain and she danced for victory.

She looked around the nest a little more. She noticed on one side, many of the gold and silver coins were melted together. She understood why the pile had been warm. Like the chickens, the family kept sat on their eggs to keep them warm. Dragons must use their fire to heat up gold for theirs. She wondered if the eggs were cold and if she should lie on them.

She also took notes of other things in the nest, looking at anything, even if it didn't look like the dragon had done anything. There was food for the little babies to eat, bread and some meat stolen from the cities. There were claw marks on the wall where the dragon had been sharpening their claws. There were ash marks in several places where the dragon must have breathed fire for some reason.

By the time she had finished taking notes and making a drawing, nearly an hour had passed since the last visitor. Ivanna, she noticed, was still looking at her, disappointed.

"Oh, come on!" said Remenor. "Mom was talking about how people like that are dangerous! By lying to them so they'd go away, I was doing what Mom wanted!"

The iguana kept staring.

"Okay, fine, what she wanted was for me to stay at home. It was a lie to protect dragons, and that should count for something! And besides, it's not like there are gonna be consequences!"

"Hello?" said another voice. "Is there a sea serpent here?"

"Don't you dare," Ivanna whispered, and walked closer to the door.

She stood just out of sight behind the pile of leaves and branches. "Yes, who is it?"

"I'm the sea serpent killer," the voice answered. "I was told there was a sea serpent to kill."

Remenor felt a lump in her stomach. This wasn't anything like what her parents had thought would happen. She couldn't help feeling they were being proven right.

The worst part was she couldn't even let him in to see she was only a kid. A sea serpent killer would be even worse than a scourge of the Eluniad, whatever that was.

By this point, there had been a pretty decent period of silence. Finally, the sea serpent killer spoke. "To be honest, I didn't actually know sea serpents could talk. That's kinda weird."

Remenor's face lit up as she saw a way out. "Well, actually, it's not all sea serpents. Just me."

"Just you?"

"Yup. I'm the only one of my kind."

"Oh." She could hear the hesitation in the voice. It was working.

"But you're still a sea serpent," the voice continued. "I mean, you sink ships and eat people, right?"

"Not really," she said. "I just sit up in my cave. I like reading poetry."

The voice outside broke. "You read poetry?"

"Oh, yeah. I think it's cool when it rhymes."

"Then you have a sense of the beautiful!"

"Oh, totally. At least one."

"You have a soul then!"

"Yeah, I just saw it."

"Then I can't kill you. I have to go home and think about my place in this world. Goodbye, fellow thinker!"

Footsteps slowly walked away.

Ivanna was glaring again.

Remenor met the iguana's eyes. "Look, if you already told one lie, you're allowed to tell other lies to sort things out. Everyone knows that."

The iguana was unimpressed.

"Okay, fine. You shouldn't do that. That's bad. Like Mom said, you can turn around whenever you want to."

She laid her hand on one of the eggs. They were warm and she could feel a slight movement from inside them. She was feeling a real-life dragon, one shell layer away. It was as close as she had ever felt to being a dragon, and there was nothing better than that.

She lay against the eggs and let time slip away around her. Lying like this, she felt that nothing could ever go wrong.

She was not correct.

There was a sound, not from the door of the cave but from close by this time. It was a gentle cracking and it echoed through the cave. Remenor stood up and looked around. The sound came again, and this time she could tell where from.

It was the eggs. A corner of one of them was breaking off.

They were hatching.

She took a step back. She had wanted to see dragons ever since she had first heard of them. Now that it was about to happen, she wondered why she had thought that would be a good idea. Sure they were beautiful, but so was the fire they breathed, and she had never wanted to hug that.

As she was trying to come up with something to deal with that, there came another voice from the mouth of the cave, a female voice.

"Remenor? We know that's you. We heard the people talk about a sea serpent up here with your name."

Her parents!

There was another tap from the hatching egg. This was going to be hard to explain.

"Are you the talking sea serpent?" another voice said. "I'm from the village. I want to learn from your kind heart and wisdom!"

This was getting out of hand. She walked to the front of the cave and realized there was only one thing to do.

She stepped outside, through the branches, revealing herself to her parents and the crowd of other villagers who had come to see the serpent. It was evening, and they were all looking at her like they expected more. Maybe she felt that way too.

"Remenor!" Her father said. "You're okay!"

"She's a sea serpent?" said a voice. "She looks like a kid."

"A really embarrassed kid" added another voice.

"Maybe we're all sea serpents," said someone else in the crowd, obviously confused.

"This didn't all go exactly as I planned," Remenor said. "I'm sorry."

Suddenly, a new figure stepped in front of the villagers. "The sea serpent killer has failed. I, Tokano, the war-hardened, the Gaerian terror, the bearer of eponyms, shall finish the job!"

"Who are you and what are you talking about?" Remenor's mother snapped, shutting the angry warrior down in a second.

"I might have told a few fibs," Remenor said, almost too quiet to hear.

"And why did you do that?" her mother asked.

She was about to say something like "It's a long story" when the question was answered for her. There was a loud, piercing cry, then another and another. The parents and the villagers froze. There followed a pause that seemed endless, and finally, they came.

They were dragons! Small and young, but dragons, with all the beauty and terrifying grace. They were covered in scales of all color and had horns and sharp, orange eyes. They left trails of flame behind them as they flapped their large, bat wings, one after the other. They gripped the pieces of food the Red Dragon had left. They flew up straight into the air, one after another, and on until they were nothing more than dim lights, new stars in the night sky. They were the next generation of dragons, going off to find their own caves and grow.

A next generation that would never have been born without Remenor.

"I can explain that," she said. Her parents and the villagers stared at her, just the way Ivanna had been all day.

Remenor did explain that, and it's the same story I'm telling you. Your grandmother saved dragons from death. The funny thing is, they didn't forget her.

Somehow, they recognized her through those shells. Maybe by smell, maybe by voice, by some sense, we don't even know but dragons do. They knew who she was, and they've shown their thanks ever since.

Every once in a while, when we go out to the fields, some dragon out there will have left us a gift. A piece of magic, some treasure, food, or even just a beautiful rock they found. You've seen some of the things the dragons have brought us, and now you know why. They remember your grandmother, who had the kindness, and maybe the silliness, to save them.

So, the next time you hear about a dragon or the next time you find something precious behind the house, remember to thank your grandmother.

Totem

Robert Kramer

The old man clutched the wooden arms of his chair; white-knuckled as the coughing fit seized him. His lungs crackled with age. He sucked in the dry air until he had enough oxygen to recount the origin of his people.

"The seven Miigis gathered beneath a canopy of branches in the ancient forest. Their skin radiated a white light, mingling with streaks of sunlight breaking through. A hush fell across the wood. Everyone paused to observe the celestial beings gliding through the congregation of trees. Soon, a young bull emerged from to accompany one of them. Shortly after, a crane and a duck perched themselves on two others. The menagerie grew to include a bear, a moose, and a small ferret-like marten; each next to one of the mystical beings. Six in total, but the seventh being walked alone. His name was Animikii."

Though his body was frail and failing, the spark in his eyes was magical as he spun the tale. His words transcended reality and carried all who heard them to a different time and place.

"Together they traveled until coming across a community of people living nearby. The people approached the beings and their animal companions. However, the mystical beings retreated. They knew that if the humans came too close to Animikii, the people would die. So, the six turned to their brother with great pain and sent him across the waters. In obedience and knowing it was for the best, Animikii bowed his head. He transformed into a great bird with four wings. He flew off low over the trees and across the waters.

The remaining six Miigis divided the people into six tribes and taught them how to live with the land. They sent the six new tribes out into the world while they retired across the waters to be with their brother. They were never to be heard from again."

Joseph Achambo, a thirteen-year-old Chippewa boy, smiled at his great grandfather. He ran a hand through the shock of dark hair that sprouted like weeds on top of his head. Just as much as Joseph adored the man, he adored his stories. Ever since he could remember, Great Grandfather had enchanted him with histories and fairy-tales. Sometimes it was hard to tell the two apart.

"It is said," Great Grandfather continued, "if Animikii had remained he would have established another tribe. The tribe of the Thunderbird." The old man held up a totem with a blue representation of a great four-winged bird.

Joseph's nineteen-year-old brother, Mike, strode into the room at that very moment. He was thin and wiry, and he carried himself with the arrogance of one who thinks he knows everything. He looked at his sibling sitting cross-legged on the worn wooden floor. Great Grandfather held the small carving like a hypnotist. "Stop filling his head with that old magic garbage." Mike said, "He already has enough of a fantasy life. Teach him something useful."

"This is important," Great Grandfather said. "It is who we are."

"So, we are a bunch of crazy redskins who believe in superstition and hocus-pocus. No wonder no one will hire me."

"If you would only perform in the Sun Ceremony, then the blessings of the Thunderbird could be bestowed upon our family. You could restore the rains." He was seized by coughs that rattled his rib cage.

Mike rolled his eyes. "How has that worked out for you? My Dad, he did the Sun Ceremony too, right? That tradition is worthless to us just like the rest of those fairy tales. The rain has nothing to do with me."

"Your father got lost."

Joseph looked back and forth between the two of them as the argument intensified. He was torn between his admiration for his brother and his love for his great grandfather.

"My father is a waste who only cared about the bottle," Mike said.

"He cared—"

"About himself," the words dripped from his tongue like venom.

Great Grandfather's shoulders slumped. He inhaled weakly as the truth of the words and pain in his great-grandson's voice beat him down, "You should show greater respect."

"Family doesn't leave when things get hard."

Mikala, a weathered woman, looked 20 years older than her 43 years of age. She strode into the room from outside where she had been attempting to grow plants in the parched earth. Dust marred her jeans and fingers as she pointed at her son, "You will show respect to your Great Grandfather."

"So, we should just follow along with his nonsense?" Mike asked, incredulous.

Joseph couldn't hold his tongue anymore, "It's not nonsense."

"You will be respectful," Mikala demanded of her son again. Her words held an authority that commanded obedience.

Mike met her glare with his own. "It's not who I am. Not anymore." He spun on his heels and stormed out.

Mikala turned to Great Grandfather and placed a hand on his shoulder, "I'm sorry."

He patted her hand and nodded, "The boy needs to find his work. Without our work, we feel purposeless and can be lost to other things."

"Great Grandfather, what's my work?" asked Joseph.

"Do not fear. Yours will come."

That night, Joseph lay in bed staring at the night sky through the window of his small room. Mikala entered and sat on the side of his mattress.

"Joseph, you know those old stories are stories, right?" she asked.

He nodded still staring at the stars, "But don't all stories have some truth in them?"

"Some more than others," she bent over and kissed him on the forehead.

He continued to stare out at the stars as she left. They seemed to grow bigger and brighter as he looked.

The stars shone down on Mike and a few of his friends as they sat around leaning on the fence to the cow pasture, beers in hand. Empty bottles lay scattered nearby. Harley, a smaller, thin 18-year-old, who always seemed to be at war with his size. Luke, a big nineteen-year-old, whose broad nose and wide forehead overpowered his gentle eyes, sat with bottles of their own. Harley perched on the wooden fence tossing rocks into the field between sips.

"My great grandfather is pushing that Sun Ceremony stuff again," Mike mumbled.

"You gonna do it?" Harley asked.

"No way. Superstition doesn't change anything. He's even pinning this drought on me now."

"I was thinking about doing it,"

The other two looked at him in surprise.

"What do I have to lose?" He shrugged.

"Just skin and intellect," mumbled Mike.

"I'll try anything if it'll help me get some money or bring a little rain for the crops."

"We can keep using the water from the lake," Mike said.

"Have you seen how much the lake level has dropped?"

Luke shook his head and took the last gulp of beer from his bottle. "Plus, it's tradition."

"I'm not interested in tradition," Mike said.

Just then, a high-pitched SCREECH ripped through the night air followed by a low rumble. Harley fell off the fence and the others gathered him up. They looked at each other and crept closer together, whispering.

"What was that?"

Luke shook his head, "Nothing I've ever heard before."

"I think it was thunder," said Harley.

Mike and Luke stared at him in disbelief. He shrugged, "I thought I heard a rumble, okay?"

The terrifying sound broke the stillness again.

"I don't know what that is," said Luke. "But it's not thunder."

A mischievous glint sparked in Mike's eyes, "Let's find out."

Harley downed his beer, "I'm in."

Luke flung his empty bottle away, "Me too."

The three boys picked a path through dry and barren trees. They were battling the effects of the beer they'd consumed. They stumbled over branches and snapped twigs. They turned to each other at every little noise they made and loudly hissed, "SSSSHHHHH!" at each other then laughed as they bumbled their way through the woods. Low rumbles of thunder rattled in the distance.

"Sounds like a storm," Luke said, "We should go back."

"If it rains, I'll run home naked and do a lap around the village," Mike said.

"Please don't rain," Harley begged of the heavens above.

They laughed as they crashed through the underbrush. Streaks of lightning fractured the sky. Electricity and nerves shattered the mask of their confidence. "Maybe this isn't such a good idea."

A stiff rush of hot air kicked up dead leaves, rattling the dry branches above them as a large shadow obscured the light. They froze in terror as the monstrous form blotted out the moon and cast them into darkness. The mysterious figure soared on the warm currents with authority and dominion. It vanished from sight as quickly as it had appeared.

"Did you see that?" Mike whispered.

Harley swallowed hard, "I didn't see anything."

"It was a weird shadow," said Luke.

"That blocked the moonlight?"

"It was a cloud, then."

A loud screech erupted from not far away. They tore at their ears as an electric bolt ripped at the atmosphere around them. The ground trembled from the thunder. "That's one loud cloud," cried Harley as he grasped his ears in pain. The three of them took off toward home. They slid on loose debris and tripping over roots as they scrambled back to the village. Not one of them looked back to see the great beast fly off toward the lake.

At home, Mike slipped in through the door and gently closed it behind him, hoping to come in unnoticed. Joseph whispered from the darkness.

"Did you hear it?"

Mike looked for his brother as his eyes adjusted to the darkness inside. He spotted him sitting near the back window, staring out at the claws of light that were tearing the sky.

"What're you talking about?"

"Animikii, Thunderbird," Joseph said.

"Go to bed." Mike walked off to his room.

Joseph spoke to the darkness. "Their wing beats pull the clouds together and lightning flashes from their eyes."

Mike paused at his threshold, "Too bad it didn't bring any rain with it," then disappeared into his room and shut the door. Joseph sat in the darkness, staring into the night. He searched for what lay hidden under the veil of darkness.

The early sun had already burned away any hope of morning dew as Joseph strolled next to a fenced-in area. Cows grazed on brittle hay on the other side of the fence. As he watched the animals chewing, he noticed the large scratches on the flank of one of them. He hopped the fence and approached, but his quick motions spooked the animal and it moved away.

This caused other cows to get restless and move erratically. Soon there was an uproar as the cattle made each other nervous. The herd started to become more unsettled. William, an old reservation cowboy with skin like leather, sensed the animals' anxiety and saw the boy in with them, "Joseph! Get outta there boy!" He moved to the fence and hauled Joseph back over to the safe side, "What'd you think yer doin'?"

Joseph stammered, "I-uh … that cow. It has scratches."

William glanced at the cows. "What're you talkin' about?"

Joseph pointed at the wounded animal and William moved toward it. It shied away, nervously. He soothed the animal as he approached with soft, low words until he got close enough to examine the three large scratches on the animal's side and back. "Well, I'll be. What'd you git yerself into?"

"Could she have gotten caught in a tree or something?" Joseph asked.

"Not that kind of damage. Looks like I'm missin' a few of my herd too."

"Maybe they all got caught somewhere together," Joseph suggested. "Or …"

William eyed the boy suspiciously. "Spit it out, boy."

Joseph started to kick at the grass with his toe as he couldn't meet the rancher's eyes. "Thunderbirds."

William stared at him silently for a good moment, then erupted in laughter. He slapped Joseph on the back. "You had me goin' there for a minute. I thought you were serious." He wiped a tear from his eye, "You might as well have said Dragons." He made claws with his hands and roared as he play-scratched at the boy. Joseph smiled sheepishly.

"Now go on and git outta here," said William. "This is no place for a boy. Go find something useful to do." He shoved Joseph away and kicked at the seat of his pants. As Joseph walked away, William put a comforting hand on the cow. He traced the scratches with his finger. "Thunderbirds."

Joseph burst through the door of his home. He found his great grandfather sitting in his usual chair, eyes unfocused. He rushed to him, grabbed his arm, and struggled to pull him up, "Great Grandfather, you must come see."

The old man's gaze turned to Joseph and he began to rise from his seat, "What's the matter?"

"A Thunderbird scratched one of William's cows. I'll show you." Joseph tugged on his arm again. Great Grandfather coughed. The cough became a fit and he grabbed his chest in pain as he fell back into his chair. "How do you know?" he asked.

"I saw it with my own eyes."

"You saw Animikii?"

"No, I saw the cow. The scratches."

"Did William see Animikii?"

"No, I don't think so. He laughed at me."

"Then how do you know?"

Joseph was perplexed, "It just is. I know it."

His great grandfather patted his hand, "Then I'm sure you are right."

"You believe me."

He coughed, "When I was a boy, about your age, I too saw Animikii."

"Really? What did it look like?"

"I had a vision of a great winged beast. It rode across the water, pushed along by a storm.

It landed in the mountain by the lake," He pointed out the window at the mountain in the distance. "There."

"Did you go find it?"

He shook his head, "No one believed my vision was real and soon I began to doubt it myself until one day it was gone from my mind."

"But you remember it now."

"You have reminded me. There are a great many things one remembers that they once forgot." He smiled at Joseph, "I need to rest now."

Joseph nodded.

"Joseph, you must remember all that I teach you. One day, our traditions will be your responsibility. The tribe will be counting on you. Your brother thinks it's unimportant, but it is the soul of our people. We always need to remember."

"I will." Joseph stood taller and left his great grandfather to rest.

Mike, sweat-stained and dirty, hopped off of the back of a pick-up truck as did Luke, Harley, and a few other tribesmen. Mike looked at his friends, "No more of this day worker stuff. It's time to find a real job." He raised his arms, embracing his destiny, "Gentlemen, it is time for me to become civilized."

"Can I come?" asked Harley.

Mike laughed, "What would your parents say?"

Harley stopped in his tracks. "They've got no say."

Luke and Mike chuckled and looked at him.

"I could go if I wanted," Harley repeated. "Besides, you're not going anywhere. Aren't you supposed to be the next Keeper of Histories for our tribe?"

Mike shook his head, "Yeah, I'll stay here and tell you guys stories until I get old and die."

"But your Great Grandfather?"

"Can find someone else to take his place. Not my responsibility." Mike waved over his shoulder as he headed home. "I'll come back for you guys when I get rich in the city."

Joseph, Mike, and Mikala sat at their small kitchen table eating beans and rice. There was an empty chair and Mike glanced at it. "Where's Great Grandfather?"

"He wasn't feeling well," Mikala answered. "It's harder for him to breathe every day."

Mike nodded.

Joseph looked at both of them, "He'll be okay, won't he?"

"He's been struggling for a while now," his mother said.

"Sometimes people move on whether we want them to or not," said Mike.

Joseph stared into his rice and beans.

After a moment of silence, Mikala directed her attention to Mike, "You were able to get some work today?"

"I put some money in the jar."

"Thank you."

Mike turned to Joseph, "There were some kids your age out there today. Hard workers."

"Mike," Mikala interrupted.

"What? He shouldn't contribute?"

"He's thirteen. And he takes care of Great Grandfather during the day."

"Not for long," Mike mumbled.

Joseph watched the exchange, shamed by his brother's criticism. "Great Grandfather told me about a vision he had when he was my age." Both Mike and Mikala turned and looked at him. "It was of a Thunderbird."

Mike dropped his silverware, "Here we go."

"Michael," his mother warned.

"He sits around here all day doing nothing but listening to fairy tales told by a delusional old man. He should be out there working with me. What are we going to do when Great Grandfather dies? His pension from the war goes with him. What then?"

"God will provide," Mikala said.

"Or you could do the Sun Ceremony," Joseph said. "Ask for the Thunderbird's blessing. Then, when they bring the rain back, we can grow crops and sell them again."

"See? This is what I'm talking about," he said, "Between the two of you, I don't know who's worse. This is ridiculous." Mike thrust himself up from the table. "Our farm is through. There's nothing left here. It's time to face it and move on."

"Where are you going?" Mikala asked.

"Out." He stormed out of the kitchen and the front door slammed shut moments later.

Mikala sighed and began to clean up. Joseph watched his brother walk off into the distance. A weak cough from the other room was followed by a long sigh.

Joseph stood with his head bowed as a pastor recited a brief prayer over the grave of Great Grandfather. Mikala and Mike stood next to him and the whole tribe had turned out to honor their Keeper of Histories. At the end of the prayer, Mikala put an arm around Joseph and walked off. Mike followed behind, mentally and physically distant. Tears stained his cheeks just as they did those of his brother and mother, but he sought no comfort with them.

Joseph sat at the table staring at his Great Grandfather's chair, now empty. Mikala and Mike prepared some food in the kitchen nearby. He couldn't help but overhear their conversation.

"I've been saving some money. I'll go to the city and find a job. Then I can send you some money every month," Mike said.

"You don't need to leave."

"This place is dead," he said. "If one of us doesn't do something then we'll be buried too. I can help the whole tribe. If I get a good job, I can bring some of the others up."

"I don't want you to go."

"Now that Great Grandfather's gone, his pension stops coming." Mike paused and sighed heavily. "Joseph's old enough now that he could be finding work too."

"He's still a boy."

"It's time for him to take some responsibility. Kids are working in factories younger than he is. He can't just sit around all day anymore thinking about stories. We need to survive."

Joseph bolted from his chair and out the front door. Mikala rushed to the door after him, too late. "Joseph!" she called, but he didn't turn back, even for her.

Mike walked up behind his mother, "I'll find him." He left the small house in slow pursuit of his brother.

Joseph ran through the village. Dirt kicked up behind him as he went down the road, past the cow pasture, and into the forest. He climbed through the brush and trees, recklessly blazing a path to nowhere. He could hear his brother calling for him from far away. Needing to be alone, he searched and stumbled up the nearby mountain. He found a cave entrance hidden in the brush and ducked inside.

As his brother's voice grew nearer, he pushed deeper inside. It was dark, but there was light deep within that he could barely make out, so he pushed on. After what felt like an eternity, he found himself looking out over the small nearby lake and dried up forest. He had traveled from one side of the mountain to the other. It was almost more a tunnel than cave. Below him was a sheer drop. He found himself in a hole in the cliff face of the mountain. It was beautiful.

He stepped back from the edge and a noise alerted him to the presence of someone or something in the cave with him. He looked around, his eyes searching the depths until he noticed a large shadow, about his size move. He prayed it wasn't a bear. "Mike?"

The shadow didn't answer.

Joseph started to creep back the way he had come as the shadow moved slightly into the light. Enough that Joseph could make out a great eye staring back at him. Terrified, he quickly scrambled back deep into the tunnel. He glanced over his shoulder in fear of the creature's pursuit, but none came. Soon he was plunging headfirst through the trees until he ran straight into his brother.

"There you are," Mike said.

"I—"

"Let's go home," Mike put his hand on the back of Joseph's neck and gently guided him home.

"But, there's …"

"Come on."

Mike stuffed a bag with the few items of clothes he owned as Joseph plopped down on his bed to watch, "Do you have to go?"

"A man has to find his work, remember?"

"Family doesn't leave when things get hard, remember."

"You don't understand. It's like Great Grandfather's story about Animikii. He had to leave for the good of the people."

"Never to be heard from again."

"It's not like that with me," Mike said. "It's going to be your responsibility to take care of things around here now. You're old enough, I'm counting on you."

"You think I can?"

Mike stopped packing and looked tenderly at his brother, "You just have to get all that nonsense out of your head. Great Grandfather was the tribe's Keeper of History, not you."

Joseph dropped his head, "I miss him."

Mike nods, "It'll be good for you. And in a couple of years, when I'm established, you can come work with me." Joseph turned his tearful eyes to his brother. Mike continued, "If you've gotten your act together and grown-up that is."

Mike tossed his bag into the back of a pickup as Joseph and Mikala stared. The truck pulled out and Mike watched as his mother and brother diminished in the distance. Moments later, Joseph laced up his boots and was headed to the door when Mikala walked in.

"Where are you going?" she asked.

"I wanted to go hiking, on the mountain."

"By yourself?"

"I'll be careful."

Mikala messed up his hair, "You better be. Pack some food and be back before supper."

Joseph walked through the trees munching on dried beef. He looked all around him, trying to locate the cave from the night before. At last, he spotted it. Pausing at the entrance, he turned around to see if anyone had followed him. Then he ducked inside.

He made his way carefully, quietly through the cave to the other side of the mountain. The cool, damp air inside the mountain a contrast to the dry heat outside. It made his skin crawl. Carefully, he picked his way through the tunnel not wanting to make a sound. Half of him wanted the creature to be gone, to have been a flight of his imagination.

As he approached the end of the tunnel, he scanned the space intently looking for the beast. He nearly tripped over an uneven outcropping of stone. He could see out across the lake waters. He was afraid to reveal himself in the light, so he stayed hidden in the shadows. Still and quiet. Until he saw what he'd come for.

It was there, laying behind some large boulders, asleep. A light brown coat of feathers with a crest of white, like a bald eagle. It was easily the largest bird he had ever seen. He couldn't make out what kind it was though, it was curled on the ground of the cave almost like a dog in front of a fireplace. The strangest thing was, he could swear it had four wings. It shifted.

Joseph froze, then stepped back as it began to groom itself with its beak, picking at its feathers. One of the wings didn't move as the others did and seemed to be held at an odd angle. Joseph shifted his weight from one foot to another to get more comfortable. Mistake. Its eyes fixed on him.

He retreated until his back was against the wall. The creature stared at him as it uncoiled from its slumbering position and began to stalk toward him. Joseph was scared, really scared, but fascinated at the same time. He ripped off a piece of his dried beef and threw it toward the creature.

The beast looked at the food, partially opened its beak to gather the scent. Then it snatched and swallowed it whole. It looked at Joseph and began to move toward him again. Joseph threw the rest of his beef jerky to the other side of the cave. When the great bird went after it, he darted deep into the tunnel. Moving as quickly as he could through the darkness inside the mountain, he constantly looked over his shoulder for talons he imagined would be snapping at his shoulders. They were never there.

He burst out of the cave and practically fell his way down the mountains. He paused only when he heard a distant screech. He looked back toward the sound. Nothing was following him.

Joseph lay in bed that night, unable to sleep or to forget the creature in the cave.

The next day, Joseph packed a larger amount of dried beef in a small satchel and set off. He made his way through the woods to the cave and inside. He crept through the darkness of the cave again until he saw that he was nearly to the other side. He continued in until he spotted the sleeping form of the creature.

It woke at his approach. Its big eyes fixated on him. His breathing became more rapid under that glare. His heart raced, but he stood his ground and held out a stick of dried beef toward the creature. It eyed him, then the food in his hand, then him. Slowly, it uncurled itself and stepped toward him.

"That's it. Come on," Joseph encouraged. He made a clicking noise with his tongue. The creature stopped and tilted its head, staring at him and stopped its approach. So, Joseph tossed the food on the ground in front of it. It gathered in the scent then gobbled the food up.

It looked at him and made a small, almost cooking screech.

Joseph produced more beef jerky from his bag and offered it to the creature. This time the creature timidly snatched it from his hand and dashed backward to eat it. The quickness of the movement startled Joseph and he recoiled. He stopped to count his fingers. They were all still there.

"Animikii?"

The creature paused its eating and looked at him.

"Animikii,." Joseph spoke, more convinced as he watched the creature. It finished the food and screeched at him gently. Joseph produced another piece of dried beef. The creature unhesitatingly snatched it from him. While it was eating, Joseph tried to touch it. It lurched away from him and screeched. A warning.

"Right."

It returned to its eating as he backed off. When it was done, it looked at Joseph and gave a low, cooking screech again. Joseph held out his empty hands.

"No more."

It screeched at him again, a bit more forcefully.

"No more," he explained.

The creature started toward him, making Joseph uneasy, so he started to back his way through the cave. It followed at a distance until Joseph picked up the pace. The bird stayed back, shrinking with the distance and light. It disappeared from his sight entirely.

Weeks passed with Joseph returning and bringing food for the creature. He became more convinced of what it was as time went by. He kept expecting for it to be gone, but every day it was there waiting for him. It was less menacing the more he got to know it. Almost gentle. He found himself calling it, "Ani" for short as he continued to care for it.

After a month, Joseph returned home one evening to hear a familiar voice from the darkness.

"Where have you been?" Mike asked.

"Mike?"

Mike turned up the oil lamp so they could see better. He was thinner than before and looked somehow worn out. Joseph rushed to him and embraced him in a great hug, tears escaping from his eyes, "I didn't think you'd ever come back."

Mike pushed him away to arm's length, "You look older," he said. "Mom tells me you've been disappearing every day. She's worried about you."

"Did you find a job?"

"Never a permanent one," Mike shook his head. "So, I came back until I'm ready to go try again."

"I didn't think I'd ever see you again," Joseph hugged him again. "I'm glad you're back."

"Me too." But Mike didn't look glad, he looked defeated.

In the morning, Mike and Mikala drank coffee at the table as Joseph rolled in, "Morning," he said.

"Morning," replied his mother. "Are you going hiking today?"

Joseph nodded.

"Why don't you take Mike with you?"

"Uh."

"It'll be good for you two to spend some time together."

"But he just got here. He doesn't want to go walking up a mountainside."

Mike looked at them, "I'm in the room you know."

"It's just that I like being alone sometimes," Joseph said.

"Don't worry, I don't want to go either," Mike said.

Mikala gave him a look, "You have something better to do?"

Joseph and Mike traipsed through the woods not speaking. Mike didn't want to be there and Joseph wasn't sure that he wanted him there. His brother seemed different somehow. A stranger.

"So," Joseph began, "the city."

Mike looked up at the sky. "It's not like here," he said. "It's all buildings and ambition. No one cares about anything other than getting ahead."

Joseph nodded and plodded along, "Isn't that why you went?"

Mike sighed, "You don't know what you're talking about."

Joseph wasn't sure what he should reveal to his brother about Ani if anything. But he thought his brother looked so sad and tired. "If I could bring back the rain, would you stay here?"

"Are you joking or delusional?"

"I can do it."

Mike rolled his eyes, "You're not going to start dancing, right?"

"I'll show you," Joseph started toward the cave. "I found it when you left."

They made their way to the entrance and Mike peered in. "Great, a cave. That's not fixing a drought."

"It's what's inside," Joseph said. "Come on."

Joseph entered the cave and started to make his way deeper in. Mike hesitated outside. Finally, he resigned himself to being his brother's keeper once again and followed him in.

Joseph glanced over his shoulder and saw the shadow of his brother framed against the cave entrance. "It gets light again in a little bit," he said. The two of them dove deeper into the darkness until it started to become a light gray. Finally, they could see the sky from the other side.

Mike moved to the opening and peered out. Below him was the lake, not much more now than a glorified pond. The mountain's cliffside pushed against a dry shore. "This is beautiful, Joseph. But we already draw water from the lake, it's just not enough. We need rain."

From behind him, Joseph answered, "I know. Look."

When Mike turned around, he saw his brother with a creature slightly larger than he was. It was a great bird, like an eagle, but larger and with four wings. It ate dried beef from Joseph's hand. Mike stumbled back and braced himself against the cave wall, too stunned to speak.

"This is Ani," Joseph explained. "He's Animikii."

"There's no way," Mike choked out.

"I think he was injured, but I've been bringing him food and I think he's better now," said Joseph quickly.

"Get away from it."

"He won't hurt me," Joseph said. "We're friends."

"This isn't real," Mike mumbled.

"I told you," Joseph shook his head. "All myths have some basis in reality,"

Mike stared in disbelief at the two of them as his brother fed the great bird.

"Maybe he can bring back the rain." Joseph said.

"Does anyone else know?" asked Mike.

Joseph shook his head and Mike bounced in excitement. "You know what this means?" Joseph looked at him slightly bewildered as he continued. "Think about it," he said. "We have a mythical animal. This could save our family and the tribe. We'll all be rich."

"What are you talking about?"

"Think of the tourists, the research money. Museums, scientists. It's endless."

"No."

Mike stared at his brother in disbelief, "This is our ticket."

"No."

Anger rose in Mike's throat like bile, "You don't know what it's like out there. And here, don't you see the suffering?" He gestured in great agitation at the shrinking lake outside the cave. "There's nothing for us anymore. No future. But this gift lands in our lap."

"I won't let you."

"Don't you get it?"

"You can't have him."

"Look," Mike said, "let's bring him to the village and see what happens."

"I don't want lots of people camped out looking at him. They'll scare him away or worse."

"Nothing bad will happen. We'll put up a big net so he can't get away or something."

Joseph shook his head angrily. "He is not for them. He is for us. Great Grandfather sent him to me," he paused, "to bring back the rain."

"If this bird controls the rain, then why isn't it raining?"

"I never should've showed you."

Mike approached Ani, who hissed at him until he backed off.

"You can't hide him forever."

As the sun fell below the horizon, Mike waited. The wind started to whip up and he had a crazed look in his eyes. Harley and Luke shuffled into the village after a hard day laboring on a farm nearby. They were surprised to see their friend back home. "I need your help," Mike spit out without even a hello.

"When did you get back?" Harley asked. "Did you come to offer us jobs?"

"What if I told you that I knew where a real Thunderbird was?"

"I'd say you were crazy."

"I've seen it with my own eyes," he said. "Joseph trained it."

Luke shook his head in disbelief, "Joseph trained a Thunderbird? Are you listening to yourself?"

"You don't believe me."

"Would you believe you?"

"This is for real," he pleaded with them. "We could make enough money to save the tribe with this thing."

"You feeling okay, city slicker?" Harley said.

"Mock me one more time," Mike stepped toward Harley, menacing.

Luke put a hand on Mike's chest to stop him, "Okay, okay Mike. Relax. We're your friends here. What do you have in mind?"

He looked at Luke and calmed, just slightly, "We need to get some chains."

Joseph began to worry about his brother's reaction to Ani. Something didn't sit right and it ate at him. His mother was resting in her bedroom, so, he decided he could sneak out and check on the bird.

He made his way through the woods as the wind whipped through the trees. In the distance, he saw clouds gathering. Joseph entered the cave and came across an unsettled Ani. She was watching the gathering weather outside the cave. He stroked Ani's feathered head. "It's time for you to go." Ani nuzzled him and he pushed the creature away. "You have to leave now," he said. "Mike's going to come and get you. I can feel it." Ani nuzzled in more. "Please, you have to leave before he comes."

"Too late," Mike said, from the back of the cave. Joseph spun around and saw his brother, his eyes wild, with Luke and Harley behind him. They carried sledgehammers and metal stakes. Luke and Harley stood unmoving, amazed at the scene in front of them as Mike strode toward his brother.

"It's real," gasped Harley.

"Get out of the way, Joseph," said Mike.

Joseph backed up into Ani, "I won't let you."

"This is your last chance."

Joseph pushed on Ani, trying to force him up and out.

"Get him," Mike commanded, but Harley and Luke didn't move. Mike turned around and looked at them. "I said get him."

Harley dropped his stakes and hammer and started toward Joseph.

"Ani, leave," Joseph begged. He shoved Ani to no avail.

Harley got within grabbing range until Ani screeched at him. The ear-splitting sound caused Harley to retreat.

"Coward," said Mike. He rushed forward and grabbed his brother, dragging him away from Ani.

"Now!" he yelled.

Harley grabbed a chain and staked one end of it into the ground. Luke ran to the other side of Ani and Harley threw the chain over the great beast to Luke. He scrambled for it, but Ani moved. He hissed at Luke who lurched back, beads of terror forming on his forehead.

Ani tried to stalk around in the narrow cave, but he couldn't spread his wings fully in the confines. Mike tossed his brother aside and jumped for the loose end of the chain that Luke had missed. Catching it, he quickly hammered it into the cave floor with a stake. Luke hammered another chain down and threw it over the bird to Harley.

Ani spun the best he could, hissing at the captors. Harley grabbed the loose end of the chain from Luke's toss and fastened it into the ground. The work progressed rapidly.

Joseph lunged forward and grabbed at Luke's hammer. Luke shoved him off and Joseph fell. He got back up and leapt onto his brother's back. Mike spun around trying to rid himself of Joseph.

"Ani, go!" Joseph called.

The beast clawed toward the exit at the mouth of the cave. He pulled and one of the stakes came loose. Ani lurched toward the opening and fell out tangled with the chains. He dangled dangerously.

Mike whipped Joseph off of him and his brother's head cracked on the rock floor. He lay unconscious. Mike looked at his fallen brother momentarily then moved to secure more chains.

"C'mon, pull him in," he said.

"But, Joseph ..."

"He'll be fine. C'mon."

The three men began to hoist Ani back into the cave. The Thunderbird struggled and failed to get away. He screeched in desperation.

Across the horizon, his screech was answered.

The men stopped tugging and looked out. In the distance, closing in fast, they could make out the shapes of two more creatures flying toward them. Behind them, thunder and lightning erupted.

"Thunderbirds," Harley whispered in awe.

The creatures closed in on the cave. They were at least twice the size of Ani. Mike stood amazed at the sight of them. "Mamma and Pappa."

Luke was the first to bolt for the exit, "I'm outta here."

Harley quickly turned and followed. But Mike stood frozen as the two giant creatures landed on the edge of the cave. The largest one screeched at him and Mike fell back, crawling into the darkness.

Together, the creatures clawed and pulled with their beaks until Ani was back in the cave. They tried to bite through the chains, but couldn't break the metal. Just then, Joseph stirred. The largest creature hissed and dove in to bite him, but Ani stuck his head in the way and the creature backed off.

Joseph woke groggily and tried to figure out what was going on. He had a face full of feathers obstructing his view of anything. He peered around Ani and saw the other two creatures. They were immense and filled the cave. Luke, Harley, and Mike were nowhere to be found. He scrambled back to the wall, making himself as unobtrusive as possible. The largest beast made toward him, but Ani put himself between them again.

Joseph quickly assessed the situation and spotted a hammer nearby. He dove for it as the largest creature continued to track him and hiss warnings. But Ani stayed in his way, even while bound by chains until Joseph knocked one of the stakes free. He pulled at the chain, nothing. He moved around to another stake and knocked it free. One of the chains slid off of Ani. The other creatures watched now. They gave Joseph more time to move. So, move he did. One by one, he knocked the chains loose until Ani was completely free of all restraints. He nuzzled Joseph and looked at the other two creatures.

"You need to go now," Joseph insisted. "That's your family. And family sticks together. Go." He shoved the bird who made his way to the other creatures. Outside, a dry storm raged. The creatures all screeched gently to one another and nuzzled with Ani.

"Goodbye," said Joseph.

Ani looked back at him one last time then plunged out into the electric storm with his parents. Mike slowly emerged from the depths of the shadows where he had been hiding. Joseph glared at him.

Mike seethed. "You let it go."

"It didn't come to make us rich."

"We could have finally gotten out of this hell-hole, done something with our lives," Mike said. "We'd have been able to have a real future."

"We already do," Joseph said as he walked out, remembering his Great Grandfather and all the stories he told him. "It's tied to the past." He smiled to himself, knowing who the new Keeper of Histories was going to be.

Mike was left standing by himself in the empty cave. He stared out at the storm as lightning raked the sky and rain started to fall.

Wimp to Warrior

Carly Seemann

Elis emerged from the wooden carriage. His feet hit the dirt path as he closed the door behind him. He looked up seeing the towering tan walls before him. He turned, telling the carriage driver to go back to the palace.

The carriage driver turned the slick brown horses around and trotted away from the town. Elis watched as the carriage rode through the tall grasses along the red dirt path. Watched as the horses disappeared into the sandy hills. Watched as the carriage vanished into the orange sky. He slipped the hood of his navy cloak onto his blonde head, shading his olive-skinned face.

Elis turned. Large brown wooden doors stood before him, blocking him from entering the town. Elis walked forward, keeping his head down and his body covered.

Guards yelled from the top of the wall, demanding for him to stop.

Elis halted. He slowly raised his face to the guards. They held spears of silver, their silver chest plates shimmering in the morning sun. A smear of ruby blood was slashed across the guard closest to Elis. His nose began to crinkle as he stopped his spine from recoiling.

"I am Elis Elvador, first in line to the throne of Galdion," Elis shouted to the men. "I am here to help."

The guards started to bustle, whispering to each other as they moved to the gate's levers. They yanked and twisted the metal wheels before them. Gears churned and shifted as the door slowly rose.

Elis's knees wobbled as he took a few steps forward.

 Screams and cries emerged from behind the door.

Elis entered the gates.

People lay in the dirt path bloody and torn. Family members lay sobbing overtop of them, pleading for gods to save them.

Elis kept moving.

He weaved through the rubble of the destroyed market. Logs and beams of charred wood lay in heaps and piles, covered with banners of red and gold.

People ran past Elis bumping and shoving him out of the way as they ran with bundles of cloth.

Elis stumbled back, falling into the pile of wood. His elbows stung as he braced himself. He stood up brushing the char off his silk cloak. He watched as the people ran, disappearing between the broken arch of an alleyway.

Elis looked around. Gashed and shredded, red and orange banners flap half destroyed in the warm wind, hanging from dented torch posts. Battered bricks lay on the red dirt paths, blocking people from their homes and their city. Scanning the street, Elis saw people running from one crumbled home to another. Some carrying bundles of cloth while others showed faces of loss and grief. Elis walked further down the street, watching as a family stood, mourning the loss of their loved ones who now lay dead in the streets.

Elis kept walking trying to take in all the damage one war could do to a city. He shook his head, pulling the cloak further over his head to hide his welling eyes. He lifted his head, blinking his eyes to clear his vision.

A girl stood in the middle of the street. Staring down at a pile of wood. Her brown trousers matching the fur of a grizzly. Her tight-fitting blazer the color of the fiery blood in her veins. Golden sleeves puffed from her blazer, matching the glinting belt at her waist.

Elis strode toward her.

Her brown wavy hair lay settled on her back, swiftly falling over her shoulder. Each strand like a wave on the ocean.

Elis neared her side, silently walking up behind her. He straightened his cloak, brushing off any remaining soot and char. His heel scuffed against the ground.

She jumped, fear flashing across her face. Her fists were ready to attack in mere moments.

"I'm so sorry! I-I didn't mean to startle you." Elis stuttered. Her wide eyes were the color of the deep ocean, not quite green but not a deep blue.

She backed away from him, blocking whatever lay behind her in a protective stance.

Elis tried to look behind her, but she stepped sideways blocking his view.

"Do you need any help?" Elis asked her.

He looked at her. Her eyes were glassy, her cheeks and nose all rosy. He put up his hands and backed away as anger crossed her face.

"We needed your help three days ago. You're no help to us now." She looked Elis up and down, disgusted by his presence.

"I'm very sorry for all of your losses," Elis said, looking down at his feet.

She scuffed him off, turning on her heel. She stormed down a half-blocked alleyway, honey brown hair swishing behind her. She looked both ways before turning down another path, out of Elis's sight.

Elis lifted his head from his feet. Before him lay a monster. Its purple scaled head glistening with silver blood, its big body buried by broken beams of market stands. Elis rushed around to the other side of the pile. Huge leathery wings lay spread out, torn and gashed, oozing out shimmering silver blood. Elis couldn't believe his eyes.

He sprinted down the half-blocked ally, turning down the same pathway as the girl. He skidded to a stop. A brick wall lay before him with a single wooden door. Elis looked around him, turning in a full circle, looking for where the girl could have gone. He took off his hood scratching his head.

He admired the door. Its hinges were made of dark metal, with bars running across the dark wooden planks. A swirled handle lay on the door, snaking in an arch before coiling up at the base.

Elis wrapped his soft, hand around the cold metal. He tugged.

The door was locked.

He peered through the keyhole. A black abyss lay in front of him. He looked farther, deeper. Something far away sparked, swishing back and forth before disappearing once more. Elis backed up, then hammered on the door. He rubbed his knuckles as they started to sting.

"Hello!" he yelled.

Elis peered back through the keyhole.

An ocean eye peered back at him.

Elis yelped, jumping back, tripping and tumbling into the dirt.

The door creaked open.

The girl peeked out from behind the door, stepping into the small alley. She looked down to Elis.

Elis lay on the floor. His cloak splayed behind him tattered and dirtied. His cream pants dusted with red dirt. He stood up quickly brushing off the new red stains.

The girl tried to hold back her chuckle.

"Let's start over," Elis said as he extended his hand. "My name is Elis."

"Ah yes, Elis Elvador. First in line to the throne of Galdion," the girl said mockingly.

"Okay, okay, yes. I am Elis Elvador blah blah blah, but that's not why I'm here."

"Did your father send you? Maybe your mother?" the girl questioned.

"No. They don't actually know I'm here," Elis said timidly, scratching at his head.

"Oh ..." the girl said shocked.

"I heard that there was a battle here and I wanted to come help, but I couldn't get a carriage fast enough." Elis scuffed his boots on the ground, kicking the pebbles from under his feet.

The girl stood there, nervously chewing on her lip.

"I'm Leia," she said extending her hand toward him.

He shook her hand gently.

She smiled a bit. She opened the door wider, ushering Elis into the dusty damp hallway, and clicked the lock behind them.

A cold draft tickled the back of Elis's neck. He shivered as he walked beside Leia.

She led them down the dingy stone hallway. Dim torches lined the hallways, illuminating the golden belt around Leia's waist, reflecting off her gold puffy sleeves, shimmering in her honey hair. Elis stared at Leia. Leia caught his glance as he quickly looked away. Her cheeks turned rosy.

"Where are we going?" Elis asked.

"You'll see," Leia smirked over her shoulder at Elis.

She turned right, sauntering down another dark hallway. They reached a set of stone stairs. Elis reconsidered his decision as he followed Leia who quickly trotted down. Her boots tipping and tapping on each step like a horse.

They turned left down a large corridor. Elis admired the architecture of this hidden place. The peaking roof that soared above their heads. Each brick supported by the weight of another. A big wooden beam snaked the spine of the roof, suspended by a ribcage of smaller beams.

Elis bumped into Leia, knocking them both to the floor.

Elis apologized as he helped her back up, helping to dust off her sleeves. Elis unclipped his cloak, shaking the dust and dirt to the cobble below. He folded it over his forearm as he ruffled his blonde hair. Looking to Leia, Elis followed her shimmering gaze to the wall before them.

A stone dragon lay wrapped around a caged ball. Its wings spread wide, its head crouched, its mouth showing its glistening teeth, snarling, and glaring at their presence. Its tail snaked down the stand the metal balled perched on, coiling up in a nice curl.

Elis took a frightened step back.

Leia grabbed his wrist and yanked him to her side.

"Wimp," she chuckled.

"What? I am not!" Elis protested, snatching his wrist from her grasp.

"Okay. Prove it," she said, crossing her arms.

Elis walked toward the dragon statue confidently, turning to Leia as he stood a meter away.

"Closer," she said as she smirked.

Elis stepped directly beside the dragon's head. Elis's cheek began to flush as heat radiated from the statue.

"Touch it," Leia said, testing Elis.

"Touch it?" Elis questioned as he backed away from the statue. "You want me to … touch it?"

Leia rolled her eyes. She walked over and stood directly in front of the dragon's head. She looked Elis directly in the eyes, lifted her hand above the dragon's forehead, and smirked.

Her hand dropped.

The dragon's eyes began to glow a deep amber. Elis recoiled as the dragon uncoiled. Its stone limbs becoming as fluent as water, its wings folding into its side like a sheathed knife, and its face calming as if it was put under a sleeping spell. The statue sat atop the metal caged ball, perched like a bird on a wire.

Elis looked at Leia in shock as she stood there with her head on its forehead.

"Close your mouth. Unless you like eating flies," Leia joked as she took a few steps back to stand beside Elis.

Elis snapped his mouth shut.

The base of the statue's stand began to glow. The whole floor began to light up, one stone tile at a time.

The floor beneath Elis dropped sending Elis crumbling to the ground. Elis yelped, crying, and wailing for help.

Leia chuckled, "Open your eyes."

Like a cannon, the stones surrounding the statue had begun to sink into the ground, starting with the tile Elis stood on. Each dropped farther than the last. A spiral staircase descending from right under his feet. Elis blushed, realizing how much he had overreacted.

Leia jumped in front of him to the following step. She didn't bother waiting as she skipped down the newly made stairs.

Elis stood up, brushing off his cream pants and blue blazer, and descended the ominous staircase.

A cavern of stone lay before Elis with archways that soared into the towering roof and pillars that plunged all the way to the cobbled floor. A blue light hovered high in the center of the room, pulsing like a living heart. It illuminated the room, shedding ice blue light onto the walls. Elis walked toward the light. A large marbled stone sat hovering in the air. Elis reached out his hand, wanting to touch the smooth surface, wanting to feel the heat of the bright light.

"Don't move!" Leia shouted from behind Elis.

Elis froze. His hand almost grazing the stone.

Leia cautiously inched closer to Elis until she was standing directly behind him.

"Move – your hand- away," she whispered harshly.

Elis slowly dropped his hand, letting it slack to his side.

Leia's shoulder relaxed. "Now, step away from the egg."

Elis took three large strides backward.

Leia let out a large sigh, falling to the ground in relief. She splayed her arms out as the relief rolled off her.

"Why do you have an egg?" Elis asked quickly, still unable to move.

"Well, if you really want to know," Leia said as she sat up from the ground, "I found this egg right before the war broke out. I brought it down here for protection."

"How do you even know of this place? What is this place?" Elis asked.

Leia stood up and walked toward the egg. "When the battle war occurred last year, all the villager's kids were sent down into the bunker," she motioned to the staircase they had just come down. "The adults needed to stay above ground to help fight. But things didn't go so well down here."

Elis watched Leia as she walked around, circling around the pillars that grew from the ground.

"The intruders broke into the bunker, taking all the children they could find. I ran from them, swerving down corridors and different halls. I turned down this corridor and ran directly into the dragon statue. The floor began to glow, and the stairs appeared. I ran down them without thinking twice. The stairs closed, and the men never found me." Leia turned and looked to Elis and walked toward him. "And now I'm here. With all my friends," she said grinning widely.

"What do you mean all of your friends?" Elis asked cautiously.

Out of the corner of his eye, Elis saw something emerge from the corner of the cavern. A dragon, larger than an elephant, came into the blue light. Its red scales were as red as the blood running through Elis's veins, its chest as golden as the morning sun.

Another dragon emerged from the darkness on the other side of the cavern. Its black scales shone against the blue light. It opened its dark red wings, stretching before folding them back up against his large body.

More dragons emerged, filling the main area of the cavern. Elis stared in shock, his mouth hanging open again once more.

"Wha-Wh-W-Hu," Elis stuttered, not being able to find any words as he ushered to all the dragons that stood before him.

"I brought all the ones I could find down here when the battle started," She explained to Elis. "For safety," she added, shrugging.

"What about all the ones you didn't find?" Asked Elis.

"The king of Sehredia took them when he intruded, or," Leia said as she looked toward the red dragon, "he killed them." The dragon inched closer to her, snaking its head down toward her. She stretched out her hand, stroking the scales and tiny horns between its eyes. It stood up, towering over her as she looked back toward Elis.

"How are we going to get them back?" Elis questioned as he stepped closer toward Leia.

The dragon huffed protectively, lurching forwards. Elis jumped backward.

"Calm Namris," she said putting her hand up toward the scarlet and gold dragon, "He's not here to hurt us."

The dragon relaxed, dropping its wings to its side.

"To answer your question, Elis, first of all, we can't get them back," she said glaring back over her shoulder, "and secondly, you wouldn't be coming."

"What do you mean I wouldn't be coming? The whole reason I came here was to help!" Elis exclaimed.

"Galdion needs you to rule when your father dies. The trip to Sehredia will be too dangerous for you."

"Well, I'm not just going to stay here!" Elis said flailing his arms.

Leia stared at him.

Elis could see the wheels and gears turning and churning within her brain.

She glared at him, "Fine."

Leia turned and snaked through the crowd to the other side of the egg. Namris followed her through the crowd, each dragon recoiling into their corners of the cavern as she passed.

"Really?" gawked Elis.

"Don't make me reconsider," Leia said as she glared through the light.

She ascended a set of stone stairs leading to the shining egg.

Elis circled the room, carefully sneaking past the puffing dragons that lay in the dark. He gingerly walked up the stairs to Leia who stood watching the glowing egg.

"You're going to need a dragon," Leia said, turning to look down at Elis.

"I get a dragon!" excitement sparkled in Elis's sky-blue eyes, a wide grin blossoming across his face.

"You need to fly somehow, don't you?" she joked.

"I guess!" he said throwing his arms up in the air. "Do I get to choose?!"

Before waiting for his answer, Elis ran down the stairs and ran to one corner of the room. The black dragon emerged from the shadows, its scales flickering in the blue light. Elis smiled, giggling to himself in excitement. The dragon raised itsco chest and breathed in deeply.

Leia yelled something, but it was too late.

The dragon blew out fire, as dark as the midnight sky. The flames engulfed him, cutting out all light. Elis's skin felt ice cold, fear flooded his body. He fell to the floor, curling his knees up to his chest. He covered his ears trying to block out the voices that now surrounded his mind.

The blue light slowly faded in again. The voices vanished.

Leia stepped through the darkness; her arms folded over her chest.

"The dragon has to choose you."

"Yeah, I get that now," grunted Elis. He pushed himself up onto his elbows, pressing a hand against his pounding headache. Leia grabbed his arm and helped him up. Elis groaned as the pins and needles prickled through his legs like wildfire.

"It'll go away soon," Leia said, comforting Elis.

"So, how do I know if a dragon picks me?" asked Elis as he dusted himself off.

"You'll just know," she said wisely.

He threw his hand up in the air, "Okay!"

Elis walked the perimeter of the cavern. One dragon scurried into the darkness, another hid under its sparkly wing, and another almost squashed him with its foot.

"This is useless Leia. No dragon wants me," said Elis, feeling defeated. He hung his head low, shuffling his boots on the cobbled floors.

"Let's just try one more," Leia said hopefully. She led him to the center of the room and up the small stone staircase. She backed down the stairs and waited at the bottom. "Touch it," she said.

"You said I wasn't allowed," Elis protested.

"Well I'm not stopping you now," she said ushering him forward.

Elis looked at the egg. It shone as bright as the sun on snow, warming Elis's skin like a summer day's sun. Its polished surface sparkled like a diamond, twinkling like the night's stars. He reached out his hand, feeling the warm light burn as he got closer.

The egg pulsed before him, pounding to the rhythm of his heart.

His fingers grazed the eggs cool surface. As smooth as ice, as cold as snow, as strong as stone.

A crack sounded from beneath his fingers.

Elis retracted his hand taking a step down the stairs.

The crack spread like a spiderweb covering the polished surface.

Elis looked to Leia worriedly, but she only watched in amazement.

The light grew brighter as the cracks grew wider, bursting out from within. The cavern became filled with the blinding light.

Elis shielded his eyes.

The shell fell to the cobble, shattering like glass. The light dimmed until there was only a light blue glow.

Elis lowered his arm.

A dragon stood before him. Its body as navy as the deepest ocean, its belly as white as the first winter snow. Its eyes sparkled like the silver swirled embroidery on Elis's blazer. It bent its head down toward Elis who put his hands up in defense. It nudged its nose against Elis's hands. Its scales were as smooth as ice but as warm as a small fire.

"Is he mine?" Elis asked Leia in shock.

"Yes, but," Leia paused, "he's a she."

"That's even better!" Elis exclaimed looking back to his dragon.

It stretched its wings, like large sheets of ice they expanded, slicing through the air before folding in beside her body.

"Climb aboard!" Leia shouted.

Namris came out stood up in the back of the cavern, strutting to stand behind Leia. She turned toward Namris who laid down. Namris extended her wing allowing Leia to clamber on, climbing up to sit across her back.

"Now your turn," Leia said, ushering Elis toward his new dragon.

Elis excitedly leapt down the stairs, turning to his new dragon.

"Lay down!" Elis commanded. The shimmering dragon didn't move.

"You can't just yell what you want it to do," Leia said, "try again."

Elis flung his arm, pointing to the ground.

The dragon huffed at Elis, shifting her weight from one side to the other, but she didn't lay down.

"Please lay down, I'm begging you," Elis pleaded.

The dragon looked at him, blinking its crystal blue eye. Suddenly, she flopped to the ground, splaying her legs out and plopping her head on the floor.

"Thank you!" Elis said, throwing his hands in the air. He ran to her side and clambered up her icy wing.

He plopped down on the dragons back. She automatically popped up, expanding her wings wide.

"What are you going to name her?" Leia asked, leading Namris to the back of the cavern.

Elis's dragon followed, lurching forward.

Elis caught his balance, "I'm not really sure," Elis paused, "Glacier! That's it!"

Glacier trotted in agreement, looking happily back at Elis.

"Not bad," said Leia.

She led Elis threw a maze of caves and caverns. The rocky roofs dripped down on Elis's head. Touching his now wet hair Elis looked up. Condensation dripped from the spikes above. Elis shook the water off his head and continued down the passageways. Glacier followed Namris like a hound on a leash. Every movement Namris made, Glacier copied, learning as they winded through the cave system.

After a while of walking Namris halted. Glacier walked to stand beside her.

"Here we are," said Leia taking in a deep breath.

Elis looked past Glacier's head. They stood on the edge of a cliff, opening into the world beyond them. The golden blazing sun beat down on the sandy mountains that covered the horizon. The wind picked up the sand, brushing it from one hill to the other. The town's border walls were nowhere in sight for the sandy hills stretched as far as Elis could see.

"It'll be a bit of a rough ride at first, but she'll get the hang of it," Leia said, giving a little smirk toward Glacier.

She whistled loudly. Namris's wings extended and began to flap, sending gusts of sandy wind swirling behind her. Namris's feet left the floor as she leaned forward, soaring into the air before them.

Glacier extended her wings and began to flap. One wing flapped faster than the other, lifting one side of her body before the other.

Elis desperately wrapped his arms around her neck, clinging to stay on.

Glacier steadied out, flapping her wing in time with the other. She leaned forward, rapidly beating her wings, unlike Namris's powerful flap. Glacier lunged forward, rocketing into the air.

Elis held Glacier tighter, becoming dizzy with the sudden acceleration.

Leia whooped and hollered, cheering Glacier on as she shot through the sky. Namris swooped, lining up directly beside Glacier. Glacier steadied her beats, matching the rhythm of Namris's powerful wings.

They flew through the sky, soaring over the sandy mountains until they turned to lush rolling hills. They gained height, darting through the clouds to keep hidden. As Glacier became more comfortable in the air, so did Elis. He loosened his grip on her neck, watching as her navy scales shimmered like water in the sunlight.

They soared for a while, traveling thousands of miles at full speed.

"We're here," said Leia as Namris swooped down.

Glacier steadily followed, gliding through the air. Elis looked over her wing. A castle lay on luscious green hills, surrounded by trees of birch and pine. The dragons plummeted toward the trees, landing in a big green field.

Namris gently settled to the ground, lying her golden belly on the evergreen grass. Glacier plopped down, coming to a crashing halt. She settled, dropping her head into the long blades, flopping her wings out wide. Elis slid down her wing like it was a slide. His feet hit the ground and his knees wobbled. He stumbled forward before catching his balance.

Leia gracefully leaped off, landing perfectly. Namris stood up behind her, tucking her wings in tight.

"What do we do now?" asked Elis.

"We go find my dragons," Leia said as she determinedly walked into the trees.

Namris and Glacier stayed in the clearing, waiting until Leia and Elis free the dragons.

They winded through the trees, leaping over roots and crunching twigs. They reached the edge of the forest. A grassy plain lay before them holding a large stone castle. Elis scanned the grounds. Twelve guards sat stationed at the tops of the place walls, four more guards sat stationed at the large wooden doors, and ten walked across the grassy plains, scanning their surroundings. Elis admired the castle. Large peaking towers reached to the sky. Moss clung to the cobbled walls, inching up the sides like veins. At the base of the wall lay three large boxes, covered in a sheet of silver. Elis studied the boxes carefully. The box farthest to the left jolted to the side, rocking side to side before settling again.

"There," Elis said, pointing to the boxes. "The dragons are in there."

Leia huffed, running a delicate but calloused hand through her silky hair. She mumbled to herself. Suddenly she stood up and walked straight into the field.

Elis burst into a sprint, tackling her into the long grass.

"Are you insane," he cursed in a hushed whisper, "I've counted at least twenty-six guards patrolling these grounds! Do you want to get us killed?"

Leia tried to fight Elis off her, so she could get up and run. She punched his arms, thrashing against him as he pinned her to the ground.

"Stop moving!" Elis whispered.

Leia froze at the harshness in Elis's whisper.

Elis peeked through the tall blades to where the closest guard was stationed.

The guard looked to where they hid, trying to see what was making noise. He took a few steps toward them, listening to hear any sound of intrusion. He scanned the grassy plain before him, pointing his spear as if he would jab someone at any moment. He lowered his spear. Shaking his head, he turned away, walking back to his post in the field.

"What do we do now?" Leia asked staying as quiet as possible.

"You're asking me what to do?" Elis said shocked, "that's new."

Leia threw Elis's arm off her body, turning and laying on her stomach beside Elis.

"I say we get up and run for the cages," Leia suggested.

"That's suicide!" Elis looked at Leia like she was crazy. Danger flickered in her eyes. "I have a different idea. Follow me."

Elis shuffled back into the cover of the dense trees. He got up and started walking away from the castle.

Leia shuffled through the grass, leapt through the trees, following Elis's every move. A grin grew on her face as she caught onto the plan.

Namris's and Glacier's heads shot up, alert and ready, as soon as they saw Leia and Elis enter the clearing.

Leia ran to Namris, swinging herself up and onto her back.

Elis pleaded that his mounting skills wouldn't go like last time as he ran toward Glacier. He got to her side, she extended her wing and he clambered on. Not a smooth mount but he was on.

"You know what to do," Elis said to Glacier.

Her wings beat strong and powerful, flapping in time to Namris who was already climbing into the sky.

Elis cheered Glacier on as she rose to meet Namris. They hovered in the air. Elis looked at Leia who grinned with hunger. Elis nodded, and both riders plunged their dragons forward.

They shot like bullets through the sky.

Namris veered left splitting away from Glacier who veered right. They dove into the clearing. Namris shot like a fireball through the sky, sending flames down on the guards who tested them.

The castle alarms went off. Bells ringing and clanging through the air. Guards rushed to the fields, other lining the cobbled walls. Glacier swerved for the castle, avoiding all spears and arrows meant to take her down. As they got to the castle, glacier took in a deep breath. Ice shards shot from Glacier, destroying, and puncturing everything they touched. She aimed for the bells. A big ice shard soared from her, splitting the bell in half.

She turned around, coating the guards lining the wall in a thin sheet of smooth ice.

"Yes!" Elis shouted.

He watched as Namris set the guards in the field on fire. He watched as they ran, as they rolled in the grass to put out the fire. Leia sat mounted on Namris like a warrior on her steed.

Elis stroked Glacier's neck, feeling the cold smooth scales run beneath his fingers.

A roar sounded from down below.

Glacier plunged to the grassy ground. She landed firmly, shaking the dirt beneath her claws. Most of the guards ran at the sight of her. She froze the ones who chose to stay.

Elis slid off Glacier's wing, starting into a run as soon as his feet hit the grass.

The cages lay before him, each covered in a sheet of silver. He grabbed for a sheet. As his hand touched the cool silver the cage shook. The dragon inside lashed against the cage holding it.

Elis jumped back, stumbling into the grass. He looked at the cages, thinking of how the dragons inside must feel. Panicked, trapped, defenseless.

Elis began to sing. He recited the lines of his childhood lullaby, as he got up from the ground. He sang loudly but calmly, giving a sense of safety to those who needed it. He reached for the silver sheet once more. He pulled it down gently, continuing to sing as it fell to the floor.

A jet-black dragon sat before Elis. Silver blood shimmering across his wings and back. Its green eyes peered out to Elis, pleading for someone to set him free.

Elis reached for the gate, only to find a padlock hanging from the frame. Elis looked to Glacier, gesturing toward the lock.

Glacier didn't blink an eye before she sent an ice shard hurtling for the lock. It burst open, dropping to the grass below.

Elis opened the gate, allowing the inky dragon to slither out.

Elis moved to the next cage, slowly lowering the silver sheet. A cloud dragon lay before him. Its eyes as blue as the sky, its body pulsing from white fluffy clouds to dark rolling thunder clouds.

Glacier shot another shard, shattering the lock.

Elis opened the gate.

The dragon stepped out, stretching its wings and body.

Elis moved to the last cage, chanting the lullaby over and over. He yanked at the sheet, slipping it off in one fluid motion.

Three eggs lay in a nest in the bottom of the cage.

Glacier shot for the lock, sending it flying in the air.

"Leia!" Elis shouted as he entered the cage.

She looked at Elis, watching as he entered the cage.

Namris continued to burn the guards who fought her, sending them falling to the ground.

"Namris, go!" Leia shouted.

Namris shot to the sky, leaving the guards charred on the ground. She bolted forwards, zooming to Elis and Glacier who stood at the cages. She landed quickly.

Leia jumped off, landing in a roll before sprinting to the cage Elis was in.

"What is it?" she panickily asked.

"These," Elis said pointing to the colorful eggs that sat at his feet.

"Holy mother of god!" Leia gasped, covering her mouth. She looked to Elis, who stared at her in need of instructions.

She ran from the cage, snatching the silver sheets that lay in the grass. She draped it over the egg nearest to her.

Elis ran for the other sheets, gathering them in his arms as he ran back to the cage. He threw them on top of the eggs.

Leia picked up a sheet covered egg, pinning it beneath her arm.

 Elis quickly did the same. He scrambled out of the cage, running toward Glacier.

Glacier laid down on the grass allowing Elis to clamber on.

Leia ran out of the cage after Elis, bolting toward Namris.

The guards were closing in. More funneled out of the castle, spears in hand.

Leia launched the egg toward Namris. It tumbled through the air, landing softly inside Namris's jaw.

Leia turned and bolted back into the cage.

"Leia!" Elis called, watching as more and more guards closed in. Surrounding them, inching closer with every step.

Glacier turned, sending a warning shot of ice crashing at the feet of the guards. They jumped back, holding up their spears. She kept an eye on the multiplying guards as Elis watched Leia.

Leia snatched up the last egg, hugging it to her side. She sprinted for Namris. Reaching her side, Leia hooked onto Namris's lowered wing and swung her leg across Namris's back. Leia yelled as Namris's wings began to beat.

The snow-white dragon gained lift off before the inky shadow. They both flapped wildly, cawing as pain surged through their wings and back.

Glacier shot another warning shot at the guards who inched closer.

They didn't jump back.

She shot again.

The guards held their stance.

Glacier backed up toward the cages as the guards closed in.

"You need to go up!" Elis shouted, watching as the guards took their aim.

Glacier shot ice, connecting the guards' feet to the long grass, covering the hands that held the spears. She flapped her powerful wings. She felt the air beneath her feet and shot to the sky.

The dragons shot through the sky like bullets, away from the castle. They soared over the rolling hills until they turned to red sand.

Their feet touched down on the cliffside of the cave. Namris dropped her head, allowing the wrapped egg to roll to the floor.

"Not too bad," Leia said to Elis as she hopped off Namris.

"Not too bad at all," Elis replied. He slid to the ground, adjusting the weight of the egg beneath his arm. Bending down he scooped up the egg on the floor, securing it beneath his arm.

He looked behind him as the new dragons shook out their wings, tucking them into their sides. He looked to Leia who walked tiredly into the cave. He smiled to himself as he strutted into the dark abyss of the cave.

47 Million Years Back

Juliana Nunes

"I think I'm doing it wrong."

"You're doing it right. Just focus on letting it flow from your mind, rather than your body. Here, turn your palms so they're facing up. Now close your eyes, and imagine there's energy flowing through your veins."

"Technically, there is energy flowing through my veins. Ever heard of blood sugar?"

Harper elbowed my ribs, breaking my concentration and extinguishing the faint blue glow that was beginning to intensify around my hands. "Nerd," she muttered as she grabbed the book I was reading from my hand, reading the cover, and smirking. "Prehistoric Extinction – a Summary." She flopped into my chair smirking, and lazily tossing my book onto the floor. "What you spend hours reading in your spare time does not concern me. For now, Eli, we need to practice your power."

"Why now?"

Harper groaned. "We've been over this at least thirty times now."

"Yeah, well I'm still not so convinced. Feels like I'm just wasting my time and draining my energy for no reason." I fell back onto my pillow, staring up at the stars and constellations I drew on my ceiling when I was five. Moonlight spilled through the cracks of my blinds, illuminating the wooden floorboards that were littered with papers and studies I had yet to read. Most were focused on areas of paleontology, about fossils and dinosaurs and ancient creatures long ago extinct.

Many of my books weren't on my bookshelf, but scattered on the floor and on the bed, with certain sections cut out and pasted on the far wall.

On the bookshelf itself sat hundreds – thousands – of small figurines, fossils, any sort of dinosaur remains. I was crazy about those creatures. Posters of allosaurs, triceratops, and velociraptors hung from every inch of my walls. Those were my favorites.

I looked at my hands, examining where the energy had been. Not a trace of blue light left behind.

"You know what mom and dad said before they died. You know that we were supposed to start generating our energy as soon as we turned twelve. And you know that lack of practice in magic means complete termination of the power, if not the complete termination of you."

"What does that even mean?"

"It means that not using your power can kill you, Eli." Harper buried her face in her hands, golden hair twinkling in the warm heat the lamp provided. She exhaled deeply, attempting to regain patience. She lifted her head, staring blankly at the grey wall in front of her. "I don't think you understand. As your older sister, I am forcing you to learn the power, and just simply practice it. It's not too much to ask. Once you get the hang of it, it gets a lot easier, and you won't feel so exhausted every time you summon the energy."

"What if I don't want this power? I never really asked for this, you know?"

Harper sat down next to me on my bed, wrapping her arm around my shoulder. "I know, Eli," sympathy replaced the harsh lines on her forehead, "I never wanted it either. But there's no getting rid of it now, and we don't want what happened to mom and dad happening to us."

I knew she was right. I obviously didn't want to die, and I really did not want to die the way our parents did. Slow and painful, it was irreversible and had more of an impact on Harper than it did on me. But that was two years ago, and Harper had long ago perfected her power. Their death served not only as a reminder for her to continue practicing it, but incentive to force me to do the same.

Harper rested her arms on her knees, closing her eyes and concentrating on the yellow light that began manifesting in her palms. "Vortex generation is not a common magic in this town. You get the odd telekinesis, levitation, maybe even invisibility. But the ability to actually create gaps in the universe? Eli, this is a gift. You have the power to travel to different countries, to different eras, to different dimensions."

"That's advanced vortex generation, though. Even mom and dad couldn't do the dimensions."

"You know what I mean," Harper rolled her eyes and pushed herself off my bed. "We're done arguing. I'm going to go make dinner. Keep practicing, you're getting better at controlling the energy, now just focus on summoning it. Hot dogs okay?"

I nodded. Harper strode downstairs, and I turned to face the blank space above the bed's headboard.

I closed my eyes and focused on the small ball of heat intensifying in my core. It spread up to my throat and down to my stomach, as if I had just swallowed some very hot hot-chocolate. I let the streams of blue energy glowing from my veins through my skin travel down my arms to the very tips of my fingers. I analyzed the electricity dancing and sparkling against my skin. The heat and the deep blue color intensified the harder I concentrated on the energy. A dark, stormy grey-blue enveloped my entire body. Blue flames erupted from my eyes.

"Harper!" I yelled nervously, my hands trembling in the heat of the sparks, "Harper, come up here. Now!"

The sound of Harper scrambling up the stairs was drowned out by the roaring of blue energy in my ears.

The energy was getting stronger and stronger. The flames were getting hotter and hotter. The wall in front of me began to bend and melt. I blinked through the burning in my vision, reaching out to the grey paint that dripped from the swirling heat and sank to the ground. Blue sparks crackled and flew around me as I placed my hand into the black hole.

Harper's muffled yells didn't seem to break the trance. I think she was telling me not to reach into the melted gap of blackness, barking commands that I couldn't make out. But I could see the stars in the outer space, I could make out constellations in the distance ...

And I did not feel fear as I leaned into the stretch of black sky, plummeting timelessly through the dark.

***

I coughed up a mouthful dust. Thousands of little particles scattered the air, stinging my eyes and finding their way back into my lungs. Hacking up more dust and debris, I pushed myself off of dry earth.

"Harper?" I rasped, peering through clouds of dust floating around my limp body.

"Over here," a faint voice sounded from afar, at least a couple of yards away.

I staggered to a standing position, groaning as I extended my legs. My limbs were a couple of rusty parts, stiff and cracking as they struggled to keep me upright. It was like falling from a three-story building and trying to land on your feet. I winced as my shoulder popped back into place when I lifted my hand to block the blistering sun from my eyes.

The heat here, it was different. It swallowed my body in a huge wave of windless air and heavy dust. The skies were completely cloudless, the air almost unbreathable. Every breath burned my lungs. It was worse than the countless laps the gym teacher made me run in the spring.

"Harper?" I croaked as I limped through dust, squinting through bright sun, and panting through burnt lungs. Only a couple of steps away, I could see a body lying on the ground. I hurried over, ignoring the pain that flared from my legs and blared in my ears.

As I came closer, I could make out a faint, shallow breathing over the pounding of blood in my head. But as the smoke cleared, I got a better look at the body lying lifelessly on the ground.

It wasn't Harper.

Splayed in front of me was a large mass of black, shimmering scales. A tail twitched and pounded the ground, raising even more clouds of dust. The long, rough limb was covered in deep scratches and gaping wounds. At the very end was an array of massive steel spikes, half of them cracked and fallen to the ground, covered in a vibrant green liquid. Four legs the size of tree stumps rested limply over a pool of the same thick, oozing liquid that spilled from the stomach of the creature. A long, scaly neck protruded from a spiny back, holding an enormous head decorated in green and purple scales over a deep black leather coat of skin. Beady black eyes flicked back and forth. Ash fell from a long snout, nostrils coated in black tar over grey lips that curled over grey teeth. Fangs that were once pearly-white, now smudged and stained by smoke. The dragon was a prisoner in its own skin. It lay helplessly on the dry ground, soaked in its own blood.

I sucked in my breath. I didn't know what to make of the creature, its body ten times the size of mine. Two large wings were tucked into its body as if huddling for warmth and fighting to stay alive. I stared into its small, cavernous black eyes, feeling sorry for it. Watching its body twitch occasionally as blood spewed from countless wounds gaping from beneath its slimy scales, I was amazed, speechless – this was the closest thing to a dinosaur, a creature that I had studied my entire life. It looked exactly like the dozens of figurines I had sitting quietly on my bookshelf. But with two massive wings, each bigger than its own body, sprouting from the sides of its abdomen.

Like the dozens of dinosaurs sitting on my bookshelf. In my room, back home.

I fought to swallow the lump that was in my throat. I had no idea what kind of hole I had opened in the universe. I could be at any time period right now, at any place in the world. And I had no clue if I would even be able to bring us back home. And, on top of everything else, I had the smallest idea as to where my sister was. She had called out to me earlier, but silence clung to the air for what seemed like hours now. I carefully examined the dragon laying wounded in front of me.

I had to do something. I couldn't just leave this thing here, to die. I had never found a species quite like this one in my books. I needed to do something to keep it alive.

The dust around me was starting to clear up, and I was able to look further into the distance. Empty foothills stretched for miles and miles. Numerous trees were toppled over and charred as if burnt by the heat of midday. The sun continued to bake the earth under a cloudless sky. I wiped away beads of sweat that were beginning to drip down my forehead.

Someone grabbed my shoulder, hard, spinning me to face them. I winced as their fingernails dug into my skin. Harper's face was smeared in dirt and blood, but she looked relieved to see me. I hugged her tightly, not caring about the tears that rolled freely down my face.

"I'm so sorry, Harper," I pulled away, wiping away the snot and tears that gathered at my chin, "I couldn't control the energy. I tried to be careful, just like you said. But the hole kept getting bigger and bigger, and I could see the stars and space and the moon ..."

"Eli," Harper gazed at me with soft eyes and scraped skin, "we're okay. We're both in one piece, right?" She wiped away the tears that stained the skin under my eyes. "Now we need to focus our energies on finding a way out of here."

"Can't you just use your powers? You practice them all the time. You can get us out of here and back home, right?"

Harper looked away. "Eli, it's not that simple—"

"Yes, it is," I interrupted, "you just close your eyes and summon that weird yellow energy around your fingers. Then you open a swirly hole and we hop through the universe right back home." I was starting to get angry. "It is that simple, Harper."

"You're not hearing me out. Eli, you're the one who brought us here. Do you have any idea what that means? It means that your mind – and your mind alone -- located a place and a time that related to your fantasy, to the knowledge found in your brain. Not mine. So, even if I did have the power to generate enough energy to bring us both back, I need to know the route of travel. I need to know where we are first."

Well, that wasn't going to work. Even I didn't know where we were. I had no clue how my brain had brought us here, the middle of absolutely nowhere. A deserted land with sand dunes and hills that stretched for miles. Absolutely no civilization in site. And, to top it all off, a wounded dragon lying only feet from where I had landed.

I had forgotten about the dragon.

"I need to show you something." I spun Harper around by her shoulders. Her eyebrows raised in concern as her gaze lowered to the black beast wounded on the ground in front of her.

Harper gasped and jumped back, as if the creature somehow would have the power to melt her with its fiery breath, considering it could barely lift its head to meet her terrified eyes.

"What … what is that?" She muttered in a quiet, trembling voice.

"I don't know. Does look an awful lot like a cute puppy, though. Wouldn't you agree?"

Harper didn't acknowledge my sarcasm. She wasn't looking at the dragon anymore, either. Her gaze had lifted to a spot behind my shoulder, and her eyes widened in bewilderment.

"What? What is it?"

I spun around, trying to make out what she was staring at. The land and the hills extended for days of walking distance, but there were no animals or vegetation otherwise. Only a number of black trees toppled over, scattered randomly around the stretch of empty land.

I peered at the black trees, squinting, and blocking the sun from my view. Did I see one move? They were too far away to properly see, but it looked like the one closest to us, at the bottom of the steep hill we were on, was moving slightly. I caught my breath.

We were stuck in the middle of a land of fallen dragons.

There must've been some sort of a disaster here, an accident or a battle or something. Something that left these dozens – rather, hundreds – of dragons wounded or dead. From the looks of it, not many made it out alive. Some limbs or a random tail could be found meters away from a creature, as if something had dismembered it. The more I scanned the hills, the more certain I was that there was some kind of a fight here, a dragon war: lines of ash smeared the ground as if fire-breathing dragons once flew these skies, bright green fluid splattered the floor around us as if something had enjoyed cutting up these dragons and painting the floor with their blood, and flakes of ember still wandered down from the clouds amongst the dust and debris in the air.

Whatever had happened here, it was bad. And it had taken too many lives.

I turned to face Harper again. She was hugging her elbows, mouth covered in shock

"We need to do something," I begged.

"Do what?" Harper sputtered, "These are beasts, Eli. Dragons. As in the made-up-mystical-creatures you only read about in books and see in movies. We don't know how dangerous they are. What we need to do is find a way to get out of here."

Harper started pacing in front of the giant dragon that still lay in front of us, watching our every step with its beady eyes but still unable to move a muscle. She wringed out her hands nervously. I could tell she was thinking, hard, by the way her eyes fixed on the ground in front of her as if lasers were shooting out of them.

I knew I shouldn't break her concentration, but these were dragons we were talking about. My mind started to race. If I had somehow brought us to an ancient era in which dinosaurs existed, then it wasn't an asteroid that had killed off their population. It was a war. Maybe a battle between species, dinosaurs vs dragons. Evidently, it was not the latter that had won.

Maybe I could still find a way to preserve the species. I would go down in history. I would be the man who saved the dragon race. I would have a dragon of my very own as a pet. I could fly it to school. I could travel the world. And to think of all the unnecessary pollution all the cars are creating when we could be getting around on the back of a giant winged creature that breathes fire. This discovery would make me a hero. There may be an elevated risk of forest fires, though.

I brought my attention back to the situation. My mind was wandering a bit, as it usually did. Harper continued to pace incessantly. The wounded dragon was still splayed on the dirt, still losing blood by the second.

I had to do something.

I walked over to the beast. It didn't flinch as I placed my hand gently on its head. Its glossy eyes met mine, and through them I could see its pain. This creature was no vicious animal, it was a soldier wounded on the battlefield. It needed help. The dragon's rough coat was cold to the touch, refreshing in the suffocating heat. Every few seconds it would shiver. I assumed it was from the loss of blood, which pooled around my ankles in swirls of thick green liquid. I stroked its snout carefully, offering my sympathy for the state that it was in and what had been done to it. Through touch, I could feel the endless amounts of suffering it had endured.

I was not expecting to see my sister join me, pressing her hands against the large gash in the dragon's abdomen and locking eyes with me.

Wordlessly, we had reached an agreement.

Harper and I worked tirelessly on the dragon. She used her energy to heal the major wounds on the surface of the body, as well as any internal damage she could detect with her hands. She forbid me from even trying to use my energy. "You've done enough already," she had told me, and assigned me to minor cuts and scrapes. I used the skills that I had learned about survival in my six months of cadet camp (which I had quit once it started taking up too much of my dinosaur research time) to wrap some wounds using scraps of my t-shirt and clean some obvious infections.

After about an hour, Harper collapsed on the floor. She tied her hair into a high ponytail, wiping away at sweat that plastered hair to her bright red face. The sun was starting to set. Temperatures were still unbearable, but beginning to lower.

"There," she panted, wiping away green blood from her arms, "we helped it." The dragon did not move. It did look over to her as she spoke, though. "Now we have bigger concerns. We don't know what night is like here. We don't know the dangers that are lurking in the shadows. We need to find shelter, so that we can come up with a plan. And most importantly," Harper struggled to swallow as she spoke, "we need water."

It was difficult leaving the dragon. Exteriorly, it didn't seem to be wounded anymore. It wasn't bleeding from anywhere. It was still blinking, but had not moved a muscle. Odd.

As we trekked away in search of shelter, I turned back and looked it straight in the eyes.

Somehow, I knew we would meet again.

★★★

We spent the night in a cave. I didn't sleep; Harper shut her eyes for a bit. My mind was too busy juggling around unanswered questions as to why there were hundreds of dead dragons scattered across the land. Had there been some sort of a corruption in the dragon hierarchy system? Had there been some sort of free-for-all, where the beasts were forced to turn on one another in order to survive? It was not a natural disaster that had wreaked all that havoc. Something else was going on.

Harper and I were welcomed by a scorching morning heat once again. Skies were cloudless, but the air was still heavy from ash that continued to fly around and burn our lungs.

That's when I saw it.

The dragon was a couple hundred feet from where we last left it. Thick green blood surrounded it, its head resting on the ground, unmoving.

It was dead.

I fell to my knees. I didn't even get the chance to properly care for it. TO bring it to shelter. To truly help it. I felt like a criminal. I had left this creature, this ancient, mysterious being, to die.

The sky fell. Cloudless blue of the atmosphere spilled hot rain drops that burned through my clothes and dirt as they hit the ground.

"Acid rain!" Harper yelled, yanking my arm and pulling us back toward the cave. I winced as drops of heat sizzled through my skin, tears swelling in my eyes. I took one last glance behind my shoulder, watching as the rain slowly burned through the dragon's body. Eventually, it would destroy the corpse, along with any evidence of that dragon ever existing.

I felt hollow.

When we reached the safe haven of the dark cave, I ripped off my shirt and threw it in a corner. It was useless. Full of small burnt holes now anyway.

"Are you okay?" Harper patted my arms and my back, quickly scanning my entire body for any major wounds.

"Aside from the handful of acid droplets covering my skin?" I spat. "Aside from the image of that beautiful, dead dragon out there? Yeah, I'm okay."

Harper sighed at my bitter sarcasm. I crossed my arms. How could she be so careless about that creature out there that had just lost its life? That we had left to die?

"I'm sorry, Eli. I really am. I know much you cared about it. It's just that we really have to get out of here. We have no clue when or where we are. We don't know what kind of danger we might be facing. We don't even have the slightest idea if we're going to survive to tomorrow. And I have a feeling that that," Harper pointed outside the cave, "was just the beginning."

I sucked in my breath.

"What?" Harper looked at me with puzzled eyes.

"I just—" I stammered. "The acid rain ... I remember something. Something in one of the books I read."

"Well?" My sister's eyes were wider than any gap in the universe I had ever opened. "What is it?"

"That book I was reading back home—the one about prehistoric extinction. The one that you threw on the floor after calling me a nerd."

Harper chuckled. It was the first time she had laughed, really, since the incident. "What about it?"

"Prehistoric extinction. Meaning extinction of ancient beings. And I don't think they just meant dinosaurs, Harper."

"You're going to have to spell it out for me here, Eli."

"The book. It mentioned acid rain. I remember reading about it in the first chapter. Acid rain was a leading cause of extinction of ancient creatures. They used the word creatures, not just dinosaurs. But of course, no one would think of dragons, because they don't exist, right?"

"Wrong. We just saw, like, fifty"

"Wrong." I looked Harper straight in the eyes, arrows targeting a bull's eye. Adrenaline coursed through my veins. "They don't exist. Not anymore, not in our time period. But here, they do. And they didn't live long enough to tell their story."

"Eli, I don't see how this gets us any closer to getting back home."

I smiled. "Acid rain was the leading cause of species extinction in a certain time period. The Permian period."

Harper gasped. "Tell me you know what year that period is."

"Harper," I took in a breath. "We are about 47 million years in the past."

★★★

Creating a portal in the universe back 47 million years had not been easy. Creating a portal in the universe to go 47 million years back to the future, though, that was a different story. Harper gave me a quick crash course on manifesting my energy in the right amounts and then controlling it so that what happened last time would not happen again. We created a swirl of blue and yellow colors on the cave wall, illuminating the black, cold space.

I looked into the molded energy. "We're coming back, aren't we?"

"Is that what you want?" asked Harper.

I nodded. I had the power of saving the dragon race from extinction. I had the power to return to the Permian period and save the lives of hundreds – thousands – of dragons.

I knew, when I had looked into that creature's beady black eyes, that we would meet again.

"Then let's go."

This time, I did not feel fear as I fell through the hole in space once more.

Contributors

Adriana Zadravec

Adriana Zadravec is currently living in Vancouver, British Columbia. She has way too many hobbies, including, but not limited to fencing, painting, reading, writing, and napping.

She is currently working to get her fiction and poetry pieces published, and she has some non-fiction pieces in the works.

CAMERON CORDICH

Cameron Cordich has been hooked on writing since middle school. With an appreciation for both fantasy and sci-fi, he enjoys exploring the unusual and unexpected in his writing from his home in Southern California.

Carly Seemann is an athlete, singer, and writer, who you can often find spending her free time training at the track. She enjoys spending her free days with friends or in her room drawing a new piece of art.

E. W. Farnsworth

E. W. Farnsworth is widely published on line and in print. A veteran of the Dot Com revolution, he has written many stories about the heady days of the transition to the new Millennium.

Inaya Bhimani

Inaya is passionate about writing.

JEFFREY DAVIS

Born in Upstate New York, Jeffrey Davis spent many years in Boston before returning to his hometown. He still likes to travel whenever and wherever he can.

While he holds a degree in Computer Science and has spent many years as a programmer, he now spends his time freelance writing as well as telling tales of science fiction, fantasy, and horror.

Over the years he's accrued a slew of hobbies including motorcycles, martial arts, and cooking. His quieter moments are spent with his two cats, Malcolm and Deckard, playing video games. He will also use that quiet time to read anything from classics to comic books.

John Dewald

An adventurer and aspiring novelist, John Dewald spends his time exploring whatever intrigue he can find. From guiding backpacking trips up volcanoes to working in scuba diving, John has stayed busy on a multi-year trip around the world.

He is currently teaching English in Brazil with Fulbright.

J. B. Charon is an aspiring author hoping to find a place in the world of fiction-writing.

John Grasso

Joshua Grasso is a professor of English at East Central University (OK), with a PhD from Miami University. As a writer and a teacher, he loves to explore the world of ancient myth and fantasy, where so much has been lost—but even more is waiting to be found.

He hopes to rescue many characters and stories from the clues left behind by Homer, Shakespeare, and the prolific poet we call Anonymous.

Juliana Nunes

Juliana Nunes currently lives in Coquitlam, British Columbia. Her passions include the languages and the sciences, and she enjoys spending her free time volunteering and finding involvement opportunities in her local community.

Karin Osterberg

Karin Osterberg grew up on the North Dakota Prairie where she perfected her ability to transform dreary winter landscapes into faraway lands. She is one of eight children and an identical twin.

Her writings explore characters making sense of their surroundings, whether that be a small town, a city, or fantastical worlds. Now living amongst the rainforests of Oregon, with BAs in both Biology and Chemistry, she analyzes chromosomes by day and creates worlds of fiction by night.

A deeply introverted dog person with a profound love for the natural world, Kelly was born overnight on Halloween, and have always been drawn to ambiguity. Grey days, storm-tossed nights, and Lake Huron are a few things that make her blood run faster.

For inspiration, Kelly is a firm believer in starting your day with sleeping in, strong coffee, and poached eggs on toast.

She loves stories. She loves honesty. She loves getting to know the loud minds that live in quiet people.

As a victim of the written word, Kelly is forever fascinated by the connection created through detailing the messy, complicated human experience.

Currently living in Waterloo Region, Canada, she works in social services.

LILLIE E. FRANKS

Lillie Franks is a writer and playwright from Chicago, Illinois. She writes about things that could never happen because she can't think of anything more honest.

MAXWELL CZYZYK

Maxwell Czyzyk received a BA from the University of Pittsburgh in 2010 with a duel major in Writing and Literature. After graduation, Czyzyk spent nearly five years working at a local animal shelter where she put her writing to good use by creating advertisements for the cats and dogs available for adoption.

Now, when she's not at her current job, she can be found snuggling with her most perfect rescue dog, Pitty Pat, while reading or researching and creating new magical beasts for her ever-growing bestiary.

Rebecca Coyte

Rebecca Coyte has been fascinated with mysterious creatures and tales of the paranormal since she was a child. After teaching fifth grade for eleven years, she decided to write her first middle grades novel, The Bigfoot Paradox, which went on to win a 2015 eLit Award for Juvenile/Young Adult Fiction, a Pinnacle Book Achievement Award for Juvenile Fiction, and Readers Favorite Honorable Mention for Children's Fantasy/Sci-Fi. Her follow-up novel, The Bigfoot Rebellion, won a 2017 Reader's Favorite Bronze medal for Children's Fantasy/Sci-Fi. She hopes that both young readers and the young at heart will enjoy her tales of otherworldly beings and intriguing urban legends.

Robert A. Kramer is a husband and father who's writing has been published in Carnegie Mellon's The Oakland Review, Abstract Magazine, Clocktower Literary Journal, and The Lakelander magazine. His feature script *Hidden Rage* was produced by the God of Moses Films and his short script *Land of the Free* was produced by Synergy Media and Biola University. He is completing an MFA at Lindenwood University.

Taylor Rigsby is an aspiring fantasy writer born and raised in her hometown of Lexington, Kentucky. While she prefers to write light horror fiction, she also enjoys writing children's stories, filled with magic and adventure, for her favorite nephew, Jamie.

A Note from the Publisher

How to Thank a Contributor

Dear Reader,

Everyone at Chipper Press would like to thank you for reading *The End of Dragons.* If you would like to thank a particular contributor, the best way is to leave a review for them. You may do so by leaving one on our Goodreads page, under the *The End of Dragons* title, by using the link below and be sure to mention the contributor directly:

http://www.goodreads.com/ChipperPress

Why should you leave a review? Reviews help budding authors build their credibility in the book industry. By posting a review on Goodreads or on other sites, you help other readers find new authors they may wish to follow, and you never know, your review may end up on an author's website one day.

Friend us on Goodreads:

https://www.goodreads.com/Chipper Press

Follow us on Facebook:

https://www.facebook.com/ChipperPress

Follow us on Twitter:

https://twitter.com/PressChipper

www.ingramcontent.com/pod-product-compliance
Lightning Source LLC
Chambersburg PA
CBHW032040050726

47590CB00001B/70